DANGEROUS TERRITORY

"The problem isn't so much that I don't trust you," Rafter said at last. "It's that you won't let yourself trust me. Face it, you have a hard time trusting anyone. You always have."

Sam's anger flared and was abruptly doused because he was right. She didn't trust easily. Even less so now after her fall from grace. She lived within a small circle of select friends, and these days rarely ventured outside it.

Pensively, she looked at him, taking in the narrowed blue eyes and wind-tousled hair falling over his furrowed brow. She felt the familiar tug of attraction, and her composure slipped a notch. Their eyes locked in a charged, I-want-you exchange as they simultaneously reached for each other.

Oh, help, she cried silently, slipping into dangerous territory as their lips fused with rough urgency and her arms wound around his strong neck. Her traitorous knees threatened to buckle under the insidious flood of need that was coming to seem disastrously familiar.

"This isn't supposed to happen," she moaned when his mouth left hers to travel up her face.

"I know. But it is." His voice was husky, sexy while he impatiently threaded one hand through her hair to turn her head for better access. "And none too soon."

PROMISES TO KEEP

JACQUELYN ROSS

ZEBRA BOOKS
KENSINGTON PUBLISHING CORP.
http://www.kensingtonbooks.com

ZEBRA BOOKS are published by

Kensington Publishing Corp.
850 Third Avenue
New York, NY 10022

All Kensington titles, imprints and distributed lines are available at special quantity discounts for bulk purchases for sales promotion, premiums, fund-raising, educational or institutional use.

Special book excerpts or customized printings can also be created to fit specific needs. For details, write or phone the office of the Kensington Special Sales Manager: Kensington Publishing Corp., 850 Third Avenue, New York, NY 10022. Attn. Special Sales Department. Phone: 1-800-221-2647.

First Printing: November 2003
10 9 8 7 6 5 4 3 2 1

Printed in the United States of America

CHAPTER 1

"The problem, gentlemen, is that the minute she finds out the governor has appointed me to fill Judge Christiansen's seat, she'll be out the door. Samantha Parker won't want to work for me any more than I want her as my law clerk."

If Nick Rafter were a more sensible man or perhaps simply a less intrepid one, he might have bolted the minute her name came up. But Nick had never been one to shy away from adversity. And he certainly wasn't about to walk away from a bright future on the court because of Samantha Parker. That explained why he remained seated across the conference table from two of the most politically powerful men in the state discussing how to persuade a woman he would rather forget ever knowing to remain in a job where he would have to see her daily.

U.S. Attorney Robbie O'Neal shot an impatient glance at Nick, his former right-hand man. "Well, the fact remains that state authorities insist on keeping her in place until they finish this ridiculous investigation. So you better figure out something soon because the governor plans to announce your appointment to serve out Christiansen's term this morning. She'll fly the coop while we're sitting up here on our asses." Robbie sent a black look around the chief judge's vast seventh-floor chambers, which were bigger than his own.

Chief Judge Hall, the room's third occupant, ignored Robbie's remark. "She may not have many options if she wants to continue paying her rent. I don't expect she'll have an easy time finding another position."

Hall didn't explain. He didn't need to. Despite having a brilliant legal mind, Samantha Parker was a pariah in local legal circles, with good reason as far as Nick was concerned. Nonetheless, Christiansen had astonishingly gone out on a limb and hired the beautiful Ms. Parker as his law clerk when no private law office in Kent County would consider hiring her. Nick knew no private firm would touch her because he'd pretty much made sure of it. But it had never occurred to him that a judge, an elected official, would risk tainting his reputation with such an association.

"Maybe if I talked to them, they'd agree to cut her loose," Nick mused, wishing the matter could be resolved that simply. "Hard to imagine Christiansen would confide anything incriminating to his legal assistant."

"Forget it. They want her," Robbie snapped, with another impatient glance at Nick.

Robbie O'Neal was a bantamweight crusader who had scraped his way to the top. He was not an easy man to work for—zealots rarely were—but Nick counted him one of the good guys. As the district's top federal prosecutor, he'd built a virtuous reputation rooting out crime and corruption, high and low. But Robbie's manner could be abrasive, and right now Nick knew Robbie was in bad humor because he considered continuing the investigation a waste of resources now that the subject of it was legally, if not physically, dead.

Hall nodded his beefy silver head in agreement with Robbie. "Like it or not, Judge Rafter, Miss Parker may be their best hope for resolving the matter. She knows more about what went on in that office than anyone else."

The sound of Nick's new title caught his attention. He turned it over in his mind. *Judge Rafter.* He liked the sound of it.

But across the table, Robbie looked as if he'd caught a whiff of something unpleasant. Nick suspected that Robbie was privately furious at the governor for stealing away his top assistant, best prosecutor, and number one workhorse. Worse, he perceived Nick as giving up the good fight for the cushy life of a judge.

Nick didn't see it that way. And after six years on Robbie's watch, dutifully doing his bidding while climbing the office hierarchy, Nick had come to feel like Robbie O'Neal's chief lackey. He was ready to make his own mark.

Nick shook off his reverie and turned his attention back to the chief judge. "I understand that so far she's denying Christiansen's involvement in any wrongdoing."

"Frankly, I believe her," Hall said. "Anyone else . . ." He shook his head, face gloomy. "Matt was a man of unshakable principle. Christ, we called him *Saint* Matthew because he could be such a pain in the butt. Always wanting to rehash every remotely plausible argument, writing dissents and concurring opinions as if we were Supreme Court justices when we're drowning in a flood of appeals."

Robbie settled back in his chair. "I agree. If anyone in that office was on the take, I'd put my money on Samantha Parker. She has the track record."

Nick was careful to keep the disbelief off his face. While he'd be the first to agree that Samantha Parker was not to be trusted, thus far no evidence linked her to any wrongdoing in this instance. On the other hand, Christiansen's involvement seemed certain. Whatever shortcomings Robbie had shown over the years, blatant disregard of the facts was not typically one of them.

"You both seem to have more faith in Christiansen than he had in himself," Nick pointed out. "My understanding is that he was the one who contacted state authorities. It's unfortunate that he suffered the heart attack before his initial debriefing." Nick didn't say more. They were as familiar with the facts as he was.

Further near-fatal attacks in the ensuing days and weeks had left the poor bastard in a persistent vegetative state. His doctors now thought he was likely brain dead. They were only waiting for sedatives and other drugs to clear his system to make sure—and giving the family time to adjust—before disconnecting life support. Meanwhile authorities were left with many questions and few answers.

But one thing was abundantly clear to Nick: Whatever wrongdoing occurred in that office, Christiansen was in it up to his eyeballs. He'd wisely croaked rather than being sent off to prison. Inmates were not kind to ex-judges.

"You'll just have to put aside your aversion to Ms. Parker and convince her to stay," Robbie was saying. "What about talking to her boyfriend, that assistant DA? The guy that ran for the state senate in the special election last year and lost . . ." He searched his memory for the name and, like a good politician, managed to pull it out of an impressive mental Rolodex. "Kingsley. Wasn't he a friend of yours? Maybe you can enlist his support."

"Ex-boyfriend," Nick corrected. "He won't be any help. Brian Kingsley dumped Ms. Parker when we fired her."

On a Friday morning in early July, as she dodged across the usual rush of traffic on Ottawa Street and hurried along the sidewalk to the State Office Building in downtown Grand Rapids, Samantha Parker guessed that her luck was about to run out.

The modern glass and concrete tower still shimmered overhead in the summer heat. The Pinkerton guard inside still waved her by security with a bored wrist flick. Nevertheless, while waiting for an elevator on the far side of the institutional lobby, she grimly calculated the odds of still having her job at the end of the day and decided they were not looking good. One of her friends from law school, presently working in the state capital, had called her at home this morning to give her a heads-up—the governor was expected to appoint Judge Christiansen's replacement as early as today.

The elevator pinged, breaking into her gloomy thoughts. Sam looked up and started when she spotted her former boss, U.S. Attorney Robbie O'Neal, among the small knot of people stepping out into the lobby. His cold, censorious gaze rested on her for a moment before he moved by without a word of acknowledgment.

Heart pounding, Sam lifted her chin and entered the elevator—by now accustomed to the snubs but still bothered by them more than she let on. She waited for a few stragglers before pushing the button for the fifth floor.

What would bring O'Neal to these lowly parts? She mulled it over as the elevator jerked into motion. Although the vast domain of the U.S. attorney was only a short hop away geographically, it had little else in common with the various state agencies and offices housed here in the State Office Building.

A pair of law clerks, both political groupies, got on the elevator at the second floor juggling vinyl briefcases and Styrofoam coffee cups while loudly debating the outcome of the hotly contested gubernatorial election coming up in a few months. The incumbent, Governor Walter Graham, considered a shoo-in for a second term until a disgruntled former mistress surfaced, was now fighting for his political life.

"Samantha," one of the clerks called out over the heads of others in the elevator, "did you hear about Graham's ex-girlfriend? She's supposed to give a press conference on the steps of the Capitol today and admit that she was a prostitute."

Sam took in his fresh-faced enthusiasm while he waited for her response with deference he had not shown the other clerk. He made her feel old and jaded. At thirty, Sam *was* a year or two older than the other law clerks in the building. At least most of them didn't snub her, unlike many lawyers in the local legal community.

"Well . . ." Sam's mouth quirked up as the elevator glided to a stop at her floor. "At least we finally have someone in the Capitol honest enough to admit she's being bought."

That drew appreciative chuckles from the elevator's other occupants, all veteran state employees.

When Sam entered the small suite of rooms comprising the judge's chambers, Liz Kauffman, Judge Christiansen's longtime secretary, was on the phone. A few years older than Sam and the mother of twin, hellion boys, Liz had reserved judgment and ignored the rumors swirling around Sam when the judge hired her. And gradually over the course of the past year, as Sam began to whittle away at the tiresome backlog of cases accumulated by previous law clerks, they had become friends and allies.

Liz glanced up and put a hand over the mouthpiece long enough to say, "The chief judge wants to see you at nine. Governor Graham has appointed a replacement." This announcement was accompanied by a sad, dispirited glance at the judge's private office before she returned to her phone conversation.

Sam followed the direction of Liz's glance and saw that the door stood open and unlocked for the first time since the judge's heart attack. Investigators from the Michigan Attorney General's Office had descended hours after he was stricken. They had sealed the records room and installed new locks on his inner chamber, keeping everyone else out while they carried on their mysterious search for God-only-knew-what behind closed doors.

Curious, Sam stepped inside the expansive, corner office. Everything looked the same. Law books lined the inner walls. A large walnut desk dominated the room, its surface dusty but otherwise clear of clutter, just the way the judge left it most nights. A separate seating area filled the near side of the room. Sam sank down on a worn leather sofa where she had spent many hours debating the law, discussing the opinions they would write, listening to Matthew wax on about his grandchildren's latest triumphs. She dropped her head into her hands in despair.

So it had happened. The governor wasn't even going to wait until Matthew actually died before

appointing his replacement. With the court's huge
backlog of cases, it was to be expected, she supposed. Everyone knew he wouldn't be coming
back. But she had hoped to have more time. Once
the new judge arrived, Sam had little doubt she
would be let go. Liz would be okay, but Sam was a
liability. She came with too much negative baggage
for a new judge to reasonably want to take on.

Fate had put her career on the Hindenburg while
most of her law school classmates were riding in
Learjets. She'd had a few heady years after law
school before her fall from grace—a successful
year in a coveted federal court clerkship and then
almost three more with the U.S. Attorney's Office.
For a brief, spectacular time, it had seemed she
could have it all. Then disaster struck, and she'd
been grateful to get a much lesser clerkship with
Matthew than the one she'd scored her first year
out of law school.

It would have been easier if she could have
packed up and started over someplace else, someplace where no one had ever heard of her. *If only.*

Sam shook her head in dismay, baffled by the
way everything had careened so wildly out of control. Recent events seemed unreal. Matthew's sudden heart attack. Investigators descending on the
judge's chambers, their very presence implying
that they suspected him of some kind of corruption. It would have helped if she'd known exactly
what he was supposed to have done.

Sam felt like banging her head in frustration.
She needed more time if she was going to have a
prayer of convincing them that Matthew was innocent of whatever they suspected him of doing—
and she never once doubted that he was innocent.
She owed him for taking her on when no one else
would. But she had another, entirely selfish mo-

tive, too. If the attorney general started throwing mud, some of it was bound to land on her. And innocent or not, that just might be the final blow to her beleaguered career.

But how to prove Matthew innocent of unknown charges? The investigators had been maddeningly tight-lipped. They had reviewed all the judge's case files and asked Sam and Liz endless questions. Had they witnessed any personal contact with litigants' lawyers? Telephone calls, letters, lunches? Had their usual routine ever varied with certain appeals?

Tears suddenly stung Sam's eyes and she wanted to cry. She hadn't toughened up as much as she thought.

This should not be happening again. Matthew Christiansen was one of the good guys. If the press got wind of the probe, Matthew's reputation would be shot and his family put through even worse torture than they were suffering now.

During the last weeks, Sam had agonized over the possibility that her own tattered reputation might somehow have aggravated or even precipitated the attorney general's interest in Matthew. Now, she had a more immediate problem: What would she do to survive if she lost this job?

Nick didn't rise from his seat at the conference table when Clayton Hall crossed the huge chief judge's office to greet Samantha Parker. It had been nearly two years since Nick had seen her, and he seized the opportunity to study her from the shadowy reaches of the room without her being aware of his scrutiny. She took one step into the room and Nick felt the punch.

"Come in, come in," Hall said warmly, closing the door behind her.

Nick watched the man transform. Hall's earlier grim demeanor fell away. He sucked in his gut and beamed at Samantha and generally made an ass of himself, while his eyes did a furtive survey down her V-neck knit top to the long, glorious legs revealed below her fawn-colored skirt. For all his judicial cloak of dignity, the twice-divorced chief judge had a well-known weakness for the opposite sex.

Nick had seen other men make fools of themselves over Ms. Parker. He placed himself at the top of the list. She was a strikingly beautiful woman with high cheekbones, a slender nose, a wide mouth, and a smooth mane of shoulder-length dark brown hair. She was also engaging, with a brilliant smile that Nick had seen disarm a number of mean, SOB litigators. She turned it now momentarily on Hall in response to his patter, before her face settled back into an anxious frown as she anticipated the point of her summons.

"I hear the governor has filled Judge Christiansen's seat on the court," she half-stated half-asked in a voice that reminded Nick of whiskey and smoke and women's lingerie.

Nick looked away from her. He'd learned a long time ago that he didn't need to act every time a woman gave him that feeling in his gut. Anyway, his gut had proved pretty damn unreliable when it came to Samantha Parker.

Hall ushered her toward the conference table, where Nick sat. She spotted him, and her step faltered. Surprise and fear and suspicion chased across her face before a cold mask settled into place.

Nick rose from his chair. "Hello, Sam."

"Rafter." She gave him a brusque nod, eyeing him as if he were a particularly nasty piece of human refuse.

She was tall for a woman, about five-eight, Nick

guessed, but at six-three, he still topped her by a full head. While most women liked his height, some didn't, perhaps finding it intimidating. Nick suspected that Sam fell into this latter group. Her ex-boyfriend, Brian Kingsley, was about her height.

"What is this about?" she asked, briefly glancing at Hall. She evidently had not yet drawn the connection between Nick's presence and Judge Christiansen's replacement. Or chose not to.

"Yes, well . . ." Hall pulled out a chair at the table. "Let's sit, shall we?"

Samantha perched on the edge of the seat, looking ready to bolt. Her wary gaze moved between Nick and the chief judge. "Does this have something to do with the AG investigators snooping around Judge Christiansen's chambers?" Worry momentarily creased her forehead, but then she smiled without humor across the conference table at Nick. "You think you finally have something you can nail me on, Rafter? Wasn't your smear campaign satisfying enough?"

Nick took the high road and said nothing. He figured that right about now Hall was beginning to appreciate the challenge it would be to get her to stay on board.

"No, no, my dear," Hall said quickly. "I'm afraid you've misunderstood the reason I asked to see you." He paused, looking suddenly uncomfortable. "Judge Rafter has been appointed to serve out Matthew's term."

Samantha glanced from Hall to Nick, a flash of disbelief quickly changing to an expression of grim resignation. For a moment, Nick almost felt sorry for her.

"I guess congratulations are in order," she said, although Nick noted she didn't actually extend them. "You seem to lead a charmed life, Rafter."

"So it would seem," he agreed.

"I'll just clear out my desk then." She began to stand and Nick knew it was time to step in. Hall couldn't pull this off on his own.

"Wait." He motioned her back to her chair and was a little surprised that she actually did sit again. "We want you to stay on for a while."

Her eyes narrowed, but she was listening. "In what capacity?"

Nick met her gaze. "Exactly where you are now."

She made a noise halfway between a snort and a laugh. "You must be out of your mind, Rafter, if you think in your wildest dreams that I would ever consider working for you again."

"Not for me so much as for Judge Christiansen. I understand he left a considerable backlog of cases."

"Not as bad as some judges are carrying." A defensive note crept into her voice. "We've cut ours in half from a year ago."

Hall was quick to soothe her. "You've done an amazing job helping Matthew reduce his backlog. That's why we want you to stay and finish the job."

"But how can I with Matthew gone? I assumed those cases would have to be reassigned to a new panel of judges."

"Not as long as the other two judges can agree," Hall explained. "That's how we've handled similar situations in the past."

"So, as long as there's a majority . . ." Sam murmured.

Nick saw a flicker of hope cross her face. She really wanted to stay. She must be harder up than he'd guessed.

"Right." Hall nodded. "How long would it take?"

"Three or four months, I suppose, if I wasn't getting new cases." She glanced across the table at

Nick. "And I wouldn't have to work with Rafter in any way?"

"Very little."

Her attention sharpened at Hall's equivocal answer.

"Judge Rafter will replace Matthew on next month's panel," he explained. "You did bench memos on those cases already."

She seemed surprised that the chief judge had that information.

"Judge Rafter's investiture ceremony is scheduled for Monday," Hall continued. "That will give him barely more than a week to prepare for oral arguments. We'll assign him a law clerk from the research pool, but you're already familiar with next month's docket. You're also familiar with how this court operates. I would expect you to put aside whatever ill feeling you may have and help Judge Rafter prepare."

Sam stood, the cold mask firmly back in place as she glanced from Nick to the chief judge. "I'll need some time to think about it."

CHAPTER 2

Desperate to be alone, Sam took the staircase down to the fifth floor. Mercifully Liz wasn't at her desk. Sam closed the door to her small office and slumped down in her chair. But she was too agitated to sit for long and stepped over to the wall of windows. For a time, while her thoughts churned, she watched pedestrians scurrying by, small creatures five stories down trying to beat a rapidly approaching summer storm. Dry litter cartwheeled down emptying streets under an ominous bank of purple sky moving over the hot city.

Sam shivered and sucked in a long, steadying breath. The unexpected encounter with Rafter had rattled her deep down below the surface calm she'd spent years perfecting. She had hoped never to see him again, yet here he was popping up like some particularly sick joke. She needed this job, but how could she possibly stay with him here? Not so long ago he had been her judge, jury, and executioner.

Sam closed her eyes and let her mind drift back to that awful, desperate time two years ago when she was still an upwardly mobile assistant U.S. attorney in Robbie O'Neal's office. She had not known Senator Philip Wentworth was the subject of an FBI probe when she went to the Wentworth mansion on that early fall evening.

Philip had known though. Of that she was sure, although she had reached that conclusion only in hindsight. He must also have realized that her job, her very career, would be jeopardized by her visit. He'd evidently hoped the authorities would assume she was one of his conquests rather than his spy, probably because he hadn't wanted to tip them off that he knew about their surveillance.

Just his Machiavellian little version of keeping one's enemies close. Philip was arrogant. He enjoyed taunting his foes.

His impromptu strategy might have worked if other condemning evidence against her had not come to light. So in the end, Rafter and O'Neal had believed that she was both Philip's spy and whore.

Her life had tumbled like dominos from there. O'Neal had fired her—quietly to protect his own reputation. Then Brian had bailed on her.

When Sam thought of Brian Kingsley, it was always with a lingering twist of pain. She no longer blamed him; he'd been in the middle of a heated battle for the state senate and had his political image to protect. For a time, though, she had foolishly hoped that Brian could fill an empty place in her heart. But in the end, he had only helped her relearn an old lesson—in the world she came from, she could depend on only herself.

After Brian cut his losses with her, his good pal Rafter made it all but impossible for her to find another job in the local legal community. Sam had never appreciated the true strength of the shadowy good-old-boy legal network until she discovered that no one would hire her, no matter how dazzling her résumé. Quietly, without a whisper to the press or the Attorney Grievance Commission, Rafter had effectively blacklisted her.

That her onetime friend and mentor would do that to her—that he could ever believe she would intentionally sabotage a federal investigation—had wounded her deeply. Much as she was loath to concede it, over time Rafter's defection had hurt worse than Brian's.

Now that she'd managed to scrape together some semblance of a life again, had he returned to take another whack at it? Because the offer Hall and Rafter just made to her had "hidden agenda" written all over it. The chief judge could assign one of the research attorneys to draft opinions for the backlog cases. She might be able to work through the backlog more quickly, but any of them could get the job done eventually.

So what did Rafter hope to gain by having her stick around longer?

Late in the afternoon, Sam returned from the law library to find the door to Matthew's office closed again.

"He's inside," Liz mouthed theatrically.

"Who?" Sam asked, dreading the answer she expected.

"Judge Rafter. The chief judge brought him by after lunch to show him around, and he stayed." Liz sent Sam a reproachful glance, but her eyes danced with excitement. "For heaven's sake, why didn't you warn me that he's a hunk?"

Sam lifted an eyebrow. "I assumed you were a happily married woman."

"I can still enjoy the view." Liz smirked. "Oh, baby, are we in for a time of it when the ladies in the building get a load of him."

Sam rolled her eyes and continued to her office. She closed the door, steeled herself not to obsess any more for now over the dreadful decision ahead, and tried to get to work on the bench memos she had almost finished for next month's call. But she couldn't concentrate. And the reason she couldn't concentrate was sitting on the other side of a thin wall. She could hear his muted voice occasionally talking on the telephone or to Liz.

After reading the same page of a brief three times without remembering what it said, she gave up and stared unseeingly at the case reporters and digests lining the walls of her small office. What was Rafter up to? His job as assistant U.S. attorney was federal, not state; it was the state attorney general investigating Matthew. Still, federal and local jurisdiction in public corruption cases often overlapped and limited resources were often pooled. Was there a connection between Rafter's appointment and the attorney general investigation?

Abruptly Sam stood, strode out of her office, and rapped on the door to the judge's inner chamber. She waited an instant until Rafter bade her to enter, then stepped inside and closed the door behind her.

He glanced up over the top of some papers, looking surprised to see her. "I thought you'd gone home to think things over."

Sam took a few steps into the large room and stopped halfway to the desk. Filled boxes lined one wall. Apparently, Liz had begun packing up Matthew's personal files. Sam dragged her gaze from the boxes to Rafter. "What are you doing here? You haven't been sworn in yet."

He shrugged. "I'm not looking at cases. Just learning as much as I can before the opening bell. What can I do for you?"

Sam squared her shoulders and plunged in. "Why were you picked to replace Judge Christiansen?"

Rafter leaned back in a big, hunter green leather chair Sam had never seen before and considered her. "The usual reasons, I expect. The governor probably thought I could make a go of the job without mucking it up too badly."

He had on his courtroom face: sincere, reasonable, trustworthy. Sam used to go and watch him work his magic in court. She had often seen him employ his leading man charm to woo a jury, and she wasn't fooled by it for an instant.

She used to believe that his reputation for integrity and fairness was deserved. She'd privately wished Brian's ambitions had been better tempered by those very qualities she admired in Rafter. Until two years ago, Sam would have defended Rafter against any naysayers. But not anymore.

Liz would see only the black hair, sky blue eyes, cleanly sculpted features, and effortless charm. But Sam had felt up close and all too personally a ruthless side she wouldn't have believed existed had he not ruined her career. She would never again let her guard down around him.

"It's a political appointment," she said flatly. "You used to avoid the political limelight. So I can't help wondering how you managed to score a plum appointment like this when there must be a dozen party insiders who would love to wear a robe."

He shrugged. "Robbie O'Neal golfs with the governor. He must have sung my praises."

Sam wasn't buying it, but she didn't waste time pursuing it further. "Why are you and the chief judge so eager to have me stay?" Before he could answer, she added, "Hall could get someone from research to reduce the backlog."

He nodded. "Right, but it's customary in these situations for the new judge to take on the departing judge's law clerk to bridge the information gap. And we're concerned about letting you go before you have a chance to find a new position."

Sam snorted in disgust at his gall, his crocodile concern now after doing his best to ruin her two years ago. "You don't give a damn about my well-being."

Rafter hitched a shoulder noncommittally. "Okay, so it's Hall who's concerned about your future. He likes you."

Sam shook her head. *The man was shameless!* "I know when I'm being manipulated. You must think I'm really stupid."

He smiled at that. There was humor in it but no warmth. "Oh no, Samantha, I have the greatest respect for your intelligence. What possible reason could I have for manipulating you to stay?"

"Oh, I have a pretty good idea."

"Enlighten *me* then."

Sam ignored his gesture for her to sit. "I think you're part of this witch hunt to get Judge Christiansen. And you're hoping to finally catch me up in your net as well."

Rafter calmly steepled his hands. "Well, you're wrong. I know the AG was looking at an allegation against Christiansen. Hall filled me in on that much as a matter of courtesy. But I certainly was not appointed as an undercover agent to get you. Frankly, that sounds a bit paranoid."

"Does it? After what you did to me, I have every reason to question your presence here." Sam glared at him sitting smugly behind Matthew's precious antique walnut desk and saw red. Rafter wasn't fit to take Matthew's place. He didn't know the meaning of the word "justice." "You tried, convicted, and punished me without bothering with any legal niceties like a fair trial. You ruined my career with your backroom manipulations."

He finally dropped the good-guy façade and returned her glare with icy eyes bluer than an alpine sky. "Yes, yes, what I did to you. Let's talk about what *you* did. You compromised a federal investigation. *My* investigation. Over a year's work down the drain and a crooked senator still in office, thanks to you."

"I was accused, counselor. Not convicted."

"You can thank O'Neal for that. I would have thrown the book at you."

"Perhaps he wasn't so convinced that the evidence was conclusive."

"Yeah, right," Rafter snapped. "Or maybe he simply didn't want bad publicity for the office."

"The evidence was meager and circumstantial. For your own reasons, whatever they were, you were hell-bent on ruining me."

Rafter pointed an accusing finger at her. "You were photographed by our FBI surveillance team entering the residence of Senator Wentworth, and you remained inside with him *alone* for two hours on a Saturday evening."

"My presence was unrelated to your investigation. I didn't even know about it!"

"You weren't so eager to talk when you had the chance."

No, she hadn't been. Philip had offered her thirty thousand reasons in desperately needed cash not to. "I told you then that my visit had nothing to do with your investigation."

"But you refused to explain what your visit did have to do with, other than to say it was personal."

He regarded her with utter contempt. "I guess we know what that means."

"You know nothing," Sam said coldly. "But you couldn't wait to run to Brian with your suspicions. You always took care of him, didn't you? And Brian always took your advice. God, you destroyed me personally and professionally without batting an eye."

"And you still deny everything without offering a single explanation," Rafter shot back. "You at least owed me that. Anyway, I don't give a rat's ass whether you fucked the senator, although a phone call he made after you left sure as hell gave that impression." He ticked off on his hand, "One, you were caught with him on video while he was under investigation and you refused to explain why. Two, we know he got wind of our interest in him about that time. And three, one of my files on the case was found in your desk, a highly confidential file you were not authorized to see."

Sam tried to control her fury—at Rafter for his conceit in his own judgment and his damned loyalty to Brian that had blinded him to the obvious, and at Philip for setting her up to take a fall far more deliberately than she'd realized before. With one phone call, Philip had sacrificed her career to his own ends. Her career might have been over anyway with the subsequent discovery of the file in her office, but Philip's disgusting manipulation had sealed her guilt.

"I don't doubt that Senator Wentworth knew of your investigation," Sam said, struggling to keep her voice even. "But it wasn't from me. You would do well to consider who it might have been because someone else left that file in my desk and set us both up. I certainly wouldn't have made such a stupid mistake if I were spying for the senator."

Her voice rose. "And I certainly would not have gone to his home if I'd known he was being watched." Without waiting for a reply, Sam turned on her heel and left.

Nick stared thoughtfully after her. She had put her finger on the one chink in his case. She should have been too smart to keep the incriminating file in her own desk.

For a long time back then Nick had clung to the foolish hope that Sam could explain away all the damning evidence. But Robbie had eventually convinced him that he was too close to be objective.

Sometimes arrogance simply led smart people to make careless mistakes. As a federal prosecutor, Nick had counted on such lapses. More often than not, it was the simple mistakes that brought the most brilliant criminals down. As for Sam visiting the good senator's bed while he was under surveillance, well, she evidently had not known about that. But ignorance about the surveillance, standing alone, did not exonerate her.

Nick's fingers drummed a slow tattoo on his desk. Their plan wasn't working. She was too savvy to buy that the court wanted her to stay for any of the reasons he and Hall had given her so far. Anything less than the truth, or some variation of it, probably wasn't going to be enough to persuade her to stay no matter how much she might want to. He pulled out his day planner, located the phone number for his contact at the Attorney General's Office, and picked up the phone.

A few minutes later, Nick followed Sam out into the central reception area of his spacious new office suite and glanced into her empty office.

"She left," Liz said. She, too, was packing up for the day.

"Does she still live on the Hill?" Nick wandered over to Liz's desk.

Liz nodded, watching him anxiously. She had undoubtedly heard their raised voices.

"Write down the address for me, please."

He waited while she thumbed through her Rolodex and jotted it down. She hesitated before handing it to him, a worried frown creasing her brow. "At times Sam may be a little too passionate about her work, but she's a hard worker and very capable. I think you'll come to appreciate her. Matthew did."

At this, Nick knew that Liz had not heard the particulars of their argument. He smiled reassuringly. "Don't worry. I know Samantha is very skilled. I was her supervisor at the U.S. Attorney's Office."

Liz's mouth formed a horrified "Oh," as the implication of that information registered.

Which meant, Nick surmised, that Liz knew Sam had been fired from her position as assistant U.S. attorney. What else did she know, he wondered, and just how far did her loyalty to Sam extend?

Liz finally, reluctantly handed over the slip of paper. "She probably won't be home now. You're more likely to catch her at the bookstore-café around the corner."

"My life must have a sign on it that says 'kick me,'" Sam grumbled to her friend Kat as she joined her at their usual table in the Jungle Café.

Despite being always stressed and always tired from a generally thankless job as director of the local legal aid office, Kat's gamin face peered cheerfully up at Sam over a plate of Japanese pan noodles. "Here," she said, pushing a drink across the table. "I ordered a double. You can have half."

Sam eyed the mystery drink and shook her head. "Thanks, but I'm already in a shitty mood. If I start drinking, I'll be sloppy and shitty."

Run by middle-aged hippies, the Jungle tilted toward tofu and whole wheat, but in a schizoid or pragmatic twist—Sam had never figured out which—it also offered a full bar, which gave the place a pub feel and occasionally resulted in some very odd mixed drinks, like carrot juice martinis.

Sam's gaze followed Billy, proprietor of Billy's Books next door, who was balancing a bowl of chowder in one hand and a plate of some kind of rice casserole in the other as he crossed the creaky hardwood floor to them. Part of the common wall between the café and bookstore had been removed so patrons could wander freely between the two establishments. In a practiced move, Billy snagged an empty chair with one foot and sat.

"Why are you feeling shitty?" he muttered, setting up his dinner in front of him. "I'm the one being hounded by the IRS again." Tall, ash blond, and totally disorganized, Billy managed to keep the overflowing bookstore afloat, barely, on a combination of his offbeat charm and a Kodak memory for trivia in general and books in particular, gifts the IRS failed to appreciate. He and Kat were Sam's closest friends.

"I think she has a right," Kat answered testily, because she was always a bit testy with Billy, "considering everything—Camille, her job . . ."

Sam grimaced. "And today it got a whole lot worse." She filled them in on Rafter's appointment to the court.

They sat in pensive silence after Sam had finished. Kat swiped at an untidy lock of blond hair falling into her face, her brow furrowed in thought; solving people's problems was her job. She also knew

Rafter slightly through a family connection; a cousin was married to one of Rafter's sisters.

"Does this mean you may consider quitting even though they want you to stay?" Billy asked after a time.

Sam looked at him, nonplussed that he could even ask such a question. He knew her entire rocky history with Rafter. Yet for all Billy's brilliance with books and the odd fact, he could sometimes be a tad slow on the draw when it came to ordinary human interactions. "Well," Sam answered patiently, "that does look a *little* less likely."

Billy covered her hand with his. "You should tell that jerk the truth. Maybe he'd back off." Lifting his chin to strike a literary pose, he recited in a full, ringing baritone, " 'This above all: to thine own self be true, And it must follow, as the night the day, Thou canst not then be false to any man.' "

"Shakespeare?" Sam asked matter-of-factly, accustomed to these theatrical displays.

"Hamlet," Billy confirmed.

Sam smiled wryly. "In this case, I don't think the truth will set me free. In fact, it might make things worse. A lot of people could be hurt, including you." Discussing this topic with Billy inevitably led to arguments. So before Billy could protest, Sam changed the subject. "I'll give you a hand with your records this weekend after I see Camille."

Fortunately, Kat chose that moment to propose her solution to Sam's mess. "You could come work for me at legal aid."

With her office's high attrition as lawyers left for better-paying jobs, Kat was undoubtedly thinking she could squeeze her budget awhile until something opened up.

"Thanks. I'd take it in a flash if I could afford to."

Kat hesitated, then said gently, "Camille may not be an issue much longer." Before Sam could respond, Kat's eyes narrowed on something across the café. "Oh Christ, cold front moving in!"

Sam glanced up and froze. Framed in the old and slightly seedy entry, his sooty hair glistening with raindrops and looking for all the world like a schoolgirl's daydream, Rafter scanned the café's funky interior. An eager waitress offered him a table. Smiling, he shook his head and resumed his search. That crooked smile used to make Sam's heart race. Now she gritted her teeth with utter loathing.

Billy scoped Rafter, then caught Kat's eye in question. She leaned over and whispered something to him. Billy's hand tightened on Sam's, and despite being distracted, she noticed his face assume that stubborn, confrontational look he got just before he did something rash.

Rafter finally spotted them at their table in the rear near the arched opening into the bookstore. Sam gave him a frosty look, but he wound his way toward them anyway and stopped beside their table. He nodded at Kat. "Katherine."

Three stony gazes greeted him.

"Interesting place," he said, flicking a glance over the smattering of other diners and then back to Sam. "How's the food?"

"What are you doing here, Rafter?" Sam said coldly. "Because I have better things to do than trade more insults."

"Can we talk in private?" he asked, glancing briefly at Billy and Kat. "I came to give you some answers."

Sam hesitated, still smarting from their earlier encounter in Matthew's office. She wanted to brush him off but was also curious to hear what he had to say. Nodding once, she rose and led Rafter to an isolated table near the front door. In the rear, Duane and Sally, the café's owners, were fiddling with an amplifier; Friday was open mike night. It gave an annoying squawk.

Sam signaled a waitress for two cups of coffee, then looked at Rafter. "I'm listening." She watched him adjust his lean-hipped, broad-shouldered frame to the small chair.

"First off," he began, "I'm not part of any witch hunt to sully Christiansen's name. I've been appointed to serve out the remaining three years of his term and that's what I intend to do, period." He held up a hand to forestall the disbelief he apparently could read on her face. "But you're right that the chief judge and I had another reason for making our offer, in addition to those we've already stated. We were asked by the attorney general to keep you in place, if possible, until they finish their inquiry."

"For God's sake, what is it they think Matthew did?" Sam asked in a rush, temporarily putting aside other questions in her need for this answer.

Rafter leaned back in the too small chair, eyeing her levelly, as if debating what, if anything, to reveal. "I don't know much," he said finally. "Just the bare facts. You know how it is with investigators—everything is always need-to-know."

"Yes, yes," Sam said, impatiently urging him on.

"A suspect in a white-collar fraud case gave up Christiansen and another lawyer in an attempt to cut a deal. He claimed the lawyer rigged at least one of Christiansen's cases."

"But that's absurd! Anyone who knows Judge Christiansen would never believe that. Matthew was incorruptible. He was known for his unflinching integrity." Sam leaned forward intently, willing him to believe her on this at least. "I have met pathetically few truly honorable men in my life, but Matthew was one. I'm so sure he couldn't be influenced on a case that I would bet my life on it."

Rafter shrugged, not looking in the least moved by her fervent defense. "I'm afraid you'd probably lose that one. You see, it was *Christiansen* who called the AG to confess his crimes. They set up a meeting for the next morning, but he had his heart attack that night before they could debrief him."

Sam was momentarily shocked silent but quickly rallied, her mind racing to explain away the phone call. "They really have nothing, then. Just that he wanted to tell them something. They don't know that he wasn't going to expose some other judge or attorney. They've searched his office and case files and come up empty." She felt a sudden, dizzy mix of relief and outrage. "This isn't a legitimate investigation; it's nothing more than a fishing expedition."

"Not quite," Rafter said. "I saw a transcript of the phone call. It's clear that Christiansen felt he'd personally done something wrong, something bad enough to require his resignation. And he did plan to resign, Sam."

She hesitated, thrown by this astonishing additional information. She couldn't wrap her mind around it. Matthew *resign*? Matthew do something bad enough that he *had* to resign? It was inconceivable! But such a statement from him would explain how investigators had convinced a judge they had legitimate reason to search his chambers, a detail Sam had been unable to account for.

"He may have overrated his own culpability in whatever he thought he'd done," she finally offered, hating that she sounded less certain.

"And you have no idea what that might be?"

"No." She stared into the distance, trying to make sense of the unimaginable, and finally gave up when she felt Rafter's eyes crawling over her, probably measuring her every expression for proof of guilt. He was good at reading people; he'd had years of practice on witnesses.

But when she glanced at him, he was looking at her with a hotter emotion that made her shift uncomfortably in her chair as old, best-forgotten memories sprang up of a New Year's Eve party when they'd both had too much to drink. In the chaos of popping corks and shrieks of "Happy New Year!" they had shared an extended, disturbing kiss. Its heat had taken them both by surprise. She wasn't sure what might have happened next if Rafter hadn't been her boss and if she hadn't already been dating Brian. After that, much to her relief, Rafter stopped socializing with Brian when she was along and kept a bit more distance at work. She only wished he'd avoided her a lot longer.

He gave her a mocking smile, and Sam had the feeling that he sensed the embarrassing direction of her thoughts. Irritated, she straightened in her chair. "Why didn't they tell me all this in the first place?"

Rafter took his time composing an answer. Sam didn't wait. "I suppose they think I might be involved, don't they?"

He shrugged. "I doubt you're very high on their list, but they have to consider all the possibilities."

"They're welcome to search my office. I have nothing to hide."

When Rafter didn't say anything, his hard, handsome face carefully expressionless, the realization dawned that they already had.

"So, they've done that," she said flatly. "And I suppose they downloaded my hard drive, too?"

Rafter sighed. "Now, Sam, you know that employees have no right to privacy with their employers' computers."

She knew, but felt violated nonetheless. "Who is the other person implicated with Judge Christiansen?"

"I couldn't give out that kind of information even if I knew." He watched her thoughtfully. "So, do we have a deal? You stay on, help me out with next month's call, finish off Christiansen's backlog, and cooperate with the AG investigators? That gives you time to find a new job, and in a few months you go on your merry way."

Sam thought a moment, weighing her options. Visions of excruciating hours cozied up with Rafter over cases made her want to reject the deal out of hand. In the end, though, her decision came down to two facts. First, no matter what was on that telephone recording, Sam still believed every word she'd said in defense of Matthew. There had to be some other explanation for his decision to resign than the obvious one Rafter and the authorities were eager to embrace. And second, Sam desperately needed the income.

"You're not my boss," she clarified.

"Wouldn't want to be. You report directly to Hall."

"How do I know you're not feeding me another pack of lies?"

"You'll just have to trust me."

Sam looked at him, shaking her head, and smiled humorlessly. " 'Trust' is not a word that comes to mind with you." She pushed back her chair and stood, the smile disappearing. "Okay, it's a deal, for now. But know this, Rafter—don't think I'll let you get away with your bully tactics another time." She aimed a warning glance at him and calmly delivered a parting shot. "Because if you ever slander me again, I'll sue your ass off."

Feeling rather powerful and vindicated for a change, Sam left him sitting there looking slightly less sure of himself than usual. Then Billy swooped toward her with a face like thunder. Before she grasped his intention, before she could stop him, he swept past her. Sam winced, her tiny burst of elation abruptly doused.

"And this time she won't be standing alone against your tyranny and injustice!" Billy proclaimed, his booming baritone rolling out over the café as he came to an abrupt halt next to the table where Rafter still sat.

Rafter rose with a bemused expression, eyeing Billy. He was several inches taller than Billy and at least twenty pounds heavier. He looked like the weekend rugby player he'd once been, and, for all Sam knew, still was. Nervously, Sam started toward them.

"And who might you be?" Rafter asked Billy in a mild and reasonable voice.

Billy straightened his slender shoulders and pulled himself up to his full height. "Billy Wentworth. I own yonder establishment." He pointed toward the bookstore.

Oh, blast. Sam saw surprise, confusion, and then the inevitable questions register on Rafter's face when he caught the Wentworth name.

"Any relation to the senator?" Rafter asked.

"My esteemed father," Billy answered with the trace of sarcasm he always reserved for his father. " 'I am the family face,' " Billy recited, lifting the narrow, patrician face that so resembled Philip's, " 'Flesh perishes, I live on.' "

Sam looped an arm around the waist of her errant white knight and held on. "Everything is all right," she said to him in an undertone that warned him to let it go. "Rafter and I came to an understanding."

"Oh." Billy relaxed and looked relieved. "Well, good." His arm dropped familiarly around Sam's shoulders.

Rafter watched their little interaction with penetrating interest. Sam could almost see the wheels turning in his nimble brain as it raced to process the nature and significance of her relationship to her supposed ex-lover's obviously eccentric son. But when she started tugging Billy away, Rafter asked only, "What was that about flesh perishing?"

"Thomas Hardy, *Heredity*," Billy called back over his shoulder. "I've got a copy in my shop if you want it."

CHAPTER 3

Sam had always liked to sleep in on Saturday morning after a long week at work. But during the last few months, she'd actually grown to dread getting out of bed because every Saturday she drove an hour to the Stanley Care Center and marked the downward course of her Aunt Camille's life. So the following morning at seven, when she heard Billy let himself into her apartment, she groaned and rolled over in bed.

Her apartment was a small, one-bedroom walk-up in a renovated Victorian mansion that she, Billy, and an odd assortment of neighbors called home. It was located in an old part of town where lumber barons once built their painted ladies on the cliffs overlooking downtown and the Grand River. What it lacked in size and modern appliances, it made up for in character.

Billy rented an apartment downstairs. He could afford his own house—he had a nice little trust fund from a Wentworth grandparent—but he liked historic Heritage Hill and its creaky old mansions, and he liked its convenience to the bookstore.

"Rise and shine, Sammy," he called out in an obnoxiously cheerful voice from her front door. A second later he gingerly sat on the edge of her bed and held out his peace offerings: a newspaper in one hand and a Jungle latte in the other. Blatant bribes. He knew the sooner she did her thing with Camille, the sooner she would be available to help him put his hopeless records into some semblance of order for the IRS.

Sam pulled the sheet over her head, blocking out both Billy and the dappled sunlight dancing across her bed through an open French window. "Go away. And give me back my spare key."

"Sorry," he said, not sounding sorry in the least. "You have too much to do to spend this beautiful summer morning in bed."

Sam moaned again but was out the door and on the road by nine. Normally she spent the hour-long drive west toward Lake Michigan thinking about Camille, worrying about mounting medical bills, and wondering if she'd see some progress this time instead of the steady decline that was coming to seem inevitable. But today her thoughts often veered to Rafter.

She'd be a fool to trust him. It would take more than a change of title and a black robe to make her believe he was defanged and declawed. The thought of working near him again made her feel queasy. She may have gotten what she wanted—to keep her job and income, at least temporarily, and perhaps the opportunity to do something for Matthew—but at what price?

The Stanley Care Center was a new, state-of-the-art facility specializing in the care and rehabilitation of patients suffering from head injuries and various neurological diseases. Despite its airy, skylight-bathed hallways and cheerful colors, it still carried a faint institutional odor of wasted bodies and chemical disinfectant.

On the way to Camille's room, Sam stopped to talk to a middle-aged man motoring down the hallway in his wheelchair. She knew from her aunt that he had ALS, Lou Gehrig's disease. Today, he appeared stronger than the last time she'd seen him. Sometimes, by adjusting medications and boosting physical therapy, the highly specialized medical staff were able to effect dramatic improvements, allowing a lucky few patients to return home. That was the glimmer of hope Sam clung to for Camille.

In the meantime, half of Sam's salary went to the Stanley Care Center to cover what Medicaid didn't. Camille's savings were long gone, sucked up by years of expensive drugs and home nursing expenses. All that remained was a modest Cape Cod, which Sam was reluctant to sell as long as any hope lingered that Camille might return to it someday. Camille had lived there until four months ago when a stroke hastened the relentlessly downward course of Parkinson's Disease. That added blow had made home health care impossible, even with hired help during the day and Sam there at night.

Sam stopped in the doorway to Camille's room, examining her aunt's frail, bent frame for any sign of change. She looked thinner. The Parkinson's made it difficult for her to chew and swallow. Her once attractive face was wasted by the disease, making her appear at least a decade older than her fifty-two years. She was slumped over in a wheelchair—a manual model because she hadn't mastered a motorized one. Although CNN blared on the television, Sam couldn't tell if Camille was awake or asleep. The twitching that had plagued her for years had diminished as her muscles settled into more permanent paralysis.

Sam observed her with a myriad of complicated emotions.

Camille had been more mother to Sam than her own mother, Rosalind. The sisters had not gotten along. But to Sam's eternal gratitude, Camille, the plainer, stabler sister and older than Rosalind by two years, had been willing to take Sam in whenever Rosalind flitted off chasing fame and fortune, which happened frequently, or when Rosalind's current husband or boyfriend didn't want to bother with a kid. Actually, Sam had liked some of those men better than the ones who did want her around. Rosalind's first husband gave Sam his name and promptly disappeared a few months after her birth.

With all Rosalind's chasing off after rainbows, Sam was with Camille more often than not. But on and off, Sam lived the life of a gypsy with her mother until it ended one hot night in Laguna Beach when Sam was twelve. Sam was alone, asleep in their shabby little apartment, when Rosalind got high for the last time at the ocean-side villa of a has-been B-movie director, walked naked into the ocean, passed out, and never came out. Camille wired money for a ticket home, and a policewoman put twelve-year-old Samantha on a plane east the next day. After that, she'd lived full time with her aunt.

Sam took a deep breath, summoned a cheerful smile, and stepped into the room. "Hi, Camille."

Sam had never referred to her as "aunt." In personality, the sisters had been almost opposites—Camille was a reliable workaholic who never married and lived her entire life in Michigan. But one thing they had shared: Neither young woman had wel-

comed the aging label of "mother" or "aunt" from
Sam.

Camille opened her eyes and mumbled a greeting in a garbled monotone Sam had grown adept
at deciphering. Her face was frozen in a slack, expressionless stare. Sam took her aunt's frail hand
and began entertaining her with the latest news and
gossip from the court. Camille was particularly keen
to hear about Governor Graham's appointment of
Nick Rafter to fill Matthew's seat on the bench and
about the governor's latest troubles in the polls.

"Harry always said Graham needed a lock on his
zipper," Camille mumbled.

Sam smiled. This was what Camille lived for, these
twice-weekly visits that brought her news from a
world she'd lived and breathed for twenty-five years
as personal secretary to Governor, and later Judge,
Harrison "Harry" Wentworth—Philip's father, Billy's
grandfather, and, Sam suspected, the love of Camille's life. Camille had grieved as deeply as Harry's
widow when Harry died six years ago.

Two hours later, Sam could see that Camille was
exhausted and rose to leave.

"Will you come tomorrow?" Camille asked.

Sam shook her head. "I'm going to start looking
through the court files if I can get at them. See if
the investigators left behind any clues about what
they were looking for." Even more, she wanted to
get into Rafter's office to see if he was hiding anything more from her, but she didn't burden Camille
with that worry. "I'll come Tuesday."

"Be careful."

"I will."

Camille seemed reluctant to let go of Sam's
hand. "You look like Rosalind."

Sam waited, half-expecting her to add the admonition Sam must have heard dozens of times as a teenager—*Don't grow up to be like your mother*—usually in conjunction with staying away from boys and drugs. When Camille didn't, Sam said softly, "But I'm nothing like her."

"I know." Camille mustered the energy to squeeze Sam's hand, her face useless to express anything. "More like me."

Early the next morning, dressed in shorts and a tank top to beat the heat because air-conditioning in the State Office Building was nonexistent on weekends, Sam used her keys to let herself into the building and then into the judge's office suite. She tested the door to the records room immediately to her left and, not surprisingly, found it locked. That obstacle didn't faze her because, as of Friday, access to the records had shifted from the investigators back to Liz.

Before Matthew's heart attack, all the doors within the suite itself, including records, had been routinely left unlocked. Security had not been a concern since the files were duplicated in other court locations and were a matter of public record anyway. The only unique and privileged parts of the files they kept here were the judge and law clerk's private notes.

Sam stretched across Liz's desk, flicked open the upper door of her office organizer, and examined the choices on the key rack while her mind raced ahead. Each judge on the court decided several hundred appeals per year, which translated into thousands over the course of Matthew's nine years on the bench. Last night Sam had realized that it would be impossible to look through that many files within any reasonable time, and also pointless considering that her goal was to exonerate, not incriminate, him.

That aside, she truly believed there was nothing incriminating in the case files to find. Which was why she really needed to discover precisely what information the attorney general had acquired. And Rafter's office was the easiest, quickest, and only place she could think of to start looking.

Just as she was reaching for that key, Sam registered a sudden chill in the room and, simultaneously, another presence where there should have been none. Reeling around, she discovered Rafter, arms crossed, casually leaning against the doorjamb to his office.

"You!" She had spun around so fast that she steadied herself against Liz's desk with one hand while the other went to her tank top above her wildly thundering heart. "Didn't anyone ever teach you that it's not polite to lurk about in shadows scaring innocent people out of their wits?"

Sam realized that she probably looked as flustered and guilty as she felt, but there was nothing she could do about that now except brazen it out. Rafter continued to regard her through unfriendly eyes. Dressed in faded jeans and a short-sleeve rugby shirt, he looked devilishly handsome, if one liked the tall, athletic look. Sam didn't in particular, although she could appreciate it from a safe distance.

"Is that what you are, innocent?"

Sam refused to engage in that debate here, now, when she was feeling anything but innocent. "Sorry I interrupted whatever you're doing. I just stopped by to pick up something in my office."

He didn't budge. "Don't you have your own key?"

Sam pulled a silly-me face and shrugged. "Forgot it."

Reaching across Liz's desk again, she bypassed her original target and quickly plucked up the key to her own office. Then, ignoring Rafter, she slipped past him into her sanctuary, which unfortunately turned out to be unlocked. Had he noticed? She closed the door behind her.

After taking a few minutes to collect her wits and give Rafter plenty of time to bug off, Sam deliberately banged her desk drawer a couple of times for show before she left her office. Thankfully, he'd returned to his own. His dark head was bent over a clutter of papers spread across Matthew's desk. Sam called out a farewell and ducked out before he could decide to continue his interrogation.

Outside the building, Sam spotted a black BMW parked at the curb that she was almost sure had to be Rafter's from its vanity license plate, ALLBLKS. Rafter's rugby team was called the All Blacks after the storied New Zealand union team. Brian had taken her to one of Rafter's games a few years ago, but Sam had failed to understand the appeal of watching grown men charging down a field in order to brutally tackle each other. She felt pretty much the same about football and hockey, and she refused to even classify boxing a sport. Tennis, though—now there was a game Sam could appreciate for its necessary combination of mental and physical skills.

Sam returned to the bookstore to help Billy prepare for his audit, but twice during the afternoon she hopped into her aging Saab and cruised by the State Office Building, feeling ridiculously like a robber casing a job. Both times, the black BMW sat in the same spot at the curb. At seven, after she and Billy knocked off for the day, Sam drove by again. This time the BMW was gone, so she parked and got out.

She was in the elevator before it occurred to her that security cameras would be recording her presence in the building. That alarmed her for a moment until she remembered she had a perfect right to be there; law clerks were given keys to the building because it was expected they would need to have access on weekends.

After quietly letting herself into the office suite, Sam stopped and listened closely for any sound coming from the judge's inner office. Fortunately, there were no security cameras here. Hearing nothing, she tiptoed past Liz's desk and tested Rafter's door.

Locked. He was gone. Sam blew out pent-up breath in relief and turned back to Liz's desk for the key. She opened the cabinet door and automatically started to reach for the prize before registering that it wasn't there. Hanging in its place was a small yellow sticky note with something written on it.

She ripped it off the key hook. *Go Home Sam,* it said.

Clenching her teeth in fury and frustration, she barely stopped the impulse to crumple the note in her fist and fling it across the room. He'd removed the records room key as well, she noted. After muttering a string of curses telling Rafter where *he* could go, Sam carefully replaced the paper on the hook, smoothing the upper sticky edge so that the tear was not noticeable except on close examination.

By eight-thirty Monday morning when Sam arrived at work, the office was already a bustle of activity. Rafter's investiture, scheduled for later that afternoon, was to be a bare-bones affair aimed simply at getting him sworn in so he could take Matthew's place on call next week. A more elaborate ceremony would come at a later date. Yet even a small ceremony, especially one pulled together at the last minute, entailed considerable coordination between judges, the court clerk who handled the administrative end of the court's business, the governor, and the press.

The fanfare made Sam, who felt she had every reason to despise Rafter, long to go home and spend the day with her face buried in a pillow. This celebration of his soaring career, while hers went south, was galling in the extreme.

Liz, looking harried, held up an index finger for Sam to wait while she continued a rapid-fire exchange of information over the phone. When finished, she glanced up at Sam. "Judge Rafter said to send you in as soon as you arrive."

Sam wondered nervously if this was about her thwarted attempt to breach his office last night. At the same time, she bristled at the imperious summons. "Maybe he needs a reminder that I don't actually work for him."

Liz frowned, her mouth pursed in a thin line of disapproval. "I see now why you weren't pleased to find out he was taking Matthew's place. He had something to do with your leaving the U.S. Attorney's Office, I assume." She didn't wait for Sam's response. "Considering that he's willing to let bygones be bygones, maybe it would be wise if you did the same." Her lowered voice held a sharply critical edge that Sam had never felt directed at her before. "It seems generous of him to be willing to keep you on."

Hurt, Sam didn't know what to say. Liz had always been her ally. She could hardly believe it. In just one day, Rafter seemed to have gotten Liz under his forked thumb.

"I'll take that under advisement," Sam said evenly, continuing toward her office.

Liz followed, a worried expression pushing aside her disapproval. She softly closed the door to Sam's office behind her back and nodded in the direction of the judge's office next door. "Another AG investigator showed up a few minutes ago. He's in there now with Judge Rafter. I think that's why he asked to see you."

Sam blew out a breath as she pondered the implications of this depressing news. "I'd hoped they'd given up."

"Me, too."

"Thanks for the warning." Liz nodded once and turned to leave. "Liz, wait," Sam said. "I want to return the favor, even though you may not want to hear what I have to say." Sam looked at her hard. "Think well of Rafter if you like, but take some advice from someone who's worked for him—watch your back."

Liz lifted an eyebrow. Sam sensed she was hoping for more. "Fair enough," she said when she realized that was all Sam was going to volunteer. On the way out, she reminded over her shoulder, "Don't forget, the ceremony is at two."

"I'm not sure I can make it."

Liz swung around and aimed a stern glance at her. "You'd better try. The chief judge wants a lot of bodies filling up the seats." Then she smiled slyly. "And I do believe the chief judge is your boss, isn't he?"

A minute later when Sam tapped on the partly open door to the corner office, Rafter rose from the sofa. "Sam, come in," he said in an almost friendly tone that made Sam eye him suspiciously. He motioned her toward the seating area where the AG agent was standing and closed the door behind her. "This is Josh Foley, with the AG office."

Sam turned her attention to the agent and offered her hand. This one was younger—about her own age, she guessed—and greener looking than the previous agents. That hinted that the AG was, if not dropping the inquiry, at least scaling back resources, perhaps as more provable malfeasance drew their attention elsewhere.

Which was good, Sam thought. Yet she couldn't get Rafter's account of Matthew's phone call to the AG out of her mind. Matthew had wanted to tell them something. What that something could be had nagged her all weekend. It had to be important enough that he was willing to sacrifice a career he loved to expose it.

Rafter motioned for them to sit, prompting Agent Foley to drop Sam's hand and bringing her wandering focus back to him. Foley was dressed in the obligatory dark business suit, but the white shirt was rumpled and the suit had a lived-in look that Sam guessed was a deliberate fashion statement. It coordinated well with inch-long spiky brown hair. He was medium height, fit, and boyishly handsome.

His gray eyes watched her with mixed interest and suspicion that made her feel like a Mata Hari and made her also question Rafter's guess that she wasn't too high on their list of suspects. If Foley wanted a long future with the agency, he really would have to acquire the poker face most veteran investigators wore as if it were part of their uniform.

Rafter had the look nailed. Sam could read

nothing in his bland expression as they all settled around the coffee table.

"Agent Foley is here to continue looking through Judge Christiansen's files," Rafter began, answering Sam's unspoken question. "The AG requested that you assist him in this task, and Judge Hall gave his approval."

She stilled, for a moment unable think beyond the immediate ramifications of this unexpected development. Was it somehow the result of her clandestine visit last night? Perhaps Rafter had passed along the suspicion that she had been attempting to gain entry to court records.

Rafter went on, "In order to accommodate your other work, you and Agent Foley will finish each day at noon." He gave them a minute to work out precise times. Sam responded automatically while mentally calculating the pros and cons of this latest development.

When they'd finished, Rafter snapped to attention and rose, evidently eager to be rid of them. "I think you'll find that Sam is eager to help out with your search," he said to Foley, sending an enigmatic look Sam's way.

At the door, after Foley passed through into the reception area, Rafter's arm shot across the threshold, baring Sam's exit. He leaned his head close to hers, inches away. Sam could smell his aftershave and feel his warm breath on her cheek as he warned in a soft voice, "Watch your step, Sam. You're strolling on razor-thin ice."

She shivered and her pulse leaped. So he had figured out she'd come back last night. But what could he prove? At most only that she'd returned and read his note. Flustered and suddenly overheated by his close proximity, Sam stepped away.

Almost in the same awkward instant, Rafter lowered his arm.

She pretended to misunderstand. "Agent Foley looks relatively harmless. But thanks, I do intend to be very careful."

She caught up to the agent at Liz's desk and explained to her what she and Foley would be doing during the ensuing mornings. After Liz grudgingly cleared a workplace for him in the records room, she pulled Sam out into the reception area.

"I don't like this." Liz shot an unhappy glance toward the open door. "Why are they back?"

Sam shook her head thoughtfully. "At least we no longer rate their first string."

Although she didn't say so to Liz, Sam thought Agent Foley just might be their first bit of luck, a chance to get some information out of a green agent and access to the case files at the same time. Now if only Rafter would bugger off. Sam rubbed at the beginning of a headache. "Frankly, I'm more concerned about what Rafter's presence here means."

Liz rolled her eyes, conveying her skepticism with apparently anything Sam had to say about Rafter. Then she seemed suddenly to remember all the details still needing her attention for the afternoon's ceremony. Circling her desk, her focus already switched, she asked, "Anything else I can get for you?"

Sam was still scowling at Rafter's closed door. "How about his head on a stick."

"_Sam_ . . ." Liz said in tart warning.

"Yes, yes, I know," Sam grumbled, waving Liz off.

In the records room, Agent Foley already had his nose buried in a file. He was beginning with cases assigned to the last panel the judge sat on, even though no decisions had yet been issued for them.

These were cases for which Sam would write opinions following Matthew's initial vote. If both of the other judges on the panel agreed, a decision would be issued without a rehearing.

Foley, a lawyer it turned out, soon settled into a routine. He ignored the criminal half of the docket altogether but painstakingly combed through each civil case file. On a legal pad, he tracked the various votes and recommendations from the initial research recommendation to the final court disposition, if the appeal had progressed that far.

After scrutinizing a file, he would hand it to Sam for her opinion on whether there was anything out of the ordinary about it. If the judges didn't follow the recommendation of the research attorney or if they changed their minds between the initial vote taken after oral argument and the final written disposition, Foley wanted to know why.

The work was both tedious and nerve-racking. Sam was glad to finally have the chance to see first-hand what investigators were doing, but she constantly worried about what they might find.

On the surface, she rattled on about the cases in a friendly way, trying to make Foley comfortable enough to open up in return, perhaps even to drop some hint about what they were looking for. He listened closely but volunteered nothing of importance in return. After a while, Sam realized that Agent Foley was not as green as he looked.

Later in the afternoon, shortly before Rafter's investiture was to commence, Sam dutifully filed into the appellate courtroom and squeezed into a middle bench beside Liz. As courtrooms went, this one was neither large nor impressive. Oral arguments at the intermediate appellate court level rarely drew much of an audience beyond the lawyers arguing the appeal and the judges hearing it.

"See," Liz whispered, "what did I tell you about the ladies." She smirked knowingly.

Sam saw that Liz was right in her earlier prediction. The women in the building, from the two women judges all the way down to the cleaning women, were out in force, their eyes focused like telescopes as Rafter, clad in a brand new judicial robe, took a seat facing the gallery.

He had a remarkable presence that went beyond the physical. Even Sam had to admit that. He was perfectly comfortable with who he was and confident of his place in the world. To Sam, who felt as if she was floundering through life, these were enviable traits.

Maybe only lucky people who grew up in perfect families inside perfect homes had much chance of ever achieving that level of serenity, she mused. All the other poor slobs were doomed to spend their lives chasing rainbows, like her mother, or running away from themselves, like Camille. Sam firmly shook off her gloom and surveyed the crowd.

Part of Rafter's perfect family sat near the front of the gallery. His parents had retired to Myrtle Beach, but his two younger sisters were on hand to share the joy. Love and pride for their big brother beamed across the room at him, a palpable force, while Chief Judge Hall gave Rafter a nauseatingly laudatory introduction before the swearing-in began.

"He certainly looks the part," Liz sighed.

"Only if you think reptiles look good in robes," Sam whispered back crossly.

For once, Liz didn't chastise her. "I was thinking he looks more like Leopold in that Meg Ryan movie." She looked almost dreamy-eyed.

Sam stared at her in alarm. "*That* is truly dangerous thinking, Liz. And please wipe the drool off your chin. It's very unbecoming."

The following day, Agent Foley dug into the next batch of cases, continuing their backward progress through the docket. So far, as Sam expected, they'd found nothing of any particular note, at least as far as she could see. Foley continued to play his investigator cards so close to his wrinkled white shirt that she didn't have a hope of seeing them. After they finished for the morning, she couldn't even tempt him into grabbing a sandwich at one of the trendy pubs she thought might be his style.

At three, already frustrated over her lack of progress with Agent Foley in the morning, she set her teeth and trudged into Rafter's office to begin helping him prepare for next week's oral arguments. They had agreed to meet for a couple hours at the end of each day until then.

Of the approximately thirty cases on the docket, Sam had written bench memos on the more legally challenging half. Because the appellate court's sole function was to determine whether significant error occurred in the trial court below, no new evidence was heard on appeal; the parties presented their case in written briefs. So when Sam showed up in Rafter's office at the appointed time, she lugged along a large briefcase containing copies of briefs and her bench memos for every case Matthew had asked her to review.

Rafter, looking *GQ* casual in twills and a white shirt, pulled up a chair for her on the opposite side of his desk.

"How is it going with Agent Foley?" he asked

with a cool look that made Sam wonder what he was getting at.

She shrugged, eyeing him narrowly. "Why do you ask?"

"I overheard you trying to lure him out to lunch." Rafter settled back in his green leather chair.

Sam gave him a withering look. "I really don't think that's any of your business."

But he wouldn't let it go. "If you succeed in the game you're playing, Agent Foley just might end up losing a job he lives for."

She stiffened at the accusation. "I don't know what you're talking about."

"Oh, I think you know exactly what I mean." He gave her a caustic smile. "You should at least have the decency to work on someone in your own league. He's hardly more than a kid."

He spoke so calmly that it took a moment for the insult to fully register. Then, it hit—he thought she was trying to seduce Foley into disclosing confidential information. Practically sputtering with indignation, Sam surged to her feet. "How dare you! You sit there on your throne arrogantly passing judgment, making me out to be some sort of evil temptress." Sam struggled to check her temper, knowing she could ill afford to let him rile her. In a frosty but calmer voice, she continued, "You know nothing about me, Rafter."

He didn't look very convinced of that.

Sam shook her head, a helpless gesture of defeat. "This is crazy. It's never going to work. I come in here to help you out and I walk into an ambush." She bent over his desk and began stuffing papers back inside her briefcase. "I'm out of here."

From the other side, Rafter reached over and stilled her hand. "Don't. You're right. And I apologize." Sam snatched her hand away. Abruptly he stood and wandered over to the window, staring out.

Sam repeated her mantra while she kept close watch on him: She couldn't afford to do anything foolish. She needed this job. She was one paycheck from the street and Camille was not far behind.

After a time, he broke the charged silence. "This is more difficult than I had imagined," he said, rubbing his forehead. "If we're going to work together without resorting to great bodily harm, we're going to have to set some ground rules." He turned to her. "I propose a truce. We pretend we just met. No baggage."

"I don't think I can do that," Sam said flatly. There was simply too much between them.

"I didn't say you have to believe it. Just pretend you do."

Sam rested stiff hands on her briefcase, considering his proposal. "I don't think you can either." She tossed the challenge at him.

He lifted an eyebrow. "Well, when you put it that way, how can I resist proving you wrong?" Amazingly, his blue eyes warmed and a lazy smile played around his mouth.

Sam's stomach did a little flip-flop before she saw that he was pretending. She looked hastily away, already regretting throwing down the challenge. She wasn't sure which was more dangerous, a nice Rafter or a nasty Rafter.

"How about we just aim for being indifferent business colleagues," she said dryly. "It will make me nervous if you suddenly act chummy."

His grin widened. "Fair enough. Let's settle for Friday casual."

"I'd prefer formal Monday."

"Deal," Rafter declared, taking his seat.

Once they turned their attention to the docket,

Sam found that working with him wasn't as excruciating as she'd imagined. The law had always fascinated her. It represented order and security in a chaotic universe.

They soon squared off over one of the more interesting appeals on the call. They'd done this so often in the past that it was eerily familiar. In a weird way, it felt almost as if they'd been transported back to a time before her downfall, a time when they were still friends.

The case raised the question of whether a ritzy church parsonage located miles away from the church proper and occupied by a lawyer, who also happened to be an unpaid assistant pastor, was entitled to property tax exemption. A strict interpretation of the pertinent state statute said yes. Sam argued that the legislature couldn't have intended such a result.

"Agreed, but isn't that a loophole for the legislature to close?" Rafter pointed out. "We're not equipped to legislate."

Sam sat forward intently. "But we do it all the time. And if the legislature doesn't like it, they can clarify the statute."

They went a few rounds until Rafter finally asked, "What would Saint Matthew do with this one?"

Sam smiled and admitted, "He'd probably take your position. He'd be appalled, of course, by the misuse of the exemption, but he would abide by the clear language of the statute." She tilted her head in thought. "What he liked to do in a case like this was tweak the legislature's nose, goad them to change the language by pointing out the absurdity of the result." She gestured toward the case reporters filling the bookshelves. "And then make sure the opinion is published."

Rafter looked at Sam thoughtfully. "Your judge sounds like a wise man."

"That he was." Sam felt her eyes start to mist and briskly moved on to the next appeal. Promptly at five, she began gathering the documents she'd strewn across the desk.

Rafter frowned and glanced at his watch. "I hoped we could get through at least one more before we quit."

"Sorry," she said, not budging. "Any other day, but I can't stay late on Tuesdays." Tuesday evenings were reserved for Camille.

Liz pounced as soon as Sam emerged from Rafter's office. "Everything go okay?" she asked, concern written across her face.

Sam paused. "Yes. We buried the hatchet."

"Not in his back, I hope," Liz muttered, not quite managing to hide a smile of relief.

"I wish." Sam laughed and headed for her office.

CHAPTER 4

The next afternoon, the news Sam had been waiting for, dreading, arrived. Matthew's family had finally relented and allowed doctors to turn off the machines keeping his body functioning. Shortly after lunch, a noticeably somber Judge Hall strode past Liz's desk and was closeted with Rafter for several long minutes before summoning Sam and Liz.

"The funeral is this Saturday in Grosse Pointe," Hall told them after breaking the news. "Both Matthew and his wife were from the Detroit area," he explained to Rafter. "Their families are still there."

Sam saw Liz furtively swipe at a tear and closed her own eyes briefly to gather herself. They'd had weeks to prepare for this moment, but it still came as a dreadful shock.

"We'll organize some kind of car pool to get over there and back on Saturday," Hall was saying. "I know a lot of folks in the building will want to go." He stood to leave, glancing sympathetically from Sam to Liz. "Feel free to take the rest of the afternoon off."

Neither did, but little work got done as they drifted about in a daze and commiserated with colleagues from other offices who stopped by to express their condolences. Gloom prevailed throughout the State Office Building as the news spread. Judge Christiansen had been better liked by the support staff and law clerks than by other judges who'd had to deal with his exacting standards. Sam appeared in Rafter's office at three as scheduled but had difficulty concentrating. She was relieved when he knocked off early and sent her home.

Later, curled up in the dark on the sofa munching her way through a bag of pistachios while watching shadows rearrange themselves on the walls, Sam jumped when a sharp rap on her apartment door broke the silence. She ignored it at first. She didn't want to face anyone with puffy eyes and a red nose, not even Kat, with whom she'd drunk her way through a bottle of wine earlier. But the persistent knock grew annoying, and Sam finally stumbled over and threw open the door. She groaned when she saw it was Rafter.

"What do you want?" She left him standing in the open doorway while she shuffled back to the sofa. Without giving him a chance to answer, she waved him off. "Never mind. Go away." He was the last person she wanted to have see her blubbering over an empty wine bottle in her ratty old flannel robe.

Rafter stepped inside and stopped, squinting at her through the dim light spilling in from the hallway. His expression might have passed for genuine concern but for their little deal. "I stopped by Billy's Books to see if you were okay. He said you hadn't been by."

"That gave you a good chance to pump him for information, I suppose. Get anything useful?" Sam asked peevishly, too embarrassed by her tatty state to look at him directly.

"He didn't spill any of your secrets, if that's what you mean. He recited some rubbish about standing in the shadow of truth and not being able to see it. Any idea what he meant by that?"

Sam shook her head, relieved that Billy hadn't said more. He was not reliably discreet. "Not a clue." She supposed she should be livid that Rafter evidently *had* used the occasion as an excuse to ferret information out of Billy, but her heart wasn't in it and her brain wasn't working at full wattage either.

"Thought not." Rafter's cool gaze raked over the dim interior of her small living room and landed on the empty wine bottle sitting in an embarrassing clutter of pistachio shells and Kit-Kat wrappers. "You're going to have a hell of a hangover tomorrow if you drank that entire bottle yourself."

"Only half," Sam muttered sourly, wishing he would just go. "As you can see, I'm fine. You've done your duty and are excused." She waved him off, refusing to look at him, and focused instead on the trash-littered table in front of her. Big mistake. The sight made her stomach roll.

"Okay, I'll leave you to it." She darted a glance at him and caught him staring at her. "Take tomorrow off if you want," he added gruffly on his way out.

"Good riddance," Sam mumbled under her breath as the door swung shut.

Driving home, Nick considered the misguided impulse that had prompted him to intrude on Sam's grief when she quite obviously would have preferred that he never darken her doorway. Curiosity, he supposed. Mild concern. Nothing more. He was certainly not in danger of falling under her spell again, he assured himself. She was simply a mystery he wanted to crack.

This afternoon in his office, she had gone through the motions of briefing him on cases, but it had not been very satisfying. She'd been pale and spiritless, unnaturally ready to agree with anything he said no matter how provocative, her hazel eyes dull and indifferent.

Maybe that was it. Over the years she had directed many emotions at him, but never indifference. For some perverse reason that he was reluctant to examine too closely, her indifference annoyed him.

And made him ponder again the kind of relationship she'd had with Christiansen that she would take his death so hard, especially now considering that he'd really been gone for weeks. Christiansen was old enough to be her father. But he had rescued her after Nick derailed her career. Beautiful young women hooked up with rich, powerful, and married older men all the time. Sam had already walked that sordid path with Senator Wentworth.

Still, Nick would never have expected to find the Samantha Parker he'd constructed in his head sitting in the dark crying into her wine over any man. It was a sight he would rather not have seen. No matter what Christiansen had been to her, her suffering made her seem too damn human. It made him feel sorry for her. Worse, it had made him not want to leave her sitting alone in the dark.

There was a time when he wouldn't have. But that was a time he would rather forget.

Nick parked the Beemer in its subterranean lair, took the elevator up to his overlarge, characterless apartment, and for once paused to really look at

the place he called home. He was thirty-five years
old and still living in an apartment. For years, his
accountant had advised him to stop throwing his
money away on rent and buy something, at least a
condo. But his punishing work schedule had kept
him too busy to shop for anything bigger than the
Beemer and a sleek sailboat he raced on summer
weekends when he could spare the time.

Nick collapsed into an ultramodern chair a former girlfriend had picked out and glanced around
his sterile living room. Compared to Sam's flat in
the beautiful, old Italianate mansion on the Hill,
his apartment was massive, but it had all the warmth
and charm of a hospital waiting room. Maybe it
was time to call a realtor and go house hunting. As
long as they steered clear of Heritage Hill.

On Saturday morning, Sam was watching out
the bay window of her flat for the gang from the
chief judge's office when, instead, a black BMW
pulled up and Rafter got out. Heart sinking, Sam
grabbed her purse and a black linen jacket she intended to put on as soon as she reached some air-
conditioning and went down before he could
come up.

"I'm supposed to be riding with Judge Hall," she
said, meeting him on the front porch. She really
didn't want to spend three hours each way cooped
up in a car with Rafter. She was still mortified that
he'd caught her blubbering and pissed Wednesday
night. The irony was she rarely drank much at all,
the legacy of being the daughter of an addict.
Rafter probably thought she'd become a sot since
he'd ruined her. Not that she gave a rap anymore
what he thought, she reminded herself.

Rafter's gaze had slithered down her sleeveless

black shift and now rose to settle on her face. "Good morning to you, too," he said with a sardonic half-smile. "Hall's car is packed. He asked if I could bring you and Liz. That okay?"

He peered at her with a bland expression that hinted at amusement. He knew full well that this was not acceptable to her and probably enjoyed her predicament.

"Fine," she agreed halfheartedly. At least Liz would be aboard to ease the awkwardness.

"Mind sitting up front with me?" he asked as she went for the backseat. "I was hoping you might be willing to go over a few cases on the way. I understand if you don't feel up to it," he added quickly.

Sam hesitated. Rafter's gaze shifted away, and hardly giving her time to reply, he said, "Forget it. I shouldn't even be asking today of all days."

Thrown, Sam glanced at him, noting the tired, pinched look around his eyes. He was nervous, she suddenly saw. Oral arguments began on Wednesday, his first big test on the bench. The realization floored Sam; it was so contrary to her image of him. Nick Rafter, the hugely successful former first assistant U.S. attorney, used to running a law office as big as a blue-chip Wall Street law firm and simultaneously handling the office's toughest cases, was anxious about cutting it on the other side of the gavel. The glimpse of this completely unexpected insecurity made her feel almost sympathetic.

If she hadn't been absorbed in her own worries and grief, she might have spotted his apprehension earlier. All week, he'd been pumping her for information about the court and how it worked, mining the boatload of both legal and practical data she'd acquired over the last year and a half working for Matthew. Rafter was driving himself to learn it all overnight.

"Wait." Sam caught the back door that he'd opened for her, stopping it. "I don't mind."

"Really?" He looked hopeful.

"Really. It will be a good distraction."

Her slightly-above-the-knee-length dress hitched up when she climbed into the passenger seat and squeezed in beside his briefcase. Sam saw Rafter's eyes stray briefly to her legs. Not too nervous to look, she thought, scoffing at her momentary softening. She'd best remember that he was most dangerous when he was being nice.

They drove in silence to Liz's home in a new subdivision not far from the interstate. The first thing Liz said upon slipping into the backseat was that she wouldn't need a ride home from Grosse Pointe after the funeral. "I'm going to stay overnight with my sister. Dan's coming over with the kids in the morning."

Lovely, Sam thought sourly as Rafter headed for the westbound on-ramp. If she'd known that earlier, she would have driven over on her own.

Feeling stupid for not having done just that when Rafter first showed up, Sam was more argumentative than usual as they went to work on the few cases left. Two hours later they hit the Detroit suburbs and their most heated disagreement at the same time. A single mother was appealing the trial court's termination of her parental rights. Sam had seen too many similar cases. Plus she had a long-standing personal bias.

"Affirm the trial court's ruling," she insisted. "The kids are better off without her."

But Rafter, not so sure the situation called for permanently severing the mother's parental rights, offered a spirited argument for reversing the lower court's termination.

"She's a drug addict!" Sam protested. "She abandoned them. Her boyfriend beat them."

"Past tense," he pointed out. "Even the prosecution admitted that she's gotten her act together somewhat."

"Only in the past couple months and for about the tenth time. Don't be naïve. How long do you think it will last this time?" Sam scowled across the car at Rafter, who was negotiating through heavy suburban traffic. "I'll tell you—maybe a month or two if those kids are really lucky."

"You don't know that."

"Yes, I *do*. Trust me, no kid should have to put up with that kind of life. Always on the move. No consistency. Constantly changing schools. Half the time no food. A parade of strange men they're supposed to call 'uncle' but who watch them in a way no 'uncle' should, and a mother who's usually too wasted to notice or care. She's there one day and either physically or mentally gone the next. And one day, she doesn't come back at all."

Sam stopped abruptly. Even after all these years, the horror could still make her stomach churn and her heart pound. She drew a deep breath, regaining control.

Rafter glanced at her curiously. "You okay?"

"Fine."

"The kids want to stay with her."

"Of course—they love her. They're terrified of losing what pathetically little security they have." She paused. "Look, Rafter, this isn't like the perfect family you probably had growing up. These kids are in a living hell. This is a chance for you to really make a difference."

"And you think the foster care system is better?"

"The foster care here is an aunt and uncle. But

they won't take the kids if they have to deal with an addict. Who can blame them?"

"It almost sounds as if you're speaking from personal experience." He shot her another laser-eyed look.

Sam shrugged. She certainly wasn't going to admit to him that she'd lived it. The last thing she wanted was Rafter's pity. "Let's just say, I've seen it all before."

The funeral was held in Christ Church, a huge, old, Gothic pile of stones. According to Liz, it was the center of WASP activity in this upscale community where Edsel Ford and other auto industry giants built their estates along the shores of Lake St. Clair. They arrived a little early and Liz drew Sam aside while Rafter parked his car.

"Geez Louise," she hissed, staring at Sam as if she'd sprouted horns. "You two really go at it over those cases. Is it like some kind of kinky foreplay or something?"

"*What?*" Sam gaped at her. "That's crazy!"

"Well, you sure could have fooled me," Liz said under her breath. "You never argued like that with Matthew." Rafter walked up, cutting the conversation short, and they joined the stream of mourners filling the church.

That didn't give Sam a chance to clear up Liz's ridiculous misconception. If she'd had the chance, she would have explained that perhaps they did get a little carried away sometimes, but only because it was an acceptable outlet for their mutual antipathy, not because of whatever Liz thought she saw.

The service was a long and touching tribute to a man who was well known and highly respected in state government. Sam spotted the governor and other notables from both public and private sectors among the overflowing crowd, even a few who would likely know of the investigation. By the end of the service, it was all Sam could do to maintain her composure; she was determined not to break down with Rafter sitting next to her.

Afterward, mourners were invited back to the widow's childhood home in Grosse Pointe, where her brother now lived. Agreeing to stay only long enough to offer their condolences to Hattie Christiansen, the three piled into Rafter's car and cruised down Lake Shore Drive searching for the address. When Rafter turned into the drive, they gaped at the sprawling Georgian Revival mansion. Lake St. Clair glittered under a high sun. An attendant directed them to park under tall trees on a lawn as thick and plush as fine wool carpet.

Rafter whistled. "To the manor born."

"Matthew's wife is from one of the old auto families," Liz said from the front passenger seat.

A somber crowd had already gathered inside by the time they entered. Sam immediately recognized a half-dozen prominent lawyers, judges, and politicians mingling in groups scattered down the length of a long front gallery. She noted among them her old boss, Robbie O'Neal, talking to Governor Graham and Marty Davis, a well-known defense lawyer in the state.

"Looks like a gathering of the state's movers and shakers," Rafter commented beside her after Liz wandered off in search of the powder room.

"A lot of these guys went to Madison Law School with Matthew," Sam said. The crowd shifted and she spotted Senator Wentworth. Good, she thought, even though her heart tripped nervously. She hoped she could catch him alone for a minute.

"The Madison Mafia," Rafter said under his breath.

Sam smiled. "Sour grapes?" Like Sam, Rafter had attended the University of Michigan Law School, a top-tier national law school and more prestigious than Madison. But Michigan alums, having their pick of top law firms and government positions across the country, often left the state, thereby leaving state politics to Madison lawyers.

"No." Rafter returned her smile. "I wouldn't like the payback that goes with all the favors."

Sam sensed she was being watched and looked up. Across the gallery, Brian Kingsley, the man who'd broken her heart, the man she sometimes still dreamed about, gave her a familiar, heart-squeezing smile of greeting. She didn't need to wonder if he'd moved on with his life. He leaned down in a familiar manner to say something to a petite blond woman at his side, and together they started in Rafter and Sam's direction.

She really shouldn't have been surprised to see him here. After his defeat in a special election for the state senate, he'd moved across the state to take a job in the Detroit prosecutor's office, for him a political repositioning. Sam doubted Brian had known Matthew except in passing, but he rarely passed up an opportunity to nurture political connections, the lifeblood of the politically ambitious.

Sam looked around for a convenient escape. She did not want to see Brian again here, now, when she still felt raw after Matthew's funeral, but her choices seemed to boil down to making a dignified stand or an undignified exit. She dithered a moment before pride and practicality won out. She pasted on a bland, store clerk smile as she watched them thread their way through the crowd.

This was the first time she'd seen him since he'd

called it quits. He had called a few times early on, until Sam had grown tired of having to make him feel better about the whole thing and started screening her calls.

From the corner of her eye, Sam caught Rafter's assessing gaze on her as Brian approached.

"Hello, Sam." Brian smiled as he leaned in to give her cheek a chaste buss. "You're looking fantastic as usual." His friend kept hold of his arm, and Sam dismally noted that she was spectacularly attractive—a small, well-toned woman with a shiny waterfall of sleek, blond hair and bottomless blue eyes that were sizing Sam up with the frosty look of an adversary at ten paces. Her diminutive perfection made Sam feel like a gangly giraffe.

Brian introduced "Helen" to Sam and Rafter, and Helen held out a slender hand to each in turn, taking Rafter's with far more pleasure than Sam's. But it was for Brian that she reserved the full force of her adoring attention, hanging on to his every word as he smoothly prattled on about Judge Christiansen's tragic death and Rafter's appointment. Helen's ego-stroking, pompon-waving ilk had always bewildered Sam; such women seemed almost hardwired to please a man. And please them they evidently did.

Sam extricated herself as soon as she could and went off in search of Matthew's widow. Walking away, she was surprised and relieved to discover that she felt almost nothing after seeing Brian again, not even jealousy. Curiously, he seemed more alive in her imagination than in the flesh. It suddenly struck her that she no longer wanted *him*—she wanted the idea of him. Indeed, if anything, she'd found his canned patter mildly irritating. That realization was vastly liberating.

The gallery connected a variety of smaller living

spaces across the rear of the house overlooking the lake. It was from one of these rooms that Sam spotted Hattie Christiansen emerge. They had talked several times on the phone over the past weeks, and although Sam had met her in person only rarely, she liked the ferociously blunt, outgoing woman with her bright red hair and quick movements. Grief had etched new lines across her freckled face. Nevertheless, she held court in her extravagant surroundings with staunch dignity.

Sam waited while a couple ahead of her finished expressing their condolences. "Samantha, dear." Hattie turned to acknowledge her with a warm, firm hand. "How good of you to come all this way."

Sam took one look into Hattie's haunted green eyes and began to lose her own thin composure. "I can't tell you how sorry I am about—" Hattie pulled her into a tight hug, cutting short Sam's unsteady warble of sympathy.

"It's so unfair," Sam sniffled as Hattie released her. "He was a truly wonderful man."

"I know." Hattie smiled sadly. "He thought the world of you, too. He said you were the best law clerk he'd ever had."

Sam was losing the battle with tears that refused to be suppressed.

"Come with me," Hattie said, drawing Sam toward an arched opening leading into one of the back rooms.

"But your guests," Sam protested weakly. Glancing across the gallery, Sam saw Rafter marking their little tableau with great interest.

"Hang them!" Hattie said under her breath. "Most came to network or troll for campaign contributions."

Hattie drew her into a quiet sitting room with

an expansive view of the water. "This is lovely." Sam fumbled in her purse for a tissue.

"It's called the Lake Room," Hattie said, giving her a chance to regroup. After a time, she looked at Sam hard, worry deepening the cobweb of lines crisscrossing her face. "Anything new with the investigation?"

"No. An agent is still at the office, but the good news is we only rate the second string now." Frowning, Sam shook her head. "It's got to be nothing—a wild-goose chase."

Hattie didn't look quite so certain and that alarmed Sam. Hesitantly, Sam asked, "Did Matthew ever say anything to you about contacting the attorney general?"

For a moment Sam thought Hattie wasn't going to answer. Her chin trembled. Finally, she said, "Not in so many words. Something was bothering him though."

"Matthew would never do anything wrong," Sam declared loyally.

Hattie sighed and patted Sam's hand. "Thank you, my dear. But I've learned in my life that even the best people stumble from time to time."

Just then, Philip Wentworth drifted into the room with Marty Davis and gave them a casual look-over.

"Let's talk about this at home," Hattie said in a lowered voice. "Too many ears here. Call me tomorrow." She gave Sam another quick hug and sent her in the direction of the powder room.

When Sam came out, Philip was waiting for her. Barely looking at her, he held open a French door leading outside. Heavy, hot air billowed in. "Care for a stroll?"

Bracing herself for what was to come, Sam nodded and brushed by him onto a vast stone patio spanning the rear of the house. They were alone; the heat kept everyone else inside. She silently waited for him to make the first move. They'd always been like opposing chess players using an uneven board. He took his time, first admiring the elegant courtyard and then staring at a Jet Ski buzzing like a chainsaw across the lake.

In the unforgiving afternoon sun, he looked older, his sharp, aristocratic features beginning to sag. But if anything, age made him look more formidable, less merely-a-handsome-face, Sam thought.

Finally he asked, "You still seeing that Kingsley chap?"

"No."

"He's here, you know."

"Yes."

"You're not talking about it."

"Nothing to talk about." And that, Sam realized, was the happy truth. Not that she would ever confide in Philip under any circumstances.

He shrugged indifferently. "How is Billy?"

Which, Sam knew, was the real reason for this little tête-à-tête. For all his many faults, Philip still cared about the son who wanted nothing to do with him. "He's fine. Dodging another bullet from the IRS."

"Why, those bastards!" Philip's face flushed with sudden anger. "I'll see about that."

"No, Philip. Billy wouldn't appreciate your interference." Sam cautioned him for Billy's benefit, not Philip's. "If you want his respect, don't use your influence."

"You don't understand. They're probably targeting him because of me."

Sam smiled. "You can only say that with a straight face because you haven't seen what passes for Billy's records."

Calming down, Philip blew out a frustrated breath. "Will you let me know if anything comes of it?" He shot her a quick glance.

"Yes, I promise."

Finished with her now that he'd gotten what he wanted, Philip straightened. Sam forced herself to speak, hating having to ask him for anything; it made her feel like an unwanted teenager begging for Wentworth crumbs again. "I need your help."

"Samantha, if this is about more money . . ." He gave her a reproachful look.

"Camille can barely speak anymore," Sam pressed on quickly, making her case before he could cut her off. "There are things that can be done, more therapy, a special computer that can help her talk, but it's all expensive."

Philip's face hardened. "Are you sure she really needs these things? With all due respect, it sounds as if she doesn't have long anyway. And frankly, I'm not in a position to help you out right now."

Stung and outraged, Sam struggled to maintain her composure. Philip was perfectly comfortable asking for money, but he hated giving it away, even when morally it wasn't his to withhold. The only way to work on him was by threats or payoffs, and she had none of the latter to offer at present.

"That money is mine. You promised Harry you would see that we got it as we needed it," she reminded him evenly. "Well, we do, desperately. You know full well that for all these years I've kept my end of our dirty little bargain. Now it's time for you to deliver."

Instead of exploding, which he often did when pushed, Philip's face relaxed. He leaned against a stone pillar. "You look like Rosalind," he observed mildly, out of the blue.

The sudden change of subject confused Sam.

On full alert for the thrust experience had taught her to expect next, she watched him warily.

"You must be about the same age she was when she died. Always thought you inherited your father's intelligence though." He shook his head in disapproval. "You might want to curb those rash tendencies. They didn't serve your mother well. I would hate to see you meet her end."

Sam's mouth went dry. "Is there a threat somewhere in there?"

Philip smiled thinly. "No threat. Just concern that you seem to have forgotten your manners."

"Manners? This from the man who set me up to look like one of his little toys?" Sam glared at him. "You owe me for that, too."

"Why, you ungrateful little bitch!" Philip spat, his urbane mask disintegrating in a flood of temper. "Your pretty little ass was cooked the minute you walked up to my door. It wouldn't have mattered what I did—you were finished at the U.S. Attorney's. And for your information, you caused me a lot of trouble. But I made sure you landed on your feet. I took care of you. And this is my thanks."

"What do you mean, you took care of me?" Sam stared at him, suddenly afraid of what she would hear.

"Can you really be that naïve?" Philip smiled slyly, now enjoying himself. "How do you think you got a job with Christiansen? You think Saint Matthew was willing to risk tarnishing his precious reputation with you out of the goodness of his heart?"

"No!" Staggered, Sam shook her head, sick to her stomach. "I don't believe you. Matthew couldn't have been pushed to do something he didn't want to do."

"Don't be stupid, Samantha. Politics is nothing more than mutually beneficial alliances."

* * *

Nick met up again with a temporarily solo Brian inside the dining room, where a huge buffet was laid out. "So how's it going with you and Sam?" Brian casually asked between bites.

"It's complicated." Distracted, Nick scoured the packed room for Sam but didn't see her. Earlier, he had found Hattie and expressed his condolences, but Sam was nowhere to be seen.

"I'll bet it is." Brian gave him a knowing, just-between-us-guys smile.

Nick frowned at him. "What's that supposed to mean?"

"Come on! I always figured you had a thing for her. This is your big chance."

"You don't say." Nick nodded to Governor Graham as he passed by in the center of a small knot of hangers-on. "I shouldn't need to remind you of all people what she did. You cut her loose because of it."

Brian looked mildly embarrassed. "Look, Nick, maybe I was looking for an excuse to get out of it with Sam. We were never really right for each other. She's this goody-two-shoes brainiac. We didn't even like the same things. We barely talked by the end. But look at her! I was going to give that up?"

"What exactly are you getting at?" Nick cast him a narrow-eyed look.

Brian lifted his hands in a helpless shrug. "I sort of kept hoping she would end it, but she was determined to make it work. Frankly, I always wondered if deep down she didn't have a thing for *you*. Anyway, when you came to me and had all that dirt on her, and I had the campaign to think of, well, that was it." Brian caught Nick's dark look and gave him a sheepish smile.

"Are you implying that you don't believe she did

any of it?" Nick asked slowly, disregarding for a moment the surge of satisfaction he felt hearing Brian confirm the possibility that his former attraction to Sam may have been reciprocated.

Brian held up a placating hand. "I didn't say that. Look, as a prosecutor, I've been wrong about people so many times I no longer trust my instincts. You told me off the record that Sam leaked information and slept with a suspect, and I accepted that. Did I have doubts? Yes. Because the woman I thought I knew would not have done any of it. She was too damn loyal." He shrugged. "But like I said, I've been wrong before. And she wouldn't account for her actions, even to me."

Nick muttered an oath, closing his eyes a moment as he recalled Sam's accusation that Brian did whatever Nick told him to. It was a pattern they had played out over and over when they'd been friends in high school; Brian had always been a terrible coward in matters of the heart. His relationships tended to last about as long as a bad movie—except, much to Nick's consternation at the time, with Sam. And Nick had helped him out of one mess after another.

"Maybe misplaced loyalty *was* her motivation," Nick said, meaning misplaced loyalty to Senator Wentworth. Otherwise, if Brian was right, the nagging guilt he'd been trying to quiet for two long years might be entirely justified.

Liz wandered over to join them, interrupting their conversation. Which was a good thing as far as Nick was concerned because the careless charm that had seemed cool in a high school buddy suddenly looked repulsive in a grown man.

"You ready to shove off?" he asked her.

"Anytime."

"I'll try to find Sam," Nick said and escaped.

He finally tracked her down on the patio. Her back was to the house, and at first, she appeared to be alone gazing out across the water. When Nick began to open the door, he heard another voice and stilled. There, standing in the shadow of an ornately carved pillar a short distance away from Sam, was none other than Senator Philip Wentworth. And they were in the middle of a heated argument. Nick's guilt began to evaporate like so much mist under a hot summer sun.

"Maybe I should just clear up this whole mess right now," Sam was saying, her normally butterscotch smooth voice shaking with anger and bitterness. "Tell the whole world!"

Wentworth's face contorted with fury. "Go right ahead. But to what end? You'll never see another dime if you do."

"And if I don't, what then, Philip?"

At Sam's taunt, Wentworth looked ready to explode but caught sight of Nick and abruptly doused his anger. Following the senator's gaze, Sam whirled around. Nick stepped outside. Embarrassment and guilt flashed across her face, quickly followed by irritation.

"You really do need to find yourself another hobby, Rafter," she said with what Nick regarded as impressive aplomb under the circumstances.

CHAPTER 5

"We need to go," Sam said abruptly to Rafter as soon as Philip disappeared inside the mansion. In hindsight, she hugely regretted approaching Philip for money here, now. She'd wrongly assumed neutral ground would make the task easier, or at least more civil.

Rafter snagged her arm in a vise grip as she passed. "Hold on a minute. When I came out here, I heard you arguing with the good senator and I want to know about what."

Sam stalled, wondering how much he'd overheard. "And just what do you think it was about?"

"It sounded damn close to blackmail. Come on, Sam—what do you have on him?" He caught her other arm as well when she tried to twist away.

"It's none of your business."

They stared each other down, so close together that Sam could see her reflection in his hard blue eyes and feel his uneven breaths on her cheek. Anyone who happened to look outside might think they were embracing. If she moved just the tiniest bit, their mouths would meet. For a crazy moment she saw the same awareness in Rafter's eyes, and her pulse galloped faster. She must be mad, she thought in the next instant.

Abruptly, Sam broke the standoff. "Let go of me this instant or I'll scream bloody murder," she promised in a cold, clipped voice and meant every word.

He dropped her arm as if it were a live wire and dug his hand into his scalp in exasperation. "It damn well is my business. This isn't over."

"Oh, I'm sure I can count on that," Sam tossed back on her way across the patio, quick to put distance between them.

Other than the hiss of the air conditioner, heavy silence descended inside the tan leather interior of Rafter's car after they'd dropped Liz off at her sister's. Sam closed her eyes, blocking out both Rafter and the questions she knew he meant to pursue. After a few minutes, she was feeling so sorry for herself over everything that was going wrong in her life that pesky tears started backing up behind her eyelids again. Horrified, she fought them back.

"You okay?" Rafter asked after a time.

Sam stiffened, caught off guard by the gentleness in his voice. "No. I'm suffering. Break out the bubbly."

She heard him sigh and pull out a tissue. "Believe it or not, I don't want you to suffer. I never have."

"Stop it." Reluctantly she opened her eyes and took the tissue he held out. "I get nervous when you're nice." Eschewing ladylike dabbing, she blew her nose loudly.

He smiled and that flustered her even more.

When he took the next exit, Sam sat up. "What are you doing?"

"Stopping for something to drink."

At a drive-through coffee shop, he ordered two iced teas. When she took one from him, her hand shook faintly, revealing how much the day's events had rattled her. She knew Rafter's eagle eyes cataloged every detail.

"You're entitled to mourn him," he said after they charged back onto the expressway. "Liz told me you were close."

"We were."

"How did you happen to get a clerkship with him?"

Sam was not fooled by the offhand delivery of the question or his sudden friendliness. Like any good prosecutor, he was simply changing tactics. "I wasn't sleeping with him," she said acidly. "I assume that's what you're really asking."

"No, not after I saw you with Hattie Christiansen."

"Ah, I see. So you want to know how I did it *without* sleeping with him, especially after you'd gone to so much trouble to destroy my reputation, is that it?" Her mouth twisted into a cynical half-smile.

"Something like that."

Sam stared unseeingly at cornfields flashing by. *Why had Matthew hired her?* After Philip's bombshell, that particular question had her stomach tied in a knot. Perhaps it made no difference at this point anyway. She knew Matthew had eventually come to respect and trust her. Yet the possibility that Philip had possessed some kind of influence with Matthew, and had used it to get Sam her clerkship, was not only highly repugnant but, considering recent events, downright sinister.

She glanced at Rafter's profile, thinking, and finally said, "All I can tell you, all I *know,* is that when Matthew asked me if rumors that I had tipped off the subject of a federal investigation were true, I said no, and he said 'okay.' That was it. He never mentioned it again."

Rafter nodded. Whether he believed her, Sam couldn't tell, but suddenly it mattered a great deal that he did believe her on this at least. Never one to shrink from hard truths, Sam reluctantly acknowledged that even now after all that had happened and despite telling herself repeatedly that his good opinion didn't matter, it did. What she found harder to admit was the horrifying possibility that she could still be attracted to him.

"Tell me about Senator Wentworth, Sam," he said softly, gently, as he might coax a reluctant witness.

Sam let out a weary sigh. "Tell you what?"

"How he found out about the investigation. When he found out."

"I have no idea."

"It's just between us now," he went on as if she hadn't spoken. "Whatever you say will never leave this car. Why not tell me? From what I heard, there's no love lost between the two of you."

"You need to stop spying on me, Rafter."

"He's not worth it, Sam. He's the worst kind of politician. There's a fine line between soliciting campaign contributions and peddling influence to the highest bidder. Wentworth leaps over that line all the time. His tenure in office has been one long slither of corruption. He manipulates and pulls strings and moves people around like pawns, but no one will turn on him because they're afraid they'll go down, too."

"I can't tell you what I don't know."

But he continued to gently work on her with his seductive prosecutor's voice. "He learned at the knees of a master. Old Harry Wentworth was known for his nod-and-wink politics when he was governor."

Sam started at this new attack. "Harry was not crooked," she said defensively. "He could play hardball, but he was not corrupt."

Rafter pounced on the opening. "But Philip is?"

When she didn't answer, he urged, "Come on, Sam. I spent over a year trying to bring that son of a bitch down. It was the biggest case of my career. I was so close to nailing him I could feel his crooked neck in my hands."

"You weren't even close." Sam hesitated, then looked away, deciding that she could tell him this much at least. "He knew about the probe all along. He was toying with you. That's his way."

"Who told him?" Despite the softness of the question, Sam could feel his intense focus. The confined space inside the car vibrated with it. He didn't ask her how she knew. He was too good a prosecutor to risk a direct assault that might stop the trickle of information.

"Sorry." Sam shook her head. "I don't have a clue."

"But Wentworth knew of the surveillance from the start?" he asked, and she could see that the possibility that he'd been scammed by Philip enraged him.

She hesitated again, then met his eyes. "Yes. He knew."

He wanted more, but Sam made it clear the

conversation was over, and they drove the rest of the way home in silence.

Sunday afternoon, Sam made up for not seeing Camille the day before. Camille was eager for news of Matthew's funeral, particularly of the supporting cast of politically plugged-in mourners. "Funerals make great networking opportunity," she managed to push out, her brown eyes alert. Sam sensed the biting humor behind the statement. She dredged up every detail she could remember for Camille to dissect except her run-in with Philip. Camille would not approve of her asking him for money.

That evening she called Hattie Christiansen, who was as eager to talk as Sam, but not over the phone. So directly after work on Monday, Sam crawled through rush-hour traffic, following Hattie's directions to the Christiansen farm half-an-hour outside the city off a winding county road. As Sam bumped along the lengthy, unpaved track approaching the house, the car kicked up a hot plume of grit behind. Near the end, woods closed in on both sides, forming a cool, twisting tunnel that opened up to a lovely meadow after the final curve.

It was not a working farm, Hattie explained to Sam as they left the sprawling, antique-filled farmhouse for the horse barn.

"Matthew grew up in Detroit. He always dreamed of having space. And I adored the privacy after growing up in that mausoleum in Grosse Pointe." She talked on, filling the enormous silence of the place while they climbed a sloping rise to the stable.

Inside, the barn was cool and dark and smelled of hay and healthy animals. "I'm just going to let them out in the yard now that it's not so beastly hot."

Sam, who had never been on a horse in her life, watched Hattie fuss over a large, white stallion from a safe distance.

"This one's a lamb," Hattie said, talking Sam into petting his velvety pink muzzle before leading him out.

She repeated the process with his two smaller stable mates, then joined Sam, hooking her arms over the yard's fence. In companionable silence they watched the horses cavort in the dusty field.

"You said Matthew was upset about something," Sam began after a time.

Hattie was silent a moment, collecting her thoughts. "I didn't want to talk about it after the funeral, especially when Marty Davis came into the room."

At Sam's questioning look, she explained, "Matthew called Marty shortly before the first heart attack. They were fraternity brothers in law school at Madison."

"So they were friends?"

"No, that's the odd thing. Matthew didn't like Marty. He had no respect for the man. I can't imagine why Matthew would ever call him."

It didn't surprise Sam that Matthew had not approved of Marty Davis. The prominent civil defense lawyer reputedly owed his success to cunning and guile rather than any great skill in the law. The two men were complete opposites.

"Rumor has it Davis is seriously ill," Sam said. "Maybe that's why Matthew called him."

"Possibly." Hattie didn't sound convinced. "But I've been thinking that phone call had something to do with why Matthew was upset. In the hospital, when he was drugged up, he said some things—

mostly gibberish about Marty and their law school fraternity, but I think he was trying to tell me something. Once he even mumbled something like, 'Tell Marty he has to.' "

"It could have been the drugs and the fact that they'd just spoken," Sam suggested.

"If that were all, I might agree. But he said other things before he became ill. Nothing concrete." Hattie turned to Sam, her face weary and troubled. "Something was going on, and I think it involved Marty."

Sam repeated Rafter's account of Matthew's call to the attorney general. Hattie listened carefully, without any visible surprise, and when Sam finished, she said, "I'm almost relieved to know it wasn't all in my head."

"You can't possibly believe Matthew would take a bribe or anything like that?" Sam asked quickly.

"Goodness, no! But something happened. And if Marty was involved, it could go back a long time."

"We could talk to him."

"I already have. That was a dead end." Hattie stared off at the distant woods, her face set in a hard line of determination that reminded Sam of Matthew. "Sam, I want to go forward with this. I'm going to call the agent who questioned me before, tell him everything I've told you."

Sam stepped away from the fence, looking at Hattie. "Are you sure? You could just let it go, let the investigation die a natural death. It appears to be headed in that direction."

Hattie smiled wryly. "That's tempting, isn't it. But no. I want to finish what Matthew started." She left the fence after a last look at the horses and walked Sam back to her car. "But, my dear, I don't want you to get caught in the middle. That can be a dangerous place. Let the attorney general agents do their jobs."

Sam nodded, not sure what she could do in any case.

Hattie gave her a quick glance and asked casually, "By the way, is there a woman named Rachel who works in your building?"

Sam searched her memory and came up empty. "I don't think so. Why?"

"It may mean nothing." Hattie discounted it with a wave of her hand. "Matthew said that name as well in the hospital, several times in fact."

"Does it mean anything to you?"

"No. Except there was a Rachel who was very popular with some of the boys in Matthew's law fraternity. In an unsavory way, if you take my meaning." Hattie's mouth thinned with disapproval, then she sighed. "It was the early seventies—students were breaking taboos. I only met Rachel once when I came over for Madison's homecoming weekend. I admit I had some uncharitable thoughts hearing that name on Matthew's lips."

They stopped next to Sam's car. Hattie looked lost in the past and suddenly vulnerable. Sam's heart went out to her.

"Matthew's walnut desk is still in his chambers," Sam reminded her, recalling her wandering thoughts.

Hattie's brisk attention refocused on Sam. "Yes. I met Nick Rafter at the funeral, and he mentioned it, too. He's very nice, decent. I'm surprised the governor had the good sense to appoint him to finish Matthew's term."

Sam thought it kindest not to pop Hattie's delusional bubble on that score. She gently drew her back to the matter at hand. "The desk?"

"Oh, I gave it to Nick. I want to leave something

of Matthew's in his hands." Hattie made a self-deprecating face. "I know it must sound silly—I barely met the man—but I'd like to think I'm passing on part of Matthew to a worthy replacement."

Later at the Jungle, Sam and Kat sorted through the scraps of information Sam had accumulated.

"Well, given that the AG has a plug in their end of the information pipeline—" Kat halted mid-thought and gave Sam a look at once suspicious and disapproving. "You're not considering taking another crack at the citadel, are you?"

Sam glanced away with a rueful smile. "No. That doesn't seem worth the risk. If there was ever anything worth finding in Rafter's office, I'm fairly certain he would have gotten rid of it after last weekend."

Neither took any notice when Billy wandered over from the bookstore between customers. He leaned against the archway between the two establishments, following their conversation while he kept an eye on a browser.

Kat continued, "Then I'd say Madison Law School would be a good place to start if you're inclined to go further with this. It seems a long shot, but maybe something did happen when Christiansen was there."

"Hattie seemed to think that was possible."

Kat's brooding eyes were fixed unseeingly on the far wall of the café. "I've never trusted frat boys. Too many kegs of beer and too much uncontrolled testosterone. Not pretty." She absently pushed the mop of blond hair off her forehead.

Sam regarded her friend thoughtfully, not bothering to point out that she didn't trust any men. Kat had a waifish, Audrey Hepburn face with big green eyes that seemed perpetually shadowed these days. In Sam's opinion, Kat was getting burned out after five years fighting the hopeless battles of the poor. Few legal aid lawyers managed to last as long as she had. One reason why, at thirty, she was already director of the office. The other reason was that she was good at what she did. She cared about the unending stream of desperate humanity flowing through her office.

"You need to take some time off," Sam couldn't help saying, knowing her advice would fall on closed ears. Kat had a missionary mind-set. "When was the last time you took two consecutive days off?"

Kat shrugged a limp shoulder. "I'm fine. When things calm down a bit, I'm going to go visit my family for a few days."

"Things never calm down," Sam pointed out.

Billy spoke up, cutting short their digression. "How you going to dig up dirt on Christiansen's law school days? It might be dicey asking the governor or my own good father if their frat brother was involved in any nasty business."

Sam shook her head. "I hadn't really thought that far. I suppose I could start with the local newspaper."

"There might be a university history," Kat suggested, then frowned as she spotted an obvious snag in that plan. "But I suppose what you're looking for isn't going to turn up in any book."

Billy's sharp gaze made Sam suspect he was a step ahead of them. "Right, but someone who has compiled a history of the law school might know things that didn't make it into the officially sanitized text."

Sam couldn't help smiling at his smug triumph. "Okay, spill it, Billy."

He spun a chair around and straddled it, leaning over with elbows on the table. "I have a customer, a Professor Sophia Somerset," he announced grandly. "She teaches at Madison Law School. She's English—comes in because I stock some unusual British titles." He hitched a shoulder, telling them that the relationship was no big deal. None of his relationships were. "We talk, have coffee. Anyway, a while back she was working on some kind of history of the law school."

Sam perked up. "Do you think she would talk to me? I mean about the sort of things I need to know."

Billy grinned. "I'm guessing she might."

Sophia Somerset had one of those glamorous British accents Americans slobbered over. On the surface, she appeared elegant and aloof—a glacially composed English rose—with stylishly short blond hair, flawless skin, and lovely blue eyes. But as soon as she smiled, the cool mask cracked and warmth flooded her face. Sam, who had initially pegged the professor's age as mid-thirties, immediately subtracted several years.

"You're Billy's friend," the professor said after Sam had introduced herself. She cleared books from a chair and motioned for Sam to sit.

Sam glanced with interest around the cramped office. Law treatises overflowed bookcases and formed mini-mountain ranges on the floor. A utilitarian desk took up most of the remaining space. Beyond the single window, a fleet of small sailboats ripped across Lake Manitou in the afternoon heat. The private university owed its popularity in no small part to being happily situated along the picturesque shores of the small lake and only a half-mile inland from the sugar sand beaches of Lake Michigan.

"I appreciate your seeing me, Professor Somerset." Billy had called ahead to pave the way. Sam hoped the professor was as willing to talk as Billy had predicted. She'd waited until Wednesday afternoon, while Rafter was away hearing oral arguments, to make the hour-long drive northwest to Madison University.

"Please, call me Sophie. I'm glad you caught me while summer school is still in session." She pulled a face. "Junior faculty draw that little pleasure, thus ensuring that full professors don't risk missing their tee-off times at the links, you see."

Sam smiled, equally charmed by the accent and the tart irreverence.

Sophie settled back in her chair. "I understand you have some questions about Madison's history—the unofficial, uncut version."

Sam nodded. "Billy said you've been compiling a history of the law school as part of some big anniversary."

Sophie smiled broadly. "I take it you're not a Madison Law alum."

"No. Michigan."

"Ah. Well done." She nodded approvingly.

Sophie had gone to Yale Law. They spent a few amiable minutes comparing their paths after law school. Sam could tell Sophie was curious about Sam's career stumble, but she was too tactful to ask about it directly, and Sam habitually avoided talking about it.

Finally, Sophie returned to the matter at hand, explaining, "This next academic year is Madison's centennial anniversary. Our fearless leader decided we needed an official, recorded history to commemorate the occasion. As the junior-most faculty member on the law school's committee, I drew that bloody awful task as well." She shrugged. "So, what can I help you with? I must confess, I've been dying of curiosity to meet one of Billy's friends. Are you a Shakespearean scholar, as well?"

Sam nearly laughed at hearing Billy, who disdained conventional academics, described as a scholar but managed to keep a reasonably straight face. "No. Just a lawyer looking for answers."

Sam paused, feeling suddenly at a loss because she didn't know where to begin or what questions to ask. "What I have is vague, maybe adding up to nothing." She gave an apologetic shrug. "Just a time—the early seventies. A place or maybe a group—a new Madison law frat. And a few names—Marty Davis and Matthew Christiansen, who were both members of the fraternity, and a girl—"

"Rachel," Sophie whispered, looking suddenly a good deal more serious.

"So something did happen," Sam said unhappily, her hope that she was on a wild-goose chase fading fast.

"I'm not sure anything happened involving the fraternity or any of our alums," Sophie said cautiously. "I'll tell you what I do know, with the warning that some people were quite touchy about the subject when I asked a few questions."

Sophie rose and paced over to the window. "I had work-study students looking through local and school newspapers for items relating to the law school—that's how we stumbled across it. Rachel Holtz was a twenty-year-old townie who disappeared in 1973 after last being seen at the Sigma fraternity. Apparently she was a frequent guest there, liked to party with the law students, do drugs."

Sophie turned from the window and continued. "You get the picture. They probably considered her white trash. When she disappeared her parents made some noise and the local police asked a few questions, but the story died quickly."

"What explanation did the fraternity give?"

"They admitted she'd been at the frat house having a bit of a private party with one of their pledges. But two or three brothers claimed she'd gone off with some mystery man who came by the frat to collect her. They said they thought maybe she left the state with this chap." Sophie grimaced. "Sounds suspicious, doesn't it? She never turned up again."

"And the parents accepted that explanation?"

"I doubt they had much choice." Sophie wandered back to her desk and perched against it. "This is a college town. Thirty years ago there were three fairly rigid classes of residents: academics at the top, students from mostly affluent families in the middle, and townies on the bottom. Tourism has helped blur those boundaries and blunt the economic dependency on a single revenue stream, but it's still largely a one-employer town. I imagine everyone, including the authorities, had an interest in protecting the reputation of the school."

"I'll try to get a membership list from the fraternity."

"Good luck. It went defunct after only a few years. Residential fraternities are not popular among graduate students."

"Maybe the national organization would have a membership list," Sam mussed aloud.

Sophie dashed that possibility as well. "They were never affiliated with a larger organization. As for Marty Davis and your former boss—I don't know anything about them other than that their pictures are in what the students call our rogues gallery."

Sam raised a brow. "I'm sure there's a story there."

"We have a wall of portraits of prominent alums of the law school." Sophie heaved a sigh. "Unfortunately, several have been indicted for various misdeeds in recent years. Hence the tag."

She regarded Sam steadily, her expression reflecting concern. "These are powerful men. You'll see for yourself if you read the news articles. I don't know why you're interested in this, but keep in mind that men in high places have lots to lose. If they are hiding something, or even if they're not, they're not going to want any trace of suspicion landing on them now."

With Sophie's warning on her mind, Sam drove down the side streets of Harbour Grace to the local library. The village was perched on a hilly peninsula with its front to Lake Michigan and its back to Lake Manitou. During the summer when the campus was largely deserted, it doubled as a popular resort community. The university was tucked behind the town along the shores of the smaller lake. According to a historical marker in front of the small library, a turn-of-the-century visionary had snapped up the land cheap during the economic decline following the gilded lumber age and turned it into one of the state's most popular campuses.

Inside, Sam found that the library had back issues of the local newspaper stored on microfiche. Armed with Rachel's full name and the pertinent time period, she quickly located the relevant articles. They contained little additional information beyond what Sophie had already told her and were remarkable only in their brevity. Philip Wentworth's name popped out as president and spokesman for the fraternity, though Sam already knew from Billy that Philip and Governor Graham were among the half-dozen original Sigma members.

On the ride home, Sam wrestled with where to go from here. Sophie's warning had struck a responsive chord. Several of the most politically powerful men in the state were possibly involved in the disappearance of a young woman. The risks involved in pursuing the matter were suddenly frightening. Sam was enough of a fatalist to fear that, on her own, she would be an easy casualty. In the interest of self-preservation, she decided not to delve further into Rachel's disappearance. She would sit tight, keep her eyes open, and wait to see what the AG investigation produced.

That evening, she called Hattie Christiansen and passed the information along for her to do with as she wished. Sam assumed Hattie would hand it over to the AG, but she didn't ask. If Hattie decided to drop the matter at this point, that was her business.

After spending the next morning closeted with Agent Foley, Sam was working at her desk during the afternoon when Rafter stuck his head in the doorway. "Got a minute?"

Sam nodded. "How did oral arguments go?"

"Not bad." He leaned against the threshold, looking more relaxed now that they were over. "Hattie Christiansen called this morning."

"Oh?" For an awful moment Sam wondered whether Hattie had told Rafter about Sam's jaunt to Madison University. She didn't relish another interrogation.

Her unease must have shown because he regarded her quizzically before continuing. "She didn't want us to overlook Liz's birthday tomorrow."

"Oh . . . Yes." Sam hid her relief. "Matthew always took her out to a nice restaurant for lunch and then gave her the rest of the afternoon off."

"Hattie said you should come along, too, so it doesn't look like I'm having a dalliance with my secretary. She was most insistent that I protect my reputation from the appearance of impropriety." His grin showed that he was vastly amused by the notion. "So the three of us have a reservation at one at Elsa's. Is that okay for you?"

Recognizing this as another of those occasions when she could not graciously avoid Rafter's company, Sam agreed. "One is fine."

"Good."

She waited for him to leave, but he relaxed against the doorjamb and crossed his arms over his chest.

"Remember *People versus Percy*—the teacher convicted of voluntary manslaughter in the shooting death of his schizophrenic father?"

"Yes."

"You think there was sufficient evidence to sustain the jury's verdict? You didn't say in your memo."

Sam shrugged. "It's a close call. You're the judge."

Rafter's eyebrows shot up in mock astonishment. "Do you mean to tell me *you* have no opinion?"

Sam gave him a grudging smile acknowledging his score. "There is sufficient evidence on which a jury could reasonably base a guilty verdict—so yes, technically the court should affirm the verdict."

"But . . . ?"

"But I'm not convinced he did it."

"Despite all the evidence pointing to him?" Rafter regarded her steadily.

"Sometimes evidence is not what it seems." She met his gaze. "No one actually saw the defendant shoot his father."

"Then why didn't he offer a defense?"

"Maybe he felt he had more to lose if he did."

"So you think he's protecting another family member, is that it?"

"Possibly. Family relationships are complicated." Sam shifted uneasily, fairly certain they were no longer talking strictly about the Percy case. "If you think there's sufficient evidence to affirm, why ask me? You're the judge."

He finally released her gaze and stared past her out the window. "Because the crime doesn't fit the guy's profile."

"Getting soft, Rafter?" Sam's mouth twisted into a stiff smile as she reminded him, "You used to believe people had to assume responsibility for their offenses regardless of their background. It's all about evidence. This defendant even had a fair trial."

His impatient gaze returned to her. "Of course criminals must be made to assume responsibility for their actions, but that doesn't mean I want to condemn an innocent man."

But that's close to what he'd done to her, Sam reflected. "So kick it back on the jury instruction error," she said coolly. "The prosecution may decide not to retry." She picked up her pen and focused on the brief in front of her, indicating that the conversation was over.

Rafter was not so easily dismissed. "Look, Sam, this is completely different from your situation—"

She cut him off. "Let's not keep rehashing the past. It doesn't get us anywhere."

"No, it doesn't seem to," he agreed stiffly. "At least answer my curiosity about one thing. You were up in arms about that parental rights termination case. But this one, where you think the poor slob might actually be innocent, you did nothing. Why?"

"He's an adult. For all we know, a guilty adult. If he is innocent, he's probably protecting someone." Sam met his cool blue gaze. "That's his decision, isn't it?"

"No, it isn't. Obviously our entire justice system is jeopardized if innocent people are convicted."

At his words, she gave him a pointed look. He hadn't hesitated to sentence her on less evidence, and unlike poor Percy, a jury hadn't found her guilty.

Rafter opened his mouth to respond, then promptly shut it. Shaking his head in exasperation, he started to leave but evidently couldn't resist a parting shot. "Look, if you don't have the guts to talk openly about the big blue goblin that's always in the room with us, don't try to make me feel guilty by continually cueing the violins."

Sam was still sputtering with outrage when he walked out. Of all the nerve! He was the one who kept bringing up the past.

CHAPTER 6

That evening, Sam listened to her phone messages while she kicked off her shoes and began unpacking a bag of groceries. She stilled when a voice she hadn't heard in years came on inviting her to tea the next day at three. "Please call and leave message eef you are not able to make it, Samantha, dear."

Sam had not seen Harry's widow since shortly after his death six years ago, but age had certainly not diminished the steel in her cultured, faintly accented voice. However couched as an invitation, Sam recognized the call as an imperial summons and wondered why it came now after all these years of silence.

She ran it by Billy later in his apartment downstairs when he came home from the bookstore. Although he was often baffled by the complicated inner workings of his grandmother's mind, he guessed the invitation probably had something to do with Sam's attempt to put the squeeze on Philip. "Why don't you take some of the money from my trust fund," he urged. "You deserve it more than I do."

They'd been over this before, and Sam gave him

the same answer. "Your trustee wouldn't allow it, and besides I don't want to take your money."

"Well then, good luck with the old battle-ax," Billy muttered as Sam was leaving. Sam smiled at this description of his tiny, birdlike grandmother.

Liz's fancy birthday lunch at Elsa's the following day dragged on well into the afternoon. Finally, Sam glanced apologetically at her watch and announced, "I've got to run. I have an appointment at three."

Across the table, Rafter, looking like a dark prince in a black suit and crisp white shirt, signaled for the waiter.

"No," Sam protested. "Stay and finish your coffee. I'll catch a cab." She rose, leaving them no choice, and bussed Liz on the cheek. "Happy Birthday."

Nick watched her dash off through the elegantly set tables. Lingering diners paused to admire her as she flashed by. Their reaction was natural; she was a beautiful woman. Lately, those long legs had starred in a few of Nick's own nocturnal fantasies. In truth, he was finding it impossible to be constantly around her without becoming confused. Quite aside from the beautiful shell, they used to click on a personal level. Surprisingly, when they managed to put aside their hostility, they still did.

"Now where do you suppose she's off to this time," he wondered aloud.

Liz gave him a thoughtful look and then glanced after Sam. "She said she was having tea with royalty."

Nick looked at her quizzically.

"Don't even ask," Liz laughed. "I don't know."

The elegant, three-story Tudor was one of the oldest and largest homes in the long-established neighborhood of upper-income conservatism surrounding Reeds Lake. Not much inside had changed in the six years since Harry's death. Sam had visited only a time or two since then and never when Marie was in residence. She spent an increasing amount of time in her native south of France.

An unfamiliar housekeeper showed Sam to the library office, where she had spent many happy hours as a child reading books while Harry and Camille worked nearby at the big oak desk. Other memories crowded in too, not all good, but some, mostly of Billy, that she treasured.

"Samantha." Marie Wentworth held out gnarled hands. Regal in magenta silk, she perched on a chintz sofa. As imperious as ever, Sam decided, leaning down and dutifully bussing the soft, wrinkled cheek offered up to her. Marie was a little Napoleon standing just five feet tall in her trademark powder blue pumps. As a child, Sam had been terrified of her.

"You are looking well, my dear." Her keen eyes were inspecting the sleek, bone-colored suit and colorful silk scarf Sam had carefully selected for the occasion. She nodded her approval. "Eet has been a long time." Her accent bore traces of her French aristocratic roots.

That Marie was seeing her in the library rather than the sitting room was a distinction not lost on Sam. This was a business meeting.

At nearly eighty, she continued to rule the Wentworth household with a firm hand and sharp wit. Philip, who saw no reason to incur the added expense of setting up separate housekeeping when he spent so little time in the state he represented, was content with the arrangement. His wife, Virginia, couldn't abide her overbearing mother-in-law and spent even less time here than Philip. She preferred life as a Washington hostess, finding Grand

Rapids entirely too provincial for her Saks Fifth Avenue tastes.

While the housekeeper set out tea, Sam scanned an area of wall near the ceiling for the camera. If she hadn't known exactly where to look, she would never have spotted it because it was so much smaller than the one she remembered from her childhood. The tiny lens almost disappeared into the hunt-scene wallpaper background. Sam wondered if they were currently on candid camera. She was probably one of the few people, outside of immediate family, aware that many of the rooms in the mansion were wired and that the old-fashioned-looking mirror surrounded by bookshelves was in fact one-way glass. She and Billy used to hide in the secret little cubbyhole behind it.

"I understand from Philip that you are having financial difficulties," Marie began when the housekeeper left. She gave Sam a stern look. "You should not be bothering heem with such things."

Sam began to explain Camille's grim circumstances.

Marie cut her off. "In the future, you will come to me. I have spoken to the director of the Stanley Care Center about your aunt." Sam's eyes widened in surprise. It seemed more than a little strange for Marie Wentworth to involve herself in the medical affairs of her aunt.

Marie read her thoughts. "You think it's odd that I would concern myself with my late husband's mistress."

Sam nearly sloshed tea onto her lap.

Marie gave a tiny shrug, and continued. "We French have a healthier attitude about these matters. Americans are so prudish about such things. The British, too. And they can't cook, either," she added with an indignant smack of her hand on the chintz arm, as if one deficiency logically flowed from the other.

Riveted by Marie's personal revelations, Sam paid scant attention to her interesting take on cultural differences.

"I had physical problems that prevented me from meeting Harry's needs," Marie continued. "It was natural for heem to satisfy those needs elsewhere." She regarded Sam with reproach. "Unfortunately your aunt was foolish enough to fall in love with heem." She clucked her tongue. "And he, twenty-five years older."

Sam was uncertain how to respond to this unprecedented candor. While Camille's affection for Harry had been readily apparent to her, this was the first Sam had heard anyone openly acknowledge that their relationship had gone beyond platonic. "I know my aunt was fond of the governor," she began diplomatically, "but—"

"Bah!" Marie waived a dismissive hand. "I am French and almost eighty years old. My sensibilities are not so easily upset. But we will speak of it no more." To Sam's relief, Marie picked up where she'd left off earlier. "The director of the nursing home thinks your aunt will not benefit significantly from this computer."

Sam leaned forward. She, too, had heard this from Camille's doctors. They were pessimistic about Camille's prognosis and had even suggested moving her to a regular nursing home to cut down on expenses. But Sam was not ready to give up. "I know she can still communicate minimally now, but if she doesn't get the computer soon, she may not be able to master it. More importantly, if her ability to communicate declines any further, I'm terrified that she's going to give up entirely. And there are special treatments and therapies that might help her regain mobility."

Marie contemplated Sam a moment. "Well, *chérie*, the doctors may not agree with you, but I do admire your commitment to your aunt." She stood, and Sam assumed their meeting was over. Instead, Marie circled Harry's huge old desk, sat, and pulled out her checkbook. "You may use this in any way you want, but I urge you to wait on that speaking computer."

A few minutes later, grateful and hugely relieved, Sam walked out with a check for ten thousand dollars, enough—she hoped—to cover both the computer and some of the other treatments.

Nick parked in front of Billy's Books and scanned the street to make sure Sam's decrepit Saab wasn't lurking about anywhere. After dropping Liz at her car, he had impulsively decided to start the weekend a few hours early and pay Billy Wentworth a visit while Sam was otherwise occupied. He was fed up with her cat-and-mouse games and sly innuendoes. It was long past time to find out exactly what had happened two years ago. He was not proud of the way he'd acted back then, and her little digs were constantly jabbing a sore spot.

Nick got out of his car and slipped off his jacket and tie, squinting through the sun at the bookstore's aged brick façade. Looking back, he knew that the critical mistake O'Neal had made two years ago was in not forcing Sam's hand, effectively leaving her in control of the flow of information. That was a mistake he intended not to repeat.

A bell jingled when Nick stepped inside the musty interior of Billy's Books. Dust motes danced in a shaft of sunlight between packed bookcases. Around the exterior of the shop, shelves climbed walls all the way up to the molded plaster ceiling;

varnished wooden ladders on tracks provided access to the upper reaches.

Billy looked up from a book he was reading behind the counter next to a cash register, the only modern-looking piece of equipment in sight. "I expected you would turn up again sooner or later," he said matter-of-factly, showing no surprise at Nick's appearance. He set aside his book.

"Why is that?"

"You want information." Billy watched him with lively interest. He finally cracked a smile. "A beer might loosen my tongue."

Nick knew when he was being toyed with. "It didn't work last time," he pointed out. "All I got out of you were riddles."

Billy shrugged. "Maybe I needed time to check you out. Then again, maybe I just like free beer."

Or more likely, Nick thought, he was bored and enjoyed matching wits. But Nick gamely tagged along into the nearly empty café. Billy snagged two Guinnesses from a tall cooler behind the counter, then spun a chair around, straddling it.

Nick considered how best to work on him while he took a long, cold swallow. He settled on the direct approach. "Tell me what happened two years ago. Was Samantha having an affair with your father?"

Billy gave him a pained look, as if disappointed that Nick needed even to ask such a question. "You were a blind fool back then, Rafter, and time doesn't seem to have improved your vision."

"Meaning?" Rafter prodded, impatient.

"Meaning no. Anyone who knows Sam knows she doesn't have a crooked or disloyal bone in her—well, everyone except for you and that twit, Brian Kingsley," Billy amended with a distasteful look that plainly said how he felt about Brian, and probably Nick, too.

Thinking to test Billy's honesty, Nick asked, "How about your father?"

"My dear father, unfortunately, has more than his share of crooked bones, as I'm sure you're well aware."

Nick hid his surprise at this matter-of-fact admission from the son who bore an almost eerie resemblance to his prominent father. Buying time with another leisurely swig at the bottle, he wondered how much Billy really knew about what happened two years ago and whether he was protecting Sam. "Are you speaking as Sam's friend or lover?"

"See, this is part of your problem. You won't think outside your narrow lawyer's box." Billy shook his head in disgust. "You can relax, though, I'm not Sam's lover."

Surprisingly, Nick *could* feel the tension ease from his shoulders at Billy's disclaimer. And that made him immediately tense up again because he didn't want to feel relieved that Sam was not involved with Billy Wentworth. He didn't want to feel anything at all for her.

Nick dragged his attention back to Billy. "If Sam was not sleeping with your father, then what was she doing at his home alone with him for two hours on a Saturday night?"

"Suffering?" Billy grinned.

Nick was not amused. "Come on, Billy. If you're her friend, tell me what's going on. You imply she's innocent, well, here's your big chance. Be a hero. Come to her defense. Because she sure as hell isn't trying to help herself." He leaned across the table, looking Billy in the eye. "If I screwed up two years ago, I promise I'll do everything in my power to make it right. Okay?"

"Do you think you screwed up?"

"So far, no. But I'm willing to listen."

"Is this an official inquiry?"

"No." The guy would have made a great litigator, Nick thought with no small measure of respect.

"Then it's personal." Billy swigged his beer, watching Nick thoughtfully. "So, 'sweet revenge grows harsh.' "

"Shakespeare?" Nick took a stab.

Billy gave a slow nod of approval. *"Othello.* Perhaps there's hope for you yet, Rafter."

Nick waited, sensing he'd just passed some bizarre test.

The front legs of Billy's chair hit the floor with a thump. He leaned forward confidentially and rested his elbows on the table. "Do you know anything about Sam's aunt?" he asked in a lowered voice.

Nick prayed that no one would come into the bookstore now because he sensed, finally, that he was about to hit pay dirt.

"I remember she had an aunt with Parkinson's."

Billy nodded grimly. "Camille. She's in bad shape. Most of Sam's salary goes to keeping her in a fancy nursing home for patients with neurological problems."

Billy fell silent, and Nick found himself the object of a long, measuring look. He met it, waiting Billy out, willing him to continue.

Finally, he did. "What you probably don't know is that she was my grandfather's personal secretary for years," Billy began.

The ensuing days passed without incident. Sam knew of Rafter's visit to Billy's Books and couldn't miss his speculative gazes on those few occasions when their paths happened to cross. She also knew it was only a matter of time before he cornered her so she made a point of staying out of his way, delaying the inevitable as long as possible. That was easier now that they were no longer meeting in the afternoons.

Meanwhile, Rafter was working more closely with the research attorney he'd chosen as his law clerk, Jake McClain. Sam had offered to trade offices with him, but Rafter had vetoed the idea. Apparently convenience was less important than keeping an eye on her. So Jake climbed the stairs from research several times each day.

In the mornings, Sam continued working with Agent Foley, reviewing a rapidly shrinking pile of cases as they forged backward through her tenure with Matthew. As far as she could tell, they had yet to find anything to suggest Matthew had engaged in any kind of judicial misconduct. Sam began to relax as the end grew near. She still didn't know for sure whether Foley intended to continue on into her predecessor's cases and, if so, whether he would want her assistance.

On Thursday, they finally finished. Foley leaned back in his chair and stretched his neck muscles. "That's it then," he said, leisurely beginning to pack up his notes.

"We're done?" Sam could hardly believe the ordeal was really over.

Foley actually smiled at her. "We're done."

Sam returned his smile with a broad one of her own. "Thank God." She felt such an upwelling of relief and liberation that she felt like hugging him and crying at the same time. Instead she continued to smile inanely while she held herself together by a thread. She would call Hattie Christiansen and tell her the good news tonight.

Foley cleared his throat and awkwardly patted her shoulder. "Hey, it's going to be okay." Ever since that first day, he had carefully avoided her gaze, but now, for once, he was really looking at her.

"Thanks." She smiled wryly. "It's just that I've been so worried."

He nodded and finished loading his briefcase. Sam walked him out to the door of the complex. They were alone; Liz wasn't at her desk. He stopped at the door and looked at her, as if engaged in a silent struggle over something.

"Samantha—" His gaze darted past her over her shoulder, and he swallowed whatever he'd been about to say. Sam knew without looking that Rafter had come out of his office. She could feel the force of his disapproval on her back. It was like the touch of a live cattle wire—unpleasant and unforgettable.

Foley's suddenly self-conscious gaze darted back to her and then away. "Maybe I'll see you around," he mumbled.

"Wait. Let me grab my lunch and I'll ride down with you," she said, wanting to avoid another confrontation with Rafter.

She needn't have bothered. Now that Rafter's race to prepare for oral arguments had passed, his former subordinates had been crossing Ottawa Street in droves to check out his new digs. Liz joked that she had become his social secretary. In the time it took Sam to dash to and from the refrigerator in the adjacent file room to grab her lunch, Meredith Pusch, yet another of Rafter's former assistants, came to call.

Meredith Pusch, called "Pushy Pusch" behind her back by the scores of other attorneys in the office, was chief of the Health Care Fraud Unit. In a profession filled with hustlers, Pushy's consuming ambition stood out. She was smart, attractive, charming, and had left as many enemies behind as she had allies strategically positioned in high places ahead. According to a coworker Sam was still in touch with, Pushy had her sights locked on the top job Rafter had recently vacated. That would be a meteoric rise, indeed, for she'd snagged the unit chief position only within the last year.

"Ah, Sam," Pushy hummed when she saw Sam come out of the records room. "So this is where you landed. I heard you got a job as a law clerk. Congrats." She smiled a saccharine-sweet smile as phony as her contact-colored green eyes.

Sam nodded without expression. "You're looking well, Meredith."

Sam surreptitiously watched her old adversary while Rafter introduced Foley to her. A few months before the Wentworth debacle, Pushy had begun maneuvering for the top job in the Health Care Fraud Unit, where both women were assigned. Unfortunately, other attorneys in the unit began indiscreetly speculating that Rafter was grooming Sam for the job. Until then, Pushy and Sam had never been more than indifferent acquaintances; Sam was of no use to the more senior attorney. But after that, Pushy's Gucci gloves came off. She undermined Sam at every turn. Never overtly. She was too smart for that. But subtle attacks from ever-shifting directions had forced Sam to be constantly on alert. To this day, Pushy was the one person in the office Sam could imagine planting that damning file in her desk.

As soon as decently possible, Sam hustled Foley out, leaving Pushy to work her wiles on Rafter. Her lust for Rafter was as well known around the U.S. Attorney's Office as her ambition. Perhaps now that he was no longer her boss, Pushy might stand a chance. They deserved each other, Sam thought, then immediately felt guilty. Even Rafter didn't deserve that fate. At least he thought he was doing the right thing. With Pushy, such issues took a backseat to her eclipsing self-interest.

Outside, Sam never did find out what Foley had been about to tell her before Rafter's interruption. They parted in front of the building with another round of "take cares" before he strode off, leaving her unenlightened.

Sam managed to avoid Rafter the rest of the afternoon. Later that evening, she stopped by the bookstore to see if Billy had seen Kat, who was being unusually hard to reach. She wasn't at her carriage house apartment or at work, and she wasn't picking up her cell phone. Under normal circumstances, Sam wouldn't be alarmed, but she knew Kat was upset because one of her young clients had turned up missing. Sam suspected Kat might be doing some amateur detective work in an undesirable part of town. Legal aid had no funds to hire a pro.

Sam was much too busy worrying about Kat to at first notice Rafter listening to a blues guitarist over dinner and a drink in the Jungle next door. She found Billy pacing the aisles separating the stacks. The IRS had offered him a settlement figure, and he had to decide whether to accept it. All too familiar with the hopeless state of Billy's records, Sam urged him to take the deal. "It doesn't seem out-of-line. It could be a lot worse." She quickly changed the subject before they got bogged down in Billy's what-ifs.

"Have you seen Kat?"

He hadn't. Sam was about to circle through the café to double-check that Kat hadn't crawled in for a late supper—a definite possibility given her brutal schedule. Instead, she skidded to a stop in the arched entryway when she spotted not Kat, but Rafter. She did an abrupt about-face on the soles of her running shoes and slipped outside through the bookstore.

CHAPTER 7

"Samantha, wait!" Rafter called out behind her as she sped up the sidewalk away from the bookstore.

"Sorry, I'm a little busy," she tossed back over her shoulder and picked up her pace to a moderate jog. She had on running shorts and a T-shirt because she'd intended to talk Kat into taking a run if she found her.

Rafter caught up a short distance down the block, jogging along beside her in worn boat mocks, khaki shorts, and a Pat Metheny World Tour T-shirt.

"We need to talk."

"I think we've done remarkably well these last few days *not* talking."

"Better here than in the office," he pointed out, easily keeping pace with her.

Reluctantly, Sam slowed. She couldn't avoid talking to him forever, and he was right: this was probably a better time and place than in the office.

He fell into step with her. "I spoke to Billy last week."

"I heard."

"He told me everything."

"Oh?"

He peered at her through the gathering twilight. "You don't seem terribly bothered by that."

"What exactly do you want, Rafter?"

"I know that your aunt was Governor Wentworth's longtime secretary and probably his mistress, too."

"So?"

They waited for a car and crossed the street. "So I know you practically grew up with Billy, and I know about your aunt's illness." Rafter stopped on the other side in the dim glow of a street lamp. Against her better judgment, Sam stopped too, intensely curious to know what conclusions he'd drawn. "Billy said you went to the senator to ask for money Harry Wentworth promised you in order to take care of your aunt." He looked at her accusingly, his eyes frosty. She could tell he was royally miffed. "Why on earth couldn't you have told me that two years ago?"

This was exactly the problem Sam had anticipated when Billy told her what he'd done. Each half-truth forced them deeper and deeper into a maze of deceit. She had no choice but to give Rafter another half-truth and hope that would satisfy him.

"Harry's money came with a price tag. I promised never to breathe a word of my aunt's relationship with him." Sam turned away from the yellow glow of the streetlight, hiding her face in shadow lest it give her away. "Nothing was ever to tarnish the Wentworth political mythology. Anyway that's why it sounded as though I was threatening Philip in Grosse Pointe. In a way I guess I was. He was balking at keeping his side of the bargain."

Rafter searched her shadowed face for the truth. "What were you thinking? You know full well that a criminal investigation should have taken precedence over any promise you may have made."

"Don't tell me that now you think I'm innocent?" Sam asked, trying to turn the subject. She had no intention of letting anything more slip. But he was not so easily manipulated.

"I see what you're doing. I know there's more to the story, and eventually I'll get it."

And that, Sam thought with a shiver, was the other reason Billy should have kept his mouth zipped.

A block ahead, near her apartment house, a car pulled over and parked. Thinking it was Kat's Escort, she began walking toward it. Rafter stayed with her.

"But to answer your question—do I now think you're innocent? Not necessarily. You still had motive and opportunity. And of course there's the file. None of the evidence is mutually exclusive. But I admit, the whole thing is more complicated than I thought."

"Doubts, Rafter? I'm impressed."

He ignored her sarcasm. "We had to fire you. You were a security risk. What was I supposed to tell the FBI—that you refused to account for your presence at Senator Wentworth's home or any of the other evidence against you, but I'm keeping you on anyway?" His voice was as defensive as it was adamant. Sam wondered cynically which one of them he was trying to convince. He glanced away from her, his expression almost embarrassed. "But I should not have hurt your reputation in the legal community, at least not the way I did and not without a full hearing. You are right about that. I'm sorry. I acted out of anger."

His unexpected apology stunned Sam into silence.

"I want to make it up to you," he went on when

she said nothing. "You'll be leaving the court in a couple months. I'd like to help you get your career back on track."

Sam found her voice. "I don't think having the reputation of slime is something that can be easily fixed."

"I'm serious. Over the last few days, I've given some thought on how to do it."

They stopped in front of her building. Sam followed Rafter's glance to the car that had passed them earlier. It was parked in front of a brick Victorian two doors down that, like hers, had been split into apartments. Sam had already realized the car wasn't Kat's. Idly, as she scrambled to reestablish bearings that Rafter had just knocked asunder, she noticed the shadow of a person sitting inside, probably waiting for someone in the house.

Dismissing the car, Sam cast Rafter a narrow-eyed look, trying to read him. "Let me see if I have this straight. You want to help me even though you still think I'm probably guilty as hell."

"Even though I'm not sure whether you are or not," he corrected. "I haven't thought this out entirely, but maybe if we . . ." He hesitated, uncharacteristic indecision and uncertainty written across his face.

"Why am I suddenly afraid of where this conversation is going?" Sam muttered. *Be careful when he's nice,* she reminded herself, resisting the tug of warmth she felt at this glimpse of softening in him. When she'd come under scrutiny two years ago, he'd been nice at first, too, pleading with her to trust him and let him help her. She hated remembering how sorely tempted she'd been to crawl into his arms and let him fix everything. She'd never dreamed that he would sabotage her career. But the hard reality was, he had.

"I thought it might dispel the rumors if we were seen together at a few events, maybe the bar association's summer ball next weekend . . ." He cleared his throat. "If you're free. That would be a good place to start."

They'd wandered up the walk to the bottom of the porch steps. Sam stared at him, appalled. "You can't be serious!"

His mouth quirked into a brief half-smile. "I am."

"There must be some other way. Couldn't you just call the people you poisoned against me and unpoison me?"

"Afraid not." He glanced away from her into the street, looking even more uncomfortable. "I only talked to a couple well-connected and notoriously indiscreet members of the bar. From there it took on a life of its own that I had not anticipated or intended. I'm sorry, Sam, but I'm afraid any attempt at a retraction at this late date would simply fuel more rumors. The good news is that, after a while, details fade and memories fog. It's been a long time. If people see us together, they'll assume they remembered wrong."

"I've always wondered what exactly those details were."

"Only the truth. The story was embellished along the way." He dug his hands into the pockets of his pants. "I said only that you were suspected of acting unethically with the subject of a federal investigation."

"Well, that certainly did the job, didn't it?" Sam said with false brightness, managing to force the words past the lump in her throat. She'd always known Rafter had engineered her career's free fall. Still, it hurt like hell hearing him admit it.

"Sam—" He reached out, touching her arm. She angrily shook it off. "How could you do that to me, Nick?" Years of accumulated bitterness and pain poured into her voice.

"I'm sorry. I shouldn't have. But dammit, Sam, what exactly was I supposed to do? By rights, you should have been stripped of your license to practice, or worse. Was I supposed to suspend all the rules for you? Was I supposed to ignore the whole thing, pretend it didn't happen, when you refused to give me any explanation? Why?"

"Because—" Their eyes locked and Sam saw the same angry frustration reflected back at her. *Why indeed?* Because she thought he knew her better than Brian ever had? Because for months before that she'd been nagged by doubts over whether she was involved with the right man? Doubts that had made her feel guilty and more loyal than ever to Brian. Ironically, Brian had suffered no such qualms when he unceremoniously dumped her a few months later.

"Because . . . ?" Rafter prompted, watching her closely.

Sam straightened. "Because we were friends. You were supposed to trust me."

"Then could *you* not have trusted me enough to tell me the truth?" he shot back, hands on hips.

She glared at him, long-festering anger and hurt overriding caution. "I did trust you. More than anyone. And for some bizarre reason that escapes me at the moment, I thought you knew me well enough to know that I would never do anything to betray you or my job. I thought you would trust me when I told you I'd done nothing wrong. We were friends, dammit!"

For a moment he didn't say anything. He simply looked at her in the yellow light cast by the porch lamp, his normally handsome features twisted with pain and regret. "You put me in an impossible situation, Sam." He sighed heavily. "Did it never occur to you that friends trust friends with the truth?"

The quietly spoken question hung in the air. Deflated, Sam didn't respond. She turned to leave, but paused. "Thanks for the offer, Rafter, but I don't think it's a good idea." She was mindful of the need to improve her standing in the legal community, but not this way. Not with him.

He smiled faintly. "Friends also help each other. At least think about it."

Behind them, the screen door banged open and Kat dashed out of Sam's building. Still dressed in her work clothes, she looked haggard and wrinkled under the stark porch light, her blond hair an untidy mop. "I've been waiting for you," she called out to Sam on the way down the porch steps. "I didn't know you were out here until I heard you arguing."

Sam watched her in concern. "What's wrong? I've been looking all over the place for you."

"Nothing's wrong with me." She brushed by Rafter and stopped in front of Sam. "I need your help, though."

Understanding dawned. "You found your missing client."

Kat nodded grimly. "She needs to be relocated to the women's shelter." Then she shot Rafter an assessing look. Sam knew Kat was considering his possible usefulness. "I could use your help, too, Nick."

"Lead on," he said gamely.

Kat had parked off the street in the poorly lit dirt lot some distance behind Sam's building. As they crossed the yard, she quickly filled them in on the plan. "I'll be driving the decoy car. You and Nick will drive Tanya and her baby. Give me ten minutes head start, then pick them up at this address." She handed Sam a slip of paper. "It's on the west side. Not a great neighborhood, so be careful. You know where to take them, Sam."

Kat thought Rafter's car would be a better cover so Sam and Rafter piled into her Escort to be dropped at his car in front of the bookstore. Halfway there, Rafter spoke up from the cramped back-seat, "I think we're being followed. It's the car that was parked on the street a couple doors down."

Kat shot a glance in the rearview mirror. "Blast. How did they know before I got there?" She pulled over and turned off her lights. The other car passed and turned the corner. Kat inched her car forward until they could just see that the other car had parked on the side street, waiting. "Anyone have a cell phone? My battery is shot."

Rafter pulled his out of his pocket and handed it up. "I'm not sure this fellow is following you, Kat."

"Doesn't matter. I'm getting rid of him anyway." She spoke briefly to someone—most likely the po-lice or someone at the shelter, Sam couldn't tell which—and within minutes a squad car arrived with lights flashing. As soon as it pulled up behind the other car, Kat sped off.

Following Kat's directions, Rafter and Sam gave her ten minutes' head start before setting out from the café. The ride was fast, tense, and except for Sam's occasional directions, quiet. The closer they got, the more the neighborhood deterio-rated. Teenage boys congregated in front of small shops on mean street corners, scaring shoppers away. This was where many of Kat's clients strug-gled to lead their less-than-perfect lives. To Sam, it represented where she'd come from and where she never wanted to go back to.

The instant Rafter pulled up in front of a dilapidated duplex, two women hurried out, evidently on the lookout for his black BMW. A pretty young Latino girl of about nineteen with a sleeping baby in her arms quickly climbed inside the back. The older woman looked on, hands covering her mouth in a useless attempt to hold back her anguish. As they drove away, silent tears streamed down the young mother's face.

"You'll be safe at the shelter," Sam said softly after a while, her heart going out to her.

The girl shook her head. "They won't keep us. It's too dangerous. They're sending us out of state. I don't even know where."

Sam watched helplessly as the girl's tears flowed harder. She was barely an adult, too young to be suddenly cast adrift from her family on her own, much less with a baby to care for. What chance did they have? And what had happened that required her to be relocated? Inevitably there was an abusive boyfriend or husband in the picture, but for everyone's safety, Sam knew not to ask.

Rafter cleared his throat, and Sam was startled to glimpse rage behind his controlled exterior. "How are you fixed for money?" He watched their young charges though the rearview mirror.

"Kat said they'll give us what we need when we get there," the girl said tonelessly.

Rafter said nothing, but a few minutes later when they pulled up in front of the shelter, he drew a wad of bills from his wallet and handed it back to the girl. "Take it. Tuck it away for an emergency."

"Thank you," the girl choked out through another wave of tears.

Sam got out of the car with the girl and hugged her briefly, taking care not to disturb the sleeping baby. "Good luck," she whispered urgently, feeling the inadequacy of the words. She hated feeling so helpless. What would become of them?

Sam and Rafter were to rendezvous with Kat at the Jungle after they made their delivery. On the ride back, wrapped up in their own thoughts, they didn't say much. Sam had participated in several of these clandestine rescues, both as decoy and driver. The experience inevitably left her feeling in awe of Kat, haunted by the women's desperate faces, and enormously grateful for the life she had. This was Rafter's first time. She gave him a reassessing look, impressed with the way he'd jumped right in without asking a lot of questions that would only have gotten in the way.

"What?" he said, catching her watching.

"That was very good of you."

"The money?"

"That, too."

They'd reached the café and Rafter parked on the street. "I take it this isn't your first time."

Inside, while they waited for Kat, Sam told him about other times she'd helped out. Observing that the mystery drink of the day was red, she took a chance on it. Red could mean tomatoes, but more likely, raspberries or strawberries.

"What do you think it is?" Rafter dubiously eyed the tall red concoction Duane put down in front of her.

Sam took a tentative sip. "Mmm. Raspberry vodka smoothie."

The blues guitarist started his last set, drawing Rafter's attention. She wondered if Rafter still played, but she didn't ask.

"I assume you're going to Hall's court retreat this weekend," he asked.

She nodded. Every summer the chief judge hosted an overnight retreat for about a half-dozen judges, their law clerks, and a few research attorneys. She'd gone last year at Matthew's insistence. He'd considered it a good way to start rebuilding her reputation. The need was even more pressing this year. Plus she hoped Hall would give her a good letter of recommendation now that Matthew could not.

"You don't look overjoyed," Rafter said.

Sam knew he was attending, too. It wouldn't do for the new judge to snub the chief judge. She shrugged, returning his commiserating smile with a faint one of her own. "I'm not big on group retreats. But this one isn't bad. It's at an old cottage association across the channel from Harbour Grace and Madison University. Think old money, tennis and boats, a formal supper club. Very snobby. No newly minted dot-commers need apply."

"Better pack my tux and cigars," he joked.

"A jacket and tie will do." Their laughing gazes met, held, and warmed. Sam knew suddenly that it felt much too good to be joking with Rafter again and looked hastily away.

Smile fading, he continued to look at her with a thoughtful, almost speculative, expression that flustered her even more. She might have snagged Billy to sit with them, but he'd already turned off the lights next door and gone home.

Thankfully, Kat dragged in a minute later and slumped down at the table. With a troubled expression, she filled them in on as much as she felt she could about Tanya's situation, carefully filtering out names and some details but, in her distress, telling them more than she normally would.

Tanya had come to Kat after a paternity test for the named father came back negative. She still insisted that he was the father, but the local child support prosecutor didn't believe her.

Kat rubbed her forehead tiredly. "I should have sent her on her way, too, but I did believe her. I know her. I know her family."

Sam didn't question Kat's judgment. She was no dewy-eyed rookie. She'd been in the trenches for years and she had good instincts about people.

"How reliable are the results?" Rafter asked.

"Usually very. But the more stones I look under, the more convinced I become that these results were somehow altered."

She caught the frowning look that Sam and Rafter exchanged.

"I know it sounds crazy, but the father's family is wealthy. The boy was ready to marry Tanya. His parents had a fit." Kat's eyes grew distant. "It wasn't until I started digging around, questioning the results, that nasty things started happening. I think they hired some muscle to scare her off."

"You're going to need more than that to convince anyone," Sam pointed out.

"How about that the parents are major stockholders in the lab that processed the results."

"Jesus," Rafter murmured. "Listen, Kat, you need to get rid of this thing. Turn it over to the authorities."

"I know. I've been trying to. Maybe now they'll sit up and take notice."

"I can probably help you out there," he said.

Kat smiled. "I was hoping you'd offer."

He handed her his card and stood. "Call me in the morning. I'll see what I can do." Sam watched him take the tab over to the cash register and pay Duane.

"Sam," Kat said, drawing Sam's attention back

to her. "This thing with Tanya makes me think about your Rachel."

Sam picked up Kat's train of thought. "They were both poor girls involved with young scions of wealthy families. Rachel disappears, and Tanya is forced into hiding."

"Maybe your Rachel was pregnant, too," Kat finished.

Sam started when Rafter reached around her and dropped a few singles on the table. If he'd heard any part of their conversation, he was for once too tactful to comment. He merely said to Sam, "Think about my offer," and left.

"What offer?" Kat asked, suddenly on full alert.

"He wants to clean up my soiled reputation by escorting me to an event or two, starting with the bar association ball. Show everyone that I'm not one of the untouchables."

"You're going to date Rafter?" Kat gaped at her as if she'd just announced she was going to bungyjump naked from the Sears Tower.

"Not date," Sam insisted. "And yes, I'm seriously considering it." Actually, tonight Rafter had given her a lot to think about.

Kat tilted her head and studied Sam. "You still fancy him," she announced, calmly sipping Sam's vodka smoothie.

"I don't either 'fancy' him—what kind of word is that? And I never did."

"Whatever." Kat waved that away. "I don't suppose there's anything I can say to talk you out of this insanity?"

"I need a job. So don't bother."

"Oh, I wasn't going to," Kat said, blithely smiling across the table. "Actually I think it's a great plan."

CHAPTER 8

The Lake Manitou Cottage Association occupied a narrow spit of wooded dunes across the channel from Harbour Grace. It was bound on the west by Lake Michigan, on the east by Lake Manitou, and on the north by the channel. Two- and three-story Victorian-era "cottages"—passed down from generation to generation in the same families—perched on heavily wooded dunes, some overlooking the Great Lake and some the inland lake. No manicured lawns or paved roads interfered with the natural rustic order. No cars were allowed past the community parking lot at the base of the small peninsula. In reluctant concession to the elderly, golf carts were permitted but frowned upon for the ambulatory.

Early Saturday morning, as Sam pulled into the parking lot and found a spot near the supper club and inn, she couldn't imagine what it would be like to grow up in this rarefied world of private schools and summer homes, of security and wealth. This was the dynastic world of the Wentworths and Christiansens. Sam didn't even know the man who'd given her his name.

Sighing, she gathered her overnight bag, briefcase, and tennis racket from the backseat and schlepped the lot through the heat to the inn. Most of the retreat attendees would have arrived Friday afternoon and were being put up in two cottages belonging to Judge Hall's family. The overflow and stragglers had to settle for small, but blessedly private, cubicles in the inn. Which was the main reason Sam had deliberately delayed her arrival. She didn't relish cozying up at a sleepover with people she worked alongside every day, especially Rafter. And as long as she was set to go courtside at the start of Hall's minitournament, he wouldn't hold it against her.

After Sam picked up her room key and dropped off her overnight bag, she made a detour by the dining room to grab an infusion of caffeine to fortify herself for the day ahead. First would come a brief meeting on procedural matters. She'd heard it all last year; it was aimed at the new research attorneys and law clerks. Every July, there was a large turnover among both groups as many moved on to long-term positions elsewhere and new grads took their places.

While helping herself to coffee and a Danish from the continental breakfast, she noticed Rafter sitting alone over coffee and a newspaper. She wondered why he was there and not with the others down at Hall's cottage. Her first impulse was to back out of the room. Then abruptly deciding to seize the opportunity to dispense with one item of business, she circled past a few early risers to Rafter's table. He looked faintly surprised to see her break with her usual avoidance tactic. By way of invitation to join him, he reached across the table to nudge out the chair opposite.

"Thought you'd be bonding with the other judges at Hall's cottage," Sam said as she organized her coffee and Danish on the table.

"I guess I must not be the bonding type. Neither, apparently, are you. Just get here?"

Sam nodded. "I'm staying here at the inn. You?"

"The same. I believe we're the only ones staying here, other than Danford." She followed the path of Rafter's glance to the pear-shaped veteran judge happily consuming a cheese Danish. "So what's on the agenda for today? Tennis, I assume." His gaze flicked over her tennis skirt.

"If it's the same as last year, we'll meet for an hour or two, then head to the courts. After lunch, everyone hangs out on the beach or sails little boats."

"The Lasers?" Rafter squinted out the window at the association's docks on Lake Manitou.

Sam shrugged. "I'm not a sailor. I think whatever's over there." Camille's tastes had run toward the sports of the rich, but sailing, skiing, and golf had been beyond their means. So she'd settled for signing Sam up for tennis lessons at the Y.

She glanced at her watch, saw that it was almost time to go, but wanted to get one thing settled with Rafter before they were swept up in the day's activities.

"I want to talk to you about . . ." She hesitated, finding it difficult to broach the subject cold. She saw that he'd guessed what she was stumbling over. His eyes lit with wicked amusement at her discomfort.

"Yes?"

"About your offer," she finished dryly.

"Good." He checked his watch and rose. "Let's

do it on the way. I have something I need to talk to you about, too." He frowned toward Judge Danford, who was helping himself to another donut and a chocolate croissant. "I suppose we should wait."

Smiling, Sam shook her head and grabbed her briefcase. Everyone at the court knew that Danford's wife kept him on a strict diet at home, which probably explained, at least in part, his complete lack of interest in retiring. "He'll ride over in a golf cart when he's ready."

Rafter held a door open for her, and they walked out the rear of the inn into a wall of heat. Across Lake Manitou, the pink sandstone buildings of Madison University glowed and shimmered under the blistering, early August sun. The sky was a clear cobalt blue, with not a cloud in sight to provide the slightest bit of relief. It was going to be beastly later on the courts with it this hot so early, Sam thought.

"So, about my offer . . ." Rafter prompted as they started down the dirt road winding through the wooded dunes. Sprawling cottages grew out of the slopes on both sides. They had the patina of age—weathered shake, cobblestone, and clapboard looked as organic as the stately trees that had grown up around them in the century since their white pine ancestors were whacked during the free-wheeling lumber age.

Sam steeled herself and admitted, "I think you may be right about how to fix my reputation." She'd given it considerable thought since Thursday night and decided she had little to lose by testing his plan. Except peace of mind. She stopped and met his gaze. "It galls me to say it, but thank you. I accept."

He ignored the hand she offered, his eyes twinkling with mischief. "I'm not sure I heard right."

Sam rolled her eyes. He wasn't going to make this easy. "I said, thank you."

"No, the other."

"It's too early in the morning for this," she complained, but he continued to wait expectantly. "I accept?" she tried.

"No . . ."

Sam groaned, knowing what was left. "I think *for once* you may be right."

"Yeah, that one." He smiled and took the hand she'd offered. "Didn't think I'd ever hear you admit it."

Sam felt the warm strength of his hand engulfing hers, the mad leap of her pulse in response, and pulled free.

"We'll start with the bar association's summer party next weekend." He sounded almost cheerful about it.

He shouldn't be. Their appearance together would likely excite considerable talk. He risked saddling himself with negative baggage he would have to overcome when he ran for reelection in a few years. But that was his problem. Perhaps he simply didn't appreciate the true strength of the backlash he'd generated against her. As that idea took root, Sam grew positively delighted at the prospect of Rafter getting a taste of what it felt like to be shunned.

This year's extravaganza was being held across the lake at Madison University. It was to be a huge do.

Sam wondered why Rafter didn't already have a date for it. In the old days, he'd never lacked for women, though he was never with any one for long. They were usually smart women, stylish women, nice women that Sam suspected would have liked more from him than a few dates. Yet another man who had trouble committing, she mused.

"There's another matter we need to discuss," Rafter went on, breaking into her thoughts.

They were nearly at the end of the road, and the hum of voices from the last cottage announced they'd reached their destination. He touched her arm, stopping her from turning onto the cottage path. The brief contact made her stomach give another little lurch. Oh, for crying out loud! It was ridiculous and dangerous to let him affect her like this.

Annoyed, Sam summoned a cool look. "What would that be?"

He imitated her, "That would be the car that was following us Thursday night."

"Following Kat."

"I don't think he was following Kat. The car was parked outside the café when we came out. I noticed because it was parked behind my car."

"So it was following you?"

"Or you." He paused a moment watching her while that sank in. "Is there a reason someone would want to follow you?"

Sam stiffened. "You mean, am I soliciting bribes or engaged in some other wicked activity that would get me into trouble?" she asked through gritted teeth. "Sorry, no. Not that you could ever let yourself completely believe me."

"That's not what I meant," he said impatiently, shoving his hands into his chinos as if to keep them from reaching out and shaking her. "Look, I know you're convinced Christiansen was an upstanding judge. I'm going to take a leap here and guess that you might be trying to protect him or prove him innocent on your own. Have you roused a sleeping bear? Made someone nervous? If you've gotten into something you can't handle, you need to call for help."

Distracted by the questions buzzing through her head, Sam nonetheless noticed that Rafter looked genuinely worried.

She slowly shook her head. "I can't think of any reason why someone would want to follow me. I haven't done anything."

Except visit Sophie Somerset. And a few days later, Sophie had left a message on Sam's answering machine to forewarn her that an AG agent had been by asking the same questions as Sam.

For a few stomach-turning, adrenaline-charged seconds, vivid conspiracy theories reared up in Sam's imagination before she firmly pushed them back into her paranoia box. Hattie must have put them on to the Rachel angle after Sam called her. The AG agents were following up on it, nothing more.

Rafter had to be wrong. No one had reason to follow her.

From the cottage, someone called out that the meeting was about to start. Sam glanced over her shoulder at Rafter as they climbed the narrow path. "Maybe he *was* following you." When he looked skeptical, she shrugged and added another possibility. "Or maybe he knew Kat hung out at the café and was watching for her there."

"Possibly," he said behind her. "But then why follow us to your house?"

She had no answer to that and was still mulling it over when they filed into the living room behind two research attorneys. One of the new law clerks waved at Sam from a sofa and motioned to the vacant seat beside her.

But sitting on her other side was Reed Boyle,

Hall's senior law clerk, who'd been with the court for three years and had carved out a niche as self-appointed leader of the research attorneys and law clerks. He also had a chip on his shoulder the size of Montana, and was right now slanting a derisive look at Sam's tennis attire.

Reed had been a thorn in her side ever since she started working at the court and had refused to instantly succumb to his cropped-blond-hair, chiseled-jaw charm. A night school graduate from a third-rate law school, he nursed a burning resentment toward those who had gone to more elite institutions and gotten an automatic pass over the bottom rungs of the legal ladder. That was Sam's most grievous crime against him.

Sam returned her wave but indicated she was going to sit in one of the folding chairs on the other side. Unfortunately, Rafter squeezed in beside her and bent his head to hers.

"What about jealous boyfriends?" He glanced pointedly across the chattering assemblage, about two dozen people in all, at Reed Boyle. "Could someone be stalking you?"

She gave him a pained look, shaking her head as Hall strode in to begin the meeting. "Hardly. You're determined to think of me as some sort of *femme fatale* even though there's absolutely no basis in fact for it." In Sam's universe, heavily influenced by Camille's bias against Sam's mother, Rosalind, *femme fatale* was just a slightly nicer way of saying "slut."

"Except what I can see," he disagreed, cool blue eyes raking over her to make his point.

Sam tossed him a murderous look, her hands itching to throttle him. It simply never occurred to her that his definition of the phrase might be different in important respects from hers.

Rosalind could have been the prototype for the amoral material girl; her beauty had been her currency. Sam had spent her entire life trying not to be like her mother. She'd rebounded in the opposite direction, doing her best to live up to Camille's standards. There had been one embarrassing experiment in college and then Brian. That was it.

Yet when Rafter looked at her, he saw another Rosalind, a seductress who wouldn't think twice about using her wiles on a government agent if it got her what she wanted. Rafter's talk with Billy may have stirred doubts about her guilt in the Wentworth debacle, yet he still automatically saw her through a dirty lens of sin and suspicion. He couldn't seem to help it. Disheartened, Sam realized that that dark chapter would likely always color his view of her. He was right—the past was always in the room with them, the big blue goblin. And there wasn't a thing she could do to get rid of it.

"A perfect day for tennis," Hall cheerfully proclaimed an hour later, having rushed the meeting to get to the courts before the heat became any more unbearable. The assembled group, dutifully clad in tennis togs, stared at him with varying expressions of doubt. Most were probably thinking he was showing signs of incipient senility. Except for a few judges, everyone else had shown up, considering it in their best interests to humor the chief judge, a well-known tennis fanatic.

Arriving at the end of Hall's pep talk after racing back to the inn to trade chinos for gym shorts, Nick swallowed a smile. He wouldn't miss this for the world. He knew Sam was something of a tennis ace and he was curious to see her in action. Plus it beat sitting through Hall's stupefying lecture on elementary court procedure, completely distracted by her sitting next to him.

She was a siren whether she chose to recognize it or not. Perhaps not to the ordinary guy on the street; she was too cerebral for that guy, her wit too subtle. She was more like a Strad than a fiddle. A BBC soap siren for the highbrow. In Nick's opinion, Brian had never fully appreciated what he had, or he would not have been so eager to unload her.

On center court, Hall was organizing doubles teams and quickly picked Sam for his partner. She was already standing next to him, and Nick had the feeling Hall's choice was a foregone conclusion. His law clerk shot Sam another pissed look. The reason for it quickly became apparent when the other judges chose their own clerks. Nick followed suit and earned a grateful smile from his own new law clerk, Jake McClain. After the remaining players paired up, they had eight teams split into two draws.

He was pleased to discover that Jake was a competent player. Nick had played in high school but, since then, had spent more time on racquetball courts. Sam and Hall played in the opposite draw on a different court, so Nick didn't have much chance to watch them until an hour and a half later when he and Jake scraped their way into the finals. By that time, duty done, most of the others had slouched off in search of shade or the beach.

Guzzling water, the four finalists met at the net to discuss terms and spin for serve. "One set. Have to win by two games," Hall dictated. He wiped his beet red face with a wet towel Sam handed him.

Concerned that Hall looked as though he was headed for heat stroke, Nick suggested they take a break. "We could wait until evening." He knew he'd said the wrong thing when, from across the net, Sam gave him an amused, almost imperceptible shake of her head.

Hall reacted with mixed irritation and humor. "What's the matter, Rafter?" he taunted. "Worried you're going to get beat by an old man and a little girl?"

By this time, from the brief glimpses he'd managed to steal, Nick had a pretty good idea that the "little girl" was, in fact, a ringer, but tactfully refrained from pointing that out. "Oh, I think Jake and I can hold our own against an old man and a girl." He knew he got it right this time because Sam rolled her eyes.

"Well, good then." Hall gave him a sly smile, eyes suddenly calculating under bushy white eyebrows. "How about a small wager on the outcome?"

Evidently, Hall was one of those sporting fanatics who loved more than anything to win and enjoyed a gentlemen's bet on the side to liven things up. "You're on. But let's make it more interesting—the winnings go to Jake or Sam."

"Agreed," Hall said promptly.

"And," Nick continued, "we play a second match, only this one in Lasers on Lake Manitou, say at two this afternoon."

"Unfair!" Sam sputtered. "You know I can't sail!"

Hall, delighted at the prospect, distractedly patted her shoulder. "No worries, my dear. I've sailed all my life." He held out a hand over the net. "A C-note on each event."

"Done." Nick shook his hand. Sam looked none too happy about the change of plan.

She played even better than Nick had expected. She wasn't a power player—she didn't have the brawn for that—rather she was a textbook strategist, using finesse and superb control to accurately place lobs, drop shots, and passing shots frustratingly just out of reach of her opponents. Hall was a surprisingly good player too, no longer up to Sam's level, but more mobile on the court than Nick would have thought.

He and Jake managed to hold serve through the first few games because they could power over an occasional ace, but they were losing badly in the volleys. Eventually their opponents' superior control began to overwhelm them. Sam played it cool, but Nick could tell she was hugely enjoying running him ragged in the heat, forcing him in particular to chase down one well-placed ball after another. He was torn between admiration and frustration, but felt only relief when the slaughter finally, mercifully ended.

"Two o'clock at the docks," Nick reminded Hall and Sam after he and Jake gave their congratulations at the net.

Sweat poured down Hall's face, but he smiled broadly. "Wouldn't miss it."

As soon as Hall and Jake split off toward the cottage, Sam rounded on Nick. "Call it off," she said flatly.

"Why? Turnabout's fair play." Nick kept trudging in the direction of the inn, anticipating a cold drink, cool shower, and at least half an hour flat on his back in his air-conditioned cell of a room before lunch. God, his legs felt like spaghetti. Sam walked with him, mopping her face and draining a liter water bottle.

"But you'll trounce us in a sailboat race!"

"So? When did you start shrinking from a challenge?"

She shot him an exasperated look and automatically passed over her water bottle when he held out a hand for it. "If you haven't figured it out by now—Hall hates to lose."

Nick chugged the rest of the water and handed the empty bottle back. "He's a big boy. Besides, what do you have to complain about—you just won a hundred bucks off me."

"But I could lose Hall's good recommendation, and I need that a whole lot more."

"Relax. I don't think you're giving him enough credit. He doesn't seem vindictive. Besides, you might win."

"I hope so." She said it with such fervor that Nick chuckled.

"So where did you learn to play? I remember Brian saying you were good. I didn't realize how good."

She was clearly pleased by the compliment and trying not to show it. "The Y and then high school."

"You were trying to kill me out there, weren't you? I bet you loved beating me." A small measure of revenge for nettling her earlier at Hall's cottage, he suspected.

She regarded him, looking annoyingly fresh, and her lovely mouth curved into a small, satisfied smile. "As a matter of fact, I did."

He groaned, climbing the few steps to the inn, and she had the gall to chuckle. "I'll get you back," he promised.

The afternoon's competition did not have quite as lopsided an outcome as Sam had feared. She and Judge Hall lost, of course. She'd urged him to select another partner—someone who at least knew a mast from a boom and starboard from port. "Nonsense," he said easily, "we'll give them a good run for my money," a hint, she hoped, that he fully expected to lose and didn't really mind.

Ashamed at having underestimated him and grateful to be let off the hook, Sam threw herself into whatever task Hall yelled her way over the noise of gusting wind and splashing neon blue water. The small, open boat tilted alarmingly on its side as they tacked back and forth, chasing Rafter's boat down the length of Lake Manitou. They were not far behind when they rounded an orange buoy in front of Madison University but lost ground on the return leg.

The boat was "running" now, Hall explained. The wind was at their back, the sail out wide, as they made a more sedate jaunt west past the association docks. But as soon as they rounded the last buoy and headed for home, they were sailing into the wind again. Hall, being the kind of competitor that would rather risk it all than play it safe, hauled in on the sail until the boat was heeled over at a gravity-defying angle. Sam gamely followed his example, leaning far out over the raised side into thin air to keep the boat from tipping over.

They were flying, gaining on Rafter and Jake, when a sudden gust capsized the boat and dumped them unceremoniously into tepid water. Sam bobbed up sputtering, grabbing for her sunglasses, and searching in alarm for Hall, who, being an old hand at this, had managed to snag the side of the boat on its way over. He grinned at her, and shrugged a wet, Izod-clad shoulder. "We almost had them."

Exhilarated, Sam laughed, bobbing in her life vest. "We sure did!"

Rafter and Jake zigzagged by on a victory lap a few minutes later, celebrating their win. Sam and

Hall had capsized only about one hundred feet off
the association's shoreline smack in front of the
gathered court gang. On-shore bettors whooped
and hollered as they chugged victory or consola-
tion beers.

Rafter pulled off his shirt and jumped in to help
right Hall's Laser. After they gave Hall a boost
aboard, Sam and Rafter swam to shore.

An adequate though not exceptional swimmer—
the result of being mostly self-taught in a series of
low-budget, outdoor motel pools—Sam was nonetheless glad to be wearing a life vest. She could
have made it without, but she was enjoying the
leisurely, low-energy paddle to shore and in no
particular hurry to trade the wonderfully mild water
for blazing heat.

"You're no coward, Ms. Parker." Rafter treaded
water on his back beside her. His muscles, tanned
from weekends of sailing, gleamed and flexed with
each lazy stroke. Sam watched from behind the
safety of her sunglasses, disgusted with herself but
mesmerized all the same. He must still belong to a
gym, she thought. Shouldn't he be at least starting
to lose his looks? It wasn't fair.

"I've seen seasoned crew balk at sailing heeled
over on their ear like that," he went on.

"We manipulative seductresses can't afford to
be faint of heart, you know, if we expect to succeed
in our evil ways." She tilted her sunglasses down
and gave him a coolly pointed look over the top.

His teeth flashed white in the high sun. "Hadn't
thought of it that way. Makes perfect sense now
that you mention it."

Annoyed, Sam stood in waist-deep water and
waded to shore in waterlogged tennis shoes. His
amused agreement was not what she'd wanted and

it grated. As soon as they reached dry sand, they were engulfed by the beer-bashing court gang, several of whom appeared to be already more than a little tight. The younger set, mostly twenty-somethings, outnumbered by four-to-one the older judges at the retreat and tended to be a hardworking, hard-playing bunch who took full advantage of free booze.

Sam automatically took the bottle thrust into her hand but almost immediately extracted herself from the group to change out of sopping wet clothes. She detoured by the docks to see if Hall needed a hand with the boat. But both Lasers were making another run down the lake so she headed for the inn.

"Sam, wait." Rafter caught up to her as she crossed the dusty gravel parking lot, her shoes squishing wetly. Rafter gingerly picked his way along in bare feet, his shorts making wet slurping sounds against leanly muscled thighs. He glanced down at his dripping shorts with dismay. "At this rate, I'm going to have to hit Danford up for a spare pair."

Sam couldn't help a grudging smile at the image of Rafter in baby blue seersucker. As they squished and slurped along, Sam pulled at the clingy wet fabric of her shirt until she noticed him watching with avid interest and stopped in embarrassment.

"Sam," he said, his tone abruptly serious. "You can't blow off this whole tail thing. If I'm right and you were the one being followed, you could be in danger."

"I'm not blowing it off. I will be careful. But I'm not as convinced as you seem to be that I was being followed. I haven't seen any other signs of it." When they stepped inside the inn, Sam pulled off her sunglasses and frowned up at him. "Besides, what more can I do?"

"For starters, if there's anything you're holding back from the investigators, for God's sake, tell me, or them. Tell someone. Get some protection."

Sam's spine stiffened at the renewed implication that she might be hiding something. Rafter caught her elbow when she made a preemptive move in the direction of her room, which was in the opposite direction from Rafter's.

"If you are on the level," he added in a more placating tone, "you still should keep your eyes open, your door locked, and a cell phone handy. And don't go running by yourself at night anymore."

Sam extracted her arm from his hand and made an irritated, noncommittal sound as she walked off down the hall with as much dignity as she could muster with shoes squishing rudely.

"Sam," Rafter called out behind her. "It's dangerous to ignore the message because you don't like the messenger."

Sam gave an airy wave over her shoulder without turning around and continued squishing down the corridor.

He had a point. She wouldn't ignore the message. But she also wouldn't give him the satisfaction of knowing that she had any residual respect for his instincts.

CHAPTER 9

Sam spent the rest of the long afternoon lounging under an umbrella on the big beach along Lake Michigan. The sun-bleached sand and surf shimmered in the afternoon heat. She roused herself occasionally to cool off in crystal-clear turquoise water. Others drifted by and left. The center of activity was on the other side of the spit of sand, where most of her colleagues were more actively engaged in windsurfing and sailing on the inland lake. For Sam, it was a real treat simply to sit and do nothing but listen to the lazy rush of water lapping over sand and wind rustling through pale green dune grass, and she meant to soak up every minute of it.

Later, she returned to the inn for a shower, nap, and change of clothes, then strolled back to Hall's cottage for a late barbecue. Queuing up at the buffet table on the deck, Sam found herself behind Rafter and Todd Perry, Hall's new junior law clerk. As chief judge, Hall was entitled to two clerks. Poor Todd was a bright but tentative sort, slightly built, nervous, certainly not up to challenging Reed

Boyle's despotic rule over Hall's chambers. Sam didn't envy him, having to work so closely with Reed. Todd and Rafter were deep in conversation about a case. She quickly surmised that it must be from Rafter's first call, the one he'd taken Matthew's place on, because Hall had been on that panel as well. She didn't recognize the case and wondered why.

Plates piled high, they moved off to a patio table. Curious, Sam filled her plate and followed them. "Mind if I join you?"

Rafter gestured to a vacant chair.

"Hi, Sam." Todd smiled up in welcome. "We were just going over the Benton Motors case. Never imagined one of my first cases would be such a biggie." His smile turned twitchy.

Sam understood his nerves. She'd felt them too when she first went to work for a federal judge right out of law school. Todd had scored the job he wanted, but now he realized that it was entirely his to blow.

Sam sent a questioning glance across the table at Rafter. "Benton Motors?"

"It's a class action. Hall's opinion to draft. Christiansen didn't have you do a bench memo on it."

Puzzled, Sam frowned. "I wonder why."

"Does that surprise you?" Rafter asked casually, but suddenly more alert.

Sam marked his interest and alarm bells went off. "No," she said quickly, too forcefully, and reached for a more indifferent tone. "Not at all. Matthew had experience with class action suits. The criminal part of the docket often concerned him more." Sam met his gaze with a bland expression. "So, tough case?"

"Not a particularly difficult record to wade

through. The appeal boils down to a single legal question."

"I guess that explains why Matthew didn't give it to me."

"Perhaps." Rafter shrugged. "But the issue is tricky."

Todd agreed and drew Rafter back into a discussion of the merits. Sam half-listened while privately scrambling to come up with a reason why Matthew hadn't sought her input on the case. Because despite her contrary assertion to Rafter, this appeared to be exactly the type of case Matthew liked to have a second opinion on, especially if the outcome was not clear-cut.

Ironically, considering all the time she and Foley had spent combing through Matthew's cases, Benton Motors had not made a blip on the radar screen; they hadn't even looked at the file because it had been reassigned to Rafter before oral arguments. Had they, Sam was certain Foley would have fastened on to it in an instant. It fit the profile—big case, important local company, high stakes, and perhaps most damning, a deviation from Matthew's normal routine.

The thought of that, the possibility that Benton Motors might be the key that investigators had searched for in vain, had Sam's nerves jangling in dread. She was glad the sun had set and twilight hid her overheated face.

Mustn't rush to judgment, she told herself, reaching for calm. She, more than most, should have learned that lesson. Matthew must have had a good reason for keeping the case from her—she'd been busy, he'd found the case easy—some simple explanation. Because the alternative didn't bear consideration.

"Sam?"

She looked up at Rafter's voice and noticed that Todd and many of the others in the under-thirty crowd had melted away.

Rafter answered her unspoken question. "They're building a bonfire over near the channel. Care to wander over?"

Sam shook her head, pulling herself together. There had to be a perfectly good explanation for Matthew's actions. She would figure it out.

"Thanks, but I think I'll stay put awhile." She wanted a glass of wine, a chance to think, and knew she would have about as much chance of getting either one at Reed Boyle's bonfire as at an all-night rave. "Maybe I'll come by later."

He nodded, his face unreadable as ever, and rose. Sam watched him join a couple other judges on the beach and begin tossing balls for Hall's retrievers, sending them racing wildly over the sand.

Almost simultaneously, two completely unrelated thoughts crossed Sam's mind. One, really more an observation, was that Rafter played the odd man out in this group. In his mid-thirties, he was closer in age to the research attorneys and law clerks than to the other judges, but far above them in rank. The other was the belated realization that he'd just invited her to join him for a little jaunt. Why? A purely benign explanation was highly unlikely. When Rafter wanted to talk to her, there was always a reason. Usually not good.

Before Sam had time to consider possibilities, Hall sank down in a chair next to her with a low groan.

"I'm too old for this." His wide, jowly face was red from sun and wind.

"You played harder and longer than anyone else out there today," Sam reminded him. "I needed a nap this afternoon."

"You're absolutely right," he agreed, brightening.

Sam took a sip of wine to hide her smile. "You should have seen Rafter staggering back to the inn after we trounced them."

"Did he now." His smile grew, aches temporarily forgotten. "I'd like to have seen that."

They sat for a time in companionable silence until the caterer approached to consult with him. "Duty calls." After heaving himself to his feet, he paused. "Schedule an appointment with my secretary next week, Samantha. We need to talk about your future. I have a few contacts that might be of help."

"Thank you," Sam murmured gratefully, stifling the urge to jump up and hug him.

By the time Sam wandered over to the bonfire, most of the dozen or so revelers looked at least halfway to being totally plastered. Someone had gone on a beer run; empties littered the sand around the circle. Had she not been too keyed up to sleep, Sam probably would have taken a pass. But between the sudden, joyous turnaround in her employment prospects, with both Rafter and now Hall offering assistance, and the unanswered questions about Benton Motors, she'd come looking for a diversion.

Reed Boyle hailed her with a sarcastic rendition of "Here she comes, Miss America . . ." He reigned supreme here and was a mean drunk. Already regretting coming, Sam was about to back away when she noticed Rafter. He was sitting in the dark on a low sand berm apart from the others, observing while he nursed a beer but keeping his own counsel.

Pride wouldn't let her turn tail and run while he watched. She didn't care what any of the others thought, but she hated showing weakness in front of him. Someone handed her a bottle in the dark and Sam sat down on the cool sand a slight distance beyond the circle around the fire where she could keep Rafter in view.

At first she thought they were playing spin the bottle. One of the new guys, Jamie, had stripped down to his boxer shorts. Then she realized they were playing truth or dare. And they weren't really spinning the bottle so much as pointing it at the next victim. The new people were being initiated, Sam gathered.

Lisa, a cute new research attorney and evidently Reed's latest conquest given the way she was plastered up against him, aimed the bottle unsteadily at Todd.

"Truth or dare?" Reed demanded Judge Wopner style.

"What's the dare?" Todd asked, a sheen of perspiration making his pale face glow sickly yellow in the firelight.

"Across the channel and back."

They all knew that Todd couldn't swim. Reed wanted him to pick the truth.

"And the truth?" Todd squeaked.

Reed considered him a moment, then smiled with callous glee. "Describe the most erotic thing a woman has ever done to you. In detail."

There were titters and guffaws from people so plastered everything sounded funny. Poor Todd looked mortified.

The "dare" was fairly benign for Reed, but Sam felt sorry for Todd. "You don't have to do it," she called over to him. She had refused last summer.

"From one chicken to another," Reed taunted, laughing, passing the insult off as a joke.

Sam stood, ready to leave. "Grow up, Reed. You sound like you're trying for head boy in your own *Lord of the Flies* fantasy."

"You got that right," Jake muttered.

Straight away, Reed wrapped his arms around Lisa from behind, his hands covering hers on the bottle, and whirled her around until the bottle pointed directly at Sam. "Truth or dare, Samantha?" His eyes gleamed a challenge in the firelight. "I don't believe you were ever properly welcomed."

The drunken chorus picked up the chant, "Truth or dare, truth or dare . . ."

"Oh, for heaven's sake." Sam hesitated, feeling trapped. She could feel Rafter's eyes on her through the darkness. He would expect her to refuse. They all did, especially Reed. This was his way of showing her up.

Maybe it was childish rebellion; there'd been no room for that in her actual childhood. On impulse she decided to turn the tables on all of them, do the unexpected, knowing she would probably very soon regret it.

"What are my choices?" she hedged. The box closed tighter. She had the satisfaction, though, of seeing surprise on Reed's face.

He made a quick recovery, almost rubbing his hands in sadistic pleasure. "We've all wondered how you ended up in our lowly midst. What sank your career? Who did you sleep with to get tossed out of the U.S. Attorney's Office?"

Sam had been expecting something along that line and schooled her face to show nothing more than bored indifference. "And the dare?"

Only the crackle of fire and lap of water broke

the expectant silence. Dancing firelight gave faces macabre appearances.

"Across the channel."

Jamie, in a drunken swipe at equality between the sexes, whined, "I had to do it in my underwear."

Reed's gaze flicked to Jamie. "Good point. We are officers of the court. Can't be sexist." He smiled at Sam. "Well?"

The rabble voiced their preferences for the truth or the dare—noisily and about evenly split.

Sam eyeballed the distance across the choppy, dark water to a park on the Harbour Grace side. It was wider here than at the bottleneck entrance into Lake Michigan, about 200 feet, she guessed, and widened considerably more a little farther inland. The distance didn't bother her overmuch. The pitch black water did. Sam wavered, teetering on the edge of reneging. She told herself she had nothing to prove to anyone here. Only pride stood in her way, and she knew well from firsthand experience that bruised pride was rarely fatal.

"Don't be stupid, Sam." Rafter's low-pitched voice cut through the dark and the chatter. She could hear the trace of amusement at her dilemma.

That did it. He was the last person Sam would tolerate telling her what to do. Or laughing at her. In that instant she decided to show Reed up and tick Rafter off.

"Well, seeing as how my personal life is none of your damn business," she said to Reed, "I'll take the dare."

"Sam, don't." Now Rafter's voice held a gratifying hint of alarm along with exasperation.

"You evidently didn't stop Jamie," she pointed out to him as he came to his feet in the dark.

"Jamie is a former lifeguard. It's too risky for you."

"That's what my kind do, remember? We take risks." She was already crossing the short stretch of beach to the water's edge, peeling off her shirt and shorts along the way to a raucous strip club serenade, smugly aware that her wild-colored pais-ley bra and underpants were less revealing than most bikinis on the beach that day. Besides, it was dark away from the fire until eyes could adjust to the moonlight.

One of the women, Meg, stumbled over to her. "Don't do it. Only Jamie has tried."

"I'll be fine." She paused in ankle-deep water to take another look across. The air still held the heat of the day, but there was a steady breeze inland and the water was cool.

"Do something!" Meg implored someone.

Jake spoke up. "Judge Rafter is right. Maybe you shouldn't do it."

Ignoring all of them, she waded out until she felt the bottom drop off, then eased the rest of the way in.

"Oh, hell," she heard Rafter mutter.

She alternated between the breaststroke and dog paddle. The water was choppier the farther out she swam, the going more difficult. When her arms tired, she flipped over on her back to rest. Slow and steady would get her there and back. The water felt warmer as she got used to it, not nearly so sinister now.

She turned to swim and felt a twinge of alarm. In the dark it was hard to tell, but the shore ahead appeared farther away than when she'd started. When she tired, she turned onto her back again and floated in a pitch black universe with a kalei-doscope of stars hanging above.

The surreal peace was shattered when she heard a splash nearby and spotted something dark in the water. She panicked, sank, and would have screamed if she hadn't swallowed water.

An arm snaked around her midsection, supporting her while she coughed and sputtered.

"This ranks right up there among the more idiotic things you've ever done," Rafter grumbled in her ear.

"I was fine until you scared me half to death!" Sam choked.

His arm was wrapped snugly around her bare waist just under her bra and the length of her backside was pressed against the warm wall of his chest, making her insides do funny little leaps and bounds. Her difficulty breathing was no longer due entirely to the water she'd swallowed.

"Let me go. I can make it."

He did. And as she got her bearings, she saw that the Harbour Grace shore appeared no closer. In fact, the shoreline in both directions looked alarmingly farther away than when she'd started.

"Watch your heading. You're drifting out into Lake Manitou."

Annoyed, mostly because she realized he was right, Sam adjusted her course and panted, "You can leave anytime. I don't need a babysitter." Her labored breathing somewhat diminished the conviction she was aiming for.

"Could have fooled me," he muttered, adjusting his stroke to keep pace with her. To her humiliation, he seemed to be mostly treading water while she huffed and puffed along, working hard to maintain minimal forward progress now that they were swimming more directly into the wind and chop.

Sam didn't say anything more, well aware that she had done something incredibly foolish and already hugely regretting giving in to a childish impulse. In truth, after the jolt of terror had passed, she was more relieved than annoyed that he'd come after her.

Exhausted, she rolled over onto her back, trying to do better this time at keeping on course.

"How much farther?" she groaned.

"We're about halfway. Can you make it?"

"Yes." Or she would die trying. That would be the ultimate humiliation, if Rafter had to haul her to shore in one of those lifeguard, hand-in-the-armpit choke holds. "Just want to . . . stop a minute . . . and float," she puffed. "It's beautiful."

He floated next to her. "It is amazing," he agreed softly. "I love to sail at night just for this."

After a few minutes, he touched her arm. "We have to keep moving. We're drifting farther from shore. You can hold on to my shoulder when you get tired." She didn't want to, but after another exhausting minute she gave in.

She didn't think things could get much worse until Rafter mentioned the boat bearing down on them.

"I think we're fine if it stays on course."

He was a strong swimmer, and for the first time they were actually making good headway. Sam could feel the muscles in his shoulders bunch and flex under her hands with each stroke.

She kept an eye on the cabin cruiser, saw it veer gradually in their direction as it came closer, as if to pick them up, but she knew no one on board could see them in the inky water or hear them over the steady throb of the engine. Her hands tightened on Rafter's shoulders. "I think it's coming this way."

Rafter stopped swimming and turned to look. Sam let go.

"Aw, hell." He found her hand and clasped it hard. "Hang on and kick!"

She did both for all she was worth. The boat was practically on them in seconds, thirty or forty feet away and fast closing the distance.

"We're going to dive," he called over the deep drone of the motor. "Take a breath. Now!"

There was no time to protest that she couldn't. Rafter dragged her down. Heart hammering, adrenaline pumping, Sam only had time for one gulp of air before she was dragged under. Eyes closed, she felt him pulling her down, down, until her ears hurt and her lungs felt close to bursting. The boat roared over and began to fade. They broke the surface, sucking air in great gulps.

Rafter had an arm around her waist, apparently recognizing that she would sink like a stone without his support. Her arms and legs felt as though they had lead weights attached. She didn't have the energy to push the wet tangle of hair from her face.

"Nothing like a little excitement," he puffed between breaths.

"My kind . . . thrive on it," she gasped.

He laughed. "You never give up, do you?"

It took another ten minutes to reach shore. They landed at the park but around the side, well beyond the channel. Sam didn't care. She was simply relieved to feel beautiful, solid ground under the water. They half-crawled, half-staggered up onto dry sand and collapsed with their feet at the edge of the lapping water.

Gasping air, Sam savored the hard feel of sand underneath her back. Rafter sprawled on his stomach beside her. "What'll we do now?" she puffed out. "Because I'll hitchhike back in my underwear before I swim that again."

"Ditto. We can hike around to the channel and

try to signal them to bring a boat." He was still breathing hard. "Just let me catch my breath."

After a time, she said quietly, "Thanks, by the way, for coming to my rescue."

He turned his head in her direction, watching her. "What on earth were you thinking?"

Sam sighed, weary of hearing him ask that question. What indeed? "I've had to put up with Reed's barbs for two years."

"So you let a pissant with an inferiority complex talk you into doing a striptease in front of a drunken mob and taking a midnight swim across a dangerous stretch of water."

"I didn't take everything off," Sam muttered defensively. "My underwear is more decent than most bikinis."

"For a man, it's seeing a beautiful woman strip, and strip not to her bathing suit, but to her underwear. That's erotic. Especially when the underwear looks straight out of Victoria's Secret. But you miss the point—"

"All right. The whole thing was stupid, I know." She decided to admit it all. What difference did it make now? "Actually, I was ready to bag it. Then you jumped in telling me what to do."

"And you wanted to show me up, too," he finished. He didn't seem to expect an answer, and she didn't say anything.

He rolled onto his side, hovering over her, mere inches away. Sam watched his gaze make a slow tour down her body.

She shivered, but it wasn't cold she felt. It was heat. The skin on her breasts and belly and thighs tingled as though he'd actually stroked them. She stifled a groan of horror and desperately willed herself not to feel anything. Not now when she was lying practically naked next to him, close enough that she could feel his body heat. But it was too late.

Their eyes met and held. Awareness leaped between them. For once Rafter's face was as easy to read as a neon sign. He wanted to ravish her, and in that reckless moment all Sam could think about was how much she wanted to ravish him right back.

Insanity! Madness!

Feeling unbalanced and out of her depth, Sam swallowed hard and parted her lips to suck in air because suddenly she couldn't seem to get enough of it. His gaze dropped to her mouth.

The charged silence was so thick it drowned out the night sounds of water and wind and crickets. All her senses were focused like a spotlight on what was happening between them.

He leaned in. Her breath hitched as he experimentally brushed his lips back and forth across hers.

"I don't think this is a good idea," she croaked, a perfunctory swipe at preventing the inevitable because she knew she should. But she didn't turn away.

Rafter plowed sandy fingers into her wet hair, cradling her head for better access. "I know it's not."

His mouth settled on hers, and Sam returned his rough kiss with increasing abandon as raw need swamped her. There was nothing proper or polite about this kiss. There was no room for finesse or tenderness. This was a wild, semihostile, desperate taking of forbidden pleasure that had them heedlessly rolling in a tangle of limbs over gritty sand into the shallow water until it lapped sluggishly at their waists.

Sam had never felt an intense, toe-curling need

like this before—passion so exhilarating, so intoxicating it ripped through barriers as though they were constructed of toothpicks in the face of a hurricane.

"Nick, what is this?" she gasped.

He had her bra off, using it to lap water over her breasts to remove sand. Then he tossed it over their heads onto dry beach.

"Seismic sex," he rasped, running his tongue over a breast and simultaneously tugging at his shorts.

She moaned when he sucked hard on a nipple, then wailed, "But I hate you!" And she'd never wanted a man more. She, who didn't even like sex all that much, was desperate to feel him inside her. Her body was a stranger who seemed to have overdosed on Viagra.

He managed a chuckle and muttered, "You know what they say about love and hate."

A rushed desperation propelled them onward, as if each realized that any pause would give them time to think, and thinking was the last thing either wanted to do. His mouth fused hungrily with hers. She could feel him wrestle with his shorts and used her foot to help shove them down. He dropped them next to her, then boosted her onto them so that her back was protected from the abrasive wet sand.

Wrapping her limbs around him like ivy, she dragged him close, moaning at the skin-to-skin contact. With one hand, he yanked down her bikini briefs and moved on to more intimate territory—parting, stroking, delving.

Sam gave a high cry of pleasure. His clever fingers pushed her close to orgasm, a jointly participatory orgasm, a feat she hadn't managed to accomplish in two-plus years of awkward experimentation with Brian. Not once.

"Damn, Sam, you feel so incredibly good," he muttered against her mouth. "I knew it."

She briefly wondered at that last, but the question scattered as her insides gathered and gathered and tightened and tightened into a nuclear-charged ball. She cried out as pulsing, mindless pleasure burst from the epicenter and rippled through her. It was incredible, wonderfully unexpected. Her eyes filled with tears while little aftershocks exploded here and there like those last few overlooked fireworks after the grand finale. If ever an almost coupling could make a woman fall hopelessly in lust, this was it.

Floating in a blissful haze, Sam cupped Nick's heavy erection in her hand. He groaned with pleasure. Even with the edge knocked off her need, she still wanted him inside her. She longed desperately for that final completion.

"Make me a happy man and tell me you're on the pill or something."

"I'm not." Her tongue felt thick and sluggish. She barely recognized the throaty whisper as her own. "But—" She was about to say that it didn't matter, that the timing was safe.

"Shh. Wait." He stilled.

She heard the call then, "Sam? Judge Rafter?" followed by the creak of oars somewhere in the dark.

"Jake," Rafter whispered to her.

Horrified, Sam sprang away and frantically groped over moonlit sand for her bra and bikini briefs. She heard Rafter mutter a curse under his breath while he chased after boxers that were floating away. Sam got her briefs on but was having more difficulty fastening her sand-encrusted bra.

Rafter fished his shorts out of the water and began

hopping up and down, struggling into them before he called out to Jake. Sam guessed Jake had already spotted them and quite likely seen them scrambling into their things because he seemed to be hovering discreetly offshore, giving them time to make themselves presentable.

Maybe it was a sign of impending mental and physical meltdown as she pushed the limits of endurance on both fronts, but when Sam looked over and saw Rafter wrestling with his sand-blocked zipper, she suddenly found their predicament hysterically funny.

Rafter's head snapped up at her giggle and he growled in disbelief, "You think this is amusing?"

She nodded. "And mortifying," she managed to croak out between helpless giggles. "It reminds me of Billy's Benny Hill video."

Rafter abruptly stopped in the midst of frantically trying to yank up the zipper. She saw the flash of white teeth in the moonlight. "I'm partial to Monty Python myself."

Sam laughed so hard she couldn't stop. Then the roller coaster she was riding careened in the opposite direction and a lump lodged in her throat.

A few minutes later, she huddled miserably on the cold metal seat in the bow of the rowboat, berating herself for all the stupid mistakes she'd made that evening, starting with stopping by the bonfire in the first place and ending with eagerly jumping Rafter's bones. Despite the warmth of the night and the beach towel she had wrapped sarong-style around her waist below Jake's borrowed T-shirt, she shivered and shook.

Rafter sat on the bench in the stern, exchanging a few words now and then with Jake, who was rowing in the middle with his back to her. Sam was too embarrassed to look at either of them. Rafter, though, appeared remarkably nonchalant about what had happened.

Men seemed to have an amazing capacity to compartmentalize and separate such things as sex and emotions, Sam mused. James Bond, that male hero icon, thought nothing of sleeping with his enemies, as long as they were female and beautiful.

She knew that Rafter had lots of experience with women. On cold reflection, she decided that he could not have been nearly as carried away as she. He'd even had the presence of mind to think about birth control. Sam squeezed her eyes shut as a mortifying possibility occurred to her. Perhaps he'd thought it fun, a sort of payback, to screw the enemy who'd foiled his big operation two years ago, stroking his ego and humiliating her at the same time.

If humiliation was his goal, he'd succeeded. Big time. She was also embarrassed, ashamed, and horrified by what she'd done—except for one small part of her that couldn't help being pleased. Because with Rafter, she'd remarkably, unexpectedly, and oh-so-easily breezed over a sexual barrier she'd never managed to hurdle with Brian.

And it could never happen again. Attraction was one thing; going to bed with him a different matter altogether. He was the enemy, she reminded herself, a fact she kept forgetting lately.

From the stern, Nick watched Sam, stoic and silent in the bow behind Jake. He didn't have to worry about her catching him staring because she was diligently avoiding meeting his eyes. All traces of levity from the beach had disappeared. He wondered what was going through that fascinating, maddening brain of hers. She appeared anything but happy with what had happened on the beach.

He wasn't sure how he felt about it beyond stunned. He'd expected her to push him away, to be angry, to hold the line. Instead, her wild response had been like jet fuel dumped on a fire.

Christ. There were good reasons why he should stay away from her, starting with that he didn't entirely trust her. He sensed she was still holding out on him. But exactly why that meant a fling with her would be such a bad idea was suddenly unclear. Maybe if he slept with her, he could finally get her out of his head once and for all.

As they neared the association shoreline, Nick took pity on her and directed Jake to drop her at the dock by the inn. He and Jake could collect clothing at the bonfire and return the rowboat. That would also give him a chance to clear the air with Jake. "No point in all three of us going back."

She sent him a quick, grateful look, before her face closed up again. When the boat bumped up against the dock, she scrambled out. Nick followed and walked with her partway up the dock, making sure they were out of Jake's earshot before reaching out to stop her flight.

"Sam, I—"

"Save your postmortems, Rafter." She shrugged off his hand. "Thanks for the rescue, but as for the rest . . . Let's just pretend it never happened."

"Like hell it didn't," he muttered to her back as she fled into the night.

CHAPTER 10

Sam was pale and subdued at the meeting the next morning. In the epidemic of hangovers, her silence passed unnoticed. "We should probably talk," Nick murmured, cornering her during a break next to the overworked coffeepot in the kitchen of Hall's cottage.

She took a step away, her gaze darting nervously to see if anyone was watching. "Not here."

Irritated that she'd reverted to avoidance mode, he made a point of moving across the room to sit next to her, ignoring her narrow-eyed glare. Hall called it quits before noon, and the participants gratefully dispersed, some for the beach and others for home. Sam hastened off when Nick was held up by another judge. He caught up to her in front of the inn as she lugged her gear across the sun-baked parking lot to her ancient Saab.

"We need to clear the air," he said, falling into step with her.

Her face immediately became guarded. "I have to visit my aunt."

"You can't avoid me forever."

She spared him only the briefest glance as she dropped her overnight bag and racket next to the car and fished inside her purse for keys. "Look, Rafter, I don't want you to think that what happened last night meant anything to me." She snagged the keys and opened the back door. "We got a little, ah, friendly but—"

"Friendly?" He eyed her in disbelief.

"Yes," she said firmly, tossing her gear onto the rear seat. She shoved on sunglasses and edged past him to open the driver's door. "We're both consenting adults, but given our differences, it's not going to happen again, so—"

"What makes you so sure of that?"

"Because our reactions had more to do with the ordeal we'd just been through than anything else. And because I won't let it happen again."

Nick took that as a throwing down of the gauntlet. Not her intention, he was sure, but her cool denial of the explosion of heat they'd generated pricked his ego and made him itch to prove her wrong. Eyes narrowing, he put a hand on the driver's door to prevent her from closing it.

"Not everything is within your control, Sam."

She looked at him from behind her dark glasses. "Don't get your back up. Surely . . ." She stopped uncertainly and shrugged. "I know men look at these things differently, but surely you agree that any further . . ."

"Friendliness?" His mouth stretched into a thin smile.

"Yes."

The rare blush working its way up her face made him feel a little less ticked off. She wasn't as unaffected by what had happened as she wanted him to believe.

She continued more firmly, "You do agree that

any further *friendliness* would be a bad idea, don't you?"

"Yes, that much I can agree with."

She heaved a little sigh of relief and slid into the driver's seat, then paused, darting a brief, uncomfortable glance up at him through the open door. "I know Jake probably got an eyeful, so it may be irrelevant, but I'd—ah—appreciate it if you would be discreet about what happened."

Nick barely hung on to his temper. "Oh, gee, you mean I don't get to brag to the boys that I made you go up like a rocket?" Shame kicked in as soon as the words left his mouth, but it was too late to call them back.

She stiffened in her seat, and Nick felt her ice over behind her sunglasses. "My reputation is already shaky thanks to you. I'd rather not have it trashed entirely just as I'm about to start job hunting." She started the Saab and tried to tug the door closed, but Nick held on.

"Sam, wait! I'm sorry." He rubbed his other hand across his jaw in a gesture of frustration. "It's just that where I come from, gentlemen don't kiss and tell. But I guess you have reason to doubt me." He looked her square in the eyes and promised, "You don't have anything to worry about from me, or Jake for that matter."

She gave him a cool nod of acknowledgment, but Nick saw her mouth tremble as she backed the car out of its space. She wasn't nearly as tough as she pretended.

Camille jerked awake when a muscle spasmed in her neck. She didn't have many of those involuntary movements anymore. In earlier days she would have been thrilled to be rid of the random jerks and shakes, but that was before she'd experienced what came next. In the disease's perverse progression, voluntary movement declined along with involuntary, in her case worsened by the stroke. Now she could barely move at all. She was locked inside this dried-up shell that could hurt but not respond.

Camille's mind floated as it did increasingly of late. Sam had been by earlier, she recalled. It was Sunday. She knew because, on the television across the room from her bed, Wolf Blitzer was interviewing an Arab in a turban. Sam usually came on Saturday, but this weekend she'd come on Sunday on her way home from that old windbag Hall's court retreat. Sam had been telling a funny story about his annual tennis playoff before Camille had fallen asleep. Men and their games. Most were just overgrown boys. She would have laughed had she been able to. But there'd been other disturbing news that she couldn't quite recall, something important she worked in vain to pull into view.

Frustrated, her eyes flicked to the clock—2 P.M. The nurse would be making her rounds soon. She would want to turn off the television for a little while so Camille could rest before dinner. Camille liked it on; the voices comforted her and kept her plugged into the outside world. Time had little meaning for her anymore, yet more than ever her life was governed by other people's schedules and that annoyed her excessively.

What difference did it make whether she got her "rest"? She would be getting plenty of rest soon enough. The thought of her demise caused no distress. She welcomed being liberated from her useless old body.

Harry had believed in reincarnation, like the Hindus. Of course as a matter of political expediency, he'd publicly held to his Presbyterian roots. But Camille knew he believed that people lugged along their Karma—good and bad—from one life to the next. Lately, Camille often thought about Harry's beliefs. If he was right, he might already be six years old. She hoped they would meet again soon, and that this time she would be the right age for him, not decades younger.

But then she thought about Sam and how alone she would be. She let out a weary sigh. Sam still held out hope for, if not a cure, at least a reprieve. Camille didn't have the heart to tell her it was no use, that she hated being trapped inside this broken body and hoped every night not to wake up in the morning. But she regretted causing Sam more hurt. She'd had too much of that already in her life.

Her gaze flicked from the television to the talking computer Sam had purchased and excitedly presented to her last week. Camille wished she'd saved her money. She didn't want to use the time she had left struggling with the contraption, and she despised the mechanical sound of it. What did she have to talk about anyway? She still managed to communicate what little she wanted to say the old-fashioned way.

A stab of guilt and worry made her frown inside. *Rachel!* The name surfaced. That was what she'd been trying to remember. But it hadn't been this visit Sam had innocently uttered that feared name. No, it was last week, wasn't it? Out of the blue, Sam had asked about the old days when Harry was on Madison University's Board of Governors. She'd wanted to know if Camille had ever heard of a townie by the name of Rachel Holtz who'd gone missing when Philip was a law student.

Camille had been stunned, for once glad her

face could not betray her. Her shock had quickly turned to horror when Sam recounted Rachel's possible connection to Judge Christiansen and her trek to Harbour Grace to try to learn more. Camille had been more frozen by fear for Sam than by the disease. Oh, to hear that dangerous name again, and on Sam's unguarded lips! If only Christiansen had taken his guilt with him to the grave.

Camille had denied any recognition of the name, of course. To do otherwise would be madness. The truth might pull Sam deeper in.

She did not know what she should do, whom she could turn to with Harry gone. She certainly didn't trust Harry's widow to protect Sam. Philip maybe, as long as his own neck wasn't in the noose. Possibly Hattie Christiansen?

She fervently hoped that no action would be necessary. Sam seemed to have recognized the potential for danger on her own and wisely decided to back off. Camille was a bit rusty, but she offered up a brief, but heartfelt prayer that it wasn't already too late.

The air had little chance to clear between Sam and Rafter during the ensuing week primarily because Sam went to great lengths to avoid him. However much she might wish to dismiss what had happened on that beach, she realized it had fundamentally changed their relationship. Something had shifted inalterably between them and settled into a new place. She wasn't sure where, except that the place was a whole lot more complicated than before, impossible as that would have seemed a few short days ago. Every time she caught a glimpse of him, she remembered in excruciating, mortifying IMAX detail everything she had done on that beach with him. A good memory could be a curse at such times.

Fortunately, other matters demanded her attention and provided much needed distractions. First thing Monday morning, she made a beeline for the records room in search of the Benton Motors appellate file. Not surprisingly, considering it was a current appeal, the file was not there. A little later, Sam dropped by Jake's office. With some embarrassment she returned his T-shirt and thanked him again for rowing to their rescue. Lingering on the other side of the desk that took up most of the space in the tiny office, she casually asked how he was getting on with the July docket, eventually steering the conversation to Benton Motors.

Jake cleared a chair of briefs so she could sit. "Yeah, Todd was asking me about that case, too. I'm not familiar with it. Judge Rafter is writing the opinion on that one and a few others."

Sam hid her disappointment. She was counting on Todd having the file. Few judges on the court had either the time or the inclination to draft their own opinions from scratch. "Lucky you."

"He's letting me acclimate. Darn decent of him. Not many judges do it, from what I hear."

"It's the case load." Sam stood to leave. "Everyone is stretched."

Over the next two days, Sam kept an eye out for a chance to sneak into Rafter's office for a peek at the file. On the sly she checked Liz's copy of his appointment book to see when he would be out. Knowing his schedule in advance also helped her to avoid running into him. Unfortunately, he was in the habit of locking his door when he left, and Sam knew from Liz that he hadn't replaced the key on her key rack. In the meantime, she began to respond to comments from other judges on opinions she'd begun circulating for Matthew's backlogged cases. She also set up an appointment to meet with Hall later in the week.

On Wednesday, her success in avoiding Rafter came to an abrupt end when Liz relayed his summons. Sam took a minute and a few deep breaths to mentally compose herself before going next door to his office. Pride demanded that he not glimpse the embarrassing tangle of emotions tying her stomach in knots.

"You rang?"

Rafter looked up, laser blue eyes probing her across his desk, his face as usual impossible to read. He waved her in and gestured to a chair.

As she sat, her gaze lit on a stack of files occupying the corner of his desk closest to her. Benton Motors sat on top.

"Any sense that you're being followed?"

Sam dragged her gaze back to his and saw that he'd marked the direction of hers. "No, not at all." After keeping a careful watch for the first two days and detecting nothing unusual, she'd begun to let down her guard.

"Good." He studied her another long moment before taking a hundred-dollar bill from his wallet and pushing it across the polished walnut surface of the desk to her. "Your winnings."

"Thank you." She picked it up, slipped it into the pocket of her slacks, and waited.

"I have the tickets for the bash on Saturday. We're still on, I assume."

Sam nodded, relieved that he was still willing to make good on his offer. Necessity trumped her discomfort at the prospect of spending time with him socially. But while she didn't have the luxury of giving in to her squeamishness and backing out, she was actively lobbying Kat and Billy to attend as buffers.

Liz wandered in with a letter for Rafter to sign. He glanced from it to Sam.

"Pick you up at six then," he said, causing Liz's eyebrows to climb.

Sam nodded again. She stood to leave and hesitated, itching to grab the Benton file while he was busy reading the letter, except she knew she'd never get away with it. She could simply ask to see the file, but would then be forced to explain why. Before she could whisper pretty-please-don't, AG agents would be crawling around the office.

Rafter glanced up, evidently surprised to see her still there. "Is there something else?" He scanned her face. For a second Sam almost imagined his eyes warmed, drinking her up.

She shook it off. "No." Self-consciously, she felt both gazes following her out of the room.

Never one to let her curiosity slide, Liz cornered her a minute later by the water cooler in the records room. "Would you mind telling me what's going on between you two? You've been holed up in your office twitchy as a cat. He's prowling around here like a grouchy bear. And now you're going out together on a date?" She looked incredulous.

Sam had no time to squeak back more than a defensive and downright appalled, "It's not a date!" before someone came into the office and Liz dashed out to see what he wanted.

"Oh, for heaven's sake," Sam muttered and closeted herself inside her office for the rest of the day.

She got her big chance at Rafter's office on Thursday evening. She could hardly believe her luck when she returned to work around nine to begin putting together her résumé, flipped on the reception area lights, and saw that Rafter's door stood open. The room beyond was dark but for the path of light spilling in through the door.

Caution stopped the impulse to boldly dash in and grab the Benton Motors file. This was too easy. Rafter never left his door opened and unlocked when he wasn't inside.

She considered and rejected the possibility of an intruder. Every door coming up, including that to the office suite, had been locked. Cleaning people, she decided with a relieved sigh. They cleaned the fifth floor on Thursday night. She leaned over Liz's desk, pulled out Rafter's appointment book, and happily discovered that he was right now across town at a retirement dinner for a family court judge.

Out of a lingering sense of caution or guilt or simply because it seemed in keeping with the clandestine spirit of a nighttime raid, Sam dug a penlight from the bottom of her purse before stealthily gliding into Rafter's office and across the carpet to Matthew's old desk.

She flicked on the penlight. As its narrow beam swept across the desk, it caught several photographs. Sam swung the light back to examine them. In one, a victorious Rafter and crew held a trophy aloft in front of a gleaming white sailboat. In another his family smiled out at her on the occasion of one sister's wedding. Sam felt a pang of jealously at the happy family scene, and guilt for snooping.

She turned the light to the pile of files she'd scoped out earlier in the week. Benton Motors no longer sat on top. Careful to keep the order, she began shuffling through the pile looking for it.

When she reached the bottom without finding it, she darted the light to a stack on the credenza under the window.

A sudden creak from the other side of the room, loud in the empty building, had her jerking the penlight to the seating area adjacent to the door. In horror, Sam watched Rafter swing his feet to the floor and straighten to a semiupright sprawl on the leather couch. She cringed, waiting for the firing squad.

"I believe what you're looking for is on the desk to your right." When she continued to gape at him, he raised a hand in front of his eyes to block the jiggling beam of light. "Do you mind?"

"Sorry," she croaked and hastily jerked it away. Face burning, she shot a glance at the door, considering the merits of bolting.

"Don't even think about it," he said, somehow reading her intentions.

"I thought you were at a retirement dinner." She winced at the inanity of it, the admission that she had counted on his absence to sneak in.

"I left early."

He padded over to the desk in stocking feet and flipped on a lamp, bathing the immediate area in a soft glow. He contemplated her with a combination of mistrust and disappointment. Both rankled.

Sighing, he circled behind her and pulled out the big leather desk chair. "Sit." He pushed the chair against the back of her knees, giving her no choice in the matter. In the process, his crisp white cotton shirt brushed the back of her head. She could smell his aftershave and found it faintly intoxicating, bizarrely so under the circumstances. Was she turning into one of those crazy danger junkies? Heart hammering, she resisted the urge to inhale deeply.

He reached around her to a short stack of files

on the opposite side of the vast desk, plucked out the Benton Motors file, and dropped it down in front of her. Apparently her dissembling at the retreat hadn't been terribly convincing. He knew exactly what she'd been looking for.

"You only needed to ask."

"You would have had the AG agents swarming the office again even if it was nothing—which I'm sure it is," she added hastily. "Nothing, I mean."

"No point bringing in the wolves on mere suspicion." He crossed his arms and leaned a hip against the desk, hovering uncomfortably close. "So, read it," he urged. "You're obviously dying to. Tell me if I'm wrong."

While she nervously opened the file and tried to read, he rose and prowled over to the windows, staring out at the city lights. She felt awkward sitting at his desk. Her mind blanked with nerves. The words ran in meaningless lines down the page. How could she concentrate with him consuming all the oxygen in the room? But eventually the need to know drew her in, and she managed to tune him out.

The appeal was from the dismissal of a class action lawsuit against Benton Motors, the state's fourth automaker and the only one still privately held. The company had long held a lucrative niche in the ultraluxury auto market with its single product, the mostly chauffeur-driven Benton Classic. Only about one thousand of the handcrafted cars were made each year. But recently, the company had branched out and introduced a new model, the Zephyr, in 2001, to compete in the Mercedes-Benz, BMW, Porsche market. Unfortunately, since its introduction the Zephyr had been plagued by defects that so far had led to a record eight safety recalls.

The plaintiff-class was composed of Michigan Zephyr owners who were suing to recover costs of repairs for defects not covered by recalls plus diminished resale value. Class certification was one of the major hurdles in a class action lawsuit. Typically, until then, big corporate defendants were unwilling to discuss a settlement. After certification, the suit could force them into bankruptcy.

Except for the oddity that Matthew had withheld the case from her, Sam could find nothing unusual, no hint of impropriety. His notes indicated that he'd leaned toward deciding the case the same way Rafter was now doing—in favor of class certification and against Benton Motors.

"Well?" Rafter asked when she leaned back in the chair. He wandered over and perched against the desk again.

She shook her head, sighing in relief. "Nothing."

"That was my assessment as well."

She sent him an annoyed look. "I suppose you raced right over here after the retreat to check it out."

He shrugged. "I could tell you were worried. You know, you could try trusting me for a change, Sam."

"That goes both ways, Rafter."

He let out a weary sigh and redirected the conversation. "How unusual was it that Matthew didn't give the case to you?"

"It was unusual," she admitted.

"You do realize that if there were a problem with the case, you'd come out squeaky clean since you never saw it."

Sam bristled. "Despite what you think of me, my purpose has never been to clear my own name or rehabilitate my standing in the legal community by finding dirt on Matthew. I want Matthew's name cleared because I believe in him."

He held up a placating hand. "I wasn't accusing you of doing anything at Saint Matthew's expense. I know you believed in him." Frowning, he admitted, "The more I get to know him—I know it sounds weird, but I feel as if I do know him, through his notes, judicial decisions . . ." He glanced at a bookcase that still held many of Matthew's books. "Choice of reading material, and especially through you and Liz and Hall and everyone else around here who think he should be nominated for man of the century. The more I learn, the more tempted I am to agree with you. I just can't reconcile that phone call he made."

In evident frustration, he ran a hand through his dark hair, making a lock of hair that usually fell over one side of his forehead briefly stand on end. He looked baffled and upset and uncertain all at once. Seeing his uncertainty made her heart miss a beat. However briefly, it felt as though they were allies again, as they'd been in happier days.

Sam stared at him in dawning wonder. "That's why you didn't call in the AG investigators," she murmured. "You believe in him too."

But he shook his head. "Sorry. I'd like to. If it weren't for that damn phone call . . ."

Hugely disappointed, Sam sighed and turned to another matter that had caught her attention in the file. "There was an earlier appeal in the same case."

"Yes. A little over a year ago. That appeal was from the trial court's first order denying class certification and dismissing the case. This court reversed and sent it back to give the plaintiff-class a shot at correcting the problem."

"Which judges were on that panel?"

Rafter smiled fleetingly. "You're quick, Parker. But you're not going to like the answer. Matthew was on that appeal as well. In fact, he was the only judge to hear both appeals."

He stretched over to the credenza, picked up another file, and dropped it on top of the first. "Feast your eyes. It's two-fer night."

Her hand hovered over this new wrinkle as her barely settled nerves jangled back to life. She knew without looking that Matthew had kept this one from her as well. At the time, she would have been fairly new to the office, still not entirely clear of the cloud of suspicion she'd come in under.

"Don't wimp out now," Rafter said dryly. "You're on a roll."

Sam opened the file quickly to mask the unsteadiness of her hand. This file didn't take as long. The three-judge panel had split two to one in favor of permitting the plaintiff-class to correct the initial defect in their case. That appeared to be the correct result.

"It looks as though Matthew initially considered ruling in Benton Motors' favor and dismissing." Leaning over her shoulder, Rafter pulled out a copy of the plaintiff-class brief. In the margins and on the back were extensive handwritten arguments in Benton Motors' favor, point-by-point contradictions of those made in the brief.

Except that the notes were not in Matthew's handwriting. Rafter, not as familiar with it, hadn't picked up on the difference.

Sam tried to make sense of what she was seeing. *Ex parte* communications about a case between a lawyer and a judge were prohibited. The strict ban was meant to discourage a host of problems ranging from unfair influence to outright payoffs. These notes appeared to be a detailed blueprint for dismissing the class action. More than that, she corrected on closer examination, they were virtually a judicial opinion written in the margins.

Except Matthew hadn't used the opinion. He'd gone the other way, giving new life to the lawsuit.

Sam breathed a little easier. Perhaps the notes had been made by one of the other judges on the panel. But she knew that was unlikely. Judges didn't write notes like this. If they didn't like an opinion, they wrote a dissent. The notes in front of her had a partisan feel pointing straight at Benton Motors. And any *ex parte* communication, whether or not actual influence occurred, had to be reported by the judge approached. The judicial code of conduct required it.

"Sam? What is it?"

She looked up. He was watching her with an expression of concern. For a reckless moment, she wanted to confide in him, to have him reassure her that her fear was groundless. But she detected suspicion in his expression, too, better hidden than the concern but never completely absent when he looked at her. The past, the lack of trust, always festered between them.

She forced a thin smile. "I was just thinking about how miffed the bigwigs at Benton Motors must have been about this decision."

"I doubt one of these judges will be getting a campaign contribution next time around," he agreed.

She flipped to the front cover where the parties' attorneys were listed. "It looks like they took it out on their own lawyer first. Marty Davis represented them in the first appeal, but not the second."

"He may be too ill to handle it."

Sam nodded, and pushed the chair back, hoping to make a quick, uncomplicated exit. "Thank you for letting me see these files," she murmured, sliding from the chair and starting to edge around him.

He watched her maneuvers with his enigmatic judge expression. "I'm happy to share information as long as it's a two-way street."

"Agreed."

When she was almost past him, he reached out and caught her hand in his. He was still perched half on the desk and reeled her in until she stood between his legs, so close that she could count the little blue facets in his eyes. "Oh, and Sam, I'm letting you off easy this time. But if you ever attempt to sneak into my office again, you'd better be prepared to pay the price."

"What price?"

"The traditional currency of women spies."

"And what is that?" She hated the breathy quaver in her voice, honest enough to concede that it was as much the result of excitement as fear.

"Why, in flesh, of course."

She felt the megaton impact of his smile as he released her hand, and she swallowed hard. "Of course."

CHAPTER 11

On Saturday morning, Sam woke with jitters over the looming party and with a list of chores that needed to be dealt with before Rafter picked her up at six. Chief among these was seeing that Kat, who had finally caved under the weight of Sam's pleas and agreed to attend with Billy tonight, was properly outfitted. Kat was hopeless with clothes due to a fatal combination of lack of interest and constant penny-pinching. If Sam didn't take her in hand, she would likely show up at the ball in her usual gray work gear, partly to make a statement against the lavish lifestyles of fat-cat lawyers but mostly because she didn't give a rap what she wore. Or worse, Billy would take one look and refuse to escort her. Plus, this was finally Sam's chance to get Kat into something nice.

In case Kat took a notion to flee to her office, Sam scrambled into sweats and a T-shirt and arrived at her tiny carriage house apartment half an hour earlier than agreed. When Kat saw who was rapping on her door at nine in the morning, she groaned and staggered back to bed. Undaunted,

Sam followed her into the bedroom and made for the closet.

"What are you doing?" Kat peered at her bleary-eyed.

"You agreed," Sam calmly reminded her.

"One is not responsible for any promises made after two mystery specials," Kat muttered thickly, pulling the covers over her head.

Ignoring her, Sam quickly surmised that Kat's closet held nothing that would reasonably do for a formal evening event, at least not one held in the modern era. Sam shook her head. There was little in sight beyond functional professional suits in dull gray and beige that were not flattering to Kat's coloring and a hodgepodge of ratty shirts and jeans.

Sam was no slave to fashion; even so her closet was overflowing compared to Kat's. But then, unlike Kat, who'd grown up with money, Sam knew what it felt like to be teased because of clothes that were ragged or dirty or didn't fit. Those precarious years with Rosalind had faded but were not forgotten. She'd learned early and painfully that people *were* judged by what they wore, and she'd addressed the problem at the earliest opportunity as she would another academic discipline.

She envied Kat's self-confidence. It was a state of mind. Kat fit in wherever she went despite her appalling taste in clothes because there was still something so solidly upper-middle-class about her. She certainly didn't harbor Sam's fear of ending up back in an L.A. ghetto surrounded by crack-heads. Kat had her own problems, but they didn't include an abiding fear of poverty.

Sam gave a little sigh. "Geez, Kat, when's the last time you bought a dress?"

A muffled voice answered from under the covers. "Gran's funeral."

"Come on. We're going shopping." Using the promise of a free lunch as a bribe, she coaxed a cranky Kat into the Saab and drove across town to a funky little vintage clothing store—her ace up the sleeve.

"I scored both my Vera Wang and Armani here at a fraction of retail." Sam spotted a parking spot at the curb in front and zipped into it. Tonight she intended to wear a designer knockoff she'd bought here gently used a couple years ago.

Kat rolled her eyes, unimpressed. "In the Brian era, I presume."

Sam nodded, her smile dimming. That was one aspect of life with Brian she didn't miss—the endless political functions that had constituted their social life. It occurred to her that they'd never gotten dressed up to do something just for fun, such as going to an opera or concert or play. She wondered if he'd be at tonight's bash. Probably. He was a Madison alum.

"Have I ever mentioned how glad I am you got rid of that jerk?"

"A time or two. Although I think you've got the ridding part backward." Sam ignored Kat's muttered abuse of Brian and steered the conversation in a cheerier direction as they slid from the car. "Jimmy, the owner, has some mysterious connection to the fashion industry 'on the coast,' although he won't say which coast in what country." Sam paused with her hand on the door and whispered a warning, "Let me handle him or you might end up looking like a drag queen."

"As long as it's not red," Kat murmured. Her eyes widened as she got her first look at the bizarre collection of Frederick's of Hollywood-style lounge wear, wild drag queen getups, and high-fashion evening wear that crammed every possible inch of the small shop.

Jimmy was auspiciously absent, and his liberally pierced assistant was too busy poring over the latest issue of a heavy metal magazine to give them more than a glance. After several misfires, Sam zeroed in on the bull's-eye, a classic, creamy Ralph Lauren in Kat's tiny size four and in perfect shape.

"Try this one." With a determined gleam in her eye, Sam squeezed into the cramped fitting room.

"It only took the fairy godmother one try," Kat complained.

"Wrong movie. You're going to look like Sabrina in this." Sam lowered it over Kat's whippet-lean frame. "This had to have been a model's demo."

"Then it'll be too long." Kat's grumble was muffled in a froth of material. Several inches shorter than Sam, she stood just five-four in bare feet.

"The clerk said they can have anything we pick shortened by tonight. Jimmy does it on a machine in back." Sam zipped her in, then backed into the shop for room to assess. A slow smile of satisfaction lit her face. "Yes."

"At least it's not red," Kat said, studying herself in the mirror.

That was all the approval Sam needed. She raced off to haggle with the clerk, and would have paid for the gown out of sheer gratitude, but Kat waived her off. "Forget it. I suppose I should have something like this in my closet."

Outside the shop, Sam squinted askance at Kat's honey blond mop. "Your hair."

"I know. I made an appointment."

Her biggest chore accomplished, Sam's attention drifted to the Benton Motors appeals as she drove home. After a time, her musings were interrupted by a radio forecast calling for blue sky and another ninety-plus scorcher with a storm front moving in overnight. She felt Kat's gaze on her. "What?"

"You've got to stop obsessing about it," Kat said, reading her mind. "So what if Christiansen didn't report an attempt to influence his decision. *If* it even happened. The fact is, you know he wasn't influenced."

"That's not what really bothers me." Sam frowned, thinking about the call she'd made to Hattie Christiansen about Benton Motors. It always helped to think out loud with Kat. She was good at working through problems and had much-needed distance.

At a red light, Sam glanced across the front seat. "Hattie thinks Marty Davis must have tried to get Matthew to dismiss the case against Benton Motors and that's what Matthew was going to report to the authorities. But if she's right, why did he wait a year and a half to do it? Why not report it when it happened? And why was Davis, or whoever sent the notes, so confident Matthew wouldn't turn him in that he would risk sending something in writing? This was no sly let's-feel-out-the-judge with nothing in writing. Matthew had hard evidence."

Kat didn't say anything a moment, then, "They had something on Matthew. That's what you're thinking."

"I don't know what to think. It's inconceivable that Matthew of all people would fail to report such a blatant attempt to sway his vote. But I can't figure out another explanation for what I saw."

Kat's nose wrinkled in thought. "You're sure the notes weren't made by one of the other judges?"

"Positive." Yesterday while Rafter was out, she'd dug through files until she came up with handwriting samples for both judges. "Neither is even close. One prints and the other has a distinctive scrawl. I wish I had a sample of Marty Davis's to compare." Sam's grip tightened on the wheel as she took a right on Fulton. What was she to do now? She wished there were some primer for law clerks in her situation, the ABCs of posthumously defending one's judge in such circumstances.

"If Davis's is a match," Kat said slowly, "I suppose one question would be whether there's some connection to that girl."

"Rachel. That's a truly scary possibility, isn't it? That this could all be connected to something that happened years ago. And I'm not sure the notion is so far-fetched. Hattie is convinced that there is a connection, that that's what Matthew was trying to tell her at the end. She said that Randall Benton is another of Matthew's Madison classmates. Except he wasn't a law student."

"Randall Benton?" Kat was staring at her in dismay.

Puzzled, Sam nodded. "Benton Motors is the defendant. I suppose I shouldn't be telling you all this but—"

Kat brushed that concern away with a distracted wave. "Sam, be careful. That man is evil, I swear to God!" Her normally mellow voice vibrated with emotion.

Alarm skittered down Sam's arms and legs. "Why! What is it, Kat?"

"Remember Tanya? Randall Benton is her boyfriend's father—ex-boyfriend, I should say."

Sam pulled into Kat's drive and eyed her normally fearless friend who, at the moment, looked seriously worried.

"Sam, if he's done half of what I suspect him of,

he's a dangerous man. And if his business is at
stake, I wouldn't put much past him."

Sam pondered this new twist. "If this goes back
to Rachel's disappearance, there could be more
than one powerful man with a lot to lose."

And that was precisely why she'd decided to stay
away from it in the first place and let the AG
agents do their job.

Rafter pulled up promptly at six. Not wanting to
invite him inside her apartment, Sam grabbed her
wrap and handbag and met him in the second-
floor hallway as he came up the last few steps. He
looked gorgeous in a tux and black tie, more like a
judge out of central casting than the real thing. He
was too young, too hip, and too attractive for that.

He stopped at the top of the stairs and stared intently down the length of hallway at her without
saying anything. Her sparkly, periwinkle blue gown
was cut to drape curves, and for a nervous moment
Sam wondered if it was too clingy for her purpose
tonight.

"You look stunning," he said finally, and Sam
felt a rush of warmth and relief. As he walked the
rest of the way to her, he shook his head, wearing a
funny little bemused smile. "I'm not sure the geri-
atric set will be safe. Weak tickers, you know. You
smell good, too."

Flustered, Sam blurted out, "So do you. I mean,
you look very nice." Massive understatement. He
looked wildly attractive. The careless flop of dark
hair over his left brow and his watchful blue eyes
gave him a brooding, poetic look. She had a brief
vision of having run her hands through that same
hair in demented fashion on the beach.

Oh, help. How was she ever to look at him again while somehow managing to keep a safe mental distance? It had been hard enough to remain detached before. Now embarrassment, shame, humiliation, and yes, she allowed with considerable annoyance, a poorly timed case of reawakened lust had joined the emotional brew.

She took a hasty step toward the stairs. "We'd best be on our way."

They met Billy in the downstairs hallway on his way to pick up Kat. In his tux, Billy's patrician resemblance to his father was all the more remarkable. Sam grinned when Billy gave a wolf whistle, covered his heart with his hand, and grandly quoted, " 'O, she doth teach the torches to burn bright!' "

Laughing, Sam caught his hands in hers. "You look yummy, too, Billy. Your dance card will need a waiting list." She reached up to buss his cheek and whispered a heartfelt "thank you" in his ear for agreeing to make this rare venture into his father's world for her.

They separated at Rafter's Beemer. Sam had briefly considered telling Rafter she would ride with Billy and Kat but decided she didn't dare. After her Thursday evening blunder in his office, she felt once again on precarious probationary status and didn't want to risk doing anything to make him bail on her. Much as it nettled, she really could use his help to repair her tarnished reputation, despite, and because of, his having tarnished it in the first place!

They didn't get more than a block before he shot her a suspicious look. "Why do I have the feeling that when Billy said he'd see you later he was talking about tonight?"

"He and Kat are coming to the party."

Rafter didn't look particularly surprised or pleased by that news.

"Tell me," he said, frowning at the road as if he found some fault with it, "are they coming as your support staff, or are you thinking you need a chaperone for protection against me?"

"They're coming," Sam said with some heat, "so that I have at least two people who will talk to me. I haven't been exactly welcomed with open arms at bar association events these last couple of years."

He glanced at her. "Has it been that bad?"

"Not really. Not after someone had the decency to put me out of my misery and tell me about the rumors. That at least explained why I was being shunned. Then I stopped going and everything was just fine as long as I didn't accidentally bump into a group of good-old-boy litigators out for lunch."

He sighed, looking contrite. "Sam, I—"

She cut him off before he could use his gentle voice on her. "No need to break out the Kleenex, Rafter. Partying with a bunch of lawyers ranks somewhere below final exam week on my top five hundred list of fun activities."

"What is at the top?"

She tilted her head, considering. "Live music of almost any kind. Except rap. Concerts, plays."

"Then you must have tossed a lot of pennies into wishing wells when you were with Brian."

"I used to wish for a lot of things back then."

He squinted over at her. "But not anymore?"

She shrugged. "No more happily-ever-after pipe dreams, if that's what you mean. I still wish for things, but they're more realistic."

"Like?"

"Well, obviously a job is at the top of the list." She made a face. "Assuming that, I'd love to go to an opera at the Met or see a Broadway show. I've always lacked either the time or money to do it. How about you?"

"I'll tag along with you," he said while charging up the expressway on-ramp.

Bewildered, Sam glanced over, trying to read him. But immediately, he began fiddling with a CD, acting as though he hadn't said anything extraordinary at all. An instant later, a bluesy guitarist was appropriately crooning about having the keys to the highway, and Sam decided it must have been one of those careless, throwaway comments that meant nothing. Besides, she was much too busy fretting about the evening ahead to give it lengthy analysis, or to read much into Rafter's occasional, brooding glances in her direction as they hurtled down the highway.

Some of her nerves eased when they pulled up in front of the president's mansion on the grounds of Madison University. From the number of guests spilling out doors onto patios and lawns, she concluded with great relief that this was not a predominately local affair.

The mansion was spectacular—built for entertaining on a grand scale, and of the same pink sandstone as the rest of the campus, with acres of winding gardens sweeping down to the glittering turquoise of Lake Manitou. As they left Rafter's Beemer in the hands of a delighted student valet, they could hear the slow beat of a swing band playing somewhere out of sight. Sam could see through open doors that tables were set up inside as well as out.

"I wonder what they would have done had it rained," she murmured as they approached the entrance.

But the weather had cooperated, spectacularly.

The warm, moisture-laden breeze was a soft touch against Sam's bare arms, comfortable enough that she checked her shawl at the cloakroom.

As Rafter steered her through the heaving bottleneck inside the marble foyer, she caught a few glances already being cast in their direction, so far more curious than hostile. Time would tell whether they would remain so benign after old rumors started recirculating and people remembered who she was.

"What'll you have?" He nodded in the direction of the bar.

"Whatever burns." She caught his amused look, and grimaced. "Joking. Surprise me."

"Chin up. These folks are from all over the state. Most have never heard of you or the scandal."

"Yet." Sam surveyed the throng milling about the huge room. Though the windows and open doors along the rear, she glimpsed a large band playing in a pavilion on the lawn. "I'm going to wander that way and see if I can spot Billy and Kat."

"I'll find you," he said, moving off.

Sam caught snatches of gossip and business as she made slow progress through the crowd. Spotting the law professor, Sophie Somerset, outside, Sam eagerly set a course for her. In so doing, she ran smack into a clique of assistant U.S. attorneys from her old office, none she knew well or counted as friends, and before she could reverse course, was pounced on by Pushy Pusch.

"Samantha!" Ravishing in sparkling black, Pushy oozed sudden interest in Sam, hooking her arm as if they were chums and pulling her into their knot before Sam could back away. She made a great show of introducing her around and reminding the others who she was, when it was quite obvious that they knew perfectly well. Several apparently now worked under Pushy in the fraud unit, and a couple seemed mildly uncomfortable with the show she was putting on. She lamented over Sam's long absence from legal functions and finally slipped in the dig Sam had been expecting all along.

"It's always such a shame to see someone with as much potential as you stumble," she gassed on insincerely, beaming her faux smile at Sam. "You'll bounce back. Look at what's-his-name, that English actor who's in all the chick flicks, caught with the prostitute going down on him . . ."

"Hugh Grant," Sam said evenly. If Pushy thought to send her staggering off for smelling salts with this tepid ammunition, she had another think coming.

"See, he bounced back. I do believe in second chances, and I'm so glad to see you've turned your life around and decided to resume a more public role in the legal community."

Sam forced a bland smile, telling herself to let it go, but not quite able to. "Thank you, Pushy—sorry—Meredith, you're very kind." The use of the despised nickname made Pushy glare and others bite back smiles. "My probation officer evidently agrees with you. He thinks I've made such great progress, he let me out for the night. Sorry I can't stay and chat about old times, but must catch someone."

"Yes, you'd better run," Pushy said, then added slyly, "I saw Rafter coming this way a minute ago, and I hear you two haven't been getting along very well."

"Oh, we're managing not to murder each other." It was then that Sam sensed something amiss and glanced around to discover Rafter behind her and Pushy but in full view of the others. They collectively strained forward, tightening the knot around

Sam and Pushy in their eagerness not to miss anything juicy. Rafter didn't disappoint.

"That's why you can't believe everything you hear,
Meredith," he said casually, startling her. Pushy's
head whirled around. "Samantha and I are getting
on famously. Just like old times. In fact, she's here
with me tonight."

With no small amount of satisfaction, Sam watched sour surprise bloom on Pushy's face as she be-
held Rafter handing her one of the drinks he held.
Sam bit back a giggle. It was a rare and entertaining event to see Pushy get her comeuppance. Sam
grudgingly admired, though, how quickly Pushy
recovered.

With a smile that was both challenging and flir-
tatious, Pushy asked, "Isn't that a little cozy, Nick?"

"What?"

"Dating your law clerk," she said nastily.

Rafter sent Sam one of the enigmatic smiles she
could never read and so found enormously frustrating. "Sam isn't my law clerk. She works for Judge
Hall. And we're not dating in the way you mean,"
he added matter-of-factly. Then he directed a
question to another of his former subordinates.

A minute later, having neatly extracted them, he
tipped his head to Sam. "Okay, this is where we go
to work. Stick with me, let me do the talking, and
for God's sake try to act as though my company
doesn't give you constipation."

She stared at him. His eyes gleamed with relish.
Dammit, he was enjoying this!

He took several steps, clearing a path through
the crowd, before he looked around and realized
she wasn't following. Backtracking, he gave her an
exasperated look. "Where did I lose you?"

"Somewhere around the place where you took

over and told me to keep my mouth shut. The constipation bit wasn't one of your more charming moments either."

"It fit. Look, no offense, but by necessity I have the starring role here. All you have to do is be gracious and act as though we have a solid, friendly, professional relationship. That a problem?"

Sam grimaced. "No."

"Good. Let's get on with it." With his hand now firmly on the small of her back, they circulated.

The turnout of the political elite from around the state surpassed even Matthew's funeral. Governor Graham was on hand. She saw him talking to her former boss, Robbie O'Neal, and the state attorney general. So many of them were Madison Law grads. And where politicians gathered, businessmen and their lobbyists were sure to follow. And vice versa, Sam thought cynically. She had been to dozens of similar functions in the Brian era. The agenda didn't vary greatly.

The political luminaries were not Rafter's targets. Instead he made a point of casually running into the very people Sam, left to her own devices, would have done her best to avoid—senior partners in the area's better law firms, in-house corporate lawyers, prosecuting attorneys for area municipalities. Potential employers. He knew many of them and was warmly welcomed.

With the instincts of a born litigator, Rafter sensed when to wield a hammer and when, as now, a feather duster would be more effective. His delivery was perfect. He used such a light touch that no one listening to his easy schmoozing would think he was deliberately talking Sam up, but all were undoubtedly left with the impression that he, at least, would give her a high competency rating. But her competency had never been in question, and whether he was as successful at dusting the layer of scandal from her, she couldn't tell. She found some reason for hope in the glances being sent her way; they held more uncertainty and less scorn and hostility than she was used to, although perhaps that had more to do with the passing of time than anything Rafter was doing. Still, she was in awe of his skill at working the room and happy to stand aside and leave him to it. For her part, she smiled and made the appropriate remarks on cue.

This was the part of law and politics she disliked most. In both venues, there were rainmakers—the stars who could bring in clients or money or votes; the ones who could make things happen—and there were grunts. Grunts could be legal Einsteins, but unless they had that intangible star power, they would never be rainmakers. Robbie O'Neal was a rainmaker. So was Philip Wentworth. Billy could be if he wanted. Brian, a rainmaker wannabe, had once rather enviously said the same about her, although she thought he was wrong given that she didn't enjoy the schmoozing that was a key component in a rainmaker's arsenal. She liked life as a legal grunt. She enjoyed law as an academic discipline.

Sam considered Rafter as they circled the room. He belonged to that rarest group of all, combining the very best grunt skills with that intangible, star quality that made people gravitate to him.

Billy and Kat joined them midway through the ordeal, and Billy slung an arm around her, murmuring into her ear, "The reinforcements are here. But no blood drawn yet, I see."

Tremendously buoyed, Sam laughed for the first time that evening. In short order, she became aware of an unanticipated secondary benefit of Billy's presence. He was a minor celebrity in this crowd, and soon was attracting his own satellites, who seemed universally unaware that they could see him anytime they wanted at his bookstore.

The Wentworths were the nearest the state had to a political dynasty. Old Harry and Philip had each reached political heights most in the room only dreamed of. The Wentworths were also an attractive, charming, and old-moneyed Michigan family. If the assemblage couldn't have the senator, they would happily make do with the handsome and much more elusive son.

By the time they sat for dinner, Sam felt as though she'd run the gauntlet. Her face ached from smiling and her brain ached from excessive small talk. The seating plan had them sharing a choice table near the front with Billy, Kat, and a third couple who had not yet arrived, Rafter's brand new replacement at the U.S. Attorney's Office and her husband.

"That went well," Rafter murmured.

Kat sat gingerly, unaccustomed to wearing a ball gown, and surveyed the seating arrangements. "Power seats. Must have something to do your elevated status, Nick."

"More likely the Wentworth connection," Rafter said.

Kat eyed him. "You do that mingling thing very well."

"You should be back in a court room," Sam agreed, attempting to readjust her facial muscles to normal. "Your talents are wasted in an appellate court."

Rafter's eyebrows shot up in mock astonishment. "Is that a compliment I hear?"

"I guess that would depend on how highly I regard your appellate skills," Sam tossed back with a little smile.

The Coteys arrived at the table just then, and

Rafter introduced them all around. Sam had always admired Sandy Cotey, a shrewd veteran lawyer in the office, and was delighted that she'd recently won out over Pushy for Rafter's old job. Of the dozens of assistant U.S. attorneys, Sandy had been one of the few who had withheld judgment after Sam's disgrace, telling Sam outright that she doubted that the rumors flying around the office told the whole story.

Over dinner, Sandy, blunt as she was gregarious, filled Rafter and Sam in on the gossip around their old office and, in turn, demanded to be filled in on their lives.

At one point while Rafter was occupied talking to Billy, Sandy, sitting on Sam's right, leaned over and asked in an undertone, "So how are things really going between you and Nick? I've heard such varying accounts, and yet here you are together."

"I hadn't realized we were being watched," Sam hedged, feeling cornered because Sandy was a friend of Rafter's. Plus her good opinion mattered where Pushy's didn't.

Sandy chuckled. "Oh, yes. Our forces are debriefed after each foray across the street."

Stung, Sam's smile faded and her back stiffened against her chair. "I'm certainly glad we could provide amusement for the gossip mill."

Regret instantly replaced the humor on Sandy's face. "Oh dear. I'm sorry. That was insensitive of me. Please, let me explain." She let out a long sigh and continued in a low voice. "You have to understand first that you were well liked in the office when you worked there. Not by all, I'll admit. There were some that resented your rapid rise and rejoiced at your fall. But most were baffled by what happened and had a difficult time believing the rumors.

"Then there's Nick. Your prime backer in the office. Yet he didn't defend you. We all wondered what happened. You were friends. Some thought more. You had a great deal in common." She looked at Sam intently. "I guess most of us have been rooting for you two to patch up the rift. I certainly have."

"Thanks." Sam managed a slight smile, feeling embarrassed for having overreacted and ridiculously emotional at the kind words. In defense she tried for indifference even though she doubted she could fool shrewd Sandy. "I'm sorry to disappoint you though. Our rift is too wide to patch. Rafter and I have nothing in common beyond mutual distrust," she added airily, not thinking where they were.

Unfortunately, this bald assertion came during a lull in the larger conversation.

"Oh, I can think of one or two more things than that," Rafter said acidly from her other side.

Sam looked up to find that they had the entire table's attention, and Rafter looked seriously put out. Billy winced in sympathy, but Kat shot her an odd look of disapproval.

Mortified, Sam felt heat rise up her face. It fleetingly occurred to her that she must have the biggest mouth in a room full of big mouths in order to have fit her entire foot into it.

CHAPTER 12

"You could try being a little nicer to him," Kat chided Sam during a private moment. After the speeches, people had begun to table-hop. The Coteys were talking to someone at the next table, Billy was being courted by a state party chairwoman, and Rafter had stalked off to refill his scotch. "From what I've seen, Nick is making a major effort here to get your butt out of a bind. And you embarrass him in front of everyone."

"I know." Sam shook her head, a weary, defensive gesture. "But it's extremely vexing that I have to rely on him of all people to save said butt."

"Maybe it's time to forgive and forget. It looks like that's what he's doing."

"He doesn't have as much to forgive or forget."

"Maybe not," Kat conceded. "But you both were in an impossible situation back then. I've always thought you should have trusted him with the truth."

"Given all that happened afterward, I think it's a darn good thing I didn't."

"You used to adore him. After working for him

for three years, could you have been so wrong about him?"

"Apparently I could," Sam muttered, annoyed at Kat for bringing up a matter better forgotten. Having longtime friends could at times be painful. They had memories and perspectives that were not always convenient, and they felt they had the duty to occasionally dust them off and parade them about as necessary for one's own good.

Kat was looking thoughtfully into the distance. "You know I have a jaundiced view of relationships. I've never understood men. Maybe that's why it never occurred to me until tonight . . . seeing the way he looks at you. Now it all clicks."

"What *are* you talking about?"

Kat focused on Sam. "Why do you think he's so intent on helping you?"

"Because he knows what he did to me was wrong and he's trying to make it right."

"But why now? Maybe you should think about it."

"If you're going where I think you are, forget it. Your radar is on the fritz big time."

Kat plowed on anyway. "The man is crazy about you. He should have removed himself from your investigation altogether."

Sam made a noise of disbelief. "The most he's crazy for is a quick tussle between the sheets."

"Maybe, but my theory explains more," Kat whispered hurriedly as Rafter returned with Pushy hot on his heels. He stopped to talk at the next table, but Pushy continued over and slid into an empty chair next to Billy.

Sam glanced away from Rafter, the crowd shifted, and her gaze lit on Marty Davis, Benton Motors' former attorney. He was deep in conversation with a man she didn't recognize.

"Randall Benton," Kat supplied darkly, following Sam's gaze.

He was a nondescript man of medium height and thinning brown hair, not a figure destined to stand out in a crowd despite his millions. Sam's gaze shifted slightly to Marty Davis, who did stand out. He bore a passing resemblance to Mr. Spock without the pointy ears, except his skin had the yellow cast of a terminal cancer patient. She wished she could hear what they were saying.

She'd asked Camille about Davis, Matthew's fraternity brother, after his name popped up on the cover of the Benton Motors' brief. She'd learned that Davis had gone through several wives, each progressively younger. None would tolerate his serial adultery once her title changed from mistress to wife. Apart from that, Camille had little to tell her about him.

Sam frowned, her mind drifting to her aunt. She'd been more agitated lately, but had also seemed more alive, so maybe it was a change for the better. Suddenly, after little initial enthusiasm, she'd shown a spark of interest in learning to use the computer to help her speak.

Across the table, Pushy was flirting with Billy with the probable aim of making Rafter jealous. Sam took pleasure in observing that Pushy was failing miserably. Rafter didn't give her a glance.

"Heads up," Kat murmured, rolling her eyes toward a blond duo, Brian and his friend Helen, who unfortunately appeared to be making their way over through the crush.

"I thought he might be here." Sam grimaced. She didn't want to deal with them.

"They must have been seated in back with the commoners," Kat said with a smirk.

"I think it's time I circulated," Sam said, standing. "Want to come?"

Kat waved her off. "You're on your own. My feet are killing me. Besides, there's plenty of action right here."

Sam wandered in the direction of the powder room, thinking she could dawdle there awhile. She hoped Rafter wouldn't want to stay much longer. On the way, she was hailed by Judge Hall, coming in the opposite direction, and happily chatted with him for a time. A little farther along, she met Sophie Somerset, who introduced her to the associate dean of the law school and that led to an intriguing invitation to send over her résumé. By the time she left the powder room, no one remained at the table.

She spotted Rafter ahead of her, immersed in a laughing conversation with an attractive redhead, who was flirting with him at terminal velocity. He seemed to be enjoying himself enormously. An uncomfortable queasy feeling, so foreign to her it took a moment to identify it as jealousy, reared its ugly green head.

Oh, hell, she thought, thoroughly disgusted with herself. *Let's just complicate everything more.* She could barely tolerate the man. She certainly didn't trust him. Despite that, an awareness had been simmering and stewing between them since the beach fiasco, and she couldn't seem to stomp it out. But jealousy? How stupid! How dangerous! She wouldn't permit it.

Abruptly she changed course for the cloakroom to collect her wrap, anticipating that it would have cooled off outside. Waiting in line, she smelled Brian's cologne an instant before he looped an arm around her shoulders with nostalgic familiarity.

Blast! She really wasn't up for a trip down memory lane with Brian right now, or ever, but especially now.

"You're a sight for sore eyes, Samantha. You look terrific. You really do."

Dissipated, pale blue-gray eyes clued her in that he was half-drunk and feeling warm and fuzzy. Unfortunately, Sam saw no trace of the perfect Helen—the usually perfectly clingy Helen.

Brian beamed his crooked heartbreaker smile at her. "You and Rafter did great tonight. Why didn't you ask for my help? It's almost like you've been avoiding me," he complained.

Sam forced a polite smile. "I didn't know you still cared, Brian. I thought we'd moved on."

He gave her his familiar wounded puppy dog look. "I don't know how I could ever completely move on from you, Sam. I miss you."

"Brian."

He ignored the warning in her voice. "Maybe we could get together and talk—for old times' sake. How about it?"

"What about Helen?"

He darted a guilty look over his shoulder. "Well, the truth is, I don't think she's exactly right for me."

"Brian—" Sam shrugged off his arm and tried to put space between them, a difficult feat as they'd gotten trapped against a wall by a sudden backup of the older set waiting for their cars. "It's over for us," she said gently, although she found it hard to summon a whole lot of sympathy for him when he'd been the one to dump her.

His smile suddenly faded. "It's Rafter, isn't it?"

"No!"

"Always wondered if you had a thing for him."

"Well, I most certainly do not." At least she dearly hoped not.

Brian's gaze slid over her. "I should never have let you go."

The coat clerk finally handed over her wrap. Desperate to escape, Sam looked at him intently. "Yes, Brian, you should have. You did the right thing. The timing stank, but it was the right thing for both of us. Even I can see that now." Softening, she leaned over and gave him a peck on his cheek. "Bye."

Turning away, she made a beeline for the French doors along the rear of the room and walked outside into a fairy-tale setting. Next to the band pavilion, couples were dancing on a vast pink stone terrace lit by miniature lanterns strung like Christmas lights all around it and along winding paths through the gardens. A warm breeze off the lake made the lanterns sway and dip to the beat of vintage Glen Miller.

She finally spotted Billy milling about, and a moment later Kat limped up.

"You're on your own," Kat announced. "Billy and I are leaving as soon as he has a dance. So go dance with him, *please!*"

"Great. I'm ready to go, too. Maybe I can hitch a ride with you." Duty done, Rafter might even welcome being freed up to pursue other matters—such as a certain laughing redhead, Sam thought.

"Oh no, you don't! Haven't you ever heard? You've got to leave with the one that brung you." Kat glared a warning. "Don't you dare undo everything now."

"Oh, I suppose you're right," Sam grumbled.

When Nick wandered outside a few minutes later, he was immediately pulled aside by Robbie O'Neal. "What's gotten into you!" he hissed, a fleck of spit-

tle catching Nick on the neck. "Why are you bringing that woman here?"

Nick calmly regarded his former boss. Robbie
rarely bothered to check his temper, at least with
underlings, and right now he was hopping mad.
But Nick was no longer Robbie's subordinate and
refused to act like it. "I'm trying to help Samantha
repair her reputation so she can find a new job,"
he said matter-of-factly.

Robbie's eyes narrowed. "Is Hall cutting her loose
now that the AG has closed its investigation?"

"I hadn't heard they had. Is it official then?"

"That's the word. Privately, I always thought they
were wasting their time. Everyone knows Christiansen was as clean as new snow."

Not so privately, as Nick recalled.

"But that's neither here nor there." Impatiently,
Robbie slashed a hand through the air. "What
business is it of yours to help her find a job? The
woman betrayed us!" His angry voice rose in pitch
as he came back to his point.

"I'm beginning to wonder whether she really was
the leak."

Robbie's face twisted into a grimace of disgust.
"You know what she did. Don't get sucked in by an
appealing face. Have you forgotten that she wouldn't
even defend herself?"

Nick refused to match Robbie's volume. "Last
time I looked, we still had a presumption of inno-
cence in this country."

"Not against getting fired. Not when a government employee is suspected of undermining a government investigation." Robbie shot him a withering
look. "*Your* investigation, as I recall. All that work
scrapped because Samantha Parker couldn't keep
her skirt down."

A flare of anger clouded reason. Only by exercising rigid self-control did Nick resist the urge to wrap his hands around Robbie's short neck. "We don't know that," he said curtly.

Robbie snorted. "Oh, man, she's really gotten to you. But tell me, has she actually offered any new explanation?"

Nick shrugged. He thought about Sam's aunt, her relationship to old Harry Wentworth. For unclear reasons, he was reluctant to spill that confidence to Robbie.

Instead he asked, "Who started the rumor that she slept with a suspect?"

"I thought you." Robbie shrugged and looked away.

"No. Not that part."

"What difference does it make? It probably came from someone at the bureau. They had the surveillance tapes."

But Nick sensed it hadn't. Robbie was not that good a liar. And Nick was a pro at spotting lies. If he had to bet, right now his money would be on Robbie as the source of that rumor. But then why wouldn't he simply admit it? Most likely, Nick decided, because he wouldn't want his good political name associated with anything as base as petty revenge.

"I want you to stop this nonsense immediately," Robbie ordered. "Stay away from her. It makes us look like idiots, you being all chummy with her."

"You seem to have forgotten one important detail, Robbie. I no longer work for you." Nick guessed he'd probably regret shoving that little reality check in Robbie's face.

Robbie flushed dull red. "Then I'll presume on our long-standing friendship and give you a piece of friendly *advice*. Let someone else throw her a lifeline. It doesn't look good, for you or my office, for you to be doing it." He glanced across the patio to where Billy was dancing with Sam. "Let Billy Wentworth play hero."

As Nick watched Robbie stalk away, he felt profoundly relieved to be free of him.

His gaze shifted to Sam and Billy dancing in the glow of lights strung around the terrace. They looked good together—a matched set. She had dark hair where his was sandy, but both were tall and fine boned, and they moved with the same effortless grace.

"Hey there, soldier boy." Pushy rubbed a sympathetic hand down Nick's forearm. "I saw Robbie stomp off in high dungeon. You okay?"

"More than okay." Nick's mouth twisted into a wry smile. "Feeling very liberated at the moment."

"Must be nice." Taking his acquiescence as encouragement, she moved closer. "Robbie's nose is out of joint because you brought Samantha Parker here."

Surprised that Robbie would have been so chatty with Pushy, Nick turned his full attention on her. "He told you that?"

"Yes. And he's right—you've let yourself get sucked in by her. From what I heard, the evidence against her was irrefutable."

"Not irrefutable. Uncontradicted," he corrected. "There's a difference."

"But the file in her office—" She stopped abruptly, and her face closed up.

"How do you know about the file?" Only he, Sam, and Robbie should have been privy to that detail. Plus, following Sam's theory, whoever planted it. "Meredith." His eyes drilled into her. "Tell me."

Her gaze shifted away. "Robbie."

Slowly a suspicion formed as previously unrelated bits and pieces realigned into a new constellation.

"Pillow talk?" It fit. Meredith's adventures in bed usually furthered alliances helpful to her career.

She nodded. "It was brief. After his divorce. It shouldn't have happened at all."

"I wouldn't have taken Robbie for a talker."

"He didn't, much. He'd been drinking. He was very upset by the whole thing with Samantha. I guess he just needed someone to talk to."

Even so, Nick thought, to choose Pushy, whose discretion could be counted on only when it coincided with her own self-interest . . . Nick had difficulty wrapping his mind around it.

"Nick, he wasn't the one I wanted. Robbie and I—we were only substitutes to each other."

Nick raised a hand to stop her before she blurted out more that would only embarrass them both later. "You're a beautiful, bright woman, Meredith, but I can't give you what you want. I'm sorry."

What she wanted, Nick guessed as she walked off in a huff, was a political partner by day, stud by night. Neither role appealed to him. Some men could enjoy sleeping with a beautiful woman they didn't particularly like. Nick wasn't one.

Across the patio, Sam was watching Marty Davis contemplate the dancers with apathetic interest. A succession of questions paraded through her head. Why had Matthew called him the night of his heart attack? Was he connected to whatever Matthew had wanted to tell the AG, as Hattie believed? Did it involve the Benton Motors appeal? Was there a connection to Rachel? More and more questions with no answers.

Marty's dinner companion had left him alone on a bench in a quiet corner of the garden. The tip of his cigar glowed red in the dark. He glanced past her toward the mansion, perhaps searching for his companion, and the lanterns caught his face. He looked awful, noticeably thinner, more skeletal than at Matthew's funeral. He was said to be dying.

Tell Marty he has to. Matthew's words to Hattie. Do what? Sam wondered. And then in one of those ah-ha flashes, it all came together, a possibility that made some sense out of the baffling scraps of information she'd collected over the last weeks and months. Marty Davis was dying. Matthew would have known that. He'd offered Marty a chance to unburden his soul, clear his conscience before the end. Matthew would think that way.

Without making a conscious decision, Sam was walking toward him. Bali Ha'i called and she obeyed.

"Mr. Davis." He looked up curiously. Then, in a gesture that made her wish for a quick bath, his dissolute gaze took a leisurely stroll down the length of her gown before returning to her face. "I'm Samantha Parker. I was Matthew Christiansen's law clerk." At this a wall came up, but she forged on. "Could we meet sometime during the coming week to talk?"

His lips stretched across perfectly capped ultra-white teeth in a sadly grotesque parody of a smile. "In better days, I would have made time for you, Ms. Parker, but it wouldn't have been to talk. Under present circumstances, I really don't think we have anything of interest to meet over."

He labored to rise from the bench to his feet, taking a puff on the cigar while he paused to steady himself.

"Benton Motors." It slipped out without thought to stop him from leaving.

The brief flash of surprise on his face mirrored her own at having actually said it. Then it was gone, and he studied her with renewed interest while taking a leisurely draw on the cigar and blowing a stomach-turning cloud of smoke in her direction.

"You may be a perfectly nice if naïve young woman, so permit me to give you the same advice I gave Hattie Christiansen—leave it alone." After a last wistful ogle at her cleavage, he slowly crossed the patio and disappeared inside.

Deep in thought, Sam turned in the opposite direction and tottered along a garden path in strappy heels not designed for nature treks. She'd been right. She was almost sure of it. Matthew had wanted Marty to confess to something having to do with the Benton Motors case.

Having taken in Sam's tête-à-tête with Davis from across the terrace, Nick caught up to her before she had gone far. "What was that all about?"

She looked up, startled and then embarrassed when she saw who it was. "Well, that was about me saying something incredibly stupid," she began, misunderstanding his question. "I'm sorry—"

"Forget it." He nodded impatiently up the path toward the vacant bench where Davis had been sitting. "I meant, what were you talking about with Marty Davis?"

"Oh. Nothing. We merely exchanged unpleasantries while he peered down my cleavage." She made a face. "He's a nasty man. Sad, but still nasty."

"Maybe he's not as ill as people say."

"No. I think he is."

"Sure you weren't digging for dirt on Benton Motors?" Nick pressed, observing her closely. She looked ravishing and remote in the moonlight.

"I thought we settled all that," she evaded.

"I thought so, too. But you asked him about it, didn't you?"

"No." Her voice was firm and steady, but her eyes gave her away.

"Sam."

"Oh, all right," she said through her teeth. "If you must know, I said two words—Benton Motors."

"And he said . . . ?"

"Essentially, to mind my own business."

"That all?"

"No. He also said I was naïve!"

Nick smiled at her affront.

"Look," she went on, pointedly ignoring his amusement, "even if I did mention Benton Motors, it's not a current appeal before the court. The appeal Davis handled was decided over a year ago. So why shouldn't I ask him about it?"

She turned onto a short side path to a platform overlooking the lake, and Nick followed. What wasn't she telling him? Clearly something had made her suspicious about the case. But darned if he could see what, beyond that Christiansen hadn't consulted her on the appeal. That, standing alone, didn't seem enough to warrant the angst she'd tried to hide when she'd finally cracked the files, or warrant approaching Marty Davis about the case. What was he missing? He felt as though he were driving through thick fog. He could sense danger looming, but didn't know from which direction.

Under his quizzical look, Sam's hands fidgeted with a sparkly little evening bag.

"If there is something fishy about the case," he finally said, "and you go poking your nose into it, you could find yourself up to your beautiful neck in trouble."

"Duly noted."

Nick was about to press for more, but realized the futility and abruptly changed the subject. "I saw Billy and Kat leaving a few minutes ago."

"Yes. Are you about ready to roll?"

"Soon."

Now that they were on safer ground, he could see the tension ease from her back. She leaned against a low stone wall, staring out over the dark water of Lake Manitou. Did it remind her of last weekend? He hoped so because he couldn't get it out of his head. It was ruining his sleep and making him cranky at work. So it seemed only fair that she should suffer, too.

The breeze teased a lock of hair that had escaped the clip on the back of her head. She shivered.

"Cold?"

"A little. But I don't want to go back inside."

"I had something else in mind." He held out his arms. "Dance?"

A Nat King Cole clone was singing "Unforgettable." Their eyes met while she thought it over.

"Chicken," he mocked softly.

She gave him a you've-got-to-be-kidding look and walked into his arms.

Nick reeled her in and rested his cheek against the top of her head, breathing in the elusive spicy-floral scent she applied so sparingly it only tempted intimacy. He felt her sigh and soften in his arms as if she'd settled some inner skirmish, and she let her head relax against his shoulder. When the music ended, the last notes drifting off over inky water, neither broke the embrace.

He guided her right hand up around his neck and lifted her chin until dreamy hazel eyes met his. "What are we going to do about this?"

He shouldn't, he knew, but her breathing was coming in short little bursts and her eyes looked vulnerable as reluctance silently battled longing. He wanted to tip the scales. So he dipped his head a few inches and found himself testing her lips. With a smothered little sound of defeat, her mouth yielded to his and Rafter indulged in exactly what he'd felt was missing every night for the past week at least.

All Sam's good intentions flipped into self-destruct mode as Rafter kissed her senseless. Yet even as she dove headlong into a lusty free fall, a warning whispered that the landing would not be soft.

With considerable reluctance, she unwound her arms from Rafter's neck and squirmed away, gripping the stone ledge behind her for support because her wobbly legs were not up to the job. Rafter looked in little better shape than she was. He was gulping in deep breaths of air, his hair standing on end from her having crazily run her hands through it, and he seemed to be having difficulty regaining his bearings as he rubbed his chin in bemused fashion.

After appearing to struggle through some internal debate, he said, "It's time we talk about whatever it is that's between us."

"There's nothing between us," she denied quickly, scared even to go there.

He raised an eyebrow in pointed disbelief. "Is that so? Well, I think there's always been something there, but because of Brian and work, we pushed it aside."

Heart hammering, Sam stared at him in denial. She'd loved Brian. She never would have betrayed him that way. "That's crazy!"

"Is it?" He searched her face. "Do you believe in second chances, Sam?"

"No!" she warbled. In panic she said the first idiotic thing that came to her. "But Pushy says she does. Why don't you give her a try?"

"I don't want Pushy," he said, staring at her as if she'd gone mad.

Absurdly, amid her panic, Sam's heart was doing deranged cartwheels. Nick Rafter, a man whose good opinion had once meant the world to her, a man she'd once trusted implicitly, wanted her. Worse, she wanted him. But all the rest was past tense, she reminded herself. All except the wanting part. But wanting was one thing, acting on it, especially going to bed with him, a far more serious matter. That door had DANGER: DO NOT ENTER plastered across it in blood red.

"You agreed before that any . . ."

"Friendliness?" he offered with a stony expression.

"Yes—was a bad idea."

He nodded. "But doing nothing has proven worse."

Sam decided it was time to drag out the heavy artillery. "What is it you're looking for here, Rafter?"

As most men faced with such a question from a woman, he squirmed and hedged. "Does it matter?"

"I don't do one-night stands," she said flatly.

A ghost of a smile curved his mouth, and his black eyebrows went up. "And that's supposed to be a disincentive?"

"Your relationships last about as long as the Sunday *Times.*"

"That's because I haven't been with the right woman." Abruptly he glanced out over the water as if he found something fascinating there.

Not sure she trusted her take on what he'd just said, it took a moment to find her voice. Then she squeaked, "If you're implying that I might be the right one, that's crazy! I'm the enemy, remember?"

He scowled and snapped, "I didn't say you were the right one. How can I know that if we don't have a chance to see?"

"So I would be another of your guinea pigs." The landing was hard.

He gave her a pained look.

"We don't even trust each other," she pointed out, half-hoping he would deny it.

"No."

"I can't make love with someone I don't trust and who doesn't trust me."

He glanced over at her with a caustic smile. "That certainly didn't stop you last weekend."

Sam was unable to speak for the emotions bursting in her chest, chief among them a childish urge to cry. She turned and dashed up the path as quickly as she could hampered by her ill-suited heels. Rafter overtook her after a short distance and offered a hand under her elbow for assistance.

"Sam—"

She shook his hand off and refused to look at him, guarding her pride from further injury as she stumbled along the terrace.

Well, at least she understood now. She wasn't anything special to him, just another fling in his search for Ms. Right, if that was even his goal. How could she have been so stupid as to think even for an instant that she really meant something to him? How dangerously idiotic that her heart had lurched at the prospect.

"Hey, I'm sorry," he muttered guiltily, easily keeping pace with her. "I have a knack for saying the wrong thing to you. My ego gets in the way."

"I think we should hit the road," she said stiffly as they reached the mansion and the thinning crowd.

"I'll bring the car around." He left her in the loose mill of guests preparing to leave.

"Terrific," Sam muttered to herself, contemplating the unavoidably awkward drive ahead.

CHAPTER 13

Sam blocked him out on the ride home, stuffing CDs into the player to fill the silence. Her pride bruised, she recklessly nipped from a half-full bottle of champagne Sophie Somerset had pressed on them as they left the waning party. With her other hand, she examined a CD cover in the dim green light from the dash.

"B. B. King," Rafter said, steering into a stiff wind that heralded the approaching storm. "One of the greatest blues guitarists ever, along with Eric Clapton."

Sam didn't respond.

When eventually he pulled into her drive, Sam finally turned to him. "Thank you for what you tried to do for me tonight," she said tightly. "The networking, I mean," she clarified so as not to leave any doubt.

During the drive, she'd realized that she couldn't blame him for simply pointing out the embarrassing truth about her convenient absence of scruples on the beach. *No, be honest,* she chided herself. She couldn't blame him for only lusting after her.

After all, wasn't that exactly what she was guilty of too?

"Thanks, too, for sailing up at the perfect moment and laying waste to Pushy." She gave him a wry half-smile. "That was worth the price of admission." She waved him back when he tried to follow her out of the car. "No need for you to get out," she called over a howling wind.

Then she set off unsteadily for the Saab, where earlier she'd forgotten her briefcase. It didn't have anything important in it, but the case itself was a treasured graduation gift from Billy, and she didn't want to lose it to a car breaker.

She skirted the rattling old Italianate Victorian and crossed the deep lot to the isolated car park. Wind bent the sugar maple trees towering over the house. Storm-whipped clouds streaked past the moon, creating sinister shadows around the decrepit garage farther back. In a sudden flash of moonlight, she thought she saw a shadowy figure disappear around the side of the garage. Spooked, she fumbled in her evening bag for car keys, quickly wrenched the Saab open, grabbed the briefcase, and dashed for the house's back door.

The motion-activated light was out again. With growing unease, Sam ventured into the deep shadows around the rear stoop, eyes darting nervously in all directions. When someone skulked around the corner, she nearly fainted before she recognized Rafter and sagged in relief.

"What are you doing? You scared me!"

He held up her wrap, which she'd forgotten. It billowed in the wind. "You left this," he said, climbing the stoop to her.

Pushing hair out of her eyes, Sam darted a glance over his shoulder. "I thought I saw someone out there."

He spun around, peering into the dark. "You need a light back here."

"It's out." She pushed open the door, not needing the key because, as usual, someone had propped it open with a stick.

Raising an eyebrow at that, Rafter picked the stick up and tossed it out into the yard before stepping inside after her. She walked him down the hall past Billy's apartment to the front door, but instead of leaving, he merely checked to make sure it was locked.

"I'll walk you up." His face as usual was inscrutable, and Sam didn't bother trying to dissuade him. It didn't seem worth the effort.

Upstairs, he waited patiently while she unlocked her door.

"Sam." When she turned, he said, "I am sorry about what I said earlier—about the beach."

She hitched a shoulder indifferently. "It was the truth."

"It was still a rotten thing to say. I don't know why I did."

"We bring out the worst in each other."

He frowned, rubbing his jaw in frustration, as if he had something more he longed to say but wasn't sure it was such a good idea. "The problem isn't so much that I don't trust you," he at last blurted out. "It's that you won't let yourself trust me. You wouldn't two years ago and you won't now. Face it, you have a hard time trusting anyone. You always have."

Her anger flared and was abruptly doused because he was right. She didn't trust easily. Even less so now after her fall from grace. She lived within a small circle of select friends, and these days rarely ventured outside it.

Pensively, she looked at him, taking in the narrowed blue eyes and wind-tousled hair falling over his furrowed brow. She felt the familiar tug of attraction, and her composure slipped a notch. Their eyes locked in a charged, I-want-you exchange. Almost as if she were a helpless observer of a slow-motion train wreck, she watched the inevitable descent of his mouth as they simultaneously reached for each other.

Oh, help, she cried silently, slipping into dangerous territory as their lips fused with rough urgency and her arms wound around his strong neck. Her traitorous knees threatened to buckle under the insidious flood of need that was coming to seem disastrously familiar.

"This isn't supposed to happen," she moaned when his mouth left hers to travel up her face.

"I know. But it is." His voice was husky, sexy while he impatiently threaded one hand through her hair to turn her head for better access. "And none too soon." His other hand slid down her back to anchor her waist so she wouldn't fall as they stumbled hastily into her apartment.

He kicked the door shut behind them while fumbling with the zipper on the back of her dress. "Shit," he growled when it stuck at her hips.

Sam laughed and groaned in despair. But she was able to wiggle free, and once the gown was safely dispatched, the rest of their clothes quickly followed, making a messy trail into the bedroom.

It was only when she was lying naked on her big bed, watching Rafter shuck the last of his clothes, that Sam had a chance to truly appreciate his masculine beauty. *Oh, God,* she thought again, stomach bungy-jumping madly. *It isn't fair.*

"You're beautiful," she gasped as he came down on top of her.

He smiled briefly, his eyes drinking her up. "I'm

a hound dog next to you." He kissed his way downward, and Sam quivered helplessly under the delicious assault.

Each new touch set off small explosions in strategic locations. Basic needs begged to be satisfied. She desperately wanted him inside her while simultaneously wanting to prolong the exquisite foreplay as long as possible, having learned that the final act was often disappointingly short and, well, anticlimatic. But she worried that he was anxious to get to the main event and holding back only out of a sense of obligation to her.

"You don't have to wait for me," she gasped, riding a tsunami of lust.

"There's nothing on earth I'd rather be doing right now than waiting for you," he laughed.

Soon after, his clever hands and mouth sent her tumbling off the crest of that mighty wave. She landed in a warm lagoon of utter contentment.

He'd done it to her again, she thought, bemused. It hadn't been a fluke. Then he eased inside her, taking her to previously unscaled heights, and she couldn't comprehend it. He was a more carnal lover, more creative, more aggressive, more fun, more everything than she had imagined possible. Or perhaps, Sam thought, she was simply more of everything with him.

Afterward, they lay uncovered in a cool breeze wafting in through open French windows across the room, a limp tangle of contrasting limbs spread out over rumpled white cotton sheets. Sam languidly watched him remove a condom and drop it into the wastebasket beside the bed.

"You were prepared," she murmured drowsily against his shoulder.

"I thought—hoped—this would happen sooner or later." He pulled her close. "Glad it's sooner because you've been seriously screwing up my seven hours of sleep."

Sam stretched against him, wanting to merge into him, amazed at how perfect it felt. So right, and yet so wrong.

"You okay?" he murmured, stroking her back. His relaxed hand drifted over her hip in a warm caress that made her skin tingle and her body reawaken. She wanted him again. The notion that she would, so soon, surprised her.

"Yes. Fine." But her smile held a trace of sadness when she rose up to kiss him.

They passed the night touching and exploring. Occasionally they dozed, but not deeply, and later they would wake to make love again. Sometimes it was gentle, but more often it felt like a contest to see who could exorcise whom first.

"I want to take you away for a few days," he murmured into her hair in the wee hours of the morning.

Sam laughed. "I'm not sure I could survive several days of this."

"We could talk, too." He pushed a tangle of hair from her face and kissed her forehead.

"Shh." Sam put her hand over his mouth. "Don't. We both know this can't go any further."

He glowered. "The hell we do."

"Please, Nick. Don't ruin this." Her eyes begged him to let it go.

He sighed and rolled over on top of her. "Brian was a fool to let you go," he muttered, slipping inside her.

Shortly before dawn, Sam awoke from a light doze. She rolled onto her side and levered up on an elbow to study Rafter's sleeping face in moonlight slanting in through open curtains. The tousled dark hair that she'd always found incredibly attractive; long straight nose, a bit arrogant; generous mouth, so sexy it made her knees wilt; defined jaw line covered by dark stubble, definitely stubborn.

She filed it away because this would be a one-night stand. Her decision. She would preempt him. It could never work out for them in the long run anyway. Even if—big if—Rafter could settle in for longer than spring-break fling week, the past, the distrust, would always be between them, wedging them apart. Less painful and less humiliating to get the jump on him and make a quick cut now before she got sucked in further. Because damned if she would let Rafter breeze in and blow her world to bits again.

She gave him a last, yearning look. It wasn't fair that sleeping with the enemy should be so good!

Feeling like a coward, Sam stole from the bed, hastily pulled on sweats, and dashed off a note telling Rafter she thought it would be easiest if she left before he awoke. Her hand hovered over the paper a second. She quickly added, "Thank you for a wonderful memory." She left the note on the kitchen table, where he would be sure to see it, then slipped downstairs to Billy's spare room, where she crawled in bed and instantly fell into an exhausted sleep.

"There you are!" Kat burst into Billy's spare room shortly after noon Sunday morning. "Billy said you were here. I've been looking all over for you."

Sam peeled one eyelid far enough open to note that Kat looked unusually excited. "He at work?" she croaked, feeling as if she'd been flattened by a steamroller. Her head hurt and her throat felt as though she'd taken a walkabout in the Sahara.

Kat nodded. "Was your neighbor playing his TV too loud again?" The usual reason Sam occasionally sought refuge in Billy's spare bed.

Guiltily, she gave a noncommittal grunt in lieu of an outright lie and thanked God for Mr. Dombrowski in 2B. He'd saved her from having to account for last night. How could she explain the rash impulse that had landed her in bed with Rafter without sounding like a complete idiot? Kat might read it as evidence that Sam really did carry a torch for him. Her head began to throb in time to a thumping rock beat coming from a boom box outside.

"So what's got you all hyped up?" She squinted at Kat, who continued to hover in the doorway with barely contained excitement.

But Kat merely smiled. "Get up first. I've brought coffee." She gestured toward the living room and left.

"Well?" Sam prodded a minute later as she carefully settled onto Billy's ancient sofa next to Kat.

Kat's green eyes were shining. "Billy got a handwriting sample from Marty Davis." With a flourish, she produced a business card from the front pocket of her shirt and waved it in the air.

Sam gaped at it. "How? When?"

"I wasn't there. According to Billy, he simply admired Davis's suit and had him write down the name of his tailor." Kat shook her head in wonder as she handed it over.

Sam stared at the scrawl—*Fazio's Custom-Made Suits*—trying to recall the handwriting in the file. It might be, she thought. She would have to see them side by side to make a better guess.

Kat went on, "Billy approached him after watch-

ing me try to wangle a lawyer referral from him—
you know, thinking I could get him to write it down.
He blew me off!"

Sam smiled. "Davis is probably not much interested in the law anymore, but he's still one natty
dresser. Sometimes Billy is sheer genius."

Monday the atmosphere in Rafter's chambers
was positively chilly. Sam had screened her calls
Sunday afternoon and not responded to either of
the messages he'd left on her machine. He was likely
miffed because of that or because she'd ducked
out in the morning before he awoke. Probably both,
if she correctly read the icy glower he sent in her
direction on the couple of occasions their paths
intersected in front of Liz's desk. Being abandoned
in the sack was likely not a familiar experience for
him.

Luckily, for most of the day he was tied up with
Jake in a final push to prepare for the next round
of oral arguments coming up in a few days. Through
the wall, she could hear the low murmur of their
voices as they discussed the appeals Rafter would
hear.

At five Liz stuck her head into Sam's office.
"Well, I'm off."

"Me too." She began packing up briefs to read
at home that night, not wanting to stick around
alone with Rafter.

But on her way out, he poked his head from his
office. "A word, Sam."

His mouth was set in a cool line, but his expression was otherwise closed as she warily filed past
him and sat in the seating area he indicated near
the door. Bracing his arms on the back of the chair

opposite, he studied her for a time, a prosecutor's tactic to make a nervous suspect blab. Sam didn't bite.

At last he broke off and wandered behind her to the windows. "I never took you for a coward."

She didn't pretend not to know he was talking about her disappearing act Sunday morning. "Is it cowardly to cut losses when the percentages are against you?"

"You never used to play it safe. You risked it all for Brian."

And lost. "People change. I told you, no more happily-ever-afters." *Especially not with you.*

She felt him come up behind her chair.

"People don't change that much." He ran a light hand against her hair.

"This isn't professional," she said, knowing that sounded ridiculous after yesterday.

"Then let's go someplace where we can be un-professional." She batted his hand away, and he sighed. "Haven't we avoided each other long enough?"

He came around and sat on the edge of the sofa, leaning toward her so that their knees touched. "This is the time, Sam."

She struggled to keep her voice steady while her heart gave a confused flutter. "It seems like a bad time to me."

He shrugged. "The timing could be better. But this may be our only chance."

She looked into those sincere blue eyes and al-most drowned. For a few mad seconds, she was tempted to chuck all the logical reasons she had for sprinting to the nearest exit and enjoy however much he had to offer. But sanity prevailed and she slowly returned to earth. A protracted fling with

Rafter posed greater danger than a short one. Whether as friend, lover, or enemy, she could never be indifferent to him.

Abruptly, Sam stood. "But you see, I don't want a chance with you. I'm trying to get my life back on track, and I can't afford another mistake."

His eyes iced. "So I'm a mistake."

The biggest. She wrinkled her forehead and tried to soften it. "Nick . . . I'm sorry. We don't even—"

"Save it," he snarled. "I get the picture. I damn well don't need your pity."

Sam snapped her mouth shut and without another word escaped.

The day oral arguments began in the upstairs courtroom, Sam saw her chance to compare Davis's handwriting to that in the file. Rafter occasionally popped down to his office on breaks, and during one of these visits, Liz left for lunch while he was down the hall in the men's room. Sam was in and out in under ten seconds, barely beating Rafter's return.

Heart pounding, she guiltily settled behind her desk and flipped open the file, laying Davis's business card next to the brief.

Bingo.

Even to her amateur eyeballs, the similarity was striking, right down to the color and width of the ink. The same flourishes. A single word, "made," appeared in both. Identical.

Thank God Matthew had not agreed with Davis's assessment of the case. Had Benton Motors prevailed on appeal, the presence of the rogue notes in the file would have been damning indeed.

Sam leaned back in her chair, deep in thought. What to do now?

Kat would heartily disapprove of her sneaking

in and borrowing the file. She thought Sam should simply ask to see it again, even if that meant spilling her suspicions to Rafter. But he might want to alert the authorities, and Sam was increasingly reluctant to do that. With the investigation stalled, presumably because nothing else untoward had turned up, there seemed little reason to revive it on this. Matthew was dead, his reputation presently intact. Marty Davis was dying. Sam thought it would be best to let the matter rest. Or at least let Hattie Christiansen make the call since she and her children would be most affected.

There was also the possibility that Benton Motors was not the needle in the haystack the AG agents had been searching for. They certainly couldn't have had very specific information, judging by the wide scope of their search. But it fit. It explained Matthew's preattack phone call to Marty Davis and at least some of his drug-induced ramblings in the hospital. Not the part about Rachel, but the rest. Sam was almost certain that the Benton Motors improprieties were what Matthew had wanted to tell the AG about.

But only one person alive knew for sure: Marty Davis.

Sam reached for the state bar directory and located Davis's phone number. It was worth another try.

She managed to finagle his home phone number out of his secretary but didn't get far after that. After putting Sam on hold, the woman who answered at his home came back and said in a chillier voice, "Mr. Davis does not want to talk to you, Ms. Parker, and insists that you not call again."

"If I could just speak with him a minute, I wouldn't—" The dial tone stopped her rushed pitch.

CHAPTER 14

"These class action law suits are almost always travesties of justice," Judge Danford proclaimed, double chin wobbling. He cast a defiant glance across the conference table at Nick and Hall, who rounded out the panel, daring either to disagree.

The judges were meeting privately after oral arguments for an informal head count on each case to see where they stood. This initial tally could and often did change right up until signatures were affixed to an opinion.

"I vote to dismiss this hogwash against Benton Motors once and for all," Danford added.

Oh, hell, Nick thought, glancing at his watch. Already it was after three and no telling how much longer this would take if Danford insisted on legislating from the bench.

"And your legal position would be . . . ?" Nick sent him a deceptively casual glance, deceptive because he was on alert for any indication that Danford was speaking not from his own conviction but for Benton Motors' interests. Hall appeared to be dozing, chin resting on the knot of his tie.

"I'll have my law clerk find one," Danford muttered. "We need our industrial base. I won't sit back and let a bunch of L.A. hot-shot lawyers line their pockets while driving another of our companies into bankruptcy. Everyone loses except the lawyers. We have a responsibility to protect our industries from this sort of harassment."

Hall yawned and nodded.

"Benton Motors has a responsibility to provide a reasonably reliable product," Nick reminded them. "Keep in mind that thousands of customers are stuck with the most flawed car in recent automotive history."

"A problem the company has addressed through a number of recalls," Danford snapped.

"The model's problems are so widely known that they don't hold their value in the used car market. Recalls can't fix that."

Danford stubbornly set his chubby cheeks. "Do you know how many people in my voting district work for Benton Motors or have friends or family who do? There are similar cases pending in other states. We're the guinea pigs. If we cave here, there's a good chance the company will go belly up."

"And then they won't be around to handle any more recalls if needed," Hall weighed in, undoubtedly thinking about his own auto-industry-reliant electorate. "Frankly, I don't see how that helps anyone."

Nick didn't bother to point out that none of these concerns were relevant to their decision. As judges they were sworn to apply the law, not make it. The latter was the province of the legislature. His seasoned panel mates appeared more willing to ignore that pesky detail than to face a hostile electorate. In the end, the initial tally on the class action against Benton Motors was two to one in favor of dismissing, with Nick the dissenting vote.

Directly upon returning to his office at shortly after five, Nick looked through the stack of appeals on his credenza for the earlier Benton Motors file, deciding to go over everything again in detail. If he was going to write a dissent in such a politically explosive case, he wanted it to be perfect.

Enlisting Sam's help was tempting but out of the question. She'd made it clear how she felt about him. It was best if he kept his distance.

Nick shuffled through the stack a second time without finding the file. Frowning, he glanced absently around the room until his gaze came to rest on the common wall with Sam's office.

On the other side of the wall behind her closed door, Sam was taking another look at the suspect notes—examining language this time. No, even the wording was not in Matthew's usual precise style, she was thinking when a sharp rap broke her concentration. Before she could give permission to enter, the door jerked open.

Framed in the opening, his rage unmistakable behind his rigidly controlled features, Rafter stared at the exact spot on her desk where she'd hastily buried the file. Sam flushed, realizing she'd been caught again. Strike three.

"Is that it?" he asked softly.

Any thought of dissembling ended in an icy eye-lock. Her plan for sneaking the file back was shot now anyway. She pushed aside papers, revealing the file. Oddly, with that, his anger seemed to dissipate. He heaved a long-suffering sigh as he slumped into the chair opposite her desk.

"Smart move. Now make another. Tell me what's so all fired interesting about that file."

"Nothing." At his withering, get-real look, she elaborated. "I'm still curious about why Matthew didn't consult with me on the case. That's all. I thought maybe if I looked through it again . . ."

"Save it. I didn't believe you last week when you about went into shock looking at the file, and I don't believe you now."

When she started to utter another denial, he cut her off. "Don't insult my intelligence. Neither of us is leaving this office until I have the truth for once."

Sam's mind raced, considering various options, but she could see no way out. The jig was up. For a long moment, she stared at the wall behind his head. "Okay, I did find something." She met his hard gaze. "If I'd thought you wouldn't be on the phone to the AG in a flash, I'd have told you then. Please hear me out before you take that step."

"No conditions."

She shrugged, extracted the brief, and handed it across the desk to him. "Matthew didn't write these notes. I recognized right away that the handwriting wasn't his."

Rafter examined it. "Could have been one of the other judges."

"Unfortunately not. I found handwriting of theirs to compare. Neither is even close."

"Their law clerks?"

"I hadn't thought of that," she admitted. "But I doubt it because I found a match." She handed over Davis's business card and told him everything, even about her unsuccessful phone call to Davis.

Her tale didn't appear to mollify him—in fact, he looked thunderous again when she related Davis's warning at Madison University to leave Benton Motors alone.

At length, he held up the card. "How exactly did you get this?"

She explained Billy's maneuver at the ball, which in turn sparked uncomfortable memories of what happened later that night. Quickly, she made her pitch for not turning the matter over to the authorities.

To her surprise, after a moment's thought, he agreed. "For now, at least. If failing to report Davis is the worst thing Christiansen ever did in all his years on the bench, I guess maybe he deserves his halo. Anyway, it's obvious he wasn't influenced by this." He dropped the brief on her desk and rose to leave. "If Davis weren't already dying, we wouldn't be having this conversation. But I make no promises about the future. The situation may change."

"Wait. Do you know if Davis was the lawyer the informant identified?"

"No, I don't. But I'll make a discreet inquiry or two." He leveled a warning glare at her. "In the meantime, stay away from him. He's bad news. You're also skating pretty close to a reprimand from the attorney disciplinary committee by contacting him about a case in the first place."

"Thanks, Rafter," Sam ventured. "I owe you."

"Damn straight you do." He started to leave, then stopped.

"Sam . . ." She looked up, wondering if this was where he would exact the revenge in flesh threatened the last time he discovered her trespassing in his office. But all he said was, "You should have trusted me." Then he closed her door, leaving her alone to stew in an uneasy mix of guilt, relief, and disappointment.

To make up for her lack of progress on her own work during the afternoon, Sam stayed late to finish it. By the time she dropped another proposed opinion from the backlog on Liz's desk for circulation, it was near eight and the late summer sun hung low on the horizon. Through his open door, she could see Rafter bent over his desk still hard at work preparing for the next day's oral arguments. Not having the nerve to call out even a casual "good night" after her latest transgression, she slunk out of the office suite without a word.

In the elevator on the ride down, she reflected that he'd been remarkably decent about it. She was lucky he hadn't sicced the AG agents on her. Even more surprising, never would she have predicted that he would agree to hold off contacting the authorities about Davis's illicit contact in the case.

Preoccupied, Sam paid scant attention to her surroundings as she trudged across the vast, empty parking lot to the Saab. The lot consisted of no-frills wall-to-wall concrete enclosed by tall office buildings on three sides. When she heard footsteps behind her, she automatically quickened her pace and simultaneously dug into her handbag for her keys, on alert because the Saab sat alone in the middle of this remote stretch of concrete.

The steps behind accelerated as she neared the car. Sam started to turn around, but she was seized from behind and slammed against the side of the Saab. Her right arm was twisted painfully up against her back and pinned there by a solid wall of flesh wedging her hard against the car.

Before she could scream, a hand clamped over her mouth.

"I've been watching you, Samantha," a man's voice hissed in her ear.

She felt more fear, if that were possible, at his use of her name. Any hope that this was a simple purse snatching gasped and died.

With his right hand, he flashed a wicked-looking knife in front of her eyes, then laid the cool metal blade against her throat.

"I know where you live, where you work, who your friends are, even your aunt. I know every move you make."

The impression that this was no common street thug filtered in through her terror. His diction was that of an educated man, even though he was trying to disguise his voice, and he smelled faintly of good cologne.

"There's no place you can run to that I won't find you eventually, so don't even try. In the meantime, I'd always have Camille to punish in your stead. So listen up." He paused for emphasis, then continued in a coldly articulated rasp. "Stay out of things that don't concern you and you need never hear from me again. Make no more calls. Ask no more questions. Do you understand what I'm talking about?"

Benton Motors. Sam jerked her head in a semblance of a nod and felt the blade prick her skin.

"Good." He removed the blade from her neck and pushed her nose into the roof of the Saab. "Now keep your face against the car and count to twenty. Slowly. You should know that I can drop you with one shot from the other side of this parking lot." For emphasis, he pressed what felt like the cold metal barrel of a gun against her temple.

"Oh, and Samantha, this little chat is our secret.

If you tell anyone or if you fail to follow any of my instructions, there's a bullet in here with your name on it and another for your aunt."

As suddenly as he'd seized her, he let her go. Sam sagged against the Saab, her legs shaking too badly to properly support her weight.

On the count of twenty, she fumbled with the lock, jerked open the door, and collapsed inside. Trembling and hyperventilating, she hugged the steering wheel. Her mind reeled. She wanted to reject what had happened as too shocking to be real. She didn't even have a face to go with the hissing voice. But it had been real. She touched the nicked skin on her neck.

What a naïve fool she'd been! People had warned her to be careful—Kat, Rafter, Sophie Somerset, even Camille. She'd thought she had a new angle on Marty Davis. But her gamble with him had backfired. He was dying, but that evidently had not made him eager to confess his sins. He'd just given notice of that. Or someone close to him had. Either way, she'd carelessly put herself and Camille in danger.

A horn tapped nearby, and Sam's head jerked up on a fresh wave of adrenaline.

Rafter.

He'd pulled up so that his driver's side window was even with hers. She cranked the window down to tell him she was fine, but some residual fear must have shown on her face because he was out of his car and at her side faster than a speeding bullet, albeit a little late to save the day.

"What is it?" He hunkered down next to her open window, his concerned gaze traveling over her. "You look ill."

Sam smiled wanly at his unflattering assessment. "No, I'm fine."

"You're trembling."

"I'm a little light-headed. Low blood sugar."

He looked dubious.

"I missed lunch," she added.

"Let me give you a ride home."

"All right," she agreed readily, surprising him.

As if she were an invalid, he locked up the Saab and assisted her into his passenger seat. They drove in silence. Feeling safe for the moment, Sam closed her eyes and leaned her head against the soft leather headrest. But then she wondered if they were being followed, and looked over her shoulder to scan the cars behind them. In the fading light, all the cars around them suddenly looked suspicious, with a thug behind every wheel.

"Looking for something in particular?"

"No." Sam turned around and kept her eyes forward.

She knew him well enough to understand that this was not an offhand question. He wasn't satisfied with her explanation in the parking lot. She could see it in the blue eyes raking over her at regular intervals.

Well, he could look all he wanted. Fat chance she would satisfy his curiosity.

This little chat is our secret, the man had hissed in her ear. She was good at keeping secrets, and this one she would keep under lock and key, hers alone. Because if she didn't . . . Sam waited for the surge of terror to pass. If she didn't, he or they or whoever would carry out those ugly threats. Of that she was reasonably sure. And there wasn't a damn thing she could do to stop it without running the risk of precipitating the very mayhem threatened.

Rafter pulled up to a convenience store. "Be

right back." He came out a minute later with a couple of juice bottles and crackers. "You look ready to faint." He popped off the top of an orange juice and handed it over.

"Thanks." Truly light-headed, Sam took a slow sip.

"What's this?"

She startled when he touched the left side of her neck.

He frowned. "You're cut. What happened?"

Sam snapped the visor mirror open and stared at a short beaded line of blood on her neck slightly left of center where the knife had nicked the skin.

"I'm not sure." The blade must have been as sharp as a razor, she thought, feeling ill. "I think it may be a paper cut." She took a tissue from her handbag and dabbed at it, but the blood was mostly dried.

Openly skeptical, Rafter was now conducting a more blatant survey of her, noting a run in her stocking, a dirty smudge on the front of her white blouse, as his eagle eyes worked their way north. He seized her right hand and pushed the sleeve back from her wrist exposing reddened skin where the monster had first grabbed her.

"What the hell happened, Sam? What's going on?"

"Nothing," she lied, then rolled her eyes away from his. "Look, this is a little embarrassing. I tripped in the parking lot and sprawled against my car. That's all. No foul play."

She doubted he bought her story, but he didn't say more until they were under way. "You scare me." His voice was tight. He concentrated on the road rather than looking at her. "Sometimes you have more nerve than sense. I know you don't trust me, but for God's sake, if you've gotten mixed up in something, don't try to handle it on your own. Get help."

Sam gave Nick's reassuringly solid profile a side-long look and fervently wished she could. But she was in this one alone. For once, not by choice.

A limousine waited at the curb in front of Sam's building when they pulled up. Not one of the ubiquitous white stretch models favored by rental agencies. No, this smaller black cousin was all about understated class. A Benton Classic.

Rafter glanced at her. "Hot date?"

"I don't know who . . ." Sam started to say, then Philip Wentworth's longtime chauffeur got out. After a discreet glance in her direction, he tact-fully averted his gaze and waited at the street-side rear passenger door.

When Rafter realized that the limo actually was waiting for her, he cut short her thank-yous. "Are you in trouble, Sam? I'm not going to let you waltz over and get in that hearse if—"

"No. This is fine," she said firmly, feeling a little lurch near her heart at his concern. He was worried about her. Not just angry and frustrated. He cared.

"Lighten up, Rafter," she said with a half-smile. "It's perfectly safe. I promise."

"Who's in there?"

Sam shook her head, declining to say, but reached over and squeezed his hand before slipping out.

As she approached the limo, Nick watched her spine lengthen and her normally graceful walk stiffen. She may believe no danger waited there, but she didn't appear eager to talk to whoever lurked inside. Or perhaps no one was inside, and the driver would take her somewhere else.

While he waited for the right moment, Nick jotted down the license plate number. His timing would have to be perfect. As Sam approached and the chauffeur reached for the door, Nick stepped on the gas. The man inside leaned forward to greet her as Nick sailed past. He caught a glimpse of the startled face of Philip Wentworth caught in the glow of the interior light.

Sam watched Nick's BMW speed off down the street. What was he thinking? That she'd planned a hot evening rendezvous with the senator?

Glumly, she turned her attention to the matter at hand, wondering what could possibly have prompted Philip's unusual visit. The timing stank.

She settled opposite him, facing the rear. He signaled for his aide to proceed, and they set off down the street, gliding like a yacht over calm seas in all the quiet, cushioning luxury money could buy.

"Where are we going?" Sam asked.

"Just around the neighborhood." He looked her over, not with any real interest, but because he liked to dictate the pace of a meeting and had evidently decided to keep her waiting and off balance awhile. Stratagem and manipulation—Philip's *modus operandi*.

Sam steadily eyed him back, cataloging the familiar leonine face, still attractive in the dim interior despite the march of time.

"That was Nick Rafter, wasn't it?" Philip asked idly, taking his gaze off her to pour a drink from the well-stocked minibar.

"Yes. How did you know?"

With a glance, he offered her a drink. She shook her head. "From Christiansen's funeral," he reminded her.

Of course. Philip would have been sure to find out the identity of their eavesdropper. She glanced around the plush gray interior of the Benton Classic, wondering if this was a taxpayer-financed perk of office and trying not to fidget while she waited for Philip to get to the reason for this visit. He wasn't here for small talk.

At last he settled back against fine leather upholstery and proceeded to dumbfound her. "I've been wondering how your job search is going."

"Fine." This was what he wanted to see her about? Her job search?

"You have something lined up then?" he pressed.

"No, but my prospects look brighter than they did a few weeks ago."

"Ah, yes." He nodded. "The Madison bash. I heard." He looked bored. "Isn't it time you finally got out of here? You should be at the top of your game. Even if you can find a job remotely suited to your abilities, this place is just going to hold you back."

Particularly coming on the heels of their bitter argument at Matthew's funeral, Sam didn't know what to make of this unprecedented interest in her life. What was he up to?

"There's Camille," she reminded him flatly.

"So move her to a new place near you. Easier now than it was when she lived in her own home. You belong in New York or Washington. I have contacts in both places."

Sam studied him warily. "Why this sudden interest in my career?"

He hitched a shoulder. "I promised Dad I'd help if you needed it." From a briefcase, he extracted a manila folder. "I've listed a half-dozen possibilities. Some private sector, some public. Look them over at your leisure. With my backing—and your résumé, of course—I think you'd pretty much have a lock on anything there. Let me know."

They had circled back in front of her building. The land yacht floated up to the curb and drifted to a stop. Confused and guarded, Sam took the folder and tucked it into her own briefcase. A lifetime of being mostly ignored and occasionally kicked in the teeth by Philip made her suspicious. Yet from a deeper place came a crazy, tender hope that he might be trying to bridge the chasm between them.

"Thank you."

Sam waited. There had to be more than a newly discovered concern for her, much as she might wish otherwise.

Philip polished off the last of his drink. "I got a call about you from Marty Davis this afternoon."

"Ah." It all made sense now. "So your frat brother sent you over to warn me off, too." Sam made a poor stab at a smile. She felt foolish, pathetic, gullible, like Charlie Brown trying to kick that damn football over and over again, never learning not to trust Lucy. Would *she* never learn not to expect anything different from Philip?

"Too?" His eyes had narrowed.

"I'm surprised Davis made the link to you."

"He saw you chumming with Billy at the Madison do, then remembered the Camille connection." Impatient, he waved aside that distracting bit of flotsam. "What do you mean, Davis sent me *too?*"

"I got his first message a little while ago when I left work—not nearly so pleasantly delivered," she added sarcastically. "You can assure him that I received it loud and clear. So you see, your visit was unnecessary though unique in Wentworth family annals."

She noticed that Philip was frowning, and not his usual bored or irritated frown. A worried expression creased his face.

"Who was this earlier messenger?"

"How should I know? I wasn't given a chance to get a look at him." Hurt, disgusted with him, with herself, Sam had grabbed for the door handle to leave when an ugly new suspicion took shape and stopped her hand. "These jobs—you're trying to get rid of me. I'm an inconvenience to you and a danger to your pal, so send me off to D.C. or New York. That's it, isn't it?"

During the short silence that followed, she could read the truth of it in the quick shift of his gaze. He usually was smoother.

"Everything I said is true, Samantha. You're wasting your talents here. I'm also worried. This Benton Motors case is a battleground and you're out there in the middle of it picking daisies. I had no idea how dangerous it's gotten until now."

"Me neither, but—"

"Listen," he snapped, "if you don't get the fuck out of the crossfire, you're going to be mowed down. Stay here—I don't care. Devote your life to taking care of Camille if you want. It's your life to waste. But don't be an idiot. Get off the damn battlefield!"

CHAPTER 15

A quiet week passed, then another as summer began to slide into early fall. Sometimes, walking along the street or dashing to and from her car, Sam would feel a tingle on the back of her neck as if some dark presence watched. But when she turned to look, she could never find anyone or anything out of the ordinary. Kat sensed that something was amiss. "Everything okay between you and Nick?" she'd asked casually. But Sam was careful not to let anything slip.

To minimize as much as possible the potential danger to Kat and Billy created simply by their proximity to her, Sam made herself scarce, pretending to bury herself in work under the guise of meeting a looming two-month deadline for wrapping up the last of Matthew's appeals. Even Billy marked her absence but was too busy organizing the bookstore's fifth anniversary blowout bash to nag her much about it.

During the second week, Agent Foley stopped by the office. "Get out here, Sam," Liz yelled from her desk through Sam's closed door. Liz had taken to hollering out phone calls and visitors because the interoffice telephone communication was on the fritz again. Such was the snail's pace in state bureaucracy that broken equipment took ages to fix, a fact of life Liz was an old hand at working around.

Sam came out to find Josh Foley exchanging beaming smiles with an ecstatic Liz, and Rafter looking on benevolently. "The AG's office has officially closed Matthew's investigation," Liz chortled and danced around the room.

The cloud was lifted. Sam smiled but privately greeted the news with less enthusiasm. She now knew that Marty Davis was utterly corrupt, and wished he and any cronies in crime could be stopped. A wish, she guessed, that Matthew had shared and which had likely prompted him to make that fateful call to the authorities in the first place.

"Matthew is finally vindicated!" Liz cried, collapsing into her chair.

While Sam popped back into her office to grab her coffee mug, Foley hovered shyly in her doorway. She thought he might be working up to asking her out for a drink or dinner, but then Rafter began shooting him chilly looks. A minute later, Foley shrugged and left. As soon as the door closed behind him, Rafter disappeared into his office. Sam faced Liz's meaningful look with a baffled one of her own.

The next day, Sam met with Chief Judge Hall in his huge seventh-floor office. She gratefully accepted his offer to act as a reference and to make a few calls on her behalf to see what was currently available in the area. Whey they'd finished, they reminisced awhile about Matthew.

"I miss him," Hall said with a sad sigh. "Did you

know we'd been friends since law school? Makes me feel old."

No, Sam hadn't known. But in hindsight she recognized the kind of close bond between them that, in her admittedly limited experience, men tended to form mostly in youth, before they learned to hold their cards closer to their vests.

Had he been part of Matthew's law school frat pack with Marty and Philip and the others? She wondered but didn't ask.

In the meantime, Rafter had backed off again. He seemed more distanced and detached than ever before. Fortunately, his commitment to restoring her good reputation remained intact. Twice, he escorted her to events he deemed helpful to that end: once to a fun charity gala and another time to a dull-as-dust business awards banquet. On both occasions he assumed a Teflon façade of friendly indifference that reminded her of their Brian-era days.

Sam greeted this latest step in their inevitably complicated dance with equal parts relief and disappointment. Just when she was most tempted to take shelter in his solid security, just when she was willing to consider putting aside old-fashioned notions that sex and commitment and trust should be a package deal, he'd maddeningly withdrawn from the dance altogether.

His abrupt about-face confused her. How did one simply shut down one's feelings like that? The obvious answer upset her more than she thought it should—easy, if the feelings to begin with were only a lot of snap, crackle, and pop in a shallow bowl of milk.

Perversely, with the constant need to guard body and soul against him gone, she found herself increasingly drifting off into fantasies where, magically, their painful history of betrayal never existed and he fell madly in love with her. Not just for the length of a disposable fling, but something lasting, permanent. In her dreams, the sun always beamed brightly. The past and Benton Motors were both gone. She saw them laughing together, and sailing and swimming and making love without restraint.

It was one of those guilty, shameful pleasures she couldn't seem to control. She was annoyed with herself and irritable, and every time she ran into her blue-eyed costar in the flesh, she felt her face heat. She was, she concluded, suffering from post-Rafter letdown, and she tortured herself by imagining that she was just one of legions of Rafter's exes who had suffered similarly.

On a Friday afternoon, Sam shut down her computer and CD player and began to clear her desk for Monday. Liz had raced off for the weekend minutes earlier. In the now quiet building, Sam became aware that Rafter had someone with him next door. As the conversation rose up the decibel scale and then down again, she recognized the unlikely visitor as none other than that sanctimonious do-gooder and frequent hot head, her ex-boss, Robbie O'Neal. Until her downfall, she'd admired him enormously, but preferred to do it from afar. Now, she lingered in her office so as to avoid a chance run-in in the reception area.

From what she could hear, she gathered he'd come for Rafter's take on a matter dating from his tenure as first assistant. She thought it odd that O'Neal hadn't simply called or sent over a lackey. After a while, realizing that they could go on for some time, Sam started to leave, but her ears perked up when she heard a reference to Benton Motors.

Sam edged closer to her open door and listened intently. She could make out only parts of Rafter's more muted speech, but he appeared to be asking for O'Neal's advice on the current Benton Motors appeal.

"Danford and Hall are voting to dismiss the suit," Rafter was saying.

How very interesting, Sam thought. And of course, knowing what he did about the likely attempt at tampering with the first appeal, Rafter would be on alert.

She missed the next part of what Rafter said, then heard, ". . . not sure what to make of it."

At that, O'Neal weighed in. "These class action lawyers run around the country looking for ways to bring these nuisance suits. They're modern-day carpetbaggers."

"Despite that, in my opinion the class has a legitimate cause of action," Rafter persisted. "And my esteemed colleagues, for whatever reason, are happy to ignore the law."

"You can't accuse them of impropriety just because they're wrong. Hell, Nick, that would be political suicide." O'Neal's voice rose. "For you! Let the supreme court reverse if it wants."

Except that this might be the plaintiff-class's only chance for review. Sam filled in that hard reality. There was no automatic right to an appeal to the state supreme court; it heard only a fraction of the cases in which appeals were sought. Sam wondered if O'Neal would give different advice if he knew of the damning notes in the earlier file.

O'Neal's voice calmed, and shortly she heard them move past Liz's desk to the office suite door.

"You can come out now," Rafter called a minute later before nudging her door farther open.

Rising from the spare chair squeezed between her desk and the door, Sam pulled a face. "He's gone?"

Rafter stood in the open doorway, arms crossed, regarding her with mild amusement. "He's not so bad, Sam—maybe a little overzealous sometimes."

"Yeah, a real Boy Scout as long as you don't cross him."

His grin widened. "How much of that did you overhear?"

"Enough to know you were discussing Benton Motors with him. Are you sure that's wise? It's a pending case."

"Robbie is the chief federal law enforcement officer in these parts. Who better than him? Corruption of public officials falls squarely within his jurisdiction."

Sam felt the blood drain from her face. "Do you really think that's going on here in the current appeal? I can't imagine Hall being involved in something like that."

His expression turned grimly pensive. "I don't know. But if I do get a clearer sense that there's more going on here than just a couple of stubborn judges, I'll have to reveal the existence of those notes in Matthew's file. It would be evidence."

Sam nodded. She understood he would feel he had no choice, but dreaded the possibility. The very idea of provoking the wrath of Marty Davis and company a second time frightened her profoundly. How did one fight a well-financed enemy who didn't play by the rules? How to keep friends and relatives safe from shadowy Ninja enforcers?

In Rafter's tidy world, the system could be trusted

to keep innocents safe. Sam had no similar faith. Too often in her life, she'd been on the wrong side of the system. Marty Davis and Randall Benton were well-connected frat brothers of a governor and a U.S. senator. The tentacles of Madison alums, only half jokingly called the Madison Mafia, slithered through all parts of state government. Whom would they protect, their own or outsiders?

Sam steeled herself against the flood of panicky questions. "Be very careful if you do take any action, Nick. And please, promise you'll give me some warning before you do." She sent him a worried look, longing to give him a more concrete warning, but not daring to risk it.

Perhaps because of her rare use of his given name or perhaps because of the odd role reversal—he was usually the one doing the warning—he regarded her thoughtfully. "I will," he said at last. "But I expect something from you in return."

Sam stilled. To her shame and annoyance, her skin began to tingle and heat in anticipation. "I . . . ah . . . thought we'd settled all that."

"Not that." His faintly amused gaze flicked over her, and her face reddened at her mistake. "Bigger."

"What then?"

"You have to level with me at that point. Don't let me walk into an ambush, Sam."

Their eyes locked. "I won't," she promised and meant it. But she hoped to God it wouldn't come to that.

That night she dreamed that Rafter, clad in his black judge's robe, was licking champagne from the dip in her belly while she sunbathed naked on the deck of a bobbing sailboat. But when he threw off the robe, he'd morphed into Marty Davis, skeletal dark eyes feasting on her. She screamed.

Then Philip was there, tossing her a bathrobe and snapping, "For God's sake, Samantha, cover up! You're just like your mother."

The following afternoon on her way out of the Stanley Care Center after visiting Camille, Sam stopped off to see the weekend nursing supervisor.

"Oh, yes, Camille has been much more animated lately," the hearty, blond Amazon reported cheerfully. She maintained a remarkably upbeat mien considering the discouraging state of most of her patients. "Much more outwardly focused. Writing letters—"

"Camille is writing?" Sam interrupted in confusion, wondering for a minute if they were talking about the same patient.

"No, no, she has one of the aides write for her, you know."

"Who is she writing to?" Sam was baffled by this new development.

"Oh, goodness, I don't know. Perhaps to her new visitors."

Another shocker. Other than Sam, Camille had no regular visitors, only a few old friends who stopped by less and less as the months passed and communication became more difficult. "What visitors?"

"Hmm." She frowned in thought. "Well now, I saw a red-haired lady."

But she didn't know more. Sam pressed her, wondering aloud if they didn't keep records of visitors and who else might know more, until finally the nurse's patience wore thin.

"You'll have to ask your aunt. Our patients are not children or inmates, you know. We try to give them as much privacy as possible. They have so little of it as it is. We don't want to strip them of their dignity."

Properly chastened, Sam gave up and left. But on the ride home, she pondered what Camille was up to and why she had withheld the rare news of visitors from Sam. She supposed there could be any number of possibilities. Two concerned her the most. The first, that Camille's mental functioning, thus far very good for a Parkinson's patient, was beginning to decline. The second, that Marty Davis and/or company had sent an emissary to scope Camille out. Neither of these possibilities, though, accounted for the letters. That left Sam both worried and wondering what was going on.

On her arrival home late in the afternoon, her concerns for Camille took a rear seat. Rafter pulled up into the side yard lot seconds behind her. From the grim set of his face as he unfolded his tall frame from his Beemer, she knew he bore bad news.

"Hattie Christiansen has been in an automobile accident. She's in poor shape."

A huge lump filled Sam's throat as she took this in. In the scheme of things, she hadn't known Hattie long, but all they'd shared since Matthew's death had drawn them close.

"How bad?" She tried unsuccessfully to keep her voice steady.

"She's unconscious. They're not sure of her prognosis."

Reading her distress, he made a move toward her, but Sam knew she would fall apart if he touched her. To prevent that, she took a step back and leaned against the Saab.

"Why don't we go inside?" he suggested, dropping his hand.

"How did it happen? Was anyone else . . . ?" She stared at the dusty parking lot beyond his feet.

"No. She was alone. Lost control on a twisting country road near her home."

"And they're sure no other car was involved?" Sam persisted, replaying Marty Davis's cold warning at the Madison gala. *I'm going to give you the same advice I gave Hattie Christiansen, leave it alone.*

Had Hattie failed to heed the warning? Sam was sick with guilt. She should have contacted Hattie after the horror in the parking lot at work. She should have warned her. Why hadn't it occurred to her that Hattie could be in danger, too?

"Sam?"

She took a breath and looked up into Rafter's sympathetic face. "Where is she?"

"At a hospital northwest of here. Evidently the same one Christiansen was in."

Sam nodded. She'd been there to see Matthew. "When did it happen?"

"Yesterday. Her daughter called for you at the office this afternoon. I told her I would relay the news."

"I wonder how she even came to think of me."

"Hattie had made a note in her appointment book to call you."

Sam made a quick calculation of when she'd last talked to Hattie—at least a week ago. What had she wanted to discuss now?

"I think her daughter is curious about the note. I gather there was more to it than merely your name and number."

Abruptly, she decided to go. She wouldn't be able to think of anything else until she knew more about Hattie's present condition. "I'll go talk to her daughter."

"I'll drive you."

"Thanks, but not necessary. It's a trek over there."

"Sam, look at you." He glanced pointedly at the shaky hand that had involuntarily risen to cover her mouth. "You're in no shape to drive, and I want to go anyway."

They passed the forty-mile drive mostly in silence. Neither had much to say as they sped past sunset-bathed fields and hills, picturesque and peaceful in contrast to the gloom prevailing inside the Beemer's cushy interior. The last color faded from the sky as Sam directed Rafter to the hospital parking lot.

Inside, as Sam had anticipated, they were not allowed into the ICU to see Hattie, but they were able to send a message in to her daughter, Sally. A few minutes later, a pinched-looking, younger version of Hattie met them in the sterile corridor outside the ICU.

Sam quickly introduced herself and Rafter.

"Yes, I remember seeing you both at my father's funeral. Mom's spoken warmly of you," she added to Sam.

"How is she?"

"Not out of danger yet," Sally said unsteadily. "Still unconscious. She has several injuries, but the big concern is her head. They're watching for signs of bleeding inside her skull. I'm talking to her, trying to get her to come around, but . . ." Her pale face began to crumple under the strain of another long bedside vigil so soon after her father's.

When Sam looped a consoling arm around her shoulders, Sally sagged against her. "Are you here alone? Have you had anything to eat?" Sam asked, guiding her to a chair in a tiny adjacent waiting room.

Yes, she answered, the nurses were bringing her food, and yes, she was alone now but her sister was flying in and would be here soon. When she'd pulled herself together, she asked Sam hesitantly, "Would you want to come in and talk to her a little? I know she had something she wanted to talk to you about. Maybe your voice would ..." Her helpless grab at anything that might reach her mother wrenched Sam's heart.

"Of course."

Sally included Rafter, and together the three tiptoed in past an alarming array of machinery. On the bed, her face as pale as the hospital white sheets covering her, Hattie was hooked up to the machinery by an equally alarming profusion of plastic tubing. The only splash of color came from Hattie's hair, shocking red against the stark white sheets.

While Rafter attempted to hover discreetly by the door, Sam took the chair next to Hattie and gently picked up her hand, just as she routinely did Camille's. Except that Camille's would often jerk and twitch like a small, trapped bird in Sam's hand. Hattie's felt cold and lifeless.

Across the room, Rafter watched Sam take Hattie's hand and lean close. Although on the surface she only pattered on about the weather and Hattie's horses and other inconsequential things, everything about her was focused on beaming life into the pale ghost on the bed beside her. As ever, her butterscotch-smooth voice wrapped around him like a siren song. Only now it was also making his chest feel heavy and overfull. Ah shit, he thought. The whole tear-jerking scene severely strained his intention to keep a safe mental distance from her. He didn't need to be opening up old wounds and certainly not sustaining new ones.

He forced himself to focus on something else and observed that she seemed completely unself-conscious about what she was doing, as if it was a familiar role. Then it clicked—her aunt, the frequent visits to see her. She probably was used to the grim reality of sickrooms, if that were possible. He shuddered and turned away from the hissing, beeping machines keeping Hattie Christiansen alive, unable to imagine ever getting used to this.

They stayed, keeping Sally company until she got word that her sister had arrived and would be there in a few minutes. But before they left, Sally dug an appointment book out of a purse.

"This note to call you was one of her last entries. I was just curious whether she did."

"No. I last talked to your mother about a week ago." Sam peered at the notation Sally pointed to.

"It says, 'Call Sam about Rachel and Rosalind,'" Sally read aloud as Sam took a simultaneous look at it and was knocked back on her heels. "Know what it means? Who these people are?"

Sam shook her head and tried not to betray her alarm. *Do not panic,* she told herself firmly. There were lots of Rosalinds out there, she assured herself, lots of them besides her mother.

"Sorry, no," she murmured. Another lie, she thought with a pang of guilt. She was becoming adept at lying. But she could hardly burden Hattie's daughter with bits of possibly dangerous information when Hattie had evidently chosen not to.

Hazarding a glance at Rafter's skeptical face, she realized that she was perhaps not as adept at lying as she needed to be. He'd caught her distressed expression.

Why had Hattie pursued the Rachel angle? Sam had been under the impression that investigators had turned up nothing more on her than Sam had learned during her trip to see Sophie Somerset at the university.

They left the hospital a few minutes later, promising Hattie's daughter to keep in touch.

On the ride home Rafter brought it up, as she'd expected he would. "You really have no idea who this Rachel and Rosalind are?"

Sam sighed. "Matthew mumbled the name 'Rachel' when he was drugged in the hospital. It was one of the last things he said. I didn't want to tell Sally that."

"A name could mean nothing."

"Hattie thought he was trying to tell her something, that the name might be the key to understanding his phone call to the AG."

"Seems like a giant leap."

Deciding it best not to let any more slip, Sam agreed. She didn't know whether Rachel tied in somehow to the Benton Motors case, but she saw no reason to gamble that it didn't either.

As for who this Rosalind was and how she fit in, Sam didn't even want to deal with that now. And she had a more pressing concern. "Anything new on the cause of the accident?" she asked, having overheard him asking Sally about it while she was sitting with Hattie.

"No—other than that tests show Hattie was perfectly sober. Sally thinks she must have swerved to avoid an animal. Unfortunately, it happened at an embankment. The police say she's lucky to have survived. She's also lucky someone spotted the wreck right away."

"And no one else was involved? No other car?"

Rafter shot her a quizzical glance. "No. Not as far as the police have told Sally."

"They need to make sure."

"You're thinking this might not be an accident, aren't you? Why?"

"Hattie talked about hiring a private investigator to take an independent look at why Matthew might have made that phone call to the authorities. I'm not sure she ever went through with it, but . . ." Sam shrugged.

"She might have found something that made someone nervous," Rafter finished with an exasperated look. "Why didn't she just work with the AG?"

"She did. But I don't know if she dropped the matter when they ended their investigation." She glanced at him, feeling as if she were walking a tightrope. She was reluctant to say anything that might ultimately lead back to Marty Davis or Benton Motors. At the same time she couldn't ignore the possibility that they might have done this to Hattie. "So I thought if you know the prosecutor or the sheriff in these parts, maybe you could hint that they need to consider the possibility that it wasn't an accident. Otherwise, they might miss something."

"I've met the prosecutor. It can't hurt to call."

"Thanks. Make sure he keeps it very quiet, on the off chance it wasn't an accident."

"I will." He raised an eyebrow. "Any other orders? Or anything else you feel like telling me?" he added casually.

She shook her head and groped for something safe to talk about, finally settling on Billy's anniversary party coming up next Friday night. Then, because she'd raised the subject in the first place, she found herself inviting him.

"You should stop by. They clear a dance floor in the café and Billy always gets great bands. It's fun," she said, trying to inject some enthusiasm into her voice when all she felt was worry.

Hattie's condition did not improve during the ensuing days. As Sam waited anxiously for better news, she continued to work her way through Matthew's backlog. She operated on automatic while stewing over the cause of the accident and alternately mulling over the meaning of Hattie's note.

When she saw Camille on Tuesday evening, Sam questioned her again about Rachel, careful at first to avoid mentioning Hattie's accident so as not to upset her. Camille said nothing, seemingly not wanting to talk about it. Sometimes, though, when she didn't respond, it was not a matter of choice, but simply short-term difficulty firing the right neurons. In case it was the latter, Sam tried again.

"Camille, this is important. When Harry Wentworth was on the Board of Governors at Madison, do you remember anything about a local girl named Rachel who disappeared from the campus? She used to hang around Philip's frat house."

At first Sam thought Camille would again not answer. Her eyes stared fixedly out the window. "Told you before," she pushed out. For all her effort, the words were still badly slurred. "Don't remember."

Sam nodded and reassured her, "Yes. Sorry. I thought you might have remembered something about it since then." She decided to wade deeper. "What about Rosalind? Did my mother used to hang around Philip's fraternity house before she went away?"

Camille's hand twitched in hers. "Don't remember. So long ago. Why . . . asking?"

Sam debated how much to reveal. She had stopped talking to Camille about Marty Davis and Benton Motors weeks ago because the subject seemed to upset her, as did this Rachel business, but everything had changed since then. Their lives could be in danger. On the off chance that Camille could shed light on Hattie's note, Sam decided she had to risk upsetting her. If her mother was somehow linked to Rachel, she needed to know.

Sam looked into Camille's alert brown eyes, the only point of expression in her slack face, and told her about Hattie's accident and her worry that it might not have been an accident at all. "She made a note in her appointment book to call me about Rachel and Rosalind."

Camille's hand jerked from Sam's. She made a guttural sound of objection.

"Do you know what that might be about?" Sam pressed, trying to read her eyes. "I heard you had a visitor." Sam took a shot in the dark. One of Camille's visitors had red hair and Hattie had red hair. "Was it Hattie Christiansen?"

"Philip," Camille rasped.

"Philip! He was your visitor?" Sam pulled back in astonishment. Philip felt no loyalty or fondness for Camille. "What did he want?"

Camille groped for Sam's hand. "Just said, hi . . . nothing important. Think he was visiting center. Philip always politicking."

Sam pressed on, but Camille held to her story with increasingly monosyllabic answers and finally no answers at all. As Sam was leaving, she roused. "Be careful. You should go New York. Let Philip help you."

Floored that he had evidently discussed such a possibility with Camille, Sam mumbled something about having to think it through, and that they would talk more later.

At home that evening, she sat down with a mounting pile of bills, the largest, and currently overdue, from the Stanley Care Center. She sighed and rubbed her eyes. Marie Wentworth's check had not stretched as far as Sam had hoped. Every month she fell a little farther behind. At this rate, unless she found a well-paying job, she'd be bankrupt in months, and Camille would be booted from the center.

Sam took a deep breath. Perhaps it was time to consider selling Camille's house, or taking a reverse mortgage on the equity.

She had two job interviews lined up for next week: one that she would leap at in a prosecutor's office. She wouldn't take any action until then. Maybe her luck was about to change. Two years ago, the same office had declined even to interview her for an opening. Rafter's strategy just might be working.

Sam sorted through the pile, paying the most urgent bills and putting aside the others before turning to new mail. An invitation to Philip's fundraiser was buried in reminder notices and junk mail. It was for next Saturday evening, the day after Billy's party. "Samantha, Come and network," Philip had scrawled inside. Sam tossed it out with the junk mail. After a moment's reconsideration, she gritted her teeth and fished it out. She couldn't afford the luxury of turning down offers of help from any source.

CHAPTER 16

Hattie began to regain consciousness on Thursday. On Friday, Sam planned to take part of the afternoon off to run up and see her before going to the bookstore to help Billy with last-minute party preparations. But shortly after she returned from lunch, Liz called out that a Marty Davis was on line one for her.

The air whooshed from her lungs like a popped balloon. At once panic-stricken and angry, Sam stared at the phone. Then, jumpy because she'd kept him waiting, she snatched it up.

"You still want to know about Benton Motors?" Davis asked without preamble.

What kind of game was this? Sam examined his question for hidden meaning and took a cautious approach. "No. I got your message loud and clear. I don't know what you've heard, but I assure you, I'm out of all that."

"What message?" Then, not waiting for her answer. "Oh yes, Philip."

"Not Philip. I was thinking of your other, more

direct threat." Anger filtered into her voice and she fought to suppress it lest she provoke him.

It took her a few seconds to identify the rasping noise coming through the receiver as laughter.

"The bully boys have been busy." His laugh ended in a wheezing cough. "I didn't have anything to do with that, but I know who did. So, you want the lowdown or not?"

Sam's thoughts raced. If not Marty Davis, then who had threatened her? Randall Benton? It was making her crazy always looking over her shoulder, living with this threat hanging over her head like a sword ready to plunge without warning.

"I can't risk talking to you, Mr. Davis."

"Sister, you can't risk *not* talking to me. There's no safety in ignorance, but there is strength in information. You come talk to me. I'll help even the playing field."

"How do I know this isn't a trap?"

"You don't. Except that I wouldn't make a mess in my own backyard. Make up your mind—I don't have all week." He rasped another bitter laugh at his joke.

Sam stifled the urge to leap at the offer and forced herself to slow down and consider the pros and cons of talking to Davis. There were obvious risks, but he did make some sense. With the right answers, she'd have a shot at beating the enemy. She might get names and faces for her Ninja bad boys. If she knew precisely who the enemy was and what he or they were hiding, she would have something to take to the authorities. Rafter would help her with that.

"I'll come," she said.

He rattled off where—his Lake Michigan beach condo—and when—immediately. Sam hung up, grabbed her handbag and briefcase, and dashed through the reception area. "I'm leaving now," she said to Liz on her way past.

"Have fun at your party," Liz returned.

"Sam, wait!" Rafter strode out of his office as Sam swung open the door to the hallway.

"Sorry, can't, I'm rushed. See you at the café later," she called back as she sped out. Chances were good he'd heard Liz yell out the name of her caller. He would demand an explanation, which she had neither the time nor inclination to give.

Outside, as she was opening the Saab's door, he caught up to her and leaned against the hood. Because she'd backed into her spot, he blocked her exit.

"That was Marty Davis on the phone," he said, wearing his inscrutable judge face.

Sam saw no point in lying. Besides she was sick to death of all the lies between them. "Yes."

"And he wants to talk to you."

He'd been on the line, she realized with a flash of indignation. "Yes. But you already knew that, didn't you?"

He didn't bother to deny it. "You can't go. It's time to take this to the authorities."

"After I talk to him. Please, I have to do this. Without Davis, there's next to nothing to take to the authorities."

"It's too risky. You don't know what you're walking into."

She smiled wryly. "That's what I do, remember? I take risks."

He scowled at her. "Dammit, Samantha! This isn't a joke."

"Don't you think I know that? I'm tired of flinching at every shadow like a scared little bunny." For a moment she got lost in his Rocky Mountain–sky blue eyes, wondering if she'd ever see them again.

Abruptly she remembered what was at stake and snapped into gear. "I have to do this. Even if you can't understand, you can get the hell out of my way and let me go." She wrenched open the door.

"I'm coming with you."

"No, you're a judge. You can't."

He planted his hands on the hood of the Saab and stared her down. "We can do this the easy way or the hard way."

He'd slipped into his arrogant, stubborn mode—impossible to reason with. Sam didn't have time to deal with it. "Get in."

He tore around to the passenger door as if not trusting that she wouldn't roar off the second he no longer blocked her car. Truth was, she was relieved to have the decision taken out of her hands. The prospect of meeting Marty Davis alone scared her silly. She couldn't have picked a better backup than Rafter.

"So he's left Lansing for the lake," he mused while Sam belted up the westbound on-ramp. "Wonder why?"

"Maybe he's hiding," Sam suggested, concentrating hard on the road as she drove faster than she was used to.

After a time, he said, "Maybe you'd better tell me why you're feeling like a scared little bunny."

"Let's hear what Davis has to say first."

He shrugged. "Now or later, as long as it's today." From the front pocket of his white shirt, he pulled a small cassette recorder Matthew had used for dictation and set it on the dash. "Thought this might come in handy."

Sam glanced from it to Rafter, vexed to realize that he'd anticipated precisely this scenario before even leaving his chambers to come after her.

* * *

Marty Davis looked in markedly worse shape than just a month earlier at the Madison bash. A long plastic tube snaked from his nose to a humming oxygen machine across the room. He didn't budge from his leather La-Z-Boy throne when his burly tough ushered Sam and Rafter in.

"Found this in her purse," Davis's man growled, holding up the tape recorder.

In a surreal scene out of *The Godfather,* she and Rafter had been patted down at the door by the blond bruiser, who by rights should have been named Vinny or Johnny. In other circumstances, Sam might have found the incident amusing.

"What do I care? Let 'em tape." Davis waved a weak hand to dismiss his man. "You can go, Jimmy. I'll be fine. My nephew," Davis explained as Jimmy trudged out with a scowl of disapproval. "He worries. Thinks I should take my secrets to the grave."

His gaze slid from Sam to Rafter. "I see you brought your own protection."

"I'm afraid I left her no choice," Rafter said coolly as he turned on the tape player.

"Sit." Davis waved them to a sofa. "She's going to need help. Sounds like she's gotten herself into a pickle."

"Mr. Davis." Sam redirected his attention.

"Marty."

"Marty, at the Madison bash you weren't the least interested in meeting with me, then or ever. Why the change of heart?"

His mouth twisted into a bitter smile. "Because I'm fucking dying and bastards I used to call friends are cheating me out of what's mine. Christ! I got kids and people like Jimmy to take care of." He visibly regained control. "We had joint accounts set up to transfer assets around. I drew my attorney fees out of them, too."

"Offshore accounts, I assume," Rafter interjected.

"Right. Tax free." Davis shot him an unrepentant glance, then stared unseeingly out the window at the million-dollar view of surf and sand. "They drained them before I could get what I was due. Bastards owe me upwards of half a million, mostly off the books. Say they'll pay up—check's in the mail. That kind of rot. The doctors give me two weeks. I know they're waiting for me to die so they can pocket it."

"Who are you talking about?" Sam asked.

"Benton . . ." He watched her face as he dropped the bomb. "And Wentworth." He smiled that ultra-white smile, ghastly against the yellow pallor of his skin, appearing to take perverse pleasure in her surprise and distress.

In spite of Rafter's presence, Sam asked, "Are you implying that Philip is also behind the threat I got? Why? What would he have to do with Benton Motors?"

"Rather a lot. But we're getting ahead of ourselves. The road ends at Benton Motors, but it began many years ago at Madison University. To fully understand the journey, we need to start at the beginning."

"Rachel Holtz," Sam whispered.

"Yes, our alliance started with Rachel's death."

On Sam's other side, Nick, who felt as if he'd started watching in the middle of the tape, stifled the urge to jump in and press for immediate answers. He could hardly believe the gift being unwrapped before his eyes. After all the time and resources he'd wasted pursuing Senator Wentworth, Davis appeared to be on the brink of handing him over for free to exact his own revenge.

But reading the dynamics of this little rat feast Davis had orchestrated, Nick sensed he would get more if he stayed in the background. For some reason that he intended to get out of Sam very soon, Davis saw her as a key player in his plan. He was telling his story to her. Nick was merely tolerated as a witness.

Davis began his story with the formation of his law fraternity. "We were just getting the frat up and running—me, Wentworth, our own Governor Graham. Only had eight guys living in the house that first year—all law students—but we were recruiting more, and by the next year, we had double that. Christiansen was a first-year recruit then."

He handed Sam a photo. Peering over her shoulder, Nick saw a dozen twenty-something men sporting Princeton haircuts and seventies preppie garb standing in front of a dilapidated fraternity house. "That's the original eight plus a few recruits."

"I have a hard time seeing Matthew as a frat boy," Sam said, passing the photo to Nick.

"There's probably a lot you don't know about Saint Matthew," Davis sneered. "For instance that he came from a nothing family. Married well, but his family were all strictly blue-collar. In law school, he was eager to develop contacts. He was ready to do almost anything for the chance to travel in the same circles as the Wentworths and the Grahams."

Davis coughed and had to pause to catch his breath before continuing. "Anyway, we'd bought this big old guest house and needed to fill it up with brothers to pay the mortgage. We had no official school status at this point. Keep in mind that it was the early seventies—" Another chest rattling cough sapped his strength. "You know," he wheezed, "drugs, free love. Wentworth knew these girls, real babes, who liked to party."

Nick caught the sly glance Davis sent Sam's way.

"There were two regulars, Rachel and Rosalind. We called them the two Rs, only reading and writing were not their forte."

It was the heightened color spreading over her face and quickened breathing that broadcast Sam's distress to Nick. But he had no more inkling now than he'd had in Hattie Christiansen's hospital room why these names prompted such a reaction.

"We'd have these private little parties with a lucky recruit or two and our leading ladies, although I do use that term loosely. These were not girls you would bring home to Mama. Highly effective recruiting tools though." His lips stretched back again in a parody of a smile. Then he sighed.

"There was an accident. All the drugs, you know. Stupid really. Bound to happen sooner or later. Rachel stopped breathing while one of the pledges was"—he darted an amused glance at Sam—"with her. She overdosed."

"Who was it?" Sam asked unsteadily.

He shrugged. "I don't know. I was downstairs. It could have been almost any of them—Matthew or Benton—he was another recruit—or Wentworth."

Not for an instant did Nick believe that Davis didn't know exactly who it was, which hinted that it was neither Benton nor Wentworth, the primary objects of his revenge. As for Christiansen, anything was possible, he supposed.

"I thought Benton was not a law student," Sam said.

"Right, he was an MBA. That was fine by us. Anyway," Davis went on, "Wentworth insisted we had to get rid of the body. Make sure no one could connect it to us or we'd all be ruined. He was right, of course. So we buried her in the woods behind the frat."

Sam's face had lost all of its earlier color. "What about the other girl?"

"Yeah, Rosalind. She was another problem." He stopped to take a sip of water. "She was with someone else in another room. Wasted as usual, so that helped. We made up a story about Rachel leaving town with a guy she'd hooked up with that night—not really a stretch if you knew her. But once Rosalind sobered up, she wasn't buying it. Wentworth and Benton took care of it. Bought her off. She left for Vegas soon after."

Davis fell silent, appearing lost in the past, and Sam was staring out the window, her face shuttered. "So you had this secret in common," Nick nudged him.

"Ironically, it made us closer than all the usual fraternity bonding rituals ever could. Our unholy alliance is the way I always think of it—a little subset within the frat comprised of those who knew."

"Who are they?" Nick voiced the question that was uppermost in his mind.

But Davis merely grimaced. "Memory's not so good these days." He shrugged and rambled on, "A couple of the guys drifted away, left the state after graduation. Christiansen wasn't comfortable with it—no surprise there. But the rest of us used our connections to help each other when and where we could. Wentworth nurtured the alliance. He probably used it the most. He was a visionary in that way. Of course he was familiar with that sort of political maneuvering from his father."

Sam finally stirred. "So the Benton Motors case . . . ?"

Davis winced as he shifted in the La-Z-Boy. He was visibly tiring. "Big case, obviously. Lot at stake for Benton Motors. Otherwise we wouldn't have taken a chance with Christiansen. If the class gets certified, Randall Benton might as well kiss his Benton Classic goodbye. The company will go belly up. You saw what happened to Dow after the class action for the silicone breast implants."

Davis glanced at Nick. " 'Course that means there's a lot at stake for Wentworth, too. Benton Motors is his biggest political contributor."

Nick shook his head. "Not of record."

Davis gave a sly smile of acknowledgment. "Right. Not of record."

Nick stilled. He was close, so close he could feel it tingling in the air. "What proof do you have that Wentworth accepted under-the-table contributions from Benton Motors?"

"I was the bagman. I set up the accounts, moved the money around as needed. I handled the dirty work for both Benton and Wentworth." His dark eyes glittered. "I have the records. Two years ago you would have given an arm for that treasure trove, wouldn't you, Rafter? Interesting that we three were also key players in that little drama. And now we meet again."

It didn't surprise Nick in the slightest that Davis knew of his involvement in the Wentworth probe. To survive thirty years operating on the wrong side of the law required a keen mind, nerves of steel, and, Nick suspected, help on the inside.

Sam stymied Nick's pursuit of Wentworth by steering the subject back to Benton Motors. "Matthew refused to toss the case out. He disregarded the opinion you so helpfully wrote for him."

"The sanctimonious little shit threatened to rat us out. Didn't have the guts when it came right down to it because he knew we could reveal his role in the Rachel cover-up and he'd be ruined, too."

Davis closed his eyes, sucking oxygen through the

tube. After a minute, he went on. "When Matthew heard about my cancer, he tried to talk me into going public with him. The Attorney General inquiry really got to him, even after they left him alone. He turned into a friggin' Pollyanna as he got older."

"Who was the original informant?" Sam asked.

"I suspect a former associate in my law firm. Shot my mouth off to him when I was tight. He had a grudge after he didn't make partner. Damn twit—" Davis coughed again, this time harder and longer than before. He doubled over in pain.

Sam jumped up and tried to help him, but Davis waved her off. "I'll get someone," she said and dashed off.

She was back shortly with a stocky, middle-aged matron who bustled over and administered a dropper full of liquid into Marty's mouth. "Morphine," she explained as she placed a pillow behind his head. "He'll want to rest."

"Another minute," Nick insisted, pulling a chair closer so Davis wouldn't have to talk as loud.

The nurse looked to Marty for direction, and he nodded. "Another minute," he rasped, his head lolling weakly against the pillow.

"The FBI will want to talk to you," Nick said urgently, knowing the time for talk before the morphine kicked in was fast running out. "They'll need details."

"Not planning to spend my last days in their inept hands."

"Then U.S. Attorney Robbie O'Neal. No one has ever called him inept."

"Robbie's a smart one," Davis agreed with a smirk. "But I'll have to decline."

"You may not have a choice," Rafter threatened softly.

"I don't have to talk."

"But I have the tape."

"And I have the records. Hidden, of course. And you only have the tape if I let you walk out with it."

Nick considered. "What are your terms?"

"Yes. Let's discuss my terms. I'll make arrangements to have my records delivered to you upon my death. My gift to you. For now, you back off." He coughed again, wincing.

Nick sorted through various courses of action and their probable outcomes. "Are you safe here?"

"Should be. No one knows about this place except Jimmy and the nurse." He hitched a bony shoulder, his speech beginning to slur from the drug.

Sam stood, and took a step closer, staring at Davis with an intense expression. "Why did you choose me? Why didn't you tell all this to the authorities."

"Because I can't stand those sanctimonious shits. And because this way will be so much sweeter, like one of those Greek tragedies." Davis managed a wink and a smirk at Sam.

Nick caught the look of horror that crossed her face before she closed up. "What's that supposed to mean?" he snapped at Davis.

"Have to ask her." With another sly smile, Davis closed his eyes, ending the interview.

Over coffee at a diner, Sam dully listened to Rafter begin to lay out his plan. He didn't trust Davis to send his records. He wasn't even convinced they existed. He certainly wasn't about to leave Davis in control. "What if his real purpose for meeting with you was to get what he wants out of Benton and Wentworth? Simple leverage?"

"We have the tape," Sam pointed out. She rubbed her forehead, her mood heavy as she contemplated the misery that lay ahead. She wondered if Camille had known all along about Rachel's death and Rosalind's connection to it. It would account for her distress when Sam brought it up.

"Without hard evidence to back it up, especially once Davis is dead, the tape won't be enough. He gave up few names and fewer specifics. We have to bring in the AG and Robbie to work on him."

If he expected her to object, he was wrong. "Agreed. When?"

"First thing tomorrow. I'll call both."

Sam nodded. The sooner the better. If Benton found out she'd talked to Davis, she wouldn't get another warning. Out of habit, she scanned her surroundings, assessing the other customers for threat potential. She was nearly certain they hadn't been followed. For days now, she hadn't sensed anyone watching.

She feared Benton, not Philip. Like Rafter, she suspected that Davis had only a passing acquaintance with the truth. He'd told them what he wanted them to believe in order to manipulate them. No matter that Davis had implied otherwise, Sam couldn't believe Philip had anything to do with the threat to her life. It didn't bear thinking about. Plus, when they'd talked in his limousine, Philip had seemed genuinely surprised and worried to learn she'd been threatened.

"Sam?" Rafter yanked her back to the present. "Why does Marty Davis want you involved in his revenge? What did he mean by that cryptic comment at the end?"

Sam shook her head slowly. "I'm not sure." She'd pondered the same question, and the only explanation she'd come up with seemed hideously diabolical. She gave Rafter a close version of what she guessed was Davis's reason. "I think it must be my connection to the Wentworths. He might find it amusing to have the senator brought down by a longtime family friend or retainer. He could see me as Camille's proxy." Or Rosalind's, she thought, depending on how much he really knew.

Sam stared unseeingly at the steady stream of commuter traffic whizzing by outside, trying to fathom the evil inner workings of a morally bankrupt bully and his twisted, Godfather-like notion of revenge. "He's evil, isn't he?" she mused. "Sitting there on his death throne spinning twisted plots for exacting his revenge. Pathetic in a way, too. Where are his kids? Where are the ex-wives? Even his brothers-in-crime have abandoned him in his final hour. He's all alone except for that thug nephew and a nurse."

"All alone with only revenge to keep him warm."

"I almost feel sorry for him." Almost. Her world was tumbling down around her ears, and he was enjoying launching the chaos from his deathbed.

"Then you have a bigger heart than I. He is evil and pathetic, though, I'll give you that."

"What now, Rafter? What do you think is going to happen?"

He shook his head, his face grim. "I'm not sure. This is big, though. My guess is that it will snowball. Wentworth and Benton are obviously going to have a lot of explaining to do. The authorities will want to locate this Rosalind."

He studied the five-by-seven photo of the founding fraternity members on the table between them. Sam had slipped it into her handbag before Jimmy had swooped in to kick them out. Together they'd picked out several of the law students pictured including Senator Philip Wentworth, Governor Walter

Graham, Marty Davis, and Matthew Christiansen. They had also tentatively identified a state supreme court justice and, more startling, the state attorney general. A roll call of political leaders. Without more names to match, it was difficult to guess at the identities of the others.

"We need a thirty-year age progression," Sam muttered, squinting at the photo.

"This could turn into a political scandal on a scale never seen in this state," Rafter went on. "Who among them knew about Rachel's death? Who participated in the cover-up? What favors were exchanged because of it? How extensive was this cabal Davis described?" He rubbed at his chin worriedly, and his eyes found hers. "It's time, Sam. I need to know everything you know. We had an agreement."

"Let's do it on the road," Sam said, standing. "I've got to get back for Billy."

In the car, she briefed Rafter on the few remaining odds and ends he needed to know: Hattie's theories, her meeting with Sophie Somerset at Madison Law School, and her parking lot run-in with her Ivy League assailant. She dropped him off at his Beemer in the shadow of the State Office Building, and he followed her home, insisting on checking out her apartment for stray Ninjas. Just to be on the safe side, she planned on spending the night in a vacant apartment below her own on the ground floor.

"So you still intend to go to Billy's party?" Rafter asked, lingering in the doorway on his way out. His tone implied that he didn't think that was a good idea.

"Yes." Helping Billy with his anniversary bash might be the last bit of normalcy in her life for a good long while and she didn't intend to miss it.

"Save a dance for me then." He glanced away. "I'll arrange with the county prosecutor to put a guard on Hattie. I can still arrange for FBI protection for you tonight."

He'd made the offer before, and again she turned it down. "No. We don't know all the members of Marty's cabal. I'll feel safer just keeping quiet until tomorrow."

"My other offer stands as well," he said, and Sam knew he meant he would stay with her if she wanted.

"Thanks. I'll be fine."

Rafter nodded unhappily. "It feels like we're putting a whole lot of faith in a man who has the morals of a cockroach. Davis would shop us to his former pals in a New York minute if it got him his money."

Sam shook her head. "I don't think so. This isn't entirely about money anymore for him. This is about betrayal and revenge."

CHAPTER 17

By the time Sam arrived outside Billy's Books, it was nine and the party was going full throttle. The air vibrated with thumping rock and roll escaping the building. A carload of Billy's acting friends disgorged onto the sidewalk behind Sam and swept her along inside on a tide of bonhomie hugs and kisses that made her feel like an alien in her bleak mood.

Within seconds of entering, Billy shoved a drink into her hand, planted a sloppy kiss on her cheek, and dragged her into an enthusiastic embrace. "About time you showed up, Sammy."

She collapsed against him and hung on harder and longer than usual, savoring the contact, all the while feeling like a Judas. Years of drilled-in loyalty to the Wentworths made her rebell at betraying them. Billy was the best of them, the only one who would understand and support her even though he would suffer too. It was his suffering and Camille's that she regretted the most.

Focus on one hour at a time, she told herself.

That was the way. If she thought too far ahead and saw the big picture, she would surely be lost.

Registering the difference between this and a casual hug, Billy drew her from the crush in the café into the slightly quieter bookstore. "Everything all right?" he yelled over the throbbing music, peering at her through not-quite-focused but very dear gray eyes.

The floodgates took a beating, but she managed to hold them together and forced a bright smile and nod. "I'll tell you about it in the morning. Save time for me before you go to work?"

Distracted by a gang of friends bearing down on them, he called out something she didn't catch as they both were swept out onto the dance floor. Two drinks later, the room began to buzz from more than music, but Sam felt no great relief from either her burden or the ticking clock.

Kat waded up in wrinkled work clothes, her blond mop in usual end-of-the-day disarray, having likely come directly from the legal aid office. "You look like hell," she had the cheek to say, giving Sam a quick once-over. "Well, for you anyway," she modified, "which is still better than most of us could dream of on a really good day." She raised an eyebrow at the martini in Sam's hand. "How many of those have you had?"

"Two, I think. Probably fewer than you." Sam watched the throng begin to bop to "Hotel California."

"But I have the capacity. You don't." Kat raised her voice to be heard over the increased volume. "It's in the genes."

"Should be mine too," Sam said. "Everything else seems tied to them."

"So how've you been?"

Kat's offhand tone said she'd been more hurt

by Sam's unexplained distance than Sam had realized. Sam pulled her farther into the bookstore, away from the blast of amplifiers.

"Kat, there are things I haven't been able to tell you, for your own safety. It's why I've stayed away. If I hadn't, I would surely have spilled everything." Her eyes pleaded for understanding and forgiveness. "I'm sorry."

Kat's expression instantly changed from indifference to alarm. "What is it? Are you in some kind of danger?"

Sam smiled wanly. "I'm okay and I'm not in danger. I can't tell you about it now, but all that will change tomorrow."

"I'm not going to be here tomorrow!" Kat protested. "My stepbrother is picking me up first thing in the morning to go visit my mother and stepfather for the weekend." She wrinkled her nose and Sam could see her trying to figure a way out of a visit she didn't want to make in the first place. "Maybe I can—"

"No. You should go. I'll explain everything when you get back." Privately Sam was glad she would be safely away.

When Nick arrived at ten, the place was crammed. He spotted Kat standing in the archway to the bookstore and wended his way over to her.

"Is Sam still here?" he yelled over the music.

Kat pointed to the dance floor, and he scoured the clutch of gyrating revelers until he located her by Billy.

"Looks like she's having a good time," he said.

"Or trying hard to."

Nick flicked Kat a curious glance as she pushed off for the bar. On the dance floor, Sam swapped

partners for Billy when the band switched into slow
gear, leaving behind an abandoned partner glow-
ering unhappily after them. Sam was talking a
great deal, explaining something to Billy, who was
frowning and shaking his head. She shushed him
and continued to make her case.

With the abruptness of a car crash, it hit Nick that
she might be forewarning Billy about the noose
tightening around his father's neck. And with that
suspicion came a sick feeling of déjà vu. Was this
how the senator had found out before—through
Billy? Even a son who despised his father might act
to protect him.

As if sensing Nick's scrutiny, Sam glanced up
and located him across the heaving throng. She
seemed to read his suspicion and met it with a sad,
disappointed look. Holding his gaze, she shook
her head, the movement barely perceptible. Yet the
message couldn't have been clearer if they'd exchanged words—denial and reproach. She looked
away, dismissing him, and Nick felt as though he'd
failed a test.

If not that, then what was she up to with Billy?
Because he sensed there was something else. Something she still wasn't telling him.

"I guess you must be involved in the mysterious
problem that Sam can't talk about." Kat was back
and watching him with an oddly knowing expression, having evidently caught the silent exchange.
She handed him a bottle of beer and took a swig
from her own.

Nick shrugged.

"I'll take that as a 'yes.' Don't worry, she wouldn't
tell me anything specific. So are you allies or ad-
versaries this time around?"

"Allies, I hope."

"Good. Then you should know that your partner is teetering on the edge of losing it big time. I haven't seen her like this since the last time you raised hell in her life."

When Sam lost Billy as a partner, another moved in to take his place opposite her. It was spike-haired Pogo with the wandering hands, one of Billy's rowdy theater friends. Sam stayed anyway. This wasn't about fun. She danced in a desperate attempt to slow the ticking clock and block the awfulness tomorrow would bring. But it wasn't working. When the music ended, she slipped through the kitchen and out the rear door into the cool September night.

The alley was bathed in the orange glow of a security light mounted on a pole. Sam leaned against warm brick and sipped the fresh drink she'd snagged on the way out. Sighing, she watched the liquid tranquilizer slide over the ice, knowing she shouldn't drink this much or she could end up like Rosalind. But that threat had lost some of its punch. For years, she'd tried hard to live the straight and narrow, had largely succeeded, and still she was paying for Rosalind's mistakes. Of course, *she* was Rosalind's biggest mistake of all, Sam reflected glumly. Very deliberately, she poured the rest of her drink out onto the grimy pavement.

The metallic squeak of the screen door alerted Sam to an intruder. Expecting Pogo, she was revving up to deliver the set-down he deserved for his ill-mannered hands. But it was Rafter who stepped out into the dim alley.

She was still smarting from that accusing look he'd sent her across the dance floor while she was trying to wheedle Billy out of the keys to the vacant apartment. She should be way beyond caring what

Rafter thought of her, but she wasn't. She still wanted him to think well of her.

"I came for that dance," he said, leaning companionably next to her against the brick wall.

"I don't think that's a good idea."

"Why?"

She might have said, because once she was in his arms there would be no hope for her. She would be unable to stop herself. The floodgates would burst, and she would fall apart in front of him. And that, she was desperate not to do.

Instead, pride had her opting for another truth. "Because you run hot and cold. It's confusing."

That startled him, and he stared at her, searching for something in her face. At last he summoned a rueful smile. "I assure you that I've never run cold with you."

Sam shifted against the brick, groping for another topic. "What do you think will happen tomorrow after we meet with investigators?"

"They're going to want to talk to Marty Davis." He paused and looked into the distance as if reading the future there. "They'll also want to obtain subpoenas to search Benton's home and office and probably the same for the senator. Locating Rosalind should be high on their list. I assume they'll want to put us into some level of protective custody although I doubt it would entail much of a change in our lives. How do you feel about a bodyguard?" he joked.

"Nick, I want to stay in the background on all this," she said in a last-ditch attempt to maintain life as she knew it. "You can have all the glory and publicity. Let me remain an unnamed witness."

He swung around in angry astonishment. "That's what you think this is about for me—personal glory? A career boost? This is what you think of me?"

"No. But you have been after Philip Wentworth for a long time. It's become an obsession for you."

"Christ! I don't believe this."

"You could nail me too, if you want. I'm sure with a little help the AG could dredge up an obstruction of justice charge to throw at me for not cooperating fully with their investigation."

"And why would I want to do that?" He gave her an exasperated look. "You stuck your neck out for a judge you believed in, and it turns out you were right."

Feeling reckless, she plunged on. Her world was already caving in. She might as well help it along. "Closure? A full circle? I sabotaged your investigation. You hated me as much as you hated Philip."

"My feelings were much more complicated than that." He shook his head, eyes narrowed on her. "I'm not sure what's going on here. It's as if you want to self-destruct." He studied her. "Or you want to punish one of us," he added, hitting remarkably close to the truth, although he surely had the wrong one of them in mind. "I thought we'd gotten beyond that."

"Swept aside the past?"

"Started to."

Sam shook her head sadly. "Impossible. The past never goes away." She felt fairly confident about this assessment because she knew there was a good possibility that the past was about to bite her and a few others on the ass big time. "When you saw me talking to Billy on the dance floor, you thought I was leaking information to my"—she caught herself, barely missing a beat—"Wentworth friends, didn't you? A repeat of two years ago. It was the first thing that sprang to your mind. So you see, nothing's really changed."

Her conviction seemed to drain him. For a time, they stood in silence staring across the dank alley. Party noises drifted out to surround them.

Abruptly, he straightened. "I'd better be leaving. Here," he said, handing her his cell phone, "keep it with you. Call me at home if you need anything. I mean it, anything. You're still planning to stay downstairs tonight?"

She nodded. "Billy gave me the key. I'll wait and go home with him."

"Good. I think we're okay for tonight but it can't hurt to be cautious."

Still, he lingered. "Have you ever wondered what would have happened if we'd met for the first time this summer with none of the past and no Brian between us?" He continued to regard her for a long moment before turning and striding off down the alley.

Too often, Sam thought, watching him go. But some dreams were better left in Neverland.

Pacing through his sprawling apartment, Nick listened to the tape of Marty Davis's rambling interview. He stopped at the kitchen counter to look again at the photo Sam had snuck out. Gutsy lady, he thought with no small measure of admiration. Probably too gutsy by half.

He wished he'd insisted on either staying with her or bringing her here. He agreed that the potential danger was likely small. Even if Benton and Wentworth found out about Davis's tell-all before the morning, what could they do? Try to silence them all like Mafia thugs? Ridiculous. But the possibility couldn't be entirely dismissed. Desperate men had done worse for less. And Hattie Christiansen's accident might still turn out to be not an accident at all.

The tape ended and Nick flipped it off. Absently he reached for the cabinet-mounted TV and switched on the news. He'd blown it again with Sam. Big time, maybe forever, blown it. She wanted his trust. And he did trust her in the sense that he'd long since regained the belief that Samantha Parker was at heart as good and decent as they came.

But she was still holding out on him. And he sensed it had to do with the Wentworths, just like two years ago. So when he'd seen her conferring with Billy, he'd jumped to the worst possible conclusion. He knew she had to be torn up about all this. Even Kat had seen it. Billy was a close friend. She would hate hurting him. In frustration, Nick rubbed his face with both hands.

None of this should matter to him as long as she delivered the goods tomorrow. But it did. *She* did. All his attempts to shut off his feelings for her had failed miserably. The worst of it was that she'd managed to convince him that there was no possible future for them. And it was tearing him up.

A breaking news report cut through his recriminations, abruptly banishing them to a back closet. In shocked disbelief, he grabbed the phone.

CHAPTER 18

Across town, sitting in the dark on a mangy sofa left behind by the former tenant, Sam listened to the sound of the building's front door opening and closing. For a moment, she wondered if it was Kat coming to check on her. Kat, who would pry, but always stood ready to help those in need. That missionary zeal of hers had kicked in at the party. Sam hoped she'd defused it. She didn't want Kat involved in this mess.

Or it could be Billy coming home. After Rafter left, she hadn't felt like waiting for him and had returned on her own. Rafter wouldn't approve. But really, what good would Billy, or any of them, be against an armed assailant? In any event, if something were to happen, she wouldn't want Billy caught in the middle. That was also why she had resisted Billy's urgings to stay next door with him in a proper bed.

A pair of feet passing by momentarily blocked light from the hallway spilling in underneath the door. But whoever it was creaked on up the staircase to the second floor.

So, neither Kat nor Billy, she thought, relaxing. Both knew where they could find her.

Emotionally spent, she burrowed deeper into the sofa, wishing the entire day could be undone and put back together as it was yesterday. Awful as that had been, it beat this new place where she was caught between what had to be done on the one side and a lifetime of loyalties and promises on the other. What would old Harry have to say about all this? Would he feel divided?

A new, more immediate unease intruded on her ruminations. On alert, Sam stilled and listened intently until she heard it again—a creak in the floor overhead. Someone was in her apartment. A big someone, judging by the groans of the floorboards.

In blind panic, Sam froze like a rabbit trying to hide in plain site. Stupid, she thought, struggling to get a grip.

An instant later, she nearly jumped out of her skin at the sound of a sudden, trilling ring close at hand. Rafter's cell phone. Frantic to silence it, she dove for the duffel parked beside the sofa and managed to locate the right button to switch it on.

"Marty Davis is dead," Rafter shocked her by announcing. "His nephew is saying he drowned himself in the lake to end his suffering." His tone implied he didn't believe Davis would commit suicide. She didn't either.

Reeling from this latest blow and focused on the creaking upstairs, Sam didn't immediately respond.

"Sam? You there? I'm coming over."

"There's someone in my apartment," she whispered. "I can hear him through the ceiling."

This was met by a brief pause. "Is Billy next door?"

"He's still at the party."

"Okay. Get out of there now." He spoke quickly, calmly, but there was a chill urgency in his voice.

"Go out a window if you can. Avoid the street. Go to Billy. I'll call the police to report a break-in and meet you there. Now go!"

The line went dead. Galvanized, Sam pulled on tennis shoes, fumbling with the laces in her panicked haste. She still wore the skirt and sleeveless blouse she'd gone to the party in, ill-suited for shimmying out windows, but there was nothing for it. The intruder upstairs wasn't going to wait for her to change into track gear.

Grabbing up the duffel, she tiptoed over to a French window, unlatched an old-fashioned hinged screen, and slid out into the dark night. A short dash across the side yard and she was hidden by the neighbors' privet hedge.

By the time Sam panted back to the Jungle, the band had packed up and left and the crowd had dwindled to a dozen diehards. A few couples, one including Billy, still swayed in tight clinches on the dance floor to one of Billy's oldies CDs. Sam slumped into a chair near the rear, back to the wall like a nervous gunslinger, and watched the door for Ninjas and Rafter.

Rafter arrived first, hobbling in looking as though he'd just gone three rounds with Mike Tyson, and lost. His left eye was red and swelling with a gash underneath and his black Fender Guitar T-shirt was torn at the shoulder from the neck halfway down the left sleeve.

Terrified that he was badly hurt, Sam bolted from her chair and met him midway across the room at the same time as Billy. To their rapid-fire questions while they settled him at a table and bustled around making an ice pack for his eye, he explained that he'd been jumped between his apartment and car.

"I'll live," he assured them. "It was stupid. I parked on the street rather than underground thinking it would be faster if I had to leave quickly." He applied the ice pack tentatively to his eye and winced. Meanwhile his good eye raked over Sam until he appeared satisfied that she'd come through her flight intact.

Quickly sobering, Billy frowned back and forth between Rafter and Sam. "What's going on here? Why were you even thinking you might have to leave in a hurry, and what are you both doing back here?"

"Long story." Rafter's face became guarded. "I've got to huddle with Sam a minute," he said to Billy.

Billy glanced at Sam, and she nodded that it was okay. "Could you see if Duane has bandages around somewhere? I'll explain in a minute," she added. This was certain to irk Rafter, but she figured that sooner or later they would need to have it out. She refused to let Billy be blind-sided by what they were about to set in motion.

"Bad idea," he said as soon as Billy was out of earshot.

Ignoring that, Sam asked urgently, "What happened?"

His mouth twisted in disgust. "I got caught by surprise. Son of a bitch came at me from behind and rammed my face into my car. Practically knocked me out. Sounds like your guy. By the time I regained my wits, he was gone." He glanced up apologetically. "So's the tape. That's obviously what he was after. I didn't even get a good look at the bastard."

Billy dropped a medical kit off at the table and made a tactful retreat. Sam stood and gently pried the ice pack in Rafter's hand away from his eye. It didn't look too bad. But she thought the gash below on his cheekbone needed professional evaluation. "You might need stitches to prevent a scar."

He sent her a get-real look. "I think we have more serious problems on our hands than that. Can't you just stick a Band-Aid on it?"

She shrugged. On him, a scar would probably end up looking devilishly attractive. "Your face."

While she applied the antiseptic and bandage, Rafter planned. "I think we'd better move up the timetable—contact the authorities now, although if you have a big objection to that, we could hole up in a motel for the rest of the night. That may be what they'll do with us anyway."

"No, I'm okay with contacting them now as long as we do it in a way that we're sure not to be walking into a trap." She glanced up from the gauze she was cutting. "Who do you have in mind to call?"

"Robbie O'Neal," he said promptly and held up a hand to forestall her objection. "Yes, I know you're not his biggest fan, but he's the only one I'm absolutely sure we can trust. Both the governor and the AG were in the frat." He shook his head in amazed disbelief.

"Robbie is a Madison Law alum, too," she reminded him.

"I know. But we've heard nothing to link him to Davis's frat, and I've never heard Robbie mention belonging to any fraternity. Most importantly, the man has integrity."

She considered it, staring off across the café, which Billy, Duane, and a few others were putting back to rights in semi-intoxicated fits and starts.

"Okay. I'll have to go with your instincts on this because, frankly, I'm biased." She recalled Robbie's strong-arm tactics two years ago to get her to accept his deal—she would quietly resign and keep her mouth shut, and in return he would file no charges against her.

"There's no one I trust more," he added.

"Okay, then. Do it."

He nodded while Sam set to work trying to anchor the trimmed gauze to his cheekbone in a way that would not interfere with his vision.

"Hold still," she murmured, bending over and leaning in.

"Yes, ma'am, I'll try." His voice was laced with sudden humor, completely unexpected under the circumstances.

Sam glanced down and saw that his gaze was riveted on the Chrysler Highway view down the gaping front of her blouse.

Rolling her eyes, she straightened. "Get a good look, Your Honor?"

His mouth quirked up. "Not by half. But I especially like that lacy—ouch!" he yelped when she abruptly pushed the ice pack back into place against his eye and cheek.

Sam snapped the emergency kit closed with a faint smile and handed back his cell phone. "I'm going to talk to Billy while you call Robbie. I won't tell him much, but I can't let him be ambushed by this."

That sobered him. "Not a good idea. Even if I were completely sure Billy wouldn't run straight to his father with a warning, which I'm not, do you really want to put him in the position of having to choose between conflicting loyalties?" He surprised her by reaching out and snagging her hand. "You'd be forcing him to choose between you and his father. Christ, Sam, you're caught in a similar bind, and I can see that it's tearing you apart."

Startled that he could read her so easily, Sam jerked her hand from his. But she shouldn't be surprised, she reflected. It was that frequent, uncanny ability to read people that had elevated him from a merely gifted prosecutor to a brilliant one. It was why she was willing to trust his take on Robbie.

She had a sudden, unexpected urge to tell him everything, but it quickly passed. The habit of silence was too deeply rooted, and she didn't think she could bear seeing the look of disgust on his face if she spilled her guts now. With luck, her entire sordid story need never come to light.

"You don't know Billy," Sam ventured carefully. "You don't know what we mean to each other. He won't talk to Philip. You've got to trust me on this, Nick, just as I'm trusting you about Robbie. I won't say much, but I couldn't live with myself if I didn't give him some inkling that his world is about to be turned upside down."

Rafter didn't say anything for a few seconds. Then he shocked her. "You want my trust?" he asked, intent eyes riveted on her. "Okay, you have it. Completely. But be careful, for Billy's sake, and everyone else's."

Nick watched her cross the café to where Billy was wrestling a table into place. She touched his arm with easy familiarity, said something, and they retreated through the archway to a more private spot in the bookstore where a few tables from the café were still standing. As Nick punched in Robbie's home number, he hoped to God he'd made the right decision.

Robbie answered on the third ring, grouchy at being woken. It took only a minute for Nick to apprise him of the seriousness of the situation, longer for them to formulate a plan of action.

Throughout, Nick observed the simultaneous exchange taking place between Sam and Billy. They were huddled together over a table, their heads nearly touching, his Wentworth blond, hers a gleaming chestnut, but similar in other ways—the same graceful line of neck, the attractively defined features, the long, lean build. They could be brother and sister. They even shared some facial expressions. How had he missed it all this time?

He finished with Robbie and hung up. The epiphany broke over him like a meteor shower as piece after piece fell into place. Sam's extremely close, but platonic, connection to Billy. Her row with the senator over money. Her presence at the senator's home two years ago, along with her refusal to explain the reason for her presence. All made sense.

The senator had a reputation as a ladies' man. Sam hadn't been one of those ladies. But Nick would be willing to bet that she was the product of his union with one of them.

A sickening thought occurred to him. If his premise were true, that meant the senator had shopped his own daughter, playing on his reputation as a Casanova two years ago to make investigators believe Sam was one of his lovers rather than his informant. If Wentworth had known all along about the investigation, as Sam had asserted, then he'd had the upper hand—no doubt feeding them only what he wanted them to know. He would naturally have wanted to maintain the favorable status quo. Sam's unexpected visit while he was under surveillance would have jeopardized that. So he'd cast her as his lover, a deft move that might have worked had it not been for the later discovery of the confidential file in her office. Manipulative bastard, Nick thought. So, if not Sam, who had planted the file?

He had no answer for that, and his thoughts belted on.

Unfortunately if he was right about all this, her Wentworth roots gave her ample motive for compromising an investigation of the senator, both two years ago and now. He'd won convictions with less motive in evidence. Remarkably, Nick realized that it made no difference. Because he did trust her. No matter how torn by conflicting loyalties, she would do the right thing. He didn't know how or why he suddenly felt sure of it, he just did. The mistake he'd made two years ago was not to trust his instincts. And his instincts were telling him to trust her now.

In the bookstore, Billy covered Sam's hand with his own. Sam nodded and smiled sadly at something Billy said. Her wan gaze wandered over to Nick, then stopped and reversed course when she registered the way he was looking at her. Confusion crinkled the corners of her eyes as she focused on him, trying to decipher his expression. Nick looked away from the questions written across her beautiful face.

He would get it right this time. In that instant, he made up his mind not to confront her, hoping that she would come to him with the truth.

When they wandered over, Nick said to her, "Robbie is sending someone for us. It'll probably be half an hour." He glanced at his watch—already after midnight.

Sam sank down onto a chair. Completely sober now, and visibly shaken, Billy hovered over them. "I'm grateful for what you've done," he said to Nick, not quite meeting his eyes, "letting Sam give me a heads-up. It helps. Not sure why, but it does." He straightened and now looked Nick squarely in the eye. "What I'm trying to say is, I won't be talking to my father anytime soon—that you can count on."

"I will," Nick said, and they shook on it.

To pass the time while they waited, Sam and

Nick drank coffee and helped Duane and some of the wait staff with the end of the cleanup. The last of Billy's friends had staggered off when his mood turned glum. Nick was keeping a lookout through the front window of the café when a dark blue sedan pulled up carrying two men in suits.

"Sam, they're here," he said quietly.

For an instant she froze, her face revealing her dread. With her small duffel in hand, Billy loped up from the back. All three scoped out the car and its occupants, each silently pondering the enormous consequences of what lay ahead. Once Sam and Nick climbed inside, there would be no turning back. A black-suited agent stepped out onto the sidewalk and surveyed the area, but did not approach the door, evidently waiting for them to come to him.

"Ready?" Nick glanced at Sam, who was staring saucer-eyed outside.

She grimaced. "Do I have a choice?"

Billy gently nudged her from behind. "Go. Do what you have to do." He gave her shoulder a quick reassuring squeeze and added under his breath, "The bastard has earned it."

Sam took a deep breath, nodded, and squeezed his hand in return. "You'll be okay?"

"Fine." He hitched a shoulder and managed a faint smile. "Seems like a good time for a vacation anyway. Go."

Nick glanced away, giving them a private moment, then opened the door.

"Do whatever you have to, Sam. I mean it. We'll get through this." He sent Nick a look of warning. "You make sure she's okay."

Nick nodded. Billy followed them outside.

He and Sam hung back while Nick approached the agent. He was a solid, competent-looking professional with short brown hair and small watchful eyes that did a quick survey of Nick and lingered for an extra second on his bandaged face.

"Judge Rafter?" At Nick's nod, he opened the rear door. "We're all set for you and Ms. Parker. Please get in now."

Nick felt a twinge of unease that he put down to loss of control over the situation. "Where will you be taking us?"

From behind, he heard Billy suddenly start to warble a bawdy pub ditty, badly slurring the words, eccentric behavior even for him. The agent looked over Nick's shoulder and Nick craned his head around in confusion to behold Billy drunkenly swaying across the sidewalk. Except that he knew Billy was stone cold sober. The agent didn't though and appeared faintly alarmed when Billy staggered over to them, as if fearing Billy might vomit on his good shoes.

Billy began to loudly berate Nick for taking Sam away from him. "Bastard!" he howled. "Oh, what villainy!" he continued in a five-star performance.

What on earth was he up to? Sam seemed equally mystified, until Billy let loose a warning from the bard in ringing baritone: " 'Trust none; For oaths are straws, men's faiths are wafer-cakes, And hold-fast is the only dog, my duck.' "

They both got it at the same time. He was warning them about the agents and creating a diversion. As a grand finale, he stumbled, fell to the sidewalk at Nick's feet, and to all appearances passed out.

Sam raced to Billy's side. "Help me get him inside, Rafter."

The other agent slowly emerged from the car. The first peered down at Billy in resigned disgust.

"We've got him," Nick assured them, hoisting

Billy upright under one arm while Sam rushed to support him on the other side.

"Leave him," the agent said, "we have to get going."

Sam shot him a withering glance. "I'm not leaving him on the sidewalk."

"Give us a minute," Nick tossed back as they staggered toward the café under Billy's dead weight.

"Make it quick," the first agent grumbled.

"You don't need to be such a blasted good actor," Sam huffed at Billy under her breath. She sagged under his weight as they frog-marched him through the door. "Maybe you could revive just a little before you break my friggin' back!"

When they got him past the archway into the dark bookstore and out of sight, Sam dropped Billy's arm and caught her breath. "This better be good."

"When's the last time you saw an FBI agent wearing an Armani suit and Gucci shoes?"

"That's it?" Nick asked, unable to believe his ears. "You went through that entire charade because—"

"No." Billy looked even more shaken than earlier. "I saw that man once at the house with my father. Look, there's no time. That man is not FBI. Or if he is, he's playing both sides of the fence."

"When did you see him?" Nick persisted.

"A couple years ago."

"Billy, for God's sake!" Nick shot him an incredulous look.

"I believe him," Sam interrupted, her face ashen. "Billy has a Kodak memory for books and faces, and if he says that man met with Philip, he did."

Nick reviewed everything the agents had done and said from the moment they pulled up at the curb for any departure from normal FBI operating procedure, searching his memory for clues to corroborate Billy's assertion, and finding them. They hadn't introduced themselves. They hadn't shown identification. It was enough.

"I'm going to assume you're right and these men are impostors." He eyed Billy with increased respect. "We'll need to leave without them seeing us. Soon, before they realize we're on to them."

"Out the back." Billy hurried Nick and a stunned-looking Sam through the book stacks.

"If we're wrong about this, and I hope to God we are, we can laugh it off in the morning," Nick said.

Sam balked at the door and refused to budge, her wounded eyes focused on Billy as if he were a lifeline. "You don't think Philip would . . ." She stopped, unable to finish the thought, and Nick ached for her. This was ripping her apart and now he understood why. She was contemplating the ultimate betrayal a child could suffer at the hands of a parent.

Billy pulled her into a tight hug, comforting her as best he could in a hurry. "No, Sam, I don't think Dad would harm you. He's not a monster. But I can't vouch for his associates. Now go. Quickly! Take my car." He tossed his keys to Nick. "It's a gas-electric hybrid. Keep the lights off. It's quiet; they won't hear you leave."

"But what about you and Duane and the others?" Sam asked, her usually steady voice all over the place.

"We'll be safe. I'll play drunk and they'll only be able to say that you went out the rear."

"Come on, Sam. It's us they want." Nick managed to pull her outside into the alley, where a few oversized drops of rain plopped onto the dusty, pockmarked pavement, forewarning an imminent downpour.

"Take care of her," Billy called after them in a hushed voice as they scurried for his car.

CHAPTER 19

"About Robbie."

Twenty miles down the highway, Rafter broke the wall of silence that had risen inside Billy's hybrid after they gave the dubious agents the slip. She guessed he'd been engaged in more planning, but she'd been too numb with shock to think much about tomorrow. For the second time in twelve hours, they sped west toward Lake Michigan. He'd said he knew a place where they would be safe for the night. The earlier trip to see Marty Davis felt as though it had taken place in another lifetime, so much had happened since then. Marty was dead and she and Rafter appeared incredibly to be on the run like clueless heroes in a Hitchcock movie.

"I know you're questioning Robbie's role in all this," he went on.

Actually she hadn't, until now. She was too devastated by the possibility that Philip might want to harm her to have any energy left over for Robbie. Billy's assurances that Philip was no monster meant only that he found it too painful to contemplate the unthinkable. But that didn't mean it wasn't true.

"How do you explain what happened?" Sam countered. She stared blankly through the night at the familiar road she took twice weekly to visit Camille. When would she see her again? What would happen if Sam could no longer pay her bills?

"I think Robbie must have trusted the wrong person. Or maybe someone down the chain of command who's on the take heard something and managed to intervene."

She shrugged. She didn't like Robbie, but Nick was probably right. Robbie's dark side consisted of a childish temper, an oversized ego, and a willingness to bully to get what he wanted. But his goals were laudable. He reminded Sam of a righteous evangelist desperately trying to save an apathetic world. Ideologically, he wasn't on the same page as Benton and Davis.

Sam dismissed Robbie and returned to the question tormenting her. "Who do you think those men work for? Who's behind this?"

Rafter's gaze briefly left the road and lit on her. Disconcerted, she turned away from the outpouring of sympathy she saw there. She felt suddenly stripped bare and wondered if his radar had somehow detected her deepest secrets. It was the same feeling she'd had in the café earlier when she'd caught him staring.

"Assuming they were in fact impostors, their most obvious employer would be Benton or Wentworth or both. Could be others depending on how organized the group really is."

Dividing his attention between her and the road, he gentled his voice. "Look, we really can't know what they intended to do once they picked us up. Could be they only wanted a chance to convince us that Marty was spewing toxic smoke or to scare us into keeping our mouths shut. If they wanted us dead, the thug who took the tape from me passed up a perfect opportunity." He managed a joking half-smile. "Murder makes for good Hollywood drama, but it's usually an impractical, high-risk solution."

Outside, the storm finally broke all at once. Sheets of water rattled the roof of the hybrid. Rafter groped around on the unfamiliar dash before locating the wiper control.

"I know how hard this is for you. If there was something I could do to make it easier, I would do it in an instant. But I'm here if you need a friend to talk to."

Sam studied his profile in the green glow of the dash light, wondering again if he'd somehow managed to peer into her hidden places. "I'm fine, just heartbroken for Billy and guilt ridden that I'm the instrument of his suffering."

She thought he looked disappointed with that, but he was so blasted tough to read when he wanted to be that she wasn't sure what he was thinking.

"You take too much on yourself. You're not the instrument. His father is."

They were nearing the turnoff for the Stanley Care Center. An idea had been taking shape and now became fixed. Sam asked Rafter to stop. "I want to look in on my aunt. There may not be another chance soon."

He looked at her in mild astonishment as though fearing she'd finally cracked under the strain. "It's the middle of the night. The place is probably locked up tight and everyone tucked into bed."

"The guard will let me in. He knows me. Day and night mean little to my aunt. She's as likely to be awake now as at any other time." She added quietly, "Nick, it's important."

He caved and was pulling into the empty parking lot when his cell phone rang, startling them both. "Robbie," he mouthed to her when he answered it.

Sam loped down the deserted, dimly lit hallway of the Stanley Care Center. She was anxious to know what Robbie had to say but welcomed the opportunity to slip inside and talk to Camille privately. She had questions to ask and didn't want an audience. As ever, CNN droned on the TV. A sympathetic night nurse turned a blind eye to Camille's news addiction, as long as she kept the volume down.

Camille's eyes were closed but snapped open when she heard Sam step into the room. Their gazes locked for a moment.

"What time . . . ?" she mumbled, flicking a glance at the clock.

Sam pulled up a chair and took her hand, understanding that she would be confused by the oddly timed visit. "No, you're right, it's night, not afternoon." Sam muted the TV and decided to gamble. Watching her closely, she said, "I have some questions and really need the answers. You knew about Rachel Holtz, her death, didn't you?"

Sam saw the fear in Camille's eyes before she closed them. "Yes, from Harry."

"Thank you," Sam whispered, squeezing Camille's hand. Then she took a long, unsteady breath and tried again. "I expect you also knew that Rosalind was there at Philip's fraternity house when it happened?"

In broken, slurred spurts it came out. Harry had intervened after learning of Rachel's disappearance from Rosalind, who was frantic for her friend. When he got the truth out of Philip and the other fraternity members involved, Harry was appalled and furious at them for what they'd done and the way they were living. But ultimately he hadn't wanted an accident to ruin the boys' lives. So, for a while, to keep her occupied and out of the way, he'd bankrolled Rosalind's obsession with chasing fame and fortune in California.

"So that's how they got together," Sam mused. "Those meetings. I've always wondered."

"Who?"

"Rosalind and Harry. The original odd couple."

"She seduced him." Camille worked to spit the words out. Even after all these years, raw anger colored her disease-ravaged voice. "First Philip, then my Harry. Always liked rich . . . powerful men."

"And I was the unhappy result." Sam looked away. She'd never had a chance to hash through all this because Camille had refused to discuss it, and Rosalind had simply lacked interest in looking back. Though it was Rosalind, with her usual carelessness, who had eventually and inevitably let slip the true identity of Sam's father.

"Why did you take me in? You loved him. I must have been a constant reminder of his betrayal."

"Hated you at first," Camille admitted, darting a glance over Sam's shoulder. "Then saw you as a chance to be close to him. He loved you."

Shattered, Sam pulled away. But Camille's grip tightened in a surprising burst of strength. "Wait. Came to love you." The words were more garbled and difficult to decipher than usual. "For *you*. You were mine. Not good mother, but you mean world to me."

Sam dropped her head to their entwined hands, sealing her eyes shut to stop the tears backing up behind. For years she had longed to hear these words, guessing that behind Camille's gruff reticence she cared, but having an orphan's insecure need for the confirmation. God, how she had tried to earn Camille's love and approval.

"Please believe," Camille rasped.

"I do," Sam warbled, swiping at her eyes. "You were always there for me to come back to when Rosalind couldn't hack it. You were my safe port, the only one I could ever count on."

"Want you safe, Samantha."

"Is that why you wouldn't tell me about Rachel?"

"Wanted you to drop it. Too dangerous." Her aunt's sharp gaze again darted past Sam to the open door.

"How long has Rafter been there?" Sam asked Camille without turning around to look.

"While."

Rafter's hideaway was only a few miles up the Lake Michigan coast on the next northernmost inland lake from Lake Manitou. On the way, he explained that Robbie had contacted both the local head of the FBI and the state attorney general. "He said that we were gone before the FBI team arrived to pick us up."

"The AG sent his own boys first, I suppose."

"So it appears."

They made one brief stop along the way at an all-night convenience store. Rafter came out with a bag of groceries in one hand and a bag of ice in the other. Neither said much after that. Sam knew he was waiting for her to offer answers, but she couldn't handle talking about it just then. Not yet. The brutal one, two, three combination of Marty's revelations about both Rosalind and Philip, Billy's revelation about the phony agents, and Camille's revelations about everyone had left her dazed.

She blocked out the questions in Rafter's eyes, turning on an all-night music station to fill the silence and staring mindlessly out the window.

The rain let up as they turned down a narrow, dark, and nearly invisible two-track winding through dense woods. Less developed than its southern neighbor, the lake was rimmed by thick woods and small, rustic cottages. He nosed the hybrid out of sight behind the dark outline of a modest clapboard bungalow and cut the engine.

Their car doors squeaked loudly in the huge silence. Pine needles crunched underfoot and the air carried the earthy smell of lake and wet leaves. An owl hooted from the depths of the dripping woods.

"Whose is it?" Sam asked.

"My uncle's, but we're not staying here. It's already been closed up and winterized."

"Where then?" Sam asked with some alarm. It was two in the morning, she needed a bathroom, and she was ready to drop from exhaustion.

"There."

She followed his glance to the dark silhouette of a sailboat moored offshore.

"It has running water and a head. Bathroom," he clarified at her blank look. "If we're still here tomorrow night, I'll open the cabin."

The wooden ketch was approximately thirty-five feet in length. On the way through the cabin to use the facilities, Sam noted a large bunk aft and two small ones that doubled as seats on either side of a table next to a tiny galley where Rafter began to stow his provisions.

When she came out, she found him lounging on deck in the balmy lake breeze, snacking on crackers and cheese in the dark. He patted a dry cockpit cushion beside him and she gratefully collapsed onto it. Sam asked him about the cottage and the boat—also his uncle's, it turned out—and he filled in the details.

She stared out over inky water, watching the last of the storm front disappear over the eastern horizon. After a time she spoke quietly. "I expect you overheard enough back there in my aunt's room to get that my connection to the Wentworths is complicated."

"You're a Wentworth. I got that," he said, helping himself to another cracker.

Sam nodded. "On the wrong side of the blanket obviously." Taking a breath, she went on. "Rosalind was my mother. She died when I was twelve. A combination of drugs and drowning."

Rafter shook his head, looking shocked. He evidently hadn't picked up on Sam's relationship to Rosalind. But now his quick brain made lightning connections. "Marty Davis is a son of a bitch to have dragged you into this," he harshly proclaimed.

"I was already in it." She peered at him. "But you'd already figured out the Wentworth connection before we stopped at the nursing home, hadn't you?"

"I guessed it at the café when you were talking to Billy."

"I'm the skeleton in the Wentworth closet." She hesitated, feeling that she owed him some sort of explanation as to why she hadn't fessed up before. "The subject has always been taboo. It would have ruined my father's reputation and career."

"I'm sorry. That must have been an unbearable burden growing up."

Surprisingly she saw only intense compassion wrinkling his brow under tousled dark hair, not the disgust she'd imagined he would feel. Her battered heart gave a hopeful flutter, then a lurch when he pulled her gently into his arms.

His breath tickled the side of her face as he continued. "None of this is your fault. You have nothing to feel guilty about. There's only so much we can do to protect the people we love." His sympathy made her want to weep. "Your father has put you in an appalling position," he went on, gently stroking her hair.

She stilled in his arms, realizing then that he'd gotten it all wrong. He apparently thought Philip was her father. She knew she should explain everything, but the words stuck in her throat like taffy. She was bone tired and already on shaky ground emotionally. Once she started talking about it, she would lose her grip entirely, and she didn't want that just now when his arms felt so good. The past held minefields and the future held misery, but the present was a safe oasis.

"God, I'm sorry about everything," he went on. "I wish I could go back and undo all the stupid blunders I made two years ago. I swear, if I could I would."

"Shh. Don't Nick. Don't go there," she pleaded. "Not tonight." She found herself caught in one of his unsettling eye locks. Around them, the boat creaked and dipped at its mooring. Rigging slapped the mast in a gust of warm air.

"You're right," he said abruptly. "Hang the past!"

He smoothly exchanged the eye-lock for a lip-lock, and Sam went into familiar free fall. When he drew away a few inches and ever-so-slowly started unbuttoning her cotton blouse, giving her all the time in the world to stop what he was doing, she instead slipped her hands under his torn T-shirt and felt her way up his deliciously fit chest. She was beyond tired, operating in a strangely anesthetized state, and had an almost inebriated recklessness to match. She sensed the danger of indulging in one last night with Rafter but lacked the clear-headed will to stop it.

Half-naked, they wobbled down the companion-way to the double bunk below, shedding more clothes as they went and rolling naked onto faintly musty sheets. But this was not the desperate coupling of before. This felt of lovers savoring every look and touch, reaching out and holding on in the face of an uncertain tomorrow, as lovers might in time of war when one is bound for battle. They made slow, lin-gering love, committing every detail to memory.

After Sam climaxed, Nick spread her quivering legs and entered her. "Don't close your eyes." He touched his nose to hers, his voice a husky mur-mur against her face. "I want to see that you're right here with me."

Sam looked at his hands on her breasts, dark against her pale skin, watched his tongue circle an erect nipple. She was awash in lust and unbeliev-ably ready to come again.

Afterward, she was awed by the wonder of what-ever magnificent force of nature this was that al-ways seemed to lift them up and carry them off to some earthly realm close to paradise. But she couldn't dwell on it for long as exhaustion soon overtook them and they fell asleep in a tangle of bedding and limbs.

Early the next morning Sam woke from a fitful sleep to the gentle rocking of the boat. Rolling over on the hard mattress, she was vaguely aware of the soft lap of water against the hull and the reg-ular thwap of line against the mast. As she came nose to nose with Nick, her heart lifted. His sleep-smoothed face covered in dark sandpaper stubble caught a beam of sunlight streaming in through a porthole. Sam's sleepy gaze lingered on the stark white bandage below his left eye before wandering over curly black eyelashes, narrow blade of nose, and yummy wide mouth. With a start, she realized that she loved him.

Oh, no, she silently cried, bolting upright in the bunk and staring aghast at the gently snoring object of her dismay.

How could she have let this happen? They didn't stand a chance with all the baggage between them. And even if they could get around the past, all external signs pointed to Rafter being one of those nimble Warren Beatty types who don't settle down—leastwise not until eligible for AARP membership and after having cut a swath through the female population.

But for a giddy moment while her mind blanked those huge impediments, her heart soared. Then reality crashed in.

What was the matter with her? Any real relationship between them was doomed from the start. This was the man who had once done his best to ruin her, she reminded herself, trying desperately to back-peddle. Meanwhile, they were caught in such an awful, dangerous mess. She had no idea how or when it would end. They couldn't afford to lose focus simply because, with the most abysmal timing imaginable and despite trying to avoid it, she'd had the bad sense to fall helplessly, hopelessly, and oh so stupidly in love with Nick Rafter.

An hour later Nick stumbled out of bed in search of Sam. He was immensely relieved to find her

dozing on cushions in the cockpit. Sagging down
onto the companionway steps, he let out a pent-up
breath while he watched her long eyelashes flicker
in sleep. On waking to find her gone, he'd feared
that she'd had morning-after regrets and fled.

God, what a mess. He was too involved. It was
making everything more complicated. A replay of
two years ago, but he couldn't help it. What shitty
timing. The hard reality of the situation was that
their lives likely would not be theirs to control for
a good long while, and that was if they got out of
this trouble intact.

Nick glanced at his watch: eight. Time to put
the ball into play. Ducking below, he pulled on old
shorts and a shirt he found stowed in a locker and
concentrated on the day ahead.

"I suppose a shower is too much to hope for,"
Sam mumbled a few minutes later, crawling down
from the cockpit.

Nick, who was scrambling eggs and frying bread
because there was no toaster aboard, thought he'd
never seen a woman look more attractive with hair
all over the place, eyes barely cracked, and face
sleep-dazed. He turned down the gas stove and
caught her up in a tender embrace. For a second
she sagged against him, her forehead resting on
his shoulder.

"Sorry, no shower on board, but we're bobbing
around in a huge bathtub. Water's not too cold either." Nick kissed her soundly on the mouth. "God,
Sam, you take my breath away. Good thing I'm not
one of those guys with weak hearts."

Smiling, she straightened and patted his arm,
but he could feel her already distancing herself

from him. Well, she could try that strategy all she wanted; he wasn't going away this time.

Over breakfast they tacitly avoided talk of the day ahead, but Nick could tell from her shadowed eyes and frequent silences that it weighed on her.

He roused her from her ruminations a few minutes later. "Come on. Let's take a swim." He was already scrounging up towels, soap, and shampoo. "Then we need to talk."

On deck, he lowered a ladder over the side of the ketch away from shore. Except for a few web-footed inhabitants, the entire lake and shore appeared deserted. With a mocking glance in her direction that she interpreted as a dare, he stripped down to beautifully two-toned skin, giving Sam her first full-light, eye-popping view of him in the buff. A second later he casually plunged overboard and began soaping up. Sam swallowed hard. He was beautiful.

Knowing he was watching her every move and not to be outdone, Sam nonchalantly stripped off yesterday's skirt, a T-shirt she'd tossed into her duffel, and finally, wildly patterned bikini briefs. Then smirking at his unwavering attention, she carefully backed down the ladder and slipped into pleasantly tepid water.

"Nice." Rafter grinned and sent the shampoo bottle floating in her direction.

Working hard to keep her head above water while her hands were occupied washing her hair, she only gradually became aware that Rafter was spending an inordinate amount of time under water. "Interesting aquatic life?" she puffed out.

"Just let me check." Resubmerging, he swam closer and hovered at breast level for a long moment, then popped up, streaming water down his grinning face. "Seriously gorgeous. I usually only cry at Disney movies and major sporting events, but this . . ." He swiped at crocodile tears. "It's severely testing my manly composure."

Sam laughed. "Disney movies?"

"My nieces allow me to escort them," he admitted with an endearing trace of embarrassment. "I see every one before they hit Blockbuster."

Shortly, he had her in stitches recounting adventures with his nieces, interspersed with occasional shark stalking to the forever-chilling two-note *Jaws* refrain. Eventually his stalking resulted in a catch.

Laughing so hard she sputtered water, Sam tried to wiggle away, but he was by far the stronger swimmer. "No fair!"

His slick skin slithered against her breasts and belly, the sensation delicious agony. Within seconds she ceased her token resistance and they teetered on the brink of making love again. Several choking submersions later, Sam learned the frustrating limitations of making love in deep water. That was just as well because she was trying to keep her distance—albeit not very successfully—in order to minimize future suffering. Apparently having pre-acquired knowledge of the difficulties inherent in aquatic lovemaking, Nick was cleverly maneuvering them more or less in the direction of the boat ladder.

Collapsing naked on the cabin trunk, he squinted up at Sam while she toweled off. "I've missed hearing you laugh like that—having fun."

"The circumstances these last few months . . ." Her mouth twisted into a wry half-smile and she shrugged. Swathed in the big beach towel, she edged along the cabin trunk to a safe distance away from him before sitting. She read in his disappointed

look and sigh the understanding that their roman-
tic interlude had ended. She wondered that he
wasn't champing at the bit to get on with business
now that he at last had Philip within his sights.

Mirroring him six feet away, Sam reclined against
the cabin trunk and watched big, cotton candy
clouds coast by, savoring a last bit of peace. The
gentle rocking of the boat made her eyelids feel
heavy. It was a beautiful September day with a sky
as blue as Rafter's eyes and a balmy breeze that felt
like a soft caress against her bare arms. Odd, she
thought, that such an outwardly tranquil day should
be the backdrop for the tempest ahead. She closed
her eyes and drifted off, avoiding the inevitable as
long as possible. God, she was tired.

"Sam." Rafter roused her sometime later dressed
and shaved, wearing the same ragged shorts and T-
shirt he'd scrounged up earlier. He'd replaced her
wet gauze bandage with a smaller plain Band-Aid.
"We need to work out what we're going to do."

Sam groaned and squinted at her watch. After
nine. Her reprieve had run out.

"The longer we wait, the more time they have to
destroy evidence."

She noted that he'd carefully avoided specifying
Philip. "I know." She sighed. "But I don't have to
like it."

His mouth curved into a faint smile of sympathy. "Ditto."

When she'd dressed, they sat in the cockpit and
Rafter outlined his plan, which was to call Robbie
and try again with the FBI. Only this time they would
go to them. They would not agree to another ride
with unknown escorts.

Sam's frown grew as he answered her questions

about the length of time he guessed such an investigation and trial would take—confirming her own dismal approximations—and the security restrictions that would likely be imposed on them for the duration of it.

"That's too long," she finally said. She thought of Camille and what would happen to her if Sam couldn't visit and maybe couldn't come up with the money to keep the Stanley Care Center happy.

"We have no choice in that."

"Maybe we do," Sam mused. An idea had been taking shape. "Philip is hosting a party fund-raiser tonight. I'll bet Benton will be there, too. Instead of waiting months while the authorities go after evidence that likely was destroyed along with Marty Davis, what if we make new evidence." Sam met and held his gaze. "Philip invited me to the party. There's someone I was supposed to talk to about a job in D.C.—"

"You're thinking about moving?" Rafter had stilled.

"I don't know. Does it matter now?" She swept an impatient hand through still-damp hair, slicking it off her face. "The point is, I could wear a wire and try to talk to Philip. Benton as well, if he's there."

Rafter was already shaking his head. "Too dangerous. And you're too involved. I would never ask you to do something like that."

"You didn't. Look, Rafter, I hate this, but whether I do it or not doesn't change that I'm about to become an informant against my own family. Informants by definition are always involved on some level, but the FBI routinely works with them anyway. There's usually little choice. Robbie wouldn't hesitate." She swallowed hard. "So, do you want Philip or not?"

When he didn't immediately answer, she added, "You really don't have much choice because I'll make the offer to Robbie and the FBI, and you know they'll accept. But I'd rather have you on my side."

She could see his internal struggle and loved him all the more for it. It both stunned and warmed her that he appeared ready to sacrifice a try at Philip for her sake.

"It's a long shot," he said at last, and she knew she had him.

"I know. But it could work."

"I have one condition. You have to insist that I go in with you as your escort."

"Agreed. And I also want a guard on my aunt."

"That shouldn't be a problem." Rafter stared moodily out over turquoise water. "Although this might not fly with the bureau. They hate rush jobs."

"Then we'd best get on with it." She touched his knee. "Nick, there's one other person I want to bring in."

CHAPTER 20

Light was spilling from the ground-floor windows of the Wentworth mansion when Sam and Rafter rolled up and added his recently retrieved Beemer to the parade of vehicles lining the street and drive in front. From a half-block away, Sam could see a crowd of political faithfuls milling about inside. Outside, with touched-up trim and garden newly planted in fall colors—all lit up by high-wattage landscape lighting—the gussied-up Tudor looked smart for the occasion. Strains of Vivaldi wafted from open windows and drifted on warm currents of evening air. Overhead a last orange wisp faded from the evening sky and a harvest moon, huge and luminous, hung low on the horizon.

A perfect night. A perfect setting. But appearances could be so very deceiving, Sam thought with a shiver. As they started up the street, she couldn't shake a feeling of doom. Just nerves, she told herself.

Rafter's Beemer stuck out in the otherwise domestic mix of cars. They were in the automotive heartland and this was a political fund-raiser. Any errant Jaguar or Benz would be left at home in the garage on such an occasion.

"All the better to follow us in, my dear," Rafter muttered with a tense smile when she pointed out the discrepancy.

She hoped it wouldn't come to that.

Nervously, Sam touched the small transmitter a female FBI agent had taped between her breasts, the lower end anchored inside her bra. A tiny black microphone the size of her thumbnail was clipped to her bra next to it. About the size and shape of a small makeup compact, the unit was undetectable under the beige silk blouse and suit jacket she wore. Rafter got to wear his taped to his inner thigh under his trousers with the microphone snaked up his pant leg to his fly. The electronics expert had nixed that location for Sam. "Some guy sneaks a peak up your skirt and you're made," he'd explained.

"Hope this thing works," Sam muttered, craning her head to make one last scan along the street as they turned onto the winding drive. In answer, a hundred feet down the block, the parking lights on a tan utility van flashed once.

"Guess so." Rafter sent her a reassuring smile.

Sam tried to force a confident smile in return, but as they neared the entrance, her step faltered on a sudden wave of nerves.

"Cold feet?" Rafter cast her a quick, concerned look.

"Icy," she admitted, struggling to get a grip.

"You don't have to do this. It's not too late."

Sam shook her head. "No, we have one chance before they realize we've gone to the authorities."

The local FBI chief had been keen on the plan, and Robbie O'Neal had acquiesced. With Marty Davis dead and his stockpiled evidence of the cabal's misdeeds now likely in enemy hands, both men realized that collecting sufficient evidence to prosecute would be tough at best. Their suspects were savvy and perfectly capable of covering their tracks.

They had one small window of opportunity and nothing to lose. By tomorrow morning, the FBI should have the warrants necessary to begin searching homes and offices, although even success in obtaining those vital warrants was not a foregone conclusion. Robbie was seeing to this aspect of the case.

Because of the extreme sensitivity of the investigation along with overshadowing worry about possible infiltration by the ring, the number of agents involved had been kept to a bare minimum and then briefed only on a need-to-know basis. Robbie, as always, was fanatical about secrecy. Of the handful of federal investigators involved, only Robbie and the FBI chief knew the identity of the targets.

Sam frowned. If she and Rafter were successful tonight, the team in the van would be getting an unexpected earful.

Rafter pulled her off to the side of the front door, out of earshot of a few other stragglers making a late entrance. "Last chance. You okay?"

Sam nodded and turned away from his worried scrutiny. He half-wanted her to back out, she knew. He wanted to shield her from the danger and hurt waiting on the other side of the door. But he also wanted the chance to finally bring Philip down and he needed her help to do that. She was his ticket in tonight.

Well, he couldn't have it both ways.

Sam summoned up her earlier resolve. This was the right thing. Matthew had understood that, too. He'd spent his last conscious breath trying to expose the cabal. They had to be stopped. She couldn't protect Billy or Marie or even Camille from the fall-out, and certainly not Philip. His fault, not hers. But she felt like a Judas nonetheless.

She nodded again with more conviction. "Let's go dangle our lures."

Inside the huge central foyer with its magnificent furnishings from an earlier Wentworth era, well-heeled party stalwarts dressed in country-club evening attire mingled with familiar ease, confident of their own importance in the world. It was a convenient mix of cash-seeking politicians with their deep-pocket lobbyist and business counterparts. As relative outsiders, she and Rafter drew a few curious glances when they came in together and gave her name to a clipboard-toting sentinel. His conservative black suit did little to disguise that he was essentially a bouncer, albeit an upscale one.

Across the foyer, Randall Benton's cold eyes were fixed on them, marking their presence not with surprise but something disturbingly close to relish. Immediately he excused himself from a knot of guests and disappeared through the rear archway into the maze of back hallways.

Sam exchanged a meaningful look with Rafter, her heart beating so hard she wondered if the agents in the van were picking up the thumps. What especially unnerved her was that Randall Benton clearly knew who they were on sight even though neither she nor Rafter had ever met the man.

"The game's afoot," Rafter muttered in her ear. "Steady on."

Sam gulped. From his rock-hard grip on her arm, she knew she wasn't the only one battling nerves.

In the adjacent living room, Marie Wentworth was holding court. She spotted Sam through the grand archway and summoned her forth with a regal wave of a bejeweled hand. As reigning Wentworth matriarch, she was perched in stately splendor on a wingback chair, downsized so she wasn't dwarfed by it, but elegant enough to appease her French aristocratic sensibilities.

She examined Rafter closely while Sam made the introduction. And when, with a charmingly crooked smile and a raised brow, he obligingly let her look her fill, she offered a faintly accented assessment, "Handsome pup. Naughty, too, by the look of his eye." She sent Sam a stern warning glance. "Don't let his skill in your bed blind you to his faults, Samantha. If he's a drunk, enjoy heem awhile if you like, but don't marry heem." With that pearl of continental wisdom dispensed, Marie sat back with a satisfied air, ignoring the variously amused or shocked looks of several of the elderly ladies resting their feet nearby.

"He's a judge, not a drunk," Sam said, feeling heat rising up her face and irritated that Rafter was just standing there, trying unsuccessfully to smother a smile, finding it all amusing. Was it that obvious they'd slept together?

"They can be both," Marie pronounced, returning Rafter's smile with a sly one of her own.

With maddening aplomb, Rafter, the rotter, admitted, "I think I do feel the need of a drink. If you'll excuse me," and wandered off to find the bartender.

Pleased to be proved right, Marie nodded sagely.

At the first opportunity, Sam disengaged herself and went in search of Philip. Rafter would be tracking down Benton. Thanks to a guest list, magically produced through undisclosed means by the FBI chief, they'd known before they walked in the door that both of their primary suspects would be in attendance.

The plan was for Sam and Rafter to flush them

out by the simple tactic of attempting to strike a deal with each one separately in exchange for not going to the authorities. They hoped their mere presence might provoke some incriminating statement or action. If either bit, Robbie would have leverage to try turning him on the others. It was akin to trolling for sharks and they were the bait. Field agents waiting outside would charge to the rescue at the first sign of trouble. Only Robbie O'Neal and Sam, among their quickly cobbled together team, had the necessary invitation to get past the bouncer at the front door.

Robbie was supposed to be here already, but Sam had yet to spot him in the crush. She hoped to God that Rafter was right about him.

A second later, Sam saw Pushy ahead, lean and predatory as ever in low-cut black. *Blast!* She quickly ducked away, wanting to avoid another run-in with her here at all costs. Her name had not been on the guest list. Sam wondered with whom she had come.

Anxiously, she scanned the milling crowd in the smaller parlor on the opposite side of the foyer and finally located her subject in a far corner. He was engrossed in a private conversation with a perky young twenty-something whose rapt gaze was fastened on him. Philip could summon an abundance of charm when he pleased. It served him well in the political arena. At present the full force of it was focused on the hapless young woman. She would be either a lobbyist or a political groupie. Probably the latter, Sam decided, noting her youth and the look of dewy adoration as she gazed up at him.

When Sam began to move toward them, she caught Philip's attention, and his eyes widened briefly in surprise. In the next instant, his mouth thinned to a cold line of fury. For a queasy second, Sam faltered, chilled despite the warm air wafting into the room through open windows on two sides. Meanwhile, Philip's companion desperately banged on, trying to recapture his attention. Over her head, Philip's eyes made a barely perceptible gesture toward the rear corridor. With an equally minute nod of agreement, Sam changed course to meet him there. She watched him lean intimately close to his eager young fan and whisper something in her ear that earned him a giddy smile. Then with a parting caress of her bare shoulder, he turned and steered his way around clusters of admiring friends and supporters to Sam.

"We need to talk," she said as he stalked past without looking at her.

"Not here," Philip hissed, continuing to put distance between them and his guests.

Sam had to practically trot to keep up.

He poked his head inside the conservatory. Finding it empty, he waved her inside, closed the door, and then rounded on her. "What the hell are you thinking showing up here now!" he railed, his face flushing with fury. "I specifically remember telling you to stay out of things that do not concern you. I told you it could be dangerous and you blithely ignore me. Shit! I've tried to help you, and you throw it back in my face."

Sam edged around the side of a potted palm; Philip wasn't above striking out when he was in a rage. But she didn't want to get so far away that the recording would be compromised.

"I had no choice—"

"Shut up! You don't know the damage you've done, you ungrateful bitch."

He ranted and paced and toppled a planter with an irate kick of his foot. Sam flinched but didn't try to stem his tirade. He wasn't easy to stop when he got like this, and the longer he went on, the more likely he would be to say something incriminating. Amazingly, so far he hadn't, at least not with the degree of clarity that would hold up well in court. She needed him to get more specific.

Instead his fury propelled him into the personal. The venom spewed forth, hurtful and eviscerating—about her lowlife mother and aunt, on the one hand, and about all that the Wentworths had done for her, how much she owed them, and her answering disloyalty on the other. The blows were fast and merciless, but he saved the best for last. "Dad is probably turning in his grave wishing he'd paid Rosalind to abort you as she'd wanted, instead of paying her to have you."

Sam raised a shaking hand, desperate to stop him, horrified that this was all being picked up by the wire. She couldn't speak at first. In the next second long-smoldering resentment began to overshadow the hurt.

How dare *he* accuse *her* of disloyalty, of owing them when she'd kept their dirty little secret all these years, of damaging the family when he'd made a career of besmirching the Wentworth name! His audacity was breathtaking.

She'd spent a lifetime trying to earn her big brother's approval. In an eye-opening, liberating instant she realized that she never had, never would, and that she no longer gave a rap what he thought anyway. She hadn't failed. Philip had. He'd failed her as a brother and he'd failed the rest of his family as well because he wasn't capable of seeing beyond his own egotistical wants and needs. Why had it taken her years to learn what Billy had learned as a child?

Sam's contemptuous gaze clashed with Philip's.

"I've proved my loyalty to the Wentworths every day of my life in ways you can't begin to comprehend," she said unsteadily. With considerable effort, she reined in the gush of words suddenly ready to burst past the dam. It might feel good for a moment to let them spew forth as Philip was wont to do, but she would likely blow the operation if she did.

"Why the hell are you here?" Philip snapped, his temper beginning to sputter out. "Now that you're in over your head, you want me to save your sorry ass, I'll bet."

"I'm here to offer you a deal." Sam eyed him levelly, for once feeling strong and self-confident with him. "If you and your friends leave Rafter and me alone, we won't take what Marty Davis told us to the authorities." Keep it simple, Rafter had advised. Let his fear do the rest.

But Philip merely quirked an eyebrow, unimpressed. "Marty told you a good tale, did he? Poor guy was delusional. The drugs, you know. His own doctors will confirm that." Sam bet they just would after a little meeting with the Ninja enforcer. "Whatever crazy story he concocted can't be proved because it isn't real."

"Rachel Holtz was real," she said softly.

"We never hurt Rachel."

"Even unproved allegations can ruin a career in Washington. Your ex-colleague from California learned that the hard way. Voters don't need evidence."

Philip made an enraged noise of disbelief. "You really think you can threaten me? *You?* You have nothing but an old rumor that's got no legs and a sad, sick old friend's delusions."

"Then I guess I haven't done so much damage after all," Sam said, tossing his earlier claim back at him.

But Philip had heard enough. He glanced impatiently at his watch. "I don't have time to play games with you now, Samantha. Get out of here. And stay away from Nick Rafter. He's leading you down a blind alley. Keep your mouth shut. We'll talk in the morning and figure a way out of this."

"And just where am I supposed to go in the meantime? I've been threatened and followed. Your thug was in my apartment last night."

Philip scowled. "It wasn't my thug. You know I would never hurt you."

"Do I? Anyway I doubt your friends have any such compunction."

"I'll handle them. Now get the hell out of my house."

The conservatory had its own exit into the gardens and he crossed to it. *Now what,* she thought. He hadn't said anything seriously incriminating and already he was kicking her out.

She didn't need to force a grimace of disbelief. "You're tossing me out without any means of transportation and without letting me speak to Rafter?"

"The lady has a point, Senator," a refined, vaguely familiar voice said behind them.

Sam spun around. From behind a concealing planter of large ferns stepped a fit-looking, thirtyish man with cropped blond hair framing a narrow face. Handsome, but it was his watchful eyes that drew her attention. They were flat and pale, threatening in their steely lack of expression.

How long had he been there? She distinctly remembered Philip closing the door. She glanced at Philip and was not reassured by his wary expression.

"I think we should allow her to leave with Rafter," the intruder said.

Sam abruptly placed the voice and felt a jolt of

real fear. She'd last heard it in a parking lot calmly warning her that he had a bullet with her name on it.

While Nick waited for Randall Benton to reappear, he passed time wandering the front rooms where old familiars, touting pet issues or bragging about their latest golf scores and vacation spots, were eager to pull him into their discussions. Bali was in at the moment, he deduced, narrowly edging out last year's favorite in the south of France. Of Sam, Nick saw no sign. Nor did he see Senator Wentworth in the throng. And where in hell had Robbie gone off to? He'd seen him once briefly but immediately lost track of him.

Nervously, he checked his watch, noting the time. He'd give Sam five minutes before he went looking. She may have succeeded in luring Wentworth off alone, a necessary prerequisite to getting him to say anything useful, but that was no comfort. This whole scheme of theirs hadn't felt right from the moment they'd stepped inside and he'd caught the look of satisfaction on Randall Benton's face. Five minutes, he thought, gulping Perrier. If she had not reappeared by then, he would abort the operation and track her down.

A trio from the governor's office hailed Nick as he passed, wanting to know how he liked trading his prosecutor's cap for a gavel. Before he moved on, the governor's senior advisor gave him a chummy back slap and urged him to call the office. "I know the governor would like to hear how you're settling in."

A coded reminder, Nick understood, that he was supposed to be the governor's eyes and ears should he stumble upon any hint of corruption while on the court. Well, he had. Big Time. But it wasn't predominately on the court.

He nodded, indicating message received, although he had no intention of passing along anything to Governor Graham under present circumstances.

As he had done often during the last thirty hours, Nick pondered the likelihood that the cabal's tentacles stretched into the governor's office. Graham had been a member of the frat. Was he also part of the conspiracy? Was Nick's presence on the court meant to help dig out corruption or simply to provide the cabal with an early warning system? Certainly Graham had bypassed usual channels and gone for a back room mole in Nick.

Sam's batty stepgrandmother was observing him from across the room, and he raised his glass to her in salute before crossing the foyer to the smaller parlor where he'd last seen Sam heading. He suspected that Marie Wentworth was shrewder than she appeared on first impression.

The crowd here had thinned. People were already beginning to leave. Sam had not returned, but Nick's quarry suddenly materialized in a rear doorway.

Across the dwindling crowd, Randall Benton steadily watched him, maintaining eye contact while Nick steered his way over. A nondescript man physically—average in height, average in feature, average in coloring—Benton was anything but average in most other respects, from his brilliant business successes at Benton Motors, at least until recently, to his legendary competitive streak, whether in the boardroom or on the golf course. In the ordinary course of events, Nick suspected that he would be beneath the golden one's notice.

When he reached Benton, Nick didn't bother with preliminaries. "I think it's time we cut a deal."

"A deal, huh?" Benton turned on his heel and started down the empty corridor. Nick fell into step with him. "What kind of deal do you have to offer that might be of interest to me?"

"Samantha and I agree to forget what Marty Davis told us. In exchange, you call off your dogs."

Benton's mouth lifted a millimeter in what Nick guessed passed for a smile. "What did old Marty have to say?"

"He had an interesting story about a girl buried behind your Madison frat house. I expect her body is still there, or did you move it?" When that poke elicited no response, Nick continued, "He also had fascinating things to say about illegal campaign contributions and offshore accounts."

"But no hard evidence, I'll bet, or you wouldn't be here trying to cut a deal. And now with Marty's unfortunate death, there's just your word."

Nick shrugged. "That a risk you're willing to take?"

They turned a corner. Ahead, waiting at the next side passage, stood the bouncer formerly stationed at the front door. Benton gave him a nod as they passed, and he ominously fell into step behind.

Ready or not, it was happening, Nick thought, both excited and worried. *Where are you, Sam?*

"You're absolutely right," Benton said mildly. "It's not a risk I'm willing to take."

"What on earth do you think you're doing?" Philip demanded of Pruitt. Her Ninja's name was Simon Pruitt, Sam had learned on their forced march down the corridor to the library.

"Just following orders." Pruitt stood guard at the door.

"Benton's?" Philip snarled. "I don't have time for this."

"He'll be here in a minute. He wants you here, too."

"I've got guests out there to see off." In a huff, Philip stormed across the antique oriental carpet to the door. Pruitt wisely stepped aside.

"Suit yourself, Senator."

"Samantha?" Philip held the door for her, surprising Sam. Did he still have some residual instinct to protect her? Or did he simply resent having someone ordering him around?

"She stays." Pruitt flashed a gun holstered under his suit coat.

Philip's mouth thinned. "I'll be back in a few minutes."

After the heavy door shut with a muffled thud, Pruitt sank into a nearby armchair. "May as well take a seat and be comfortable," he said, watching her calmly through pale blue eyes.

Sam had retreated to the bookshelves on the inside of the room to put as much distance as possible between them. She nodded in response but was too much on edge to sit.

What now, she wondered, pretending an interest in the trophy photos covering the adjacent wall. They were mostly of Harry on the far end, familiar pictures of him as governor, several with Michigan's homegrown President Ford during his short stint in the White House, and later of Harry as judge. Closer to the bookshelves, the photos gave way to Philip alongside various dignitaries.

On a shelf in front of ancient blue-bound law treatises sat a five-by-seven framed photograph from

Philip's law school days. Sam had seen it so many times over the years that it had become part of the wallpaper. Now she stepped closer and really looked. It was similar to the one she'd taken from Marty Davis—a group of male students in seventies preppy threads—except that the composition of the group varied slightly from Davis's picture.

She leaned forward to look more closely at a man not included in the other one. It could almost be—

No, it couldn't be. And yet . . .

Her hand was shaking as she reached for the photograph. She stared at a skinny, dark-haired law student, different-looking from his preppy companions. He stood on the edge of the group almost out of the picture. The odd man out. Even his expression was faintly disapproving, as if he questioned whether he really belonged with this band of junior elitists.

Dizzy, she gripped the edge of a shelf for support.

No. She was tired and scared. She'd been running on adrenaline for too long. Her mind was making it up.

But even as one part of her brain couldn't comprehend it, wanted to reject it, another part knew it was true. She would recognize Robbie O'Neal's hell-and-brimstone eyes anywhere.

CHAPTER 21

Benton opened a door. A library, Nick saw an instant before registering the presence of two occupants whose heads snapped up on his entry.

Nick's gaze swept past a smartly dressed blond-haired man to rest on Sam, standing on the far side of the masculine room in front of a wall of bookshelves. He had to school his face not to reveal his profound relief at finding her. She looked wide-eyed and wary but in control, and he'd never been so glad to see anyone in his entire life.

"Ah, good," Benton said, following Nick in, "Ms. Parker is already here."

The senator entered close on their heels. "What's going on, Randall? Your man thinks he can tell me what to do in my own home."

"Relax, Philip. He'll be on his way shortly."

Nick quickly sorted out the players. Benton pulling the strings. Philip seemingly clueless and thus a potential liability to Benton. The other two were Benton's men—the bouncer obviously professional muscle, but the classy dresser's role less clear, a trusted aide perhaps.

No one moved to stop Nick as he crossed the room to Sam's side. Benton was busy placating Philip in low tones over by the enormous antique desk. The other two stood by, awaiting further orders.

Nick held out his arms and Sam practically fell into them. "You okay?" he murmured under his breath. For one precious second he held her tight.

She nodded and took a shuddering breath when he released her. "Meet my Ninja attacker," she whispered quickly. "I'm almost sure of it."

"Which? The blond guy?"

She nodded again. "Mr. Ivy League. And we may have a bigger problem." But as the huddle by the desk broke apart, she stopped and began to move away.

Nick held her arm long enough to whisper, "Hang in there. The cavalry is poised to charge."

"Check them, Pruitt." Benton flicked a glance from the blond man to Sam and Nick.

The bouncer drew a handgun from his pocket as inducement for them to cooperate. He handled the weapon with familiar ease. Nick noted the silencer. Meanwhile, from a briefcase, Pruitt pulled a hand-sized black box with an attached antenna that bore a slight resemblance to the portable metal detectors used at airports.

Oh, shit. Nick guessed that it was not, in fact, a metal detector, but rather a device to detect wires. It emitted a Geiger counter–type audio signal as Pruitt ran it up and down each of them and zeroed in immediately on the wires.

"One each, there and there." Pruitt pointed to the center of Sam's chest and to Rafter's thigh. "No weapons," he added, shutting off the device.

Wentworth swore softly, immediately recognizing the potential for political ruin. Nick could almost see him replaying every word he'd said for incriminating content. "Bitch!" he mouthed, glaring at Sam. She shifted backward as if anticipating physical retaliation.

"Put a sock in it, Philip." Benton shot Wentworth a warning glance, then turned to the bouncer. "Pull Judge Rafter's BMW around here to the back." He looked at Rafter. "The keys, Judge."

Wentworth, having slumped into the chair behind his desk, insisted, "I want to see them."

Bewildered, Nick didn't immediately hand over his keys to Benton's man. Didn't they understand that the jig was up, that any second agents would be storming in? What did they hope to accomplish?

Sam looked increasingly worried. But then, from the start, she'd had less confidence in Robbie and the FBI than he.

"The keys, *now,*" Benton repeated, as cool and mechanical as an ice machine. "Then drop your trousers so Philip can see the wire." He flicked a glance at Sam. "And your blouse. Let's go."

When neither moved to obey, Benton nodded to the bouncer. Nick braced for a blow, but instead of going for him, his glittering eyes were all for Sam as he started across the carpet for her.

"All right. You win." Nick held up one hand in surrender and used the other to shield Sam. "What the hell difference does it make anyway? This is over." Cautiously, he snagged keys from his pocket and dropped them into the bouncer's big paw.

"Go," Benton muttered to the man, opening the door.

Feigning modesty, Nick turned his back on the room, facing Sam, and muttered under his breath in the vicinity of her wire, "Anytime now, guys," as he began unhooking the tiny microphone from his fly. He lowered his trousers to his knees and faced Wentworth, who stared murderously at the damning evidence. Nick began to peel off the tape holding the device in place against his thigh below his boxers.

"Leave it." Benton motioned for Nick to pull up his pants, then turned to Sam. "The blouse, Ms. Parker."

Nick put a hand on Sam's arm to stop her. "Enough, Benton. What's the point? This is obviously a draw—"

"Shut up." Benton's impassive stare held a more blatantly evil threat than the gun his aide, Pruitt, suddenly had aimed at the center of Nick's chest.

"Do it," Pruitt said softly, staring at Sam. "Our senator demands proof."

Sam glared at all three as she unbuttoned the top few buttons of her beige silk blouse and held it open. The black box nestled like a jewel between her creamy soft breasts. For an instant Nick found himself staring before he recovered in self-disgust and stepped in front of her, blocking her from view while she buttoned up.

"It's over, Benton, at least this round is. So why don't we all say good night, and Sam and I will be on our way."

Wentworth rose and paced along the French doors behind the immense desk, his patrician face taut with anger and nerves.

"You think we're finished here?" Benton did that little lip-twitch half-smile thing again. "You still expecting the FBI to rush to the rescue? Too late. They left as soon as you stepped inside. Your wires were turned off when you came up the drive. You've been flying solo."

CHAPTER 22

A setup, Sam thought, counting off the seconds. The likelihood increased with each muted tick of the old grandfather clock that went unanswered by the pounding of rescuers' feet up the corridor until finally it hardened into certainty.

No wire. No cavalry to the rescue. A setup. It made sense. It explained how Benton seemed to have known they were wired even before checking.

Philip hadn't known. He looked shaken and vastly relieved, sagging against his desk as if his legs would collapse like green twigs without additional support. He would be ticked that Benton had let him sweat this out, she thought irrelevantly.

Who? Sam's gaze veered to the photograph on the bookshelf. Robbie. Until this very minute she'd looked for a benign explanation for Robbie's presence in that photo. Rafter trusted him and he was seldom wrong about people.

Still, after last night's double-cross, Sam had been open to the possibility that he was one of them. But the reality . . . She couldn't grasp it. If U.S. Attorney Robbie O'Neal, righteous crusader for truth and justice, was part of Marty's unholy alliance, then the world had spun crazily off its axis.

Sam shut her eyes. Was anyone what he seemed? Benton, a major CEO, and Philip, a U.S. senator, both leaders of the community, were common criminals. No, not common. Uncommon, but criminals nonetheless. And Rafter . . .

She glanced at him. He reached for her hand and gave it a steadying squeeze, a promise that they would get through this. He'd been the biggest surprise of all. The man she'd viewed as the enemy for so long had a heart as big as the Rockies, and she'd fallen head over heels for him. The real deal. The kind of helpless, I'll-follow-you-off-a-cliff kind of love. Which was why she'd swallowed her doubts and followed him back to Robbie. Sam took a deep breath and tried to control her fear. They still had a chance.

"So what now?" Rafter was asking Benton. Did he realize yet that Robbie had betrayed them?

"Now we wait until my man brings your car around and then you'll be on your way."

"I assume to some dark field where your thugs will put bullets in the backs of our heads."

"Now don't go getting all dramatic," Benton said mildly. "I'm sure my men can work out a mutually satisfactory agreement with you." He turned away from them to confer privately with Pruitt.

"No doubt similar to the one they worked out with Marty Davis," Rafter snarled, taking a menacing step toward Benton, which was brought up short by Pruitt's quickly swiveled pistol.

They meant to kill them, Sam thought. She and Rafter knew too much. Benton would never say so outright, so that he could deny it later if anything went wrong, but she knew it, Rafter knew it, and Philip did too.

She turned, facing Philip, who had dropped back into the leather chair behind his desk and was watching events unfold with a stunned expression. When he looked up at her, she said softly, "Harry would be horrified to see what you've become."

"Disloyalty such as yours," he snapped back, "was a cardinal sin in dear old Dad's book, as you well know." But for the first time in her memory, his gaze slid guiltily away.

This then was how he would live with her murder, by rationalizing that she'd brought it on with her own disloyalty.

Sam looked past Philip to the corner where the camera lens was concealed in hunt scene wallpaper. It would be on, of course. Philip recorded everything on the theory that one never knew ahead of time what might be revealed. He disposed of unwanted video later. The only real question was whether his cronies knew they were on camera.

When Benton and Pruitt finished their powwow, Benton had Pruitt's gun in hand. Pruitt crossed the room to Rafter and used Rafter's belt to bind his hands behind him.

Coolly, Rafter assessed Benton while Pruitt cinched the belt tight. "Are you sure about all this, Benton? Maybe you're the one being set up to take the fall. Because someone's going to. This has gotten too big, too many people know, for it to evaporate."

Sam knew that he was bluffing, at least in part, stringing Benton along, trying to sow seeds of doubt to force a mistake. Because without the wire, even their little insurance policy was crippled.

Sam heard a creak from behind the bookshelves and stared at the ornate mirror framed by bookcases. Was someone watching from the little cell behind? *Is that you, Robbie?*

The bouncer had returned and confirmed that the patio was clear of potential witnesses. They were evidently to leave through the library's exterior door and cross about twenty feet of patio to Rafter's car. While Benton was engaged with issuing final instructions to his men, Rafter leaned close and whispered to Sam, "Wait here."

Perplexed, Sam watched him approach Philip. Anticipating an attack despite Rafter's incapacity, Philip raised his hands, then lowered them when Rafter murmured something to him. Sam couldn't hear what was said except for Rafter's low parting words as he moved away. "Choose your poison, Wentworth."

What was that all about? But Rafter glanced away from the questions in her eyes. Whatever he'd said had gotten to Philip. His face was now ashen and perspiration beaded his upper lip as he paced the safe oasis behind his desk like a trapped animal.

When Benton broke huddle and his men began moving Sam and Rafter toward the patio doors, Philip stopped his frantic pacing. "Wait! Let them go, Randall."

Benton drilled an impatient look at Philip. "That's what I'm doing."

"Then do it without the escort." To Sam's astonishment, Philip moved to block her from Benton's men, shielding her.

"You know we can't do that." Benton's soft voice was threaded with steel.

"They have no evidence of anything. We haven't done anything wrong. If they become a problem, we deal with it then."

"They already are a problem, Philip. Now move out of the way."

"What does *he* say about this?" Philip asked.

Sam's mind frantically cast around, trying to figure out what Philip was up to and who this "he" was. Robbie O'Neal? Governor Graham?

"It's his plan," Benton snapped, losing patience. "Move aside now, Philip, before you get hurt." He nodded to Pruitt, who drew his pistol and aimed it at Philip.

"You don't understand," Philip wailed, staring in horror at the weapon in Pruitt's hand. "I can't let you murder her. She's my sister, dammit!"

Sam dimly registered Rafter's shock at Philip's revelation, but was riveted by the horror being played out in front of her eyes. Benton had to be bluffing. They wouldn't shoot Philip, would they? He was one of their own. But so had been Marty Davis.

"You crazy fool. Did you think we didn't all know that?" Benton eyed him with contempt. "It didn't stop you from making her take a fall for you before."

"I didn't murder her!"

Benton's icy gaze flicked to Pruitt. "Do it."

Pruitt fired while Philip was still shouting, "No!"

The silenced gun hissed like a deadly snake and struck Philip in the leg. He fell in howling agony, clutching his lower leg. Blood oozed crimson between his fingers.

Shocked, Sam automatically began to kneel next to him. Pruitt jerked her upright and shoved her outside onto the cement patio behind Rafter and the bouncer. Benton brought up the rear. Sam heard him say to Philip, "I'll be right back. Don't fret, you'll come out of this smelling like a rose."

The rear lights had been turned off, but the full moon reflected off the white cement, dimly illuminating the area. Beyond the patio, shrubs and trees were veiled in deeper shadows.

Suddenly they were caught in converging beams of high-intensity light. One second they were trudging along in the dark, the next blinded by light. Sam stumbled when Pruitt's entire body jerked. He abruptly let go of her arm.

"State Police. Freeze!" a disembodied voice barked from the shrubbery.

They were the sweetest words imaginable. Sam offered up a huge thank-you to the heavens. Their insurance policy was paying dividends after all.

"Throw down your weapons and raise your hands where we can see them."

After a charged moment, Pruitt and the bouncer, understanding that they'd lost, obediently tossed down their weapons and raised their hands. Pruitt's pistol landed almost at Sam's feet. The bouncer automatically assumed the captive position, linking his hands behind his head. For guys like him, doing time was an occupational hazard. They knew when to cut their losses.

Sam's relief was short-lived. After a stunned second of inaction, Benton, trailing the four, scooped up Pruitt's gun and grabbed her from behind. Using her body as a shield, he began inching backward toward the library door. Sam's heart missed a few beats, then thundered into overdrive. Stiff with horror, she stumbled on wooden legs. Benton roughly yanked her against him.

"No, please stop," she stammered.

From the other side of the blinding light, a trooper called out a warning for Benton to drop the gun. Sam braced for a barrage of bullets from both sides.

"Let her go, Benton." Slowly, Rafter turned to face them and took a small step forward. He could do nothing against a gun, particularly with his hands tied behind his back, but that might not stop him from trying.

Benton aimed the pistol at Rafter, and Sam was terrified he meant to shoot. "Nick, no!" she pleaded.

Rafter risked another cautious step in their direction. "It's over, Benton. We had backup for our backup because we weren't sure how far your tentacles went."

Benton jerked Sam tighter and inched closer to the library door behind. "You're crazy. I don't know what you're talking about. We caught you rifling the senator's files."

Sam made out shadowy figures emerging from the dark, handguns trained on Benton, and her.

"Let her go," Rafter coaxed softly. "You can tell your story to the authorities. You can hire the best lawyers. This only makes you look more guilty."

Benton was breathing hard. Short, harsh pants rasped in Sam's ear. The arm around her eased a fraction, and Sam sensed his indecision. But the gun at her side was still aimed at Rafter. She hastily tried to marshal her wits.

This was when Benton was at his most dangerous and impulsive. He understood that he had lost. He was probably glimpsing the horrors ahead. He could go meekly or he might decide to go down in a blaze of bullets, taking along as many of them as he could. Starting with Nick.

Trying not to telegraph her intent, Sam burst into action, kicking backward at Benton's shins and grabbing for the pistol at the same time. Benton jerked the pistol away from her, and it discharged with another hissing pop. Pruitt went down screaming.

With a roar, Rafter charged across the few feet separating them and shoulder-butted Benton in the solar plexus. They both landed with sickening thuds on the hard patio. The pistol skittered harmlessly across the cement.

Sam scrambled over to Rafter as Agent Josh Foley and two state troopers descended on Benton and his men. "You okay?" she asked, helping him sit up.

"Just bruised." He looked her over. "You?"

"Fine." Trying to catch her breath, Sam scanned the building's rear façade, searching for signs of activity, witnesses, she wasn't sure what. Philip had made it as far as his chair and was watching the scene unfold outside, his face twisted in a grimace of pain. Why had he taken a bullet for her? She put the question aside for later. Movement from the next room caught her eye. The edge of a curtain wavered as someone retreated from view. If someone had watched from the hidden cell behind the mirror, he would have entered via that room.

"About time you showed up, Foley," Rafter was saying. "Sam, would you get this belt off me."

"Your wires weren't transmitting. We saw the surveillance van leave and were debating what to do and watching for you to come out when we saw the big guy here bring your car around."

In short order, Foley and associates had Benton and the bouncer in handcuffs. They had their hands full between attending to Pruitt, keeping an eye on the other two, and calling for reinforcements and ambulances.

Sam knew what she had to do. A sense of urgency propelled her across the patio toward the utility entrance off the kitchen.

"Sam! Stop! What are you doing?" Rafter called after her. As she stole inside, she heard him bellow, "Someone get this damn belt off my hands!"

CHAPTER 23

The rear corridor was deserted. Sam could hear the muffled clatter of dishes from the kitchen as the caterers cleaned up, unaware of the unfolding drama outside or that their routine was about to be shattered.

Sam dashed up the narrow back stairs. Philip's suite was located here, overlooking the patio and Reeds Lake. She stopped in the open door to his sitting room. Empty. Silently, she padded across thick carpet. This had been Harry's domain. She stopped to listen at what appeared to be a closet door. Years ago, she and Billy had privately dubbed the hidden room "spy central." It was sandwiched between Philip's bedroom and sitting room. All the wires led here.

Hearing nothing but the low hum of electronic equipment, Sam nudged open the door and slipped inside. The room was narrow and about eight feet long, with a bank of video monitors dominating the long wall. Most were active, a few dark. They were motion activated to save on tape. Philip had not upgraded to digital, Sam noted, though he had expanded the areas of coverage since Harry's time. A monitor sprang to life as Sam watched, showing Rafter dashing inside downstairs and then disappearing from view.

Because the room was tucked lengthwise behind a shallow closet, Sam didn't spot Marie Wentworth at the far end until she'd stepped fully inside and then past the corner of a metal storage cabinet.

Marie stood in front of the screen monitoring Philip's library office. When she saw Sam, she unloaded the tape from the VCR underneath. "Samantha, I thought you might come. I blame you for thees catastrophe." Marie turned to the opposite counter where Sam knew she could erase the tape with a few quick swipes across the magnetic tape eraser.

"Don't do it." Sam held up her hands, not daring to move for fear of precipitating the very action she wanted to prevent.

Marie hesitated with the tape hovering over the eraser. "I have to. I'm his mother."

"If you're trying to protect Philip, don't destroy that tape. You were up here watching, weren't you?" Marie didn't deny it. Sam figured that if Marie had absolutely decided that destroying the tape would be best for Philip, she would already have done it. "Then you know the tape shows that he tried to stop Benton from having us killed. That tape will help him."

"But it links heem to Benton and those other devils," Marie objected. But she was listening, and she now clutched the tape to her chest.

"It may," Sam conceded. "I'm sorry. I never wanted to hurt any of you. But they threatened me and others. They killed Marty Davis."

"He was scum," Marie sniffed.

"But I'm not and neither is Rafter, or Hattie

Christiansen. Where would it end? Harry would never have approved of this. You know that. You also have to know that Philip's days in office are numbered whether you destroy the tape or not."

"Philip can find a way out. He always does." But Marie sounded less certain.

"Not this time." Sam shook her head, and didn't sugarcoat the likely scenario. "The feds and the state will launch a massive investigation. One of Benton's men will cut a deal. The only issue is whether Philip does jail time or not. That tape shows he isn't a murderer. It shows him doing everything he can to stop it."

"He risked his life for you," Marie mused, watching Philip on the monitor. She appeared almost as surprised by that as Sam was.

"I know. I'm not sure I understand why."

"Don't hate heem for what he said about your mother."

"How did you know?" Marie glanced over Sam's shoulder at another screen, confirming Sam's instant suspicion. Several monitors had been silently flickering on and off as staff and guests moved about downstairs activating motion sensors. No audio. Marie evidently had tuned out all but the library.

On the conservatory monitor, Pushy Pusch's red hair stood out amid the foliage. Sam's eyes widened when she realized she was seeing Pushy dispensing noncash favors on a high-ranking and very married state legislator, who was lounging on a bench with his pants inelegantly tangled around his ankles. And the entire X-rated exchange was being caught on tape.

Embarrassed for them, Sam turned away. "So you heard everything."

Marie nodded. "Try to understand heem. Harry

was hard. He had such high hopes for Philip. But you, he loved and spoiled like a doting *grandpère*, and Philip resented you for it."

But Philip was an adult and I was a needy child, Sam wanted to scream. Harry had practiced the sort of benign neglect one might expect of a grandfather but not a father. He would send money to Rosalind and never bother to check that Sam was okay. Yes, he had doted on her when she was occasionally around, but those times had been small islands of feast amid a sea of famine.

Sam looked up. "Was it true? What Philip said about my mother?"

"Yes. Harry paid her to have you. I told heem he risked his career, but . . ." She lifted a shoulder and smiled sadly. "You are more like heem than Philip. He loved you. I tried to love you, too, but it was difficult under the circumstances."

Sam struggled to pull herself together. The truth about Rosalind stung even after all these years, but was hardly a surprise, and the present required her full attention. "About the tape . . ."

"If I give it to you, you will promise to help Philip? You know these people. You can tell them he didn't know what the others planned to do to you."

"I promise," Sam said and meant it. She owed him for trying to save her. She didn't understand it, but the action itself was enough. She would do what she could for him.

Marie nodded, eyes dulled with defeat but head still proudly erect as she stepped forward and handed Sam the tape. Glancing at the conservatory monitor, she observed, "Is a good way to keep the troops in line," demonstrating yet again that she was a blue-blooded elitist to the core. "Even that crazy little federal prosecutor use."

Sam stilled. "Robbie O'Neal? He knows about the tapes? This room?"

"Not the room. But Philip gave heem a tape two years ago in return for a favor." Marie's shrewd gaze swept over the monitors. "Sometimes I watch here when certain people come. Is useful."

Sam scanned the monitors. *Where are you, Robbie?*

"I told Philip not to trust heem. He's dangerous because he thinks he's on mission from God."

"Your son got an excellent return on that investment, Mrs. Wentworth."

Sam's stomach lurched sickeningly at the sound of Robbie's voice behind her. He stood in the doorway around the short corner leg of the cramped room. Thoughts racing, she realized that he wouldn't have a clear view down the length of the room to Marie. She made a split-second decision, slipping the library tape back to a startled Marie and simultaneously grabbing another from a stack on the counter before turning around as Robbie stepped farther into the room.

He had a small pistol in his hand, and was staring in awe at the bank of monitors, his gaze lingering longest on the X-rated feature playing on the conservatory monitor. "I knew Philip had to have a surveillance system—I've been looking for this room for years—but I had no idea . . . The whole place is wired."

Unfortunately not enough of the upstairs, Sam thought, or they would have had advance notice of Robbie's approach. She gauged his degree of distraction, wondering whether she should try to jump him. She'd barely formed the idea when he jabbed the pistol at her. "Don't even consider it."

He directed them out into the sitting room, Sam first and then Marie, who'd had the presence of mind to tuck the tape out of sight under her suit jacket. Through the open window, Sam could hear the glorious wail of distant sirens. In minutes, the place would be swarming with police and agents. But even minutes might be too late.

When Sam looked into Robbie's glittering black eyes, she read her own fate. He did not intend to leave witnesses behind. She saw no hesitation, no apology, only the same terrifying evangelical fervor with which he daily blasted criminal transgressors.

"Let Mrs. Wentworth go," Sam said to him unsteadily. "You don't need her."

Robbie inclined his head in agreement. "Wait in there until I come for you." He waved Marie to Philip's bedroom. "Don't leave."

Marie blinked at him, then drew herself up to her full, five-foot height. "I don't take orders from the likes of you," she sniffed. "Especially not in my own home."

Robbie aimed a fiery glare in Marie's direction. "You better change your mind about that fast if you want my help getting your son out of this mess."

Marie retreated in a huff, and Robbie returned his attention to Sam. "The tape." He held out his hand.

Sam held tight to it, frantic for time. *Keep him talking,* she thought. "What, no attempt to continue the charade? I'm shocked."

Robbie hitched a shoulder. "You recognized me in the photo."

"So it *was* you behind the mirror."

"I guessed years ago from the look of it that it was two-way. Finding that little hidey-hole was easy. Unlike this place." He flicked a glance at the door to spy central. "Now the tape."

"Why should I give it to you? The way I figure it, I've got about the same odds of living either way."

"Because one way could be considerably more painful," he snapped, losing patience with her. He raised the gun to her upper chest, and Sam knew with terrifying certainty that time had run out. He'd evidently decided it would be easier to kill her where she stood and make his story fit the scene than to make the scene fit whatever story he already had in mind.

"No, don't!" Sam cringed, waiting for an explosion of pain. After a horrifying second, she realized that she'd won a brief reprieve. "Here," she croaked. Her hand shook uncontrollably as she held out the tape and took a jerky step toward him.

The sirens were loud now as a convoy of emergency vehicles screamed their way through the neighborhood. They camouflaged Rafter's charge down the hallway as he systematically searched the house for her. Sam saw him skid to a halt in the open doorway, and had never been more selfishly relieved or scared to see anyone in her entire life. He came in slowly, on alert, taking in the gun in Robbie's hand and the tape in hers.

"Come in, Nick," Robbie calmly invited. "I caught Samantha and Mrs. Wentworth up here destroying evidence. It seems Samantha has managed to make fools of us again. The only question is who in the FBI is the mole. Because only one of their own could have sent our surveillance unit packing."

Sam listened in stunned amazement as Robbie spun a remarkably credible web of lies to account for what had gone wrong. It was preposterous! Did he really think he could sell it?

Rafter's stony gaze swiveled to Sam.

"Nick?" When he said nothing, she looked at him in shock. "My God, you can't possibly believe that crap!" Again he said nothing, and she frantically rushed on. "He's the one in charge of it all. Can't you see that? He was a member of the frat! Or a recruit! There's a picture in the library . . ." But he merely continued to look at her with a closed, condemning expression. Devastated, Sam felt the room sway as the blood rushed from her head. "You know me. After everything we've . . . I—"

She stared at him in agony. *I love you,* she silently cried, feeling her heart breaking. *Don't do this to me. Not again!*

The wild hope that maybe, just maybe, they might have a future together flickered and died. Ridiculously, considering their already dire straits, the world seemed suddenly a grayer place.

"Get the tape, Nick," Robbie said, yanking her back to the moment. She saw a glint of satisfaction in his expression. He knew he'd won.

Rafter crossed the room to her. God, how could he be oblivious to the danger they were in? Fear pressed in, making it hard to breathe. She wanted to scream and run. Instead, she summoned the will to try again.

When he plucked the tape from her hand, she stared at him hard. "Don't be a fool a second time. He can't afford to let us leave this room alive. We know too much. Think, Rafter! How is it that the great Robbie O'Neal has been so good at rooting out corruption everywhere except here?" Sam gestured to the mansion around them. "And ask yourself why he let me off so easily two years ago? He's also one of the few people with the authority to dismiss that surveillance unit. Open your eyes! He's the link."

"Save it for your lawyer," Robbie snarled.

Rafter paused to look at her, his face in shadow

with the only lit lamp behind him. "If Robbie wanted us dead, he would have already done it."

He was right, she realized. Nothing was stopping Robbie from dropping them both where they stood. Then it clicked. "That's it," Sam said over the shriek of sirens. "You don't want us both dead, only me. Rafter is still of use to you because he's your biggest cheerleader. He'll help deflect suspicion from you," she rushed on as his plan became clear. "But you'll have to get him away from here fast so you can do your dirty deed." Even as the three of them stood locked in a tense triangle, sirens were being switched off emergency vehicles pulling up outside.

"The tape, Nick." Robbie waggled the fingers of his free hand, impatient with Rafter's lack of speed. "Now go get—"

Robbie's next order—the one Sam figured would send Rafter from the room so he couldn't witness her execution—was cut short when Rafter fumbled the tape exchange and it fell into the thick cream carpet at Robbie's feet. They both reached down. But instead of going for the tape, Rafter whipped the gun from Robbie's distracted grasp and quickly stepped out of reach with it.

Robbie snapped upright, narrowed gaze darting from the lowered pistol in Rafter's grip to his unreadable expression. "No," he said slowly, "you're going to go downstairs and bring back whoever is in charge down there while I stay here with her."

Sam, now every bit as uncertain as Robbie which way Rafter leaned, tried to say something, anything to sway him, but found that, beyond managing to utter a guttural "No!" to Robbie's plan, rational thought and composure had completely deserted her.

"You all right, Sam?" Rafter darted a glance in her direction, but his focus was on Robbie.

She gave a jerky nod. A lie. She thought she now understood how Alice felt falling down the rabbit hole. The floor seemed to have dropped away beneath her and she couldn't get her balance. Teetering on the verge of hysteria, she was still uncertain what Rafter was thinking.

Robbie was looking increasingly desperate as the seconds ticked by. Through the open window came sounds of people rushing about and urgent, low-pitched voices.

"Nick—" Trying to reassert his authority, Robbie took a step toward Rafter and reached for the gun.

At last, reluctantly, Rafter raised it to take unambiguous aim at Robbie's chest. "That's far enough. We'll wait here for our backup."

Understanding dawned on Robbie's face. "So that's how it is. You don't know what you're doing. You're making a terrible mistake. But it's not too late," he rasped urgently. "We can still help each other."

"So you really are part of the cabal." Rafter's shoulders dropped under the weight of his disillusionment.

"Cabal?" Robbie snorted. "There never was a cabal. We helped each other achieve our goals when we could. Nothing wrong with that. And look at the good I've been able to do."

"By climbing into bed with the enemy? What happened to you?"

"Grow up! It's the way the world works. Compromise is a fact of life necessary to make real gains. It takes a strong man to accept that and move on."

"So that's how you justify it? You cast yourself as the great savior making tough decisions for the greater good? Because from where I'm standing, all I see is a man willing to deal with the devil to advance his own agenda."

"Don't you dare judge me!" Robbie exploded, taking a threatening step forward. His presence always seemed deceptively large for his slight stature and even more so when riled. "Every war has collateral damage. I learned that in the jungles of 'Nam. Right and wrong are relative."

For Sam, much of the exchange that followed passed in an unreal blur. Now that her brain registered that the danger had passed and she had a future again, she couldn't hold it together any longer. She made an effort to focus on what Robbie said, knowing it could be evidence against him, but her nerves had been stretched tight for so long that now her brain simply wanted to shut down. Watching Robbie's tirade as if from a great distance, she thought he might charge and vaguely expected to see him cut down. But then, shaking with the force of his rage, he held his ground.

"Who are you to judge me?" He jabbed a finger at Rafter. "At the first opportunity, you turned your back on the fight and took a cushy judgeship. I've spent my life fighting criminals and corruption."

"Except among your own friends." Rafter looked ashen. He'd devoted years of his life to carrying out the policies of this man, his former mentor.

"Not friends. They've been my informants. Eventually they'll get what they deserve. I'll see to it."

Amazed, Rafter shook his head as if finally seeing Robbie clearly. "You think you're still going to wiggle out of this."

"Of course. I've done nothing wrong." Robbie looked surprised that Nick considered any other outcome a possibility. He believed his own spin. It was his blind spot, and in that instant, Sam guessed that it would be his Achilles' heel as well.

They waited until Agent Foley and his troopers found them. Then all, including Marie, were herded downstairs and outside into the brightly lit chaos of the patio. The place was crawling with uniformed and plainclothes personnel. Medics attended to Philip and Pruitt while agents and police officers conferred and bustled about, casting huge shadows in the stark light glaring from portable lights hurriedly being set up around the perimeter.

Rafter had his arm cinched tight around Sam's waist, and he kept asking if she was okay. In a daze, Sam made the appropriate responses at approximately the right places, but inside she felt numb and she couldn't stop shaking.

"You believed him, didn't you?" she asked through chattering teeth. "For a while you thought it was me instead of Robbie."

"No! I realized it was almost certainly Robbie in the library."

"But you had doubts. For a second you thought I'd betrayed you again." She watched Philip being loaded into an ambulance in the drive. From his side, Marie glanced up and met Sam's gaze, holding it across the distance, not to include Sam in the family moment, never that, but to remind her of her promise to help Philip. Marie had already fulfilled her end of the bargain; she'd turned the real tape over to Agent Foley upstairs. Sam nodded once.

"Sam—" Rafter caught her hand. But before he could continue, Sandy Cotey, Robbie's new first assistant, bustled over.

"Hard to believe," she muttered wearily when she'd sent an officer on his way. "This morning when we talked, I never dreamed it would actually come to this."

Rafter gave her a commiserating look. "Don't beat yourself up over it. We all believed in him."

Robbie had been hustled directly to a black sedan that sat within view on the jammed drive. They could hear him bellowing at the recently arrived FBI chief.

Sandy's sharp gaze settled on Sam. "Not all, thank God." Sandy rubbed her forehead, studying Sam closely. "I'll have Foley get you out of here posthaste." Then to both, she added, "Sorry, guys, but I have to split you up. Everything goes by the book from here on."

"Just give us one minute," Rafter insisted. "I promise that what I have to say to Sam is completely unrelated to this case."

Sandy sighed, but held firm. "Later. You know it's the appearance of you two talking that the defense can seize on."

She signaled to Agent Foley, and the next thing Sam knew he was leading her over to another sedan and bundling her into the rear seat.

"Sam!" Rafter called out as she was halfway inside. She stopped and looked back. Sandy had a hand on his arm to keep him from coming after her. "He didn't get to me upstairs. I had to play along. You've got to believe me. If he'd been talking about anyone else . . ." Nick shook his head, his anguished eyes beseeching her to believe him. "But not you. Not anymore."

His face looked haggard and deathly white in the harsh glare of the crime scene lights. It startled her. He was as desperate for her trust and faith as she'd been for his upstairs with Robbie. Just like her, she saw, surfacing from her daze.

"I know," she croaked, craning to see him past Foley's chest. "I do believe you." But her voice was drowned out by the noisy bustle around them, and then Foley slammed the door shut.

Through the rear window as the car began to creep forward, she watched him say something to Sandy, scowling as he shook off her restraining hand. At the same time, her reawakened brain processed why Rafter, ordinarily a private person, was frantic to communicate with her in the chaos of the crime scene: There might not be any other chance in the foreseeable future. In a prosecution of this magnitude, witnesses would be kept apart as much as possible. So much for her instantly revived hope that they might still have a chance together, she thought in a burst of emotion.

Oh, hell. Sam closed her eyes. She had to stop torturing herself by continually resuscitating that delusional fantasy. Drained, overemotional where before she had been numb, she squeezed her eyes shut and sucked in a deep breath.

"Well, well," Agent Foley murmured from the front seat as they inched down the congested drive behind Philip's ambulance. "Look what else got caught up in the net."

Sam opened her eyes to see a squawking, disheveled Pushy Pusch and her outraged companion being unceremoniously hustled out the front door of the mansion.

"You did good back there," Foley said, glancing at her in the rearview mirror. When she said nothing, he added, "We won."

"Yes, we won," Sam agreed, but the words rang hollow, and at the moment her only thoughts were for the man she loved not wisely, but hopelessly, and when she would see him again.

CHAPTER 24

Rumblings of a looming political scandal of vast proportions rocked weekend newsrooms the next morning. A multiagency governmental task force, hastily assembled to coordinate the investigation, had little success in keeping a lid on the rumors. Across the state and beyond, whispered speculation grew into media frenzy as the story broke over the ensuing days and weeks.

Industrialist Randall Benton and two of his aides were arrested on weapons charges. More charges were expected. In connection, Senator Philip Wentworth, recovering from a bullet wound to the leg, became the subject of a grand jury investigation and had gone into seclusion to avoid voracious reporters. U.S Attorney Robbie O'Neal was suspended from his duties while the task force also investigated his role in events at the Wentworth mansion that night, leaving First Assistant Sandy Cotey temporarily in charge. Speculation ran rampant that other top officials might also soon be ensnared in an emerging scandal of unprecedented magnitude in state history.

Scrambling for dirt behind official news releases, the frenzied press soon exhausted the ranks of the catering staff who'd worked the fund-raiser and the hospital staff who'd treated Pruitt and Wentworth. The ones they really wanted were the law clerk, Samantha Parker, and Judge Nick Rafter. But Sam had been whisked away to a safe house and Nick spent most of his time in the company of an FBI-issued bodyguard, safely cloistered in his chambers within the State Office Building—impenetrable post-September 11—or in his secure, high-rise apartment building.

In an attempt to avoid the desolation that would otherwise steal over him whenever he had time for reflection, Nick threw himself into a bottomless pit of work. But he couldn't always be working, and when he surfaced, he was miserable. The unfinished business with Sam left him in purgatory. He missed her dreadfully and was plagued by nightmares in which he raced into the senator's sitting room just as Robbie pulled the trigger, too late to save her.

He tortured himself with self-recriminations. Why hadn't he put it together for himself sooner? Why hadn't he seen Robbie for who he was? Sam had. It was all there, small clues accumulating over the years, if he'd only been willing to see past his prejudices.

If Sam hadn't insisted on bringing in Sandy Cotey and Josh Foley as added insurance . . . *God!* He couldn't bear thinking about it.

Nick was also devastated that Sam had opted to run away without a word. When he'd learned early Sunday morning upon emerging from hours of initial debriefing that Sam had already been spirited away, he stormed into Sandy's office, not caring that she was in the midst of an emergency meeting with several of Nick's own former assistants.

"Where is she?" he demanded, irrationally incensed with all of them, but mostly with Sandy. "How could you send her off like that! You knew I wanted to talk to her."

Sandy raised her hands to calm him down, which only infuriated him more. "Nick, it was her idea," she said bluntly. "She was anxious to get away before the press frenzy began. Think how bad this is going to be for her when they learn that she's the senator's half-sister."

"Fine. Just tell me where she is."

"I can't." At his murderous look she continued helplessly, "I don't know. Agent Foley handled it."

But Foley proved no more forthcoming. "I can't tell you," he insisted. "It could hurt our case."

"For Christ's sake, I'm not going to talk to her about the damn case! You can't keep her under house arrest—" He stopped mid-rant and eyed the agent with suspicion. "Or is that what you want? Keep the field clear so you have a shot at her."

Color spread up over Foley's face but he didn't take the bait, and in truth Nick felt foolish as soon as he said it.

"Take it easy. She's not under house arrest." Foley met Nick's glare with something that looked irritatingly like pity. "She can call you if she wants to. No one's stopping her. But I don't get the feeling she wants to talk much to anyone right now."

Meaning him, Nick thought, torturing himself with brutal honesty. He was haunted by the look of betrayal on Sam's face when she'd thought he believed Robbie. For her it must have been a horrible replay of his colossal betrayal two years ago.

Then to have her spirited away before he had a chance to explain and make it right . . . Nick's frustration was beyond expression.

He tried to reassure himself that given time she would see why he'd done it; she was too quick not to. But he wasn't at all confident she could forgive him the rest. He'd torpedoed her career, all the while convincing himself that she was getting what she deserved. How could he expect her to put that aside? Deep in his guilt-stricken soul, he was miserably unsure she even should.

Meanwhile, Sam was faring no better than Nick. September dragged out into the longest four weeks of her life. Foley set her up in an off-season beach rental hidden in wooded dunes along Lake Michigan, convenient to the Stanley Care Center. With her, he installed an ambitious young FBI agent introduced only as Carla, last name not offered. Suspecting that the first was phony, Sam didn't ask for a last. Her new housemate was energetic, businesslike, and bored with an assignment that didn't test anything beyond her stone-skipping skill. Sam understood; the tedium and frustration of a seemingly endless wait on the sidelines weighed on her, too. She longed to go home.

She had nothing to do except follow news of the scandal and walk the deserted beach. Judge Hall had reluctantly declined her offer to finish off the last of Matthew's opinions from her remote location. His sensitive political antenna warned him of possible public scrutiny and controversy should the rampaging media learn of the arrangement. That spelled the end of Sam's paycheck.

She scrambled to find a way to tap into Camille's

home equity to temporarily cover her nursing home bill, only to learn that the outstanding debt plus the next three months' expenses had been paid in full, anonymously. Sam detected Marie Wentworth's deft hand behind the curtain. She figured the money was both gift and reminder of her promise to aid Philip, made anonymously of course to avoid public misconceptions of payoffs and the like.

During these weeks, Sam frequently visited Camille. She had been clandestinely moved to another building at the center under an assumed name and with an FBI-trained private nurse, at Sam's insistence in case the press or a cabal deputy came calling. Now that the immediate danger to Sam had subsided, Camille seemed to take perverse enjoyment in the cloak-and-dagger break in routine. She followed news of Philip's downfall with less grief than Sam had anticipated, her remorse eased by his membership in a brotherhood that had intended to murder Sam.

Surprisingly, most in the press were treating Philip, the politician, more sympathetically than either Benton or O'Neal. This was due, Sam thought, to Philip's veteran spin-handlers brilliantly playing up that he'd incurred his injury while protecting Sam from Benton, a fact she, too, had stressed during her debriefing. Philip's own spokesperson had released the sensational information that Sam was Philip's half-sister. That prompted a mad rush of renewed digging into her background.

At first she was shocked to turn on the TV and see her own face plastered across the screen. There were pictures from years ago of her with Harry and Billy and Philip, pictures that could have come only from the Wentworths. Now, when Philip had seriously muddied the name, he apparently wanted to make her appear an accepted member of the family—one who'd been protected from the media rather than hidden.

"The press is fascinated with you," Carla had commented, riveted to the story in turn. Together they were in danger of becoming worse news junkies than Camille. "They already have money, murder, sex, and corruption in high places. You're the mystery woman. The public is hooked. The press loves it."

"And poor Pushy fills the sex angle," Sam noted, feeling a pang of sympathy for her. The press had gotten wind of Pushy's taped, post-fund-raiser tryst with the state representative and been merciless in trotting out stories of both participants' past indiscretions. Coverage of the sex scandal hadn't eased until a new development pushed it from center stage: Investigators located Rachel Holtz's body behind the old Sigma fraternity house in Harbour Grace.

As the days and weeks passed, Sam sometimes wondered why she'd agreed to this interminable exile. At the time, distancing herself from both Rafter and the looming media horror had seemed a good idea, but she'd been in shock and forgotten that waiting in the wings didn't suit her. She told herself that she was not glued to the TV largely in hopes of catching a glimpse of Rafter, but she was lying and knew it.

She missed seeing him every day, even if it was only to spar. She missed making love to him. She missed . . . him.

He could get under her skin more easily than anyone, yet she longed for him, physically ached in a way she never had for any man. And that was exactly why she couldn't afford to weaken and call him. Every second she spent with him carried the very real danger of making her fall more hopelessly in love. She was miserably aware that they had about as much chance making a go of a real long-term relationship as did Will and Grace.

Better to chop him out of her life now before she grew terminal. But sometimes it felt as though she'd accidentally severed a major artery in the process. And she was haunted by visions of Rafter moving on to other women.

Kat was less than impressed with Sam's decision to sever ties with Rafter. "So this is what . . . a pre-emptive strike?" she asked, munching an apple. In late September, Carla had finally relented and let them meet for a picnic lunch at a quiet park a safe distance from their hideout. "I tell you he called again asking if I knew where you were, and you get all uptight about even talking to him."

Sam glanced at Kat, wondering whether she'd guessed that something beyond purely professional had transpired between her and Rafter. Her ability to read people rivaled his. "No, I just see no reason to maintain a connection now that we won't be working together anymore," Sam said with a shrug. "The past makes it awkward."

"Oh." Kat put aside the apple and eyed Sam. "Because for a minute there I was thinking that maybe you're more in love with Nick now than you were back then and that maybe it was about time you did something about it."

"I loved Brian!" Sam protested, cringing away from the other part of Kat's revelation, the part about Rafter, because, if true, that might mean it was already too late, already terminal.

"Maybe you loved Nick more."

Upon her return to the cottage, dire news from the Stanley Care Center pushed Kat's troubling conjecture from Sam's head. She and Carla rushed over to find that Camille was suffering from pneumonia, a nasty complication of her illness resulting from the difficulty she had swallowing. After only a day not seeing her, Sam was horrified at how bad she looked, thin and dreadfully weak, rarely alert, and barely able to communicate when she was.

Frantic with worry, Sam badgered the doctors to do something more. To her dismay, they refused to take an aggressive approach because Camille had signed a living will requesting that no extraordinary measures be taken.

Days ran together as Sam watched Camille slip away. She held her frail hand and talked about anything she could think of. Sometimes Camille would make a whispered response, reassuring Sam that she was still there. At first, Sam was beside herself and could barely look at her without crying, and since she rarely left Camille's bedside, her eyes were constantly red. But after a while, when all hope faded, Sam prayed that she would go quickly with no more pain.

Camille felt Sam's hand in hers—strong and warm like its owner. She opened her eyes to see this daughter of her heart but could see nothing. It didn't matter. Camille could picture Sam in her mind's eye—beautiful like Rosalind but nothing like her inside. Harry's daughter in spirit.

Camille regretted it had taken her so long to understand that. Regretted the wasted years. Regretted most that her love had been tempered by nagging jealousy of Rosalind and fear that Sam would turn out like the woman she so resembled. She'd been too hurt, too angry with Rosalind for seducing

Harry, to recognize Sam as the most precious of gifts.

Ah, Sam, what have I done to you? Can you ever forgive me?

She wished she could tell her how proud she was of her and how much she loved her. But when she tried to talk, her mouth wouldn't form the words. All that came out were nasty, animal-sounding noises that made her panic and scream inside. Sam's computer couldn't help in the end.

Sam must have sensed her distress. Camille felt her stroke her forehead, heard her murmur soothing words, say something to another person in the room. Their voices faded and she floated off into that other place again where Harry waited.

At Camille's moan, Sam lifted her head from their clasped hands. "It's okay. I'm here with you," she murmured. *Don't leave me!* she selfishly wanted to wail and clenched her teeth to hold it back.

Tears streamed down her face. She'd cried buckets of them already, but still they came. Camille's doctor wanted to give Sam something to make her sleep, but she refused to leave as long as Camille clung to life. There would be lots of time to sleep later.

She stroked Camille's forehead, letting her know she was there, that someone cared. "I love you," she murmured.

Camille struggled to say something. Small whispery noises came out. Then, "forgive me." It was weak and unexpected. For a second, Sam thought she'd imagined it. Camille squeezed her hand.

Sam's face crumpled and great silent sobs wracked her shoulders. "Oh, Camille," she cried, "there's nothing to forgive. You took me in and loved me when I had no one else. You saved me."

In early October, Nick broke his mostly self-imposed seclusion to attend the long delayed reception in his honor marking his appointment to the court. He didn't feel much like celebrating anything, but Liz had already rescheduled it twice; she'd have his head if he asked her to do it again. And his parents wanted an excuse to come north to see for themselves that he was all right. He tried to keep the whole thing small and quiet. That proved impossible. It seemed that everyone invited, plus some who weren't, queued up between the potted palms in the jammed atrium of the Meijer Gardens pavilion to congratulate him and wish him well. The press, with their cameras and microphones, swarmed the garden entrance outside, giving the occasion more the feel of a pop-royalty crowning than a staid judicial ascension.

Howie Delany, his FBI-issued bodyguard, whispered between well-wishers, "Get used to it—you're an authentic hero. Not many of those around these days." Howie had been his near constant companion these last few weeks, stopping Nick from going crazy on more than one occasion. Tonight, as an added precaution until everyone was satisfied that all remnants of the cabal had been mopped up, two additional agents, comely Nicole and brawny Charlie, reinforced Howie.

From Nick's other side, Sandy Cotey surveyed a crowd comprised heavily of lawyers and offered a more cynical explanation. "They want you to remember them fondly next time they have a case before you."

Late in the evening, Brian Kingsley cornered

him by the bar. "I suppose you've heard that Sam's aunt died?" he said when the bartender moved out of earshot and for a moment they were alone.

Nick bristled. "She's been in touch with you?" he asked coldly, jealous that she'd contacted Brian and not him. *He* wanted to be the one to comfort her.

"Sam?" Brian shot him a quick, surprised look. "No. An obituary was in yesterday's paper."

"Any funeral notice?"

"No. Doubt anyone wanted to tip off the press in case they figure out Camille is Sam's aunt. But I'm sure Sandy Cotey or someone will tell you if you want to go."

"I wouldn't bet on it," Nick snarled, taking a generous belt of his malt whiskey.

He wondered how Sam was dealing with her aunt's death. God, he missed her. Distracted, he continued going through the motions of making small talk with those who approached. Everyone was too tactful to raise the one subject all secretly hoped Nick would discuss, but he didn't oblige and eventually they drifted away disappointed.

It was during one lull that Nick had an idea. Billy and Kat had known Camille. They would likely attend her funeral. If they really hadn't known Sam's location when he'd asked before, perhaps they did now.

Nick glanced at his watch. The Jungle Café would still be open. If he hurried, he might catch Billy or Kat.

The crowd was beginning to thin, but not fast enough to suit him. His mother, having finally gotten him to herself, was fussing at him worriedly. "Honey, you look awful. You're much too thin and pale. I think you must be pushing yourself too hard. Your sister says you do nothing but work."

Nick stopped her hand from feeling his brow for

fever. Giving it a pat, he smiled and agreed, "You're absolutely right, Mother. I do need a break, and I think I'm going to start taking it right now. So if you'll excuse me . . ." He glanced around for Howie, who stood propping up a potted fern a few discreet steps away. "You're on, partner. Time to rock and roll."

With police clearing a path, Howie at front guard, Nicole at his flank, and Charlie covering the rear, they ran the press gauntlet to a waiting sedan. He and Howie jumped in. "Jungle Café," he told the driver.

"You sure that was a good idea?" Kat worriedly asked Billy. Both watched Nick Rafter's heated exit after they'd refused to tell him where Sam was. His pale, drawn face brought to mind an angry ghost. "He's in love with her."

"Let him sweat." As the door swung shut in Nick's wake, Billy quoted softly, " 'Love's not Time's fool.' " He rose to lock up for the night. "Better for Sam in the long run to know whether he can go the distance. It would be a low blow if he turned out to be another flamer like Brian."

Nick was in a foul mood by the time he and Howie reached his apartment building. He was sure Kat and Billy knew Sam's location and had refused to tell him. They *had* revealed that Camille's funeral had been earlier in the day, so he suspected Sam was close by. "Let me out," he snapped before Howie could pull into the underground lot.

"Not a good idea, pal."

The night street beckoned—cool, dark, deserted. "I need a few minutes."

Resignation followed disapproval on Howie's face. "Ten, no more."

Red taillights disappeared under the building. Nick started walking east on the sidewalk. A car door creaked behind him, loud in the still silence, and he spun around. *Oh, hell.*

"Hello, Nick." Robbie O'Neal smiled wryly when Nick started backing away. He held up his hands to show he was unarmed. "Don't worry. My gunslinger days are over."

Nick's heart rate settled down, but he remained on full alert. When Robbie took a step to bridge their ten-foot chasm, Nick held up a hand. "Close enough." Robbie shrugged and stopped. "What are you doing here?"

"Finishing old business." When Nick said nothing, merely waited for him to get to the point, Robbie continued, "I want you to know that I didn't do it for money or for notches in my belt. Everything I did was for the good of my country."

"I believe you. I just can't agree that it was right."

Robbie scowled. "In case you haven't noticed, we're at war right here, right now, and not only with terrorists from abroad. We have plenty of home-grown evil. The bad guys outgun and outman us. Which is the greater evil, Nick, to use whatever resources you can get your hands on, even if they get a little dirty in the process, or to turn a fastidious nose up at them knowing innocent people will suffer because of your high scruples?"

"So you threw your lot in with the likes of Benton, Wentworth, and Davis."

"They served a useful purpose. It's easy to keep men with base goals in line."

"Not Matthew Christiansen."

"Never tried to with Matthew. I just let him carry on the good fight."

"Until the Benton Motors case."

"That was all Benton's doing. I told him no good would come of blackmailing Matthew, but Benton's a greedy bastard. He couldn't stand forking over big money to settle the case."

"And Marty Davis?"

"His time was up." Robbie waved that off.

Nick understood that Robbie's cryptic answer was all he would get on the subject of Davis's death. He was, in truth, astonished that Robbie was divulging anything at all when he knew everything he said would be admissible in a court of law.

"Rumor has it you're Washington's top choice to take my place," Robbie continued, turning the conversation in another surprising direction.

Nick was aware of the rumors. He'd even fielded feelers from Washington, though he thought them premature. Apparently in the current antipolitical climate, his nonpartisan status earned him points. "You're still U.S. attorney in this district," he noted carefully.

"Not for long."

Expecting an explosion of anger, Nick was caught more off guard by what Robbie said next than any of the rest.

"Take it, Nick. Continue the fight for me. You're wasting your talent as a judge. You can do that when you're old and gray."

For a spellbound moment, Nick watched his former mentor walk away and wondered if he'd ever fully understand him. Then he pulled his cell phone from his pocket and rang Sandy Cotey.

"You'd better move on Robbie ASAP. I think he just sang his swan song."

CHAPTER 25

The morning following Camille's simple graveside service, Sam listlessly roamed the cottage packing up her things to leave. Carla, sensing her need for privacy, had tactfully retreated to her bedroom to make phone calls to her superiors to discuss the need for new lodgings. She was upset that the security of their safe house had been breached yesterday by Kat and especially Billy, a Wentworth. Sam, though, had no intention of remaining in limbo now that Camille was gone. "Have you told her you intend to split?" Kat had asked yesterday.

Sam admitted she had not. "She would try to talk me out of it. I'll tell her tomorrow before you come back to get me."

Now, through the thin walls of the cottage, Sam could hear Carla still engaged on the phone. She glanced at her watch. Only nine. Kat wouldn't arrive until eleven. Packing her few things had taken hardly any time at all. She slumped in front of the TV for an update on the scandal, which showed discouragingly little sign of abating anytime soon. Almost daily there seemed to be some new de-

velopment that stoked the media fire, and today
proved no exception. But today's news was exactly
what she'd been hoping for in one form or another
for weeks. CNN was reporting that Benton's errand
boy, Simon Pruitt, had cut a deal with prosecutors
in exchange for his testimony against the others.
That meant her importance to the prosecution,
and hence to the cabal, just sank from leading lady
to chorus line.

Sam felt dizzy with relief. She'd just been handed
her life back. If only she knew what to do with it,
she thought with a pang. But for the first time in
days, her spirits lifted. Seconds later they plum-
meted when coverage turned to last night's reception honoring Rafter, and a huge picture flashed
across the screen of him leaving the Meijer Gardens
pavilion with a ravishing blonde.

Sam gave a sob of misery and switched off the
TV. Not wanting Carla to see her break down yet
again, she fled the cottage for the gray gloom of
the beach. She'd foreseen that he might eventually
move on to a new companion—but nothing had
prepared her for the pain of the reality.

For a moment she succumbed to the urge to
wallow in self-pity. She'd lost everything—Camille,
Nick, her job, even her freedom and privacy. She
felt alternately numb and miserable, off balance,
as if with Camille's death her world had lost its
alignment and seemed an alien place. But it was
this final loss of Rafter that hurt the most. No matter how many times she had told herself that there
was no potential for long-range happiness with him,
there had still been a minuscule glimmer of hope.

Slogging on through heavy sand across the
wide-open beach, shivering in the brisk October
wind, she tried to come to grips with her life. She
could get another job, she thought wearily, go any-

where now that Camille no longer tied her to the area. And she still had Kat and Billy. But staring out to the horizon over the cold, empty sea of choppy blue, her life seemed every bit as cold and lonely as the endless stretch in front of her.

Determined to walk off her despair, Sam set off on a hike up the deserted beach. She took grim pleasure in the blustery, moody day. A beautiful day would have mocked her. Tumultuous surf pounded at her bare feet, soaking the bottom of her jeans. A bracing wind stung her face. Gray clouds churned and boiled overhead. The trees lining the top ridge of the dunes were turning orange and already losing their leaves in anticipation of the winter ahead.

Nearly an hour later as Sam neared the cottage on her return, Kat waved across the distance and set out to meet her. "I've got great news," Kat called out as she puffed up. "You remember Sophie Somerset?"

Sam nodded. "Billy's friend at Madison Law School."

"Right. Well, she's trying to get in touch with you. They got the résumé you sent and want to interview you for a teaching position," Kat rushed on excitedly. "Trial practice, Billy thought." Kat's green eyes fairly danced. "I'll just bet that right about now the old guard over there are scrambling to jettison their good-ol'-boy image and distance themselves from the Madison Mafia before their good-ol'-boy asses are handed to them on a platter. What better way than to hire you?"

Sam tried not to get excited. It was only an interview, after all, but finally here was something worth pursuing. "They probably have a boatload of applicants."

"Maybe," Kat agreed, her smile widening, "but none who could give them great press for a change."

"Hard to believe something good could come of

all this." Sam glanced at her watch and sighed. "I'd better go up and tell Carla I'm leaving." But when she started for the cottage, Kat quickly sobered and caught the sleeve of her sweatshirt.

"Sam, I brought someone along who wants to talk to you. I hope it's okay." Sam followed Kat's nervous glance toward the cottage, where she spotted Rafter waiting and watching them. "He, ah, followed me in his car."

Sam felt her heart leap to her throat and the sand drop out from under her feet. For a crazy instant, she thought her longing for him had conjured up a ghost; even from a distance, he looked thinner than she remembered and haggard, dark hair blowing wildly across his pale forehead, making him look Heathcliff tragic in blue jeans and a leather bomber jacket.

"I can't talk to him," Sam warbled.

Kat darted an uncertain glance at her. "You've got to bite the bullet sooner or later if you're coming out of hiding. You might start by telling him you love him." Under her breath, Kat added, "Someone's got to go first."

Sam nervously blocked her out. Fortunately Rafter's slow progress across the sand gave her precious seconds to gather the remnants of her composure tightly together before he reached them. Kat mumbled something about checking in with Carla, then slipped away almost unnoticed by the other two whose gazes were locked on each other. Rafter said nothing, an odd expression on his face as if he were drinking her up after a long trek across a desert. Careful, Sam thought.

"What are you doing here?" she prompted in what she hoped was a steady voice.

He looked vaguely surprised by the question, and for a moment seemed to fumble for an answer.

Then he said, "I'm sorry about your aunt," his voice full of husky concern and his eyes full of compassion.

Sam abruptly dropped her eyes from his before she could get any more hopelessly lost in them and do something really foolish. "Thanks."

After another long silence, during which Sam didn't trust herself to speak, given her shaky emotional balance, she glanced up to find him staring out over the water, his face set. "I have news of interest to you."

"I heard they managed to turn Pruitt," Sam said, glad to move the subject in a less personal direction. "That takes some heat off us."

He nodded. "But there's more that hasn't made the news yet. Robbie is dead. Agents found him early this morning at his home with a bullet in his head. Presumed suicide."

Horrified, Sam stared at his grim profile. "Why would suicide be presumed?" Suicide was rarely presumed until all other explanations were ruled out.

"I talked to him shortly before his death and guessed what he planned to do." Rafter gave her a brief account of Robbie's surprise visit the night before. "I think he did it partly because he couldn't bear being locked up with the kind of people he'd spent his life fighting. But mostly because if he couldn't continue the good fight, he saw no reason to live."

"I'm so sorry, Nick. I know you were close once." She wished there were something more she could say to comfort him. He looked dreadfully pale and drawn.

"I should have listened to your suspicions about him."

"Not suspicions," Sam protested. "Never anything as well formed as that."

"Whatever it was, how could I have missed it all

these years?" He glanced over at her, appealing to her for an answer, his blue eyes filled with anguish and self-doubt.

"Why would anyone suspect that a righteous warrior like Robbie would climb into bed with the enemy? I know he'd somehow twisted it around to justify what he did, but I still don't understand it."

Rafter let out a heavy sigh. "Neither do I. But I think that once he did step over the line, it became easier and easier to rationalize until finally he became what he'd set out to defeat."

He fell silent for a time, squinting out at the breaking waves. Then he groaned and shook his head. "I've been the most incredible shit to you." He finally looked at her, searching her face, pleading for her forgiveness.

She'd dreamed of this moment hundreds of times, but now that it had arrived, she took no pleasure in her victory. They'd both suffered enough. "What did you do to me that I couldn't have stopped with a few words?"

He gave a short laugh of self-disgust. "What didn't I do? I ruined your career. I destroyed your reputation. I broke up your relationship with Brian. You have every reason to hate me."

Sam shrugged. "You thought I was a saboteur. All the evidence pointed in that direction."

"Yes, too obviously. I should have seen that. I think Robbie planted that file in your office, by the way."

"I think so too, but why? Philip had already done his damage control. He'd made me look like his girlfriend, not his spy."

"Robbie knew you were smart. He probably didn't want to risk having you poke around and maybe figure out how Philip knew about our investigation of him. So he planted the file and insisted you were involved up to your neck, and I bought it." Nick shook his head, mouth thin with bitter regret.

This was his real reason for coming, Sam thought, to unload his guilt so he could get on with his life. His next words turned that assumption on its head.

"Sam . . ." He hesitated, his gaze darting off to the water again. "I asked you once whether you believed in second chances—for us, I mean. Do you still feel the way you did before?" She couldn't breathe to answer, and he rushed on. "I know I don't deserve one. I can't turn back the clock, but let me at least try to make it up to you. This is finally our time, our chance. We might not get another."

Sam turned away and closed her eyes, trying to maintain her dignity. *Don't do this to me!* It was so very tempting to give in to what she wanted . . . and disastrous in the long run. *Remember Will and Grace.*

"Say something, Sam, anything, *please!*"

"Oh, Nick, this isn't about the past anymore. It's about . . ."

"About what? Say it!"

She groped for a pride-saving way of putting it. "It's just that we want different things in life. You don't stay with one woman very long, and I tend to stick like glue. It would be a disaster."

He appeared unable to speak for a moment, his face wearing the thunderstruck look of someone hit upside the head. Sam might have found it comical under other circumstances. "That's it? That's why you won't give us a chance?"

"Well, you don't exactly have a great track record," she said defensively.

"Because of you!" he roared.

Now it was Sam's turn to be astonished. "You're going to blame your philandering ways on me?"

"Abso-freakin'-lutely! It was only after I met you

that I started dating around a lot." He took hold of her shoulders as if he wanted to shake her, his laser-eyed gaze drilling into her. "Christ, Sam—I was waiting for you and Brian to realize that you were all wrong for each other, but you were taking your sweet time about it. What was I supposed to do, sit home singing the blues over my guitar every night? I didn't want to create expectations, so I went in for casual relationships with women who were like-minded while I waited for you to come to your senses."

Sam barely dared to move in case she broke heartstrings already stretched to their maximum limit. She searched his face and saw no hint of deception. "What about that woman last night?" she whispered.

"Last night?" He looked bewildered.

"You left the reception last night with her. There was a picture on the news."

"That was an FBI agent!" In frustration, he tugged on the zipper of his jacket, his face agitated and uncharacteristically vulnerable. "God, Sam, I've been crazy for you from the first. That's probably why I believed Robbie about you; I knew my own judgment was totally biased. And then after everything became clear at the Wentworth mansion, you disappeared before I could tell you what a complete fool I've been. I thought I'd go out of my mind wondering whether you were all right. I've lost twenty pounds worrying about you. Why didn't you at least call?"

"I was trying to get over you," she whispered, her voice raspy with emotions swelling inside her chest.

"Did it work?"

She touched his jaw with trembling fingers. "Not a bit."

He reached for her. With a sob, Sam fell into his

arms. He kissed her desperately, on and on, as if fearing she might any second disappear again. Sam eventually surfaced for air only to decide that breathing was highly overrated. When finally Nick pressed her head tightly over his galloping heart, Sam was trembling with such emotion her legs could barely support her.

"Oh, Nick, I've missed you so much," she gasped against his leather jacket.

"Not as much as I've missed you." He lifted his face from the top of her head, but his arms tightened, and Sam guessed he was looking across the beach to the cottage. "Your bodyguard appeared to be packing for a move. Where are they taking you next?" Sudden urgency laced his voice.

"I'm not going anywhere but home." She gave a shaky laugh. "You showed up just as I was about to go AWOL with Kat."

"You can't go home," he said flatly.

"The cabal has bigger fish to worry about than me now. Billy thinks even Philip is about to cut a deal."

"You're probably safe from them, but the press will hound you. And your apartment has no security." He paused and his mouth curved into a slow smile that eased the gaunt look of his face and, as ever, made her legs turn to wet noodles. "I know the perfect place where we can think the problem through overnight." Without offering more, he unwound her arms from around his neck and began pulling her up the beach, having clearly shifted into problem-solving mode. For the moment, sensing that their needs and desires were in perfect accord, Sam let him charge on.

"Does this place have a tendency to rock and roll?"

"See how much we already think alike?" Flashing a wall-to-wall smile, he caught her up and twirled her around in a giddy circle, sending sand flying in the wind.

Dizzy and laughing, Sam couldn't take it all in. Incredibly, what she wanted most seemed suddenly within reach. And then the tears came, welling up from some huge reservoir that should have been tapped out days ago.

Nick set her on her feet and peered worriedly into her face. "Sam, what is it? Tell me. Am I being an insensitive jerk dragging you off to ravish you when your aunt has just died? Is that it?"

"No, no." Sam smiled and swiped at her eyes with one shaky hand while the other reached up to tenderly cup his cheek. "I'm just so happy. But what will we do about our babysitters? They're not going to approve of us going off together on our own, at least I'm sure Carla won't."

"I don't think that will be a problem." His crooked, faintly abashed smile toward the cottage behind her alerted Sam that something was amiss.

She spun around to find four faces grinning at them from the deck—Kat, Carla, a brush-cut bruiser who had to be Rafter's agent, and to her astonishment, acting U.S. Attorney Sandy Cotey.

Under a midnight moon, the splendid old wooden ketch bobbed gently at its secluded mooring. Yellow light glowed from her aft portholes. Belowdecks, Nick dropped a few more sticks into the small stove keeping the night chill from the cabin before padding back to their cozy love nest and Sam. His eyes lingered on her. It seemed the stuff of dreams that she was finally here with him for real after all these years.

"Have our keepers gone to bed yet?" she asked with a wicked smile of appreciation for his naked self.

"The lights went off hours ago."

For now, Carla and Howie were tucked up in the cottage on shore for the night. What happened tomorrow would depend on whether Nick could talk Sam into moving in with him. He sure didn't want to leave her hanging out there for some other guy to poach now that he finally had her within reach. When he'd crawled back under the pile of blankets mounded on top of the bunk and pulled her close, he buried his face in her wildly disordered mane of dark hair. "I must be the luckiest chump on earth."

Sam wiggled closer. "No, I am, no contest."

"No, I've definitely got you beat because I've wanted you longer."

"That's debatable," she said.

Nick sighed. "Do you want to waste time trying to beat my clearly winning hand or do you want to hear more news?"

She laughed and kissed him. "The news."

"Now where was I . . . Oh, yes, Hattie Christiansen is doing well. She was released from the hospital a couple weeks ago. Her doctors predict a full recovery, but caution that she may never remember the time around the accident. So we may never know exactly what caused it."

"What about the private investigator she talked of hiring?"

"She can't remember doing it, and there are no clues in her house. If she did, he was either scared off, paid off, or buried."

"Well, I'm glad she'll be all right," Sam said fervently.

"Pushy and Representative Rowbotham have been cleared of any connection to the conspiracy," Nick went on, "but the videotape of them was widely viewed by investigators and stills from it have somehow found their way onto the Internet. Everyone's pointing fingers, but no one's admitting anything. Pushy's fled to Washington, probably permanently."

Sam's mouth curved into a slight smile. "At least now she's swimming with other sharks." Then, frowning, she lifted her head from Nick's shoulder to look at him. "There's something I've been wanting to ask you about from that night. Right before Philip was shot, you said something to him. What was it?"

Nick could have laid it all out to her then, but instead he looked into her bruised eyes and lied. "I told him he was a butthead and a few other unmentionables." He relaxed when this explanation seemed to satisfy her.

This would be his little secret with the soon-to-be ex-senator, how Nick had impulsively tipped him off to their secret insurance plan. Why aid his old foe? Nick supposed the biggest reason was that he hadn't wanted Sam to go through the rest of her life thinking her own brother had been willing to let her go off to slaughter without a fuss. Maybe Philip would have come through on his own—Nick hoped so—but he didn't regret having given Philip additional incentive to do the right thing. And what the heck—it was always easier to prosecute when they could turn an insider. Indeed, the senator was the first one turned. Though, as a matter of strategy, that had been kept secret.

"I'm also curious about how you learned of my aunt's death," Sam was saying. "We have different last names, and Kat insisted she didn't tell you."

Oh, hell, another subject Nick would have liked to avoid. He heaved a sigh and propped up higher against the varnished wooden bulkhead. "Brian came to the reception last night. He'd seen the obituary in the paper."

"Ah, I should have guessed he'd be at your party."

"I'm sorry that I broke you and Brian up." Then Nick grimaced, and admitted, "That's not strictly true. But I am sorry I caused you pain."

Sam anchored the blankets under her arms and rolled onto her back. "We weren't right for each other. You were right about that. My biggest mistake was trying to hang on to a doomed relationship so long. Everything Brian did I would subconsciously compare to what you would do in the same situation. You were my gold standard. It wasn't very nice of me, or fair."

"But you loved him."

She sent him a small, wry smile. "As Kat so astutely pointed out earlier, I loved you more."

Nick intently studied her face for such a long moment without saying anything that Sam grew nervous. "Are you saying you love me?" he finally asked, his face difficult to read in the shadow of the oil lamp hanging on the bulkhead behind him.

Sam felt faint with horror that she'd gotten it all wrong after all. "Isn't that what this is about?"

Then he smiled and Sam started breathing again.

"But you've never actually said it," he pointed out. "While I've been telling you how crazy in love with you I've been from the first."

"Oh, but I do love you," she cried, burrowing into his arms and kissing him again. "I thought it was obvious."

It took a long time for Nick to get his campaign back on track because Sam then felt it necessary to prove how much she loved him.

"Just a warning," Nick said as Sam was about to nod off. "When I say I love you, it's forever. We're stuck like peanut butter and jelly. I'm not one of those guys who fall in and out of love every other week like Brian."

"Then you'd better know that I'm rotten with men. The women in my family are all jinxed in that area." She yawned and waved a hand before covering her mouth. "Long history."

"Maybe you never met the right one."

"Or maybe we've just been unable to please them." Sam opened her eyes and searched Nick's face worriedly. "I could never be one of those perfect little Stepford ego-strokers." Like Brian's Helen, she thought.

Nick laughed. "Sam, if I wanted a woman like that, I wouldn't have fallen for you." Then he had to go and ruin it. "Besides, who else could handle you? You're sneaky, headstrong, and too cleaver by half."

"Is that so," Sam murmured, too tired to summon much indignation or keep her eyes open any longer.

"But two of those happen to be qualities I'm most fond of." He hooked the blankets over her chest and lifted them up a few inches to peek underneath. "And you have other qualities I'm rather fond of, too."

Sam laughed and swatted his hand away.

"Face it," he continued, "we're a perfect match. Like Bogey and Bacall, Tracy and Hepburn . . ."

"Lucy and Ricky?" she mumbled sleepily.

He laughed again. "Will that advance my case?"

Sam cracked an eye open. "It might."

"Then Lucy and Ricky it is. There's just one last thing before you wander off to dreamland. Seeing as how it only makes sense that you move into my apartment since yours has no security, I'll be expecting you to make an honest man out of me in the very near future."

Sam's smile widened but she didn't open her eyes. "I'll have to check my day planner and see if I can pencil that in."

EPILOGUE

Seven months later . . .

"Last question," Sam said firmly to the persistent trio of students camped in her tiny office.

All were nervous first-years—1Ls—from her criminal procedure class. Sam had cut them some slack and stayed beyond normal office hours. She adored her new job, but she would be late meeting Nick if she didn't boot them out soon. They had an appointment with a real estate agent to go house hunting this afternoon.

Sophie Somerset, who had the office three down from Sam's, poked her blond head in a second later and made a face. "The vultures are back."

Sam groaned and glanced anxiously at her watch. The press descended *en masse* every time something new developed in the still-unfolding scandal. They'd quickly learned that the open campus of Madison University was the easiest place to corner her. As long as they stayed outside the building, campus security tolerated their presence. Sam had learned, almost as quickly, that it was better to face them immediately and get it over with. Then they left her alone until the next big development.

Walking outside onto the high, broad, and impressively grand stone steps of the law school, Sam plucked up her courage and faced the half-dozen tenacious reporters lolling about in the mild spring weather. Spotting her, they shot to their feet, tossing aside cigarettes and pulling out tape recorders and cameras on the fly.

"Professor Parker, how would you say the prosecution is handling Benton's case?" the *Detroit Free Press* reporter called out, converging and jostling for position. "What do you think his chances are now that Jimmy Davis has agreed to testify against him?" another asked.

Today, on the eve of Benton's trial, Marty Davis's nephew, Jimmy, had pled guilty to a reduced charge for his part in helping his uncle along to the hereafter. In exchange, he'd joined Simon Pruitt in agreeing to testify against Randall Benton.

Sam gave her stock answer: "I'm not at liberty to discuss a pending case."

"Then what's your reaction to your brother getting off with only six months at Club Fed?" the *Daily Express* asked. "Do you consider that an adequate sentence?"

"I'm sorry, I have no opinion," she said. "I leave that determination to the judge."

Philip had gotten off lightly compared to Benton. The statute of limitations had run out on crimes stemming from the cover-up of Rachel's death. Who had been with her at the time of her death was still a mystery. Philip claimed not to know, so the answer had probably died with Christiansen, Davis, and O'Neal. Nor had Philip been charged

with taking part in the conspiracy to murder Marty
Davis or the attempted kidnapping and murder of
Sam and Nick.

In contrast, Benton faced an uphill battle against
a mountain of charges. With Robbie O'Neal gone,
he was viewed as the big fish, and prosecutors were
leaving no stone unturned in their effort to collect
his scalp. From Kat, Sam knew they were currently
interviewing her client, Tanya, to see if they could
bring additional charges against him.

Investigations were continuing of several other
members of the tainted Sigma fraternity, including the attorney general and a state supreme court
judge. There was also, as Robbie used to say, collateral damage. In a backlash of voter wrath against
politics as usual, beleaguered Governor Graham,
apparently not part of the cabal, was nevertheless
swept from office in the November election. And
Representative Rowbotham, Pushy's unfortunate
partner in the sex scandal, had been recalled by
angry voters in his largely rural district who'd felt
duped by a fraudulent Bible-thumper.

"Aw, com'on," the *Free Press* said in disgust. "You
gotta give us something. Do you support your
nephew Billy's run for city council?" he asked, lob-
bing her a soft one.

Sam smiled. "Wholeheartedly. Billy has my vote."
Billy, she suspected, was about to come into his
own. It would be no easy task to restore the family
name, but Sam thought that in time he just might
pull it off.

She spotted Nick slouching against his Beemer
in the parking lot below and glanced back to the
reporters. "You'll have to excuse me now," she said
and started down the stairs.

"Wait!" one called out. "Does your husband plan
to indict anyone else when he takes over as U.S. at-

torney?" The president had nominated Nick for the position. If confirmed by the Senate, he would succeed Robbie O'Neal as the district's top federal prosecutor. Sam was thrilled for him. In this she agreed with Robbie—at least for now, Nick belonged on the other side of the gavel.

"You'll have to ask him," she said.

The reporters showed various degrees of disappointment and disgust. A few began to flip off tape recorders and cameras.

"How do you like married life?" one asked with a wide grin as she brushed past.

"Yeah, how was the honeymoon?" another called out.

Automatically, Sam's gaze darted to Nick. He gave her a wink and that enigmatic smile she was gradually learning to decipher. Blushing faintly and hastily looking away, she started to laugh and tossed back over her shoulder, "Definitely no comment to that."